time's child

ALSO BY REBECCA ORE

Outlaw School

Gaia's Toys

time's child

Rebecca Ore

An Imprint of HarperCollinsPublishers

HarperCollins books may be purchased for educational, business, or sales promotional use. For information please write: Special Markets Department, HarperCollins Publishers, 10 East 53rd Street, New York, NY 10022.

FIRST EDITION

Designed by Paula Russell Szafranski

Library of Congress Cataloging-in-Publication Data

Ore, Rebecca.
    Time's child / Rebecca Ore.—1st ed.
      p. cm.
    ISBN: 978-0-380-79252-8 (pbk.)
    ISBN-10: 0-380-79252-4 (pbk.)
      1. Time travel—Fiction.

PS3565.R385 T56 2007
813'.54 22   2006052980

07 08 09 10 11 ❖ / RRDH 10 9 8 7 6 5 4 3 2 1

This is dedicated to the Net

Thanks to iMeowbot, Peter da Silva,

and various other friends and foes.

Benedetta Then and Again

A Species of Afterlife

An angel told Benedetta she was in Purgatory. Benedetta knew she wasn't in Purgatory when she saw a scab on the angel's knuckle. She didn't believe she'd died, even though her body didn't hurt as it should have from the wound she'd received. Benedetta was unsure what this afterlife was, but she was in her body and angels could be wounded. Perhaps this was a game of light and shadows, of things like puppets.

"Confess what brought you to us, sister," said the angel with the scab.

"You say you're the creature of the Lord?" Benedetta said, edging around the walls and feeling for a secret door to the room. Camera obscuras did something to have people on the wall behind the tiny round window. Only Benedetta didn't see a tiny round window, just a mist at the top of the room. This was something like a camera obscura, Benedetta thought. They'd drugged her with opium or that Arab drug the Old Man of the Mountain used, or something. She was not dead. Angels didn't have scabs on their knuckles. But perhaps she should play along if the angel had a good excuse for not knowing her history.

"I'm not the Lord God Almighty, I'm just one of his servants who takes confessions in Purgatory from the unshrived."

Oh, that's a good one. Benedetta smiled. "I was a young novice in a nunnery who was foully abducted by the French."

"That's not the entire story," the fake angel said. "You had been sexually active long enough to have had a child, and you were raped recently. And the man who died with you wasn't your most recent lover."

"Why do you doubt me?" Benedetta asked, genuinely curious.

"Because the Lord tells me you are lying."

"Oh, bullshit."

"That's more how you sounded like when your soul was being brought to Purgatory. As you lay dying."

How do I get out of here? "So, I was kidnapped a couple of months earlier and ran away from those cruel French to the Lombardians."

"And I don't believe the couple of months. Child, confess and save your eternal soul."

Benedetta wondered what the fake angel got out of lying to her. "Prove this is Purgatory and not Hell," she said.

"It would be better if you started telling us about life in the camps," the fake angel said. Benedetta hadn't felt any doors in her complete circling of the room. Maybe the fake angel got down on a rope from the area in the ceiling she couldn't see for the smoke or mist or whatever. Mirrors, perhaps they obscured the openings with mirrors.

Don't panic. Benedetta didn't want to tell the truth, because that's what this creature wanted, and being trapped in a closed room with no windows and being told she was dead and in Purgatory made her angry. The anger warred with the panic and left her momentarily confused. "I went with the soldiers rather than be bored."

"I believe you, my child."

"So you want to jerk off while I tell you about the fucking I did?"

"I'm an angel. I'm sexless."

"Let me kiss the fucking ring." Benedetta grabbed his hand and bit down hard. If she hadn't had her mouth occupied while he shrieked, she'd have told him that angels don't feel pain, much less have scabs.

Other people in weird clothes rushed through the walls, through the doors Benedetta hadn't felt and couldn't find, and grabbed her mouth at the jaw hinge. She spat out blood.

"Why did you bite me?" the fake angel asked.

"You have a scab on your knuckle. You can't be an angel. Your lingua, your Lombardian, sucks. So, what the fuck is this place?" She expected she would die now, but the people holding her simply grabbed her legs and arms and held on. Something hissed against her arm and she thought *snake* before passing out.

Not a snake, she thought when she woke up.

The angel and a woman in strange clothes sat beside her bed. The woman said, "I know you're not going to believe this either, but you're in an archival facility in the future. Think of it as a library for people. I'm here to explain your legal standing in our culture."

Benedetta wondered how many layers of lies they'd try on her.

The fake angel said, "We're trying to learn about the past and we'd like you to help us."

The woman said, "We saved your life and brought you into the future. A lot of people are more comfortable if they think they died and are in an afterlife they can understand."

Maybe they aren't lying? Benedetta thought this was all too crazy for anyone to try as a lie. Should she pretend to believe it until she could learn more, or just stay confused?

"We're sorry, but I don't understand why you bit me," the angel said. "Why so hard?"

"You were lying to me. Well, thank you for saving me from dying. I can't believe those French. I want out of here."

"We'd like to spare you the culture shock," the woman said. Benedetta didn't know how culture could cause shock.

"We've saved your life," the man said. "Not that we expect you to be immediately grateful, or to believe us. Yet. But can you begin to tell us honestly about your life. We really want to know what you saw, how you lived, what your customs were."

"I want to see the future first," Benedetta said. Her heart was beating very fast.

"You have the right to be treated as reasonably as possible. But I think you should wait," the man said. "Your heart is beating very rapidly."

I've been trapped by magicians, Benedetta thought. "I couldn't believe in Purgatory."

"Most people from the period of Christianity that had a concept of Purgatory as well as Heaven and Hell would find Purgatory believable. Nobody believes they are good enough for heaven—or at least they don't argue about it. And people are relieved to find they're not in Hell," the man said. "I'm Joseph. You can call me Joe."

"But she isn't sure where she is now, are you?" the woman said.

"In a camera obscura," Benedetta answered.

"Well, sort of," Joe said. "You probably want to get some rest and think about things for a while. All your friends are dead, in the past. If you believe us, this has to be a shock."

"What is the year?" Benedetta asked.

"By the Christian calendar, 2308," the woman said.

"Eight hundred and fucking nine years from 1499," Benedetta said. Benedetta realized she didn't know how to get out of their archival room. What was the difference, 1499 or 2308? They were men and women, like other men and women. She would have to get to know them, then figure out who would bend the rules for her. Until then, she'd tell them as many stories as they'd believe.

Joe asked, "You can do subtraction in your head?" He sounded genuinely amazed.

"Yeah, I can do subtraction in my head. You think I'm stupid because I'm a peasant girl?"

"We would never have thought that," Joe said. "It's that we didn't know women were taught to figure in your time."

"Oh," Benedetta said. She decided not to tell them she could read, too.

Raped, kicked, and left dying, she'd been brought to some fake purgatory run by creeps who'd out-clevered the Florentines with their toys of light. Purgatory wouldn't have been a good fit. Hell was where Benedetta had expected to find herself on the days when she bothered to believe in an afterlife. Most of the time, she figured dead was dead, so up in the future could be better yet. Living in the future, if she could escape the forgeries of times past in these little rooms, would be another adventure.

"I want to see this future."

"Your *immune system* can't handle current diseases. Even *immunizations* to prevent the diseases might kill you. We can't let you out that easily," Joe said.

"Explain that in words I know."

"Eight hundred years years isn't *genetically* that large a spread," the woman said, then spoke further in a strange language.

"Look, I'm not stupid. Explain what an *immune system* is." Benedetta spoke the words as well as she could remember them. The future people seemed surprised for some reason.

"I can't explain without you knowing more of our language. We have medicines to prevent diseases, for most of the deadly modern diseases. These are not without risks and while you can ask for them, you need to understand what the risks are. And it's hard to explain any of this in archaic Italian."

I'm in prison, with better food, with people to talk to, and without beatings, but it's still prison. "So teach me your language if that will help me understand better."

"What was it like being with the army?" Joe asked. "You were a camp follower, right?"

"No, I wasn't a common camp woman; I was on the artillery team with my husband." She'd never married Emelio in the church, but they'd been together long enough.

The people who'd saved and imprisoned her had another hasty conversation in their language, then Joe said, "Okay, we've suspected that the future could send people into the past just as we can move them out, so that is a possibility here, but there are accounts of women working on gun crews in Burgundy."

Benedetta shrugged. These people saved her life, but they weren't interested in setting her free. She wondered what they'd do if she lied and said she was from the future. No, she'd tell them the truth until she had a better idea of what sort of mess she was in.

Joe asked, "Where in Italy did you travel? What did you see? We're interested in learning things about how people lived that didn't get mentioned in the written records."

"We lived in Milan when we weren't on jobs."

They talked among themselves. "Really. Can you show us on a map?" They brought in a map of the streets of Milan, some different than what she'd remembered, and it didn't look like the map Leonardo drew. She found the old Sforza castle where Leonardo had lived, and found the little house near it, and said, "Some years, we lived there. And we visited one of the duke's engineers there a lot." She pointed to the old castle.

The future people went nuts for a while in that strange language they were speaking.

"Are you talking about meeting Leonardo di Vinci?"

Yeah, I'm really from the past; I was really on an artillery crew; Leonardo really tried to seduce Emelio but thought I looked nice in mountain-girl clothes. Benedetta finally said, "Milan didn't have that many first-class artillery crews, and Emelio was cute as well as bright. We spent a lot of time at Leonardo's place. He even borrowed my kid for one of his experiments."

"I know someone who'd have so many questions for you," Joe said. "Normally, the people we get didn't know anyone historically significant in the old sense of historically significant."

"I will tell you what I know if I can get out of here."

Joe said, "Did you use forks for eating at the table and for what and what did they look like? Yeah, the information on Leonardo will excite some people, but what I'm most interested in is the daily life of the past, what wasn't in books."

Benedetta remembered how weird forks has seemed when she first saw them at the table. "Saved on water, having your own fork to hold meat. And on fingers eating sticky things." She wouldn't tell them how embarrassed she'd been not knowing how to use a fork when she first saw one.

But they were excited that she'd met Leonardo. Um, something to work with there. Man's reputation lasted more than eight hundred years; Leonardo wouldn't have been surprised, though.

"If you see the future, it may corrupt what you remember of the past," the woman said.

"Did Leonardo's drawing books get passed up to the future?" Benedetta asked.

They chattered between themselves again, then said, "Yes, some of them."

"What is this *culture shock* you mentioned?"

"Most people from the past would have mental difficulties if they tried to understand our times. Most of the more modern ones, and some of the most archaic ones, finally learn where and when they're living now," Joe said. "They're happiest living in places that most resemble their own times. We try to keep them comfortable."

But they don't live long was generally the rest of that statement in Benedetta's natural lifetime. She wondered if people that had lived by the priests' rules died of shock to find themselves neither in Heaven, Purgatory, or Hell, but in another life, sometime else. "But people from the past don't live long?" Benedetta asked.

The woman said, "You didn't choose to come here, everyone you know is dead. Grief damages people."

Joe said, "She doesn't even have a model for infection in the same way we know it."

"How we deal with *transtemporals,* people from other times, was invented by scholars of humankind for dealing with an American native survivor, Issi, at the beginning of the twentieth century. We provide shelter and give you appropriate *technology,* tools you'll understand, and an afterlife that's familiar to you."

"Do I belong to you people?" Benedetta asked.

"The Philadelphia Archives has permission to bring noncitizens from the past and house them as long as they live," the woman said.

"So I belong to the Archives? What government is this?"

"You don't really belong to the Archives like a slave, if that's what you're worried about," Joe said. "We just have permission to bring you uptime and are responsible for you."

"Things are very different beyond these rooms," the woman said. "But you legally do have a right to ask us to let you out. I don't advise it right away. We're still responsible for your welfare. Our time will probably kill you. You're in a biocontainment area now, you understand quarantine? Vaccinations might help or you could have a bad reaction to them."

How do cows figure into this? "How did you get me from Lombardy then to wherever I am now, in your time?"

"We don't know precisely how the engine works," Joe said. "It appears to have come to us from the future, maybe as a jump start toward improving human genetic diversity, maybe for some amusement of the future's. We've got people working on it. But I'm a history researcher, not a temporal physicist. What languages do you know?"

"A number. I learn languages fast," Benedetta said, seeing a way to make herself useful and to get out of the room they'd trapped her in. If Joe wasn't lying, everyone Benedetta knew was dead now, over eight hundred years dead. And she didn't want to be like a body to dissect, to these people.

Joe and the woman talked their language at each other, then Joe said, "You're probably not going to catch anything lethal from anyone brought here from before the plague era."

"We had plague. If you keep clean . . ."

"Different plagues," the woman said. "Not carried by rat fleas. And they killed more than people."

In the next couple of days, they worked out that the present dialect was a distant variant of the English Benedetta knew from a couple of mercenaries in her day.

Pinholes in Time

The more the Time Team let Benedetta help them with other people from the past, the more Benedetta wanted to move into the future, but the Archives people kept refusing to let her out.

However, this week, Joe, who seemed seducible but embarrassed to find himself male, headed the Time Team. He was probably in his early twenties, though age was harder to figure with these future people who didn't dry themselves out with the sun or overwork themselves chasing armies. Joe said, "Not all people from all eras are as flexible as you are. Beyond that, I don't know how your body would cope with the diseases we have now."

"I didn't get the plague in my day."

Best not to remind him that I bit him the first day I saw him. Benedetta went to take a shower. One of the best things about the future was instant hot water. If she could find some people from the past who weren't just idiots, she could . . .

. . . bring in more idiots from the past. That shouldn't be the plan, though. Not to bring in idiots, but to find people who needed a refuge from their own times, who would find the future a kinder place. She thought in the tongue her father spoke, German of some kind, then in the future English she was learning, then in the language she'd learned in the Lombardian hill village, the past and future wheeling around in images she saw with her mind's eye: Leonardo's drawings turned into real metal and fake wood, the past turned into drawings, and the maps changed, just as the maps changed for Benedetta's father and mother.

Hey, it's all projections. The past is just another projection. You think we knew what was going on then, even the brightest of us. So I knew Leonardo da Vinci who thought I looked cute in my mountain-girl clothes.

Benedetta had fallen forward in time eight hundred years to live where Leonardo's drawings were real things, surrounded by things that Leonardo himself might not have imagined. And the Time Team tried to protect her from the future they'd saved her for.

The future was scary and marvelous, but Benedetta's past had also been scary and marvelous. If she'd been afraid of novelties and change, she'd never have run away with the Duke of Milan's army in the first place.

The Time Team tried to protect the rescued from the future, both from its diseases and its ideas. Benedetta saw through the attempt to persuade her she was in Purgatory, so the Time Team had adopted her as their special past person with all sorts of archaic languages. Now, she played supernatural interrogators from a range of strange religions. Today, she'd been a cup bearer in a Norse afterlife to some barely bearded kid who'd been thrown in the sea by Irish people he'd tried to enslave. The little shit was still trying to play tough.

The Norse boy might be perfectly okay if they just told him that he was now in the future more than a thousand years from his time.

Or perhaps not. Benedetta had tried the truth once and the old woman declared her to be a demon and kept on believing. Then the old woman died anyway.

Pre-European, post-Roman, and a number of wars away

Benedetta's father and grandfather spoke different languages than her mother, but they all seemed to understand each other. Benedetta learned both languages so she could hear her grandfather's stories, which were much more interesting than her mother's. He talked about Trento, and the Venetians seizing Bergamo and the people beyond Venice who spoke yet another language whose words for *milk, snow,* and *yes* her grandfather remembered. He told her of walking through high mountain snow even in the summer.

When her grandfather died, Benedetta's mother began to insist that Benedetta spend more time spinning and weaving.

Benedetta found a boy who spoke like her father and grandfather and wondered if she could learn more languages. A family from the Aosta Valley came through the area speaking something that sounded like baby babbling crossed with Lombardian. "French," the boy who spoke like her father said.

Her mother had another baby, which lived after two earlier babies who died almost as soon as they were born. As her brother thrived and grew, her mother began leaving Benedetta to shift for herself.

More than eight hundred years later, Benedetta couldn't remember the boy's name, though she'd learned from the Time Team that he'd spoken German, as had her father and grandfather.

Most women who spoke two languages before they bled could learn languages easily, and a mercenary army in Lombardy was a good place to have learned the ancestral and descendant languages of most of Europe. Benedetta found a new way to make herself useful to the strangers.

In Benedetta's opinion, the Time Team tended to more think about past languages than actually use them. Computers generated the scripts used to build more vocabulary to get more information. Benedetta was dismayed to find most people couldn't tell a script from a real person. Joe spoke a kind of Lombardian and wanted to practice it on her, so he was there, pretending to be an angel, when she woke up in the future.

Breaking out from There Then

When Benedetta was thirteen, soldiers camped out in a fava bean field under the mountains. Benedetta and the German-speaking boy snuck up by the sentries and lay flat under the beans the soldiers hadn't cut for horse fodder. Men played tabors and pipes while women danced barefoot, with naked breasts, around the camp fires. Children ran around, shrieking and giggling, stuffing food in their mouths as they ran.

Benedetta wanted to be part of that. When one of the women of the camp came into the village to haggle over grain, Benedetta asked her what camp life was like.

The woman smiled, then looked at Benedetta again and smiled even more. Benedetta had had enough of spinning and weaving. It was now time for adventure. "Can I just go with you?"

"I haven't even told you what the army is like," the woman said. "And you don't even know whose army we are."

"You smiled," Benedetta answered. "And I've seen the camp at night."

"If people want you back, we'll give you up. The Sforza family believes in being nice to peasants—after all their grandfather was one. War helps the poor who are clever. That's why my brother and I are with the war contractors. Ludovico is great to work for. My brother believes in keeping his money in the family, so that's why I swab cannons."

Benedetta said, "Sounds great. If anyone wants me back, I'll go back, but nobody will give a shit."

The woman asked, "My brother might need a girl. How's your cooking and weaving? And we have to check with your family."

"If I have to, I can spin, weave, and cook," Benedetta said. She could stand a little woman's work in exchange for adventure. Men who weren't the usual plowboys sounded good, too.

"I can teach you about dressing wounds, too," the woman said. "It's always a good skill to have. I'm Julia. My brother, Emelio, is a cannoneer. Cannoneers are fussy and temperamental and like things just so, only Emelio's not as bad as most. My own sweetie is a crossbow man. He kills knights, bolts through the steel. Let's talk to your people and bring a spindle and distaff if you have them."

Benedetta carried half the wheat Julia had bought from the village. She stopped by her father's house. Her mother was warping the loom. Benedetta said, "I've got a place to go to." Julia put down her sack of wheat and began helping Benedetta's mother with the warp.

Benedetta looked at both of them, feeling anxious to get moving.

Her mother said, "We don't have a dowry for you. We were going to send you off in service."

Julia said, "My brother and I are with Ludovico's military contractors. She's willing to come with us, but there's no money for the camp women."

"Benna's such an idiot for a smart girl. If she stays here, the youth are likely to rape her for being so forward. I'm surprised it hasn't happened already, but she's not quite a woman yet. If they rape her, she'd have to go to the brothel, if her father doesn't kill her first."

"This is better," Benedetta said. "I can translate for them if they invade Father's country."

"Does she knit?" Julia asked her mother, who shook her head. "You can knit while walking, a bit more tricky than spinning while walking, but a clever girl can manage."

"I don't think Benedetta wants to be a woman," her mother said. "Benedetta, don't come back here if you go with the soldiers."

"Her father won't mind?" Julia asked.

"She's bound to embarrass him whatever she does. If he has a problem with it, I suppose we can ask her to come home."

The three women nodded then. *I can be a different kind of woman.*

After the loom was warped and tied to the front beam, Benedetta and Julia walked back to the camp. "You'll need a pair of boots," Julia said. "Walking barefoot all day with packs isn't good."

"What about dressing like a boy?" Benedetta said.

"My brother would not be impressed," Julia said.

Benedetta wondered why this brother got dragged into the deal, but wasn't going to argue right now. She was getting away from that stupid village, and traveling with an army.

Julia gave the password to the sentries and they walked up to a campfire where dinner was cooking. Julia dumped the wheat sacks by the fire. A stocky man with big arms came out of the crowd and hugged her. "Benedetta, Carlo, my sweetie," Julia said. "Carlo, where's Emelio? I found him a girl."

"Tiny tits. She ripe yet?"

Benedetta said, "I should bleed soon enough."

"The Southern girls get ripe sooner," Carlo said. "Cold in the mountains."

Just then, Emelio came up and smiled at Benedetta. He was a blond skinny guy with black fingertips, from gunpowder charcoal, Benedetta learned later. He said, "You like big cannons?"

"I would like to learn about big cannons," Benedetta said, sure he was referring both to his cock and the guns he fired.

Emelio took Benedetta's chin in his fingers and looked at her. His eyes were more gray than blue, with black rims at the outside of the irises. "We'll see if I should keep you."

"I can't go back," Benedetta said. "I'd be raped and forced into a brothel if I went back."

"It might be a kinder life," Emelio said. "Most whores make good marriages after service."

"But without adventure," Benedetta said.

"War is mostly *mathematics* now." He saw that Benedetta was puzzled and said, "Numbers, the angle of the gun, the weight of the shot and powder, can be used to predict where the shots will land."

"Ah," Benedetta said. She knew angles from the slant fibers made in yarn—how they lay determined what the thread was good for. "But learning that would be an adventure, too."

Emelio said, "You're the beginnings of a beauty. Go back to your parents."

"No," Benedetta said. She decided they were teasing her; otherwise, she'd be desperate. She couldn't go back.

Emelio said, "Julia, I can see you found a sister for yourself."

"One never knows what one will pick up in these mountain villages."

Emelio said, "I'll be kind, but I do need things taken care of. Julia can teach you about making corned powder and slow matches. Walking rope is not that different than spinning, Julia says."

Benedetta missed her mother that first night in Emelio's tent more than she'd expected. But if she went back, nobody would believe that she wasn't a virgin. It wasn't just the taking by force that was a problem—it was the ritual humiliation of the raped girl that made the rape so nasty. Servant girls were fair game.

But Emelio didn't touch her.

In the morning, Benedetta said, "Emelio, I can give you pleasure."

He blushed, then said, "No force," touching her cheek with the knuckles of his hand. "It's a sin if we both aren't enjoying the act."

Benedetta didn't want to beg, so she would have to learn to be alluring.

The three—Julia, Emelio, and Carlo—fended the camp's young men off, Benedetta noticed. There were women who were wives and there were women who were common to all. Benedetta realized she really didn't want to be common to all, and getting raped by the unattached youth had the same consequences in camp that it had in any town or village. Girls who were raped became common.

The contract soldiers were in the mountains because of plague in Milan and to keep an eye on the Venetian Republic. It was 1486. Dates hadn't mattered to Benedetta before.

Three times a week, Emelio fired a cannon with carefully weighted gunpowder and shot. He didn't let anyone else set up the guns, but Julia taught Benedetta to boil rope in lye and gunpowder for the slow matches and to swab out the cannon after the shots were fired.

After the gun was fired, Benedetta ran into the field with a rod to show where the shot landed. Emelio measured how high the rod looked in the distance to figure how far the shot had gone. When the shot were traveling more than a mile, she asked for a horse to ride, rather than run. They let her ride one of the horses that pulled the cannon wagons.

When winter came, the military contractors brought them back to Milan. "War is becoming a science," Emelio told her. "One of the duke's engineers is designing new equipment for us, very fantastic. We need more artillery."

When Benedetta stopped bleeding the first time, Emelio and she worked together to break her maidenhead. There wasn't much to it. "It's because of riding the horses," Emelio said, checking first with his fingers. Benedetta was glad she had something there or Emelio might have thought she wasn't a virgin when she came to him. She and Emelio seemed more like children playing with their bodies, but the sensations fed on themselves.

Emelio fell asleep after it was over, but kissed her when he woke up and said, "You're such a clever girl."

The camp children heard the love noise through the tent and for the next two months followed giggling when Emelio and Benedetta looked like they were going to slip away for a private moment.

The next fourteen years were golden, but Benedetta didn't want to think about what she'd lost now. She'd think about Leonardo, Emelio, the duke later, and she forced it out of her mind.

Falling forward

Then she remembered the hillside, smoke, gunpowder, and the French coming at her, riding her down with their horses. One of her mercenary soldier friends ran toward her as though he would tackle the first horse. The horseman hacked at him with his sword while a second horseman came up and grabbed at Benedetta's hair. She stabbed his hand. The French rider swore. Benedetta's friend lay kicking on the ground. His bowels rolled out.

The horsemen surrounded her. The man she'd stabbed was angry, but the other four were laughing. Benedetta knew she should drop the knife and let them take her. She could survive a rape. But she got angry just thinking about that, and ran forward, stabbing a horse in the shoulder. His rider yelled at her and stabbed at her with his sword as one of the other riders hit her over the head with the pommel of his. "Ruined a good piece," she heard them say in French as she came halfway around, bleeding. They'd stepped on her hand and bruised it getting the knife away. The five French men looked at her, still probably thinking about raping her, but she was bloody. One pulled her skirts up and raped her anyway, but she didn't move even from the pain. He pulled her head around to look in her eyes. She didn't focus on him. He went limp and pulled out of her, stood up all red from her blood. "Bitch," he said, kicking her. He went to her friend and came back to shove her friend's cut-off cock in her mouth. Another one said, "I don't want cold bloody cunt." They got back on their horses and trotted off. Benedetta could feel the hoofbeats through the ground.

"Well, she'd got her man with her, doesn't she?" she heard one of them say.

No, she wanted to tell them, *he was just a friend.*

The world went black. And everything after she thought she died was wrong.

Time passed

Then Benedetta met a boy who thought he'd drowned on the way to Iceland. The Time Team were tricking him as they had tried to trick her. Most people who were brought forward seemed to be happy to be fooled, and wanted to stay in their comfortable afterlives until their gods told them they were going to be reborn, and even then, some of them didn't want to be reborn. Maybe nearly dying left them brain-damaged?

The Norse boy believed he was in his pagan afterlife. Only he was suspicious of the god apparatus and decided he'd gone into the afterlife of his trickster god, Loki.

Benedetta thought this was funny.

Live at the Archives

Ivar drowned off the coast of Iceland. The cold sucked his life as quickly as the water blocked his breath. The churls who'd seized the boat kept laughing in his mind until blackness took him.

The black shivered. Blue light streaked through. He woke up on a feather bed spread with furs in a corner of a vast hall filled with warriors drinking and singing to harps. At the head of the table sat a man with one eye and two raven companions. He looked at Ivar and said, "Welcome to the afterlife. Introduce yourself to us."

Odin? The tongue was not quite of Ivar's people, but he could understand it.

Why don't you know my name, All-knowing? "I was called Ivar." Ivar had been suspicious of the Gods. They seemed to work for their own ends against human happiness, just as men who would be king of all did.

"You died on the way to Iceland when churls seized your boat. The story went on for generations of men." Odin spoke words that could be praise with a different tone to them.

Speaking down to me. The gods are bastards even in the afterlife. Ivar nodded and began walking around the hall. Odin's raven flew up from Odin's chair-back and began picking at a plate of stew set out near the bed where Ivar had been lying. The end of the hall where Odin sat seemed impossibly far away, never getting closer. Ivar stopped walking toward Odin.

Why would a man who drowned off Ingolfshofdi be in Valhalla? The Irish monks had fled when the first ships came into Reykjavik, so it was a raw country ready for settlement, not a battleground. Churls had drowned him. Ivar seethed at the humiliation. He went to a door in the center of the hall and opened it.

The door led to white, the cold spaces between places of the dead. Ivar wished he knew more about managing the gods. This was forever; the other warriors singing seemed like dreams. Ivar was tempted to touch them, but didn't want to risk rudeness.

Three big hounds, one Irish and hugely tall, the other two with curly tails over their backs, stalked around the tables, snapping at bones tossed to the floor. The people were ruder than Ivar's people.

Odin was a distant figure sitting on a high platform, smiling from his mouth, the one good eye unblinkingly fixed on Ivar. In the center of the hall, a hearth burned without giving off smoke. The dogs moved out of his way, never letting him touch them. He wondered how his body had been pulled from the sea after he died. And remembered how cold it was as he drowned into the black. But then he remembered the flash of blue light. Here, the warriors constantly toasted Odin; the big hounds snapped the bones. Ivar wondered if his body had been found by people who didn't know him, and if a narwhal had ripped him and made the corpse look like a warrior's body rolled to shore after a battle between boats. He wondered if he'd been howed in a ship burial, if Thor had taken him as a warrior because the thralls hadn't been thralls that long and still could fight.

The afterlife. Ivar didn't question that he was dead. He'd seen the slit throats of the others and the bodies thrown overboard. And they would have cut his throat if he hadn't gone into the waves first to avoid death from a thrall's knife.

Odin's one eye gleamed while the two ravens flew around the roof beams, or landed by their master to take food from his fingers. Of all the creatures in the hall—men, Aesir, and beasts—the ravens alone seemed real. One landed by Ivar and stared at him. Ivar reached out slowly and touched the bird. The feathers bent slightly. The bird turned, then looked back over its wing at Ivar before jumping to flight. *Thought or Memory?* Ivar wondered which. *Huginn or Muninn?*

He sounded the names on his tongue. A Valkyrie he hadn't noticed before said, "Muninn, but there are many forms of Memory." Her speech was as strange as Odin's, but Ivar didn't expect his home speech in Valhalla.

Odin said, "Tell us of your deeds."

"Does someone who jumped into the sea to keep from having his throat slit by thralls end up in your hall, Lord?" Ivar asked. He sound peeved to himself and wished he'd not spoken.

"Yes," Odin said.

One of the ravens said, "Story. Tell story." Muninn. The bird's speaking was no different from his Lord's.

Ivar realized his body felt tender but not bruised. He felt down his tunic and found the scar he'd gotten falling out of an apple tree. The afterlife body was the same as the life body. Ivar didn't remember whether this should be so.

"I need to know your story," Odin said. "Perhaps after this, you'll be reborn again in another time and place."

Odin needs my story? "Give me beer for voice. I am in awe to be here." Ivar's mother spoke from his memory: *Bold against the gods, oh, that's brave. Would you be bold against Loki?* Ivar thought that he couldn't die twice but put and kept his back against the wall nevertheless, his eyes to the door. The Valkyrie brought him a horn of beer and sat beside him, her body warm in that cold place. One of the hounds brushed by Ivar. It had fur but no heat at all. He tried to remember if the raven had been warm.

Now, would Odin do him the courtesy of letting him drink before answering the questions?

The horn of beer felt real, warming to his hand. Ivar lowered it to look at the surface and saw a foam fringe like beach spume ringing the dark liquid. He looked up at the ceiling. It was murky, smoke without the smell of smoke. The foam jiggled slightly. Ivan tasted the beer, feeling as though he was in enemy hands. But he was dead. The beer tasted bitter—hops, with an undertone of sweetness—but the taste was slightly off.

The Valkyrie leaned against him and said, "You might as well get drunk and stay drunk." She was a blond girl with high breasts who had thin eyebrows and a blue stain across the top of her eyelids. She smelled slightly sour. Her skin wasn't as perfect as he'd expected a Valkyrie's to be, pouched under the eyes, but she was handsome otherwise. Ivar wondered if the Valkyries were the spirits of women who'd gone in death with their lords. And if that had brought her to Valhalla, had she lost her courage by the roughness of the strangling and the knife to the ribs? Or had she heart enough to have borne the pain soundlessly?

Ivar leaned back against her, pushing her more than she had pressed against him, trying to turn and press against her breasts. "I remember my uncle with a woman like you." Ivar remembered his uncle burning the chief and the chief's dead slave in the grave ship, sailing in the smoke to forever. He realized he was talking the memories, how the dead man's slave volunteered to die for him. She was kept drunk and fucked for the week before the Old Death Woman killed her. He's been too young to be among the men, but his uncle let him watch when the slave died.

The Valkyrie leaned away from him. He reached for her with a hand, but one of the hounds, a cold thing, pushed its teeth against his hand. Cold teeth. No growl. Ivar realized he was speaking what he thought and sat up straight. The hound lay down at his feet.

Odin hadn't blinked in either eye. Ivar looked over at the Valkyrie. She was staring at one of the ravens, tense. He remembered the Irish thralls squatting on a shingle beach while Ivar and one of the earls threw dice for them. He thought at the time that he'd been lucky. Obviously not. "How long does this afterlife go on? Is this hall the beginning and end of it for dead mortals?"

The Valkyrie turned her head toward him. "Oh, you'll be bored with being dead before you know it. For you, it's just this room." She held a bit of bread out to one of the ravens. "I always associated ravens with eating dying and dead people on battlegrounds. I never knew they could be so much fun." The raven came up and pecked the food out of her hand. Ivar began talking about real and mythological ravens, his tongue going almost as though it was separate from his watching of the creatures in the room. The dogs seemed oblivious to both food and bird. The Valkyrie cocked her head as if hearing something Ivar couldn't hear, then said, "Can you tell Odin why you were going to Iceland?"

Odin repeated, "Iceland, Iceland," and Ivar wondered why he'd said anything about ravens. Iceland had been Ivar's craving for a future full of fish, gold, water that was warm without a boiling kettle, hills that built themselves from spews of soft, hot rocks.

Iceland, over the horizon, beyond Haraldr Fairhair's taxes. "We'd heard so much good about Iceland, how warm some water was, how the winters were tempered by hot melted rocks, good for fishing, grazing cows and sheep. And empty. I went with kinsmen to Ireland to get workfolk and gold during the winter after the slaughter of the excess beasts. Fairhair was making the Northworld small. Iceland was an opening out."

Odin asked, "What about Greenland, then. Beyond Iceland?"

Ivar tried to think, but it was more important to say more about Iceland, about the Irish villages that'd given them tribute when the long ships came up the creeks. He almost drank more beer, but more would be dangerous. He had even spoken that out loud. He was talking every thought out loud, speech coming with each thought, not with a considered reflection of it. And he couldn't stop.

The Valkyrie nodded and said, "You're a bit more muscular for your size than average here, so the dose was a bit high." She flinched and pulled something, probably a flea, out of her ear.

Ivar understood that he was drugged, but trickery from the gods was something he expected. "Odin can kiss my ass. The beer should be better."

"What was wrong with the beer?" Odin asked.

"It should be mead in Valhalla." After Ivar talked his tongue and throat ragged, he tried to grab the Valkyrie's wrist. Before the cold hound could react, she twisted her hand like a slippery fish and stood back from him. He sat heavily back down on the bed. He noticed the warriors had fallen silent, just making the motions of eating and drinking, the harps and voices quiet. The hall had been silent for some time, Ivar realized. One of the ravens had found something shiny like a bit of silver leaf and was hiding it from the other raven under the rim of a platter.

"You're supposed to like me." Ivar couldn't remember if the Valkyries slept with the slain warriors. They should.

"So your uncle helped murder slave women after fucking them and you thought that was exciting. Why am I supposed to like you?"

"Odin tells you to." He wanted to drink more but the beer had been drugged to loosen his tongue to the very root of speech. He decided to drink more yet and drank so quickly he fell asleep.

And woke up to his beard being tugged. The smaller raven was on his chest, pulling at his beard hairs. The Valkyrie was watching. Ivar was annoyed that she hadn't brushed the bird away when it was pulling his beard hairs. Beside her was a small trestle table holding a bowl of porridge and an earthenware plate with a piece of cheese and flat bread.

The other raven flew in toward the table, but the girl brushed that one away from the food. Except for the girl and the two birds, the hall was empty. He touched his tongue and thought, *Good, no hounds today.* This time, his tongue didn't speak as he thought.

"After breakfast, we have things we want you to identify," the Valkyrie said. She'd learned his tongue better overnight, now sounding like a woman from Bod in Norway.

Ivar sat up, wondering if she was still angry that he participated in a burial ceremony. He tried the porridge. It had rye, barley, and oats in it and he remembered the porridge fed to people who were going to be hanged to Odin. But he was already dead.

The hall was empty. Ivar wondered where all the others went to sleep, or if they simply disappeared when Odin stopped remembering them. Maybe he was Odin's dream now.

Something was odd about being dead in a body that could be drugged, and which was now very hungry. He waved his left hand at the ravens who flew onto the table to see if they could steal his food.

After eating the bread and most of the cheese, Ivar said, "I never made it to Iceland. I wanted to, you know. I thought I'd have a second chance there." He regretted telling that to the hard woman beside him. His tone had been weaker than the words.

"Iceland? Gee, there are a lot of places that are more fun than old chilly-with-hot-springs-and-smoking-mountains Iceland."

One raven tried to land on his knee. Ivar tossed a crust of cheese out into the hall. It landed on one of the tables. The ravens squabbled over the cheese for a second, then the smaller one came back to beg for more.

Ivar said, "This place is not much fun. Whatever you call it."

The Valkyrie's body stiffened and her shoulders rose slightly. She looked hard at him for a moment, and then looked at him as though she pitied him, which annoyed Ivar. He wondered why she stiffened.

Before he could ask, she said, "We want you to identify some things. Time stretches between here and the world of the living, so things will look different than when you saw their like last." She stood up and led him to the end of the center table.

Horse bits, stirrups, saddletrees, and horse harness charms that had been bright and well wrought when Ivar last saw things like them lay rusted and worm-addled on the table. They looked as old as grave goods from huts made from stone and giant bones in the Orkney Islands. *I am somewhere other than the land of the living.* Some kinds had been old when he was a boy. Others he knew for what they were, but had never seen those particular designs. A few had been molds ready for castings when he was last in Norway, new in their day. He saw what had been a good saddletree with no leather surviving except for a shred near a nail. One gold piece gleamed from a heap of blackened silver horse charms.

And then the Valkyrie reached under the table and slid a box out full of swords, all so rusted and with the hilt leathers rotted down to corroded metal. Ivar found himself happy to see swords but dismayed to see the metal bitten with neglect.

"Is this Loki's version of the afterlife?" Ivar asked.

"Certainly not what you expected is it?"

"I didn't expect anything."

"I can neither admit nor deny that this afterlife could be run by Loki."

"I want to put my cock in you."

"No."

"You won't have sex with me. You're teasing me with swords too rusted to be useful, with hilts with the handles missing. This has to be an afterlife ruled by Loki."

Odin appeared at his table at the far end of the hall and said, "If it would work better for me to be Loki for you, I'll reveal myself tomorrow."

Life in Leonardo's Notebooks

Soft-noise machines on steel wheels

It's Leonardo's drawings come to life, Benedetta thought seeing the night lights and metal carriages rolling by on metal tracks, humming like a hive of bees, the wheels moving the carriages as fast as a horsetrotting fast could have carried them, without the clatter of hooves, the horses snorting. Those sounds were missing. The other sounds were like nothing Benedetta had heard before, really. Not so much like bees as her first impression. *Powered by soft noise.* The spectacle made her feel aggressive, not just intimidated, though she was fighting fear. The air was cold and the sky was reddish dark above the lights. Benedetta wondered for a moment if she really was dead, then decided, no, this wasn't bad enough to be Purgatory, much less Hell.

"It's a big shock for people who never knew such things could exist," Joe said. "That alone can affect your ability to fight off new diseases."

"Explain things to me," she said. Fear tried to grab her again, and she became even more determined to understand this place. "Men made this?"

"Yes, but remember it's been over eight hundred years between your time and ours."

"Are you so much smarter now?" Benedetta didn't think so, really. The people now knew different things.

"That's possible, actually. There's been a certain *evolutionary pressure.*" He used two words Benedetta didn't understand, not Italian, then. "People have been breeding themselves for more brains, I think. More of us know more things. And we know technology continues to improve—we've got the time machine."

"If men made it, I can understand it." Benedetta looked back at Joe to see if he was going to patronize her. He'd pay for any condescension.

"Well, I can try to begin to explain, but I don't know the modern Italian for some of these things, much less the Lombardian Italian you speak."

"Basically, what makes things move?"

"*Electricity.*"

Benedetta didn't understand the word *electricity,* but didn't ask for an explanation. She would find out, though. *Electricity.*

"A peculiar sort of fire, I would say."

"Many people even among us just accept that it works without understanding why. You know about amber, sparks from silk? Lightning. These are all related."

"Ah, like people were about gunpowder in my earlier life," Benedetta said. "It just went boom."

"Precisely," Joe said.

"But someone knows how this all works, so it's something like learning how to grain powder, how to make saltpeter from night soil. I can learn this, too."

A machine thing balanced on two wheels went by, a woman dressed in leather riding it. The machine made a tremendous racket compared to the cars on metal wheels. Its wheels looked like black leather. Benedetta wanted to be that woman in this time. She wore boots like a man. "What's that?"

"A motorcycle. It's a replica of an antique machine, runs on alcohol or *hydrogen* fuel cells."

"I want one. Please. Or a horse. I'm not used to not having a horse. She wore boots like a man."

"Do you want to go inside? You're trembling."

Benedetta realized she was. "Remember I thought I was dead, and now I'm here." She realized after she spoke how awed she sounded. She wished her body would catch up with her spirit. "Are there any horses at all?"

"Machines are easier to manage," Joe said. "But we do have horses. More of them in the grain lands. We were lucky to have had the *Amish,* some people who hadn't lost the skill with horses and that sort of farming, in our hinterlands. We could use the *petrochemicals* we had left for ... Ah, I'm talking things you don't understand here, sorry."

Benedetta knew she could manage a horse. "I must be able to come back out here."

"If you survive this exposure, we'll give you more opportunities to get closer. We'll even find a work range for you. Now, you have to come in and go through decontamination."

Leonardo da Vinci, who dissected a woman Benedetta had seen the soldiers drive to a Milanese brothel, would have loved this future.

Inside the Notebooks, Milan, 1495

Running and screaming with laughter in the Corte Vecchio, Benedetta chased her son, Gregorio, now four, up to Leonardo's workshop below the roof. The workshop was huge with a crane and giant doors that opened north. The large clay horse that would never be made in bronze was in the room, three times the size of a real horse, staring out over the city below through the open doors. Benedetta stopped laughing, afraid that Gregorio would go to the edge and fall into the moat.

Gregorio stopped at the horse, patting the clay fetlock of the raised hoof. Then Benedetta saw two men in bright colors and a youth in fop clothes even brighter, green and gold with slashes in the sleeves showing scarlet. The oldest man wore a short magenta coat that ended at his knees and paint-spattered gray hose below that. *Ah, Leonardo.* Benedetta knew a bit about him, his beautiful boy who stole things and pouted, the paintings of Il Moro's women, the cannons he was always designing.

Leonardo nodded when he saw she recognized him, and said, "The little artillery girl and her son."

"I've heard about your horse," Benedetta said. "And you have notebooks." Her son stopped looking at the horse and began climbing into a cupboard, and Benedetta rushed to pull him out. *At least he's not going to the doors.*

"Difficult times for the horse. The bronze that would have been for the casting went to Ferrara." Leonardo was no longer young now, and the short magenta coat looked a little sad. "Would you sit for me with your son? For sketches?"

"We're waiting for saltpeter before we can get around to graining a mess of powder, but I can sit for a quick sketch until we hear from our men." Benedetta pulled her son away from all sorts of things that looked like they'd be dangerous.

Leonardo pulled out a bench. "You're a mountain girl, I've heard."

"I've heard you like mountain girls in rags," Benedetta said.

"Women are more beautiful if they don't preen," Leonardo said.

"But you wanted to paint Caterina," the youth with a sulky mouth said. "And not the Caterina your mother."

That Caterina was another Sforza—Galeazzo's illegitimate daughter who married her captain's brother after her first husband was murdered. She had bad luck with husbands, as that one was murdered, too. Benedetta said, "Ah, the one with bad luck with husbands."

The older men laughed. The young boy looked as though he preferred everyone to think about him.

"Caterina ... my life has more than a usual number of Caterinas in it. She says she's too busy. But you and the boy will sit for me for a few moments." Leonardo nodded at the bench. Benedetta sat down and held Gregorio firmly.

Leonardo sketched. The two other men went silent. Gregorio even stopped squirming as Leonardo looked at him, at Benedetta, who didn't think anyone had looked so intensely at her ever, not even Emelio looking at her naked.

"You can move now," Leonardo said.

"Can I see the drawing?"

Leonardo sighed, but let her come see the quick sketch in the notebook. Alongside it were jottings in writing that Benedetta couldn't read, even though she'd picked up reading from Emelio. They looked backward. She wanted to see other drawings. Emelio had told her about the gun designs, how he wasn't sure they were practical.

She turned the page and saw mechanical things, flying machines. "Do these work?"

Leonardo picked up a small whirly thing with a top that was a broad, shallow screw of paper and light wood. He twisted a key in the bottom of the toy while holding the paper and wood screw. He pulled out the key, let go of the screw. The screw whirled and rose in the air, then dropped.

"We'll fly soon enough," Leonardo said. He made a movement toward the notebook, but Gregorio ran to pick up the whirly toy. Leonardo grabbed it first. Gregorio grabbed his leg and reached for the toy. Benedetta turned to pages of dissections, horrible and fascinating, then fascinating. She'd seen some of this when soldiers were wounded, but not the details.

"You really don't want to see those," Leonardo said. She freed his leg from her son, handed Leonardo the book after he put the whirly toy out of Gregorio's reach, and said, "Are we really like that inside?"

"Yes."

"Thank you for showing them to me." She wanted to see more.

Back in the quarters Emelio found for them in the city, a small house with two rooms up and two rooms down, Benedetta kept thinking about Leonardo's notebooks, what she'd heard of them, what she'd seen. Gregó ran back to the garden and started to throw mud down the well. Benedetta grabbed him and brought him back inside. He said, "I want the flying toy."

"I'll try to get one for you," Benedetta said. That would be a good excuse to go back to Leonardo's studio.

In those days, Milan was filled with people in its tawny brick and gray stone buildings, walking and riding and carried in sedan chairs through the streets and boating on the canals. The cathedral continued to grow, lacy stone against the clouds. The gossip traveled by foot, horse, and boat—the Turks were in Apulia; the Venetians sent troops into Lombardy, the French were in Sicily at Ludovico's suggestions. Emelio's commander, Sanseverino, married Ludovico's illegitimate daughter Bianca.

Benedetta felt a tiny part of the greater struggles she heard about—the artillery team. The Sforzas themselves began as peasants who contracted for war work. Emelio got permission to live inside the city during the winter rather than in a camp outside the city walls. He was trying to talk to Il Moro about bringing in smaller guns, more of them. Ludovico Sforza, now duke of Milan officially after ruling Milan for years in the name of his nephew Gian Galeazzo Sforza, was good to his war contractors and their men.

Julia agreed to take care of Gregorio while Benedetta shopped in the city. She went first to the Corte Vecchia to see about the flying toy.

Leonardo wasn't in, but an old woman and the sulky beautiful youth were arguing over towels. *Leonardo's mother?* The doors to the outside were closed and the giant horse almost disappeared in the gloom. Benedetta wondered if she could just borrow the flying toy.

"Who are you and what do you want?" the woman asked, turning from her argument with the boy.

"An artillery man's wife," the boy said. "Where's the brat?"

"Hush, Salai, and I expect the towels to be back where I left them to dry or I tell Leonardo."

"Ah, the towels," Salai said. "Leonardo lets me do whatever I want with the towels."

Benedetta said, "I'm supposed to pick up the flying toy and take it to Leonardo."

The woman looked suspicious. "Why would he need it now? He's painting a wall."

"You're cute, even if you are old," Salai said.

"He didn't say why he wanted to take a brief look at it. I'll bring it back," Benedetta said. She would need to find an artificer who could make a copy of it.

The old woman looked at Benedetta and asked, "Why, really?"

She looked as though lies bored her more than anything else, having heard too many in her lifetime.

"My boy wants one."

"You can have it copied and bring Leonardo's back to me. I can find out where you live."

"I didn't take the towels," Salai said. "This bitch did."

The old woman turned to look at him and gave him the fig, exaggerating it by wiggling her thumb between her index finger and middle finger. "Leonardo takes too good care of you, you little fuck." She went over to the cabinets with the drawing books and pulled out the flying toy. "And bring back the towels, or I'll tell Leonardo you stole this, too."

"Caterina, you are a crazy old bitch," Salai said.

"I will die soon enough, then you can have Leonardo all to yourself," Caterina said. She said to Benedetta, "Bring it back in one piece. You can find someone to forge a spring for you, I would think."

Benedetta realized the spring in the toy was a relatively valuable thing, hand-forged and coiled into the spiral. "I could pay for it."

"If the baby breaks it, you will pay for it," Caterina said. "Copy this one, bring it back to me. An armorer should be able to forge the spring. Boys are so loveable when they're babies, aren't they?" The old woman smiled, a quick upturning of the ends of the lips that changed her whole expression. Benedetta saw the resemblance to Leonardo then.

And either one of them could help her see more of the drawings. "I'll be careful and I'll get it back after I find another spring. The rest of it seems simple enough."

"There's a trick of the fanlike thing," Caterina said. "But I'm not my son and I can't tell you what it is."

Salai followed Benedetta down the stairs and tried to pinch her.

She almost hit him with her elbow, but decided she could use him. Things in Leonardo's house that went missing got blamed on Salai. Not a bad thing to know. So, she just turned her body so the pinch fell on the side of her hip.

"I'll see you again," Salai said.

"I'm sure you will," Benedetta said, wondering where she'd find a spring like this. Clockmakers might have them. An armorer could make one.

That night, Emelio looked at the flying toy and said, "Where would he find a spring strong enough to fling a man into the air? This spring is heavier than the toy itself. It only goes up for a moment, just a toy. Leonardo . . ." Emelio didn't finish the sentiment.

Benedetta took Gregorio with her when she next went to the powder mill and stopped by the armorer to see if he could duplicate the spring. He tasted it and smelled it, then scratched it with a diamond. "I'll try to make one, but you could make something of green wood that might work out."

At the powder mill, Benedetta found the saltpeter bags and thrust her arm down into each one. Five of the bags were good; one felt slightly damp, wrong stuff. She tied that bag up again with a second cord marking it as a bad sack. Someone should have checked first, but for now, the bag was set aside to return to the dealer. The other bags went into the kneading mill, then the charcoal, sulfur, and vinegar. This was for the big guns: half saltpeter, a bit more sulfur than charcoal.

"Emelio's woman is baking again," one of the mill workers said.

"I'll need the big-holed skin," Benedetta said. While the mill worked the powder mass, Benedetta set up the roller and the frame of stretched bull-hide perforated with large holes. Gregorio helped bring lumps of mixed gunpowder to Benedetta, who rolled the paste through the holes in the bull hide. They had several weeks of work ahead of them. One of the workmen set up another bull-hide sieve and began working, too. They'd need at least half the weight of the shot in powder to fire the big guns.

"You're an awful little girl to be messing with that roller," said the workman on the other bull hide.

Benedetta just grunted and kept pushing the roller back and forth, sweating as she pressed down on the roller. It was hard work, harder than kneading dough, but she decided early that the guys would pull fewer tricks, like giving her the wrong saltpeter, if she could work as they did. Periodically, she'd spread the corned powder out so it would dry faster. Then as she got tired, she asked, "We have more bags of saltpeter coming in?"

"Should."

"Be sure to get credit for that crummy damp shit they sent us."

The images from Leonardo's notebooks played in her memory. She wanted to see them again. Perhaps if she just asked him to let her see them when she brought the flying toy back.

The weather turned rainy, so Benedetta decided to work on wooden springs for the flying toy and found that she could build another one with a coil of yew. She launched it into the air for Gregorio. As it descended, the vane still whirling, he grabbed it with both hands and promptly broke it. Benedetta pulled the splinters out of his hand while he squalled between her knees.

She put the original up high.

The next clear day Benedetta took the original toy back to Leonardo's, with Julia taking on Gregorio for the day. Salai and Leonardo's mother, Caterina, still appeared to be quarreling as though they'd never stopped when Benedetta came up to the big studio. A peacock was menacing a couple of cats in the corner of the space. "Excuse me," Benedetta said. "Here's the flying toy back. Could I see more of Leonardo's drawings?"

"What can you do for us?" Caterina asked.

"Nothing," Salai said, eating from a bowl of millet and fish with his fingers. "You can leave now."

The old woman said, "I think a gunner's wife would find my son's drawings interesting."

"Leonardo brought you here because he felt sorry for you, Caterina. You don't understand what he does well enough to have a right to be proud of him."

"I don't steal from him," Caterina said. "And I asked him for a small bit of a funeral. I keep his pets fed." She looked at the cats and peacock who were now ignoring each other studiously, then at Salai with her cooking in his bowl.

"Show the bitch Leonardo's drawing books then, and see what he says to that."

"If it's that much trouble, if I need to ask his permission directly, I won't bother you," Benedetta said, perfectly happy to be polite now that she appeared to have Caterina's sympathy.

"Pity your man isn't an artist. Milan falls, Leonardo will be working for the French or the Florentines. Artillery makes you much more on one side." Caterina walked back to the shelves with the notebooks and looked through them, then brought one of them to the table. Salai shrugged and went down the stairs.

"A waste of a good asshole, that one," Caterina said. She turned her attention to the notebook and opened it. "Don't touch. I'll turn the pages."

Benedetta nodded and looked at Leonardo's map of Milan, the city in a circle. Caterina pointed, almost touching the page. "The Sforza Castle fears the city more than enemies beyond."

The castle was built up more on the city side. Benedetta had been vaguely aware of something odd there, but hadn't thought much about it. Seeing Leonardo's plan of the city made this clear.

Caterina turned the pages with the tips of her fingernails. "And here, what the inside of a head looks like." Benedetta thought the drawing was much neater than the messes of men's heads she'd seen after battle. "And, here, about waves. And about machines."

"Slow down."

"Come back and visit with me again. I'll show you more. You'll be here for a while? Or are you going fighting again?"

"I can come back," Benedetta said, her head full of the drawings, imagining them in color, as real things.

Caterina looked around sharply to see if anyone was listening. "It all depends on how stupid the Moor is going to be, of course. You should find someone to take care of your son. Is your mother still alive?"

"I don't know," Benedetta said.

"That's very sad," Caterina said, "but there are sadder things." She opened the notebook and said, "Here's what Leonardo wanted to do for the city, to make it cleaner and stop the plagues." Caterina seemed tired now. "What would you and your man do if there was no war?"

"Don't know. I wouldn't want to be just a housewife. Maybe trade, a shop?"

"Pity your man didn't pick a peaceful art."

Benedetta didn't say anything about the cannons and armored carts she'd heard that Leonardo wanted to build.

"You will forgive me what I said. Please come back. Bring the baby."

Leonardo's mother is lonely. "I'll visit again."

Surviving the exposure

The bed was confusing, too hot. Benedetta remembered talking to her son, who seemed to have grown up and resented her for an obscure reason having to do with the fact that she thought she was dying whenever this was. The bed held her firmly. Then Leonardo's mother came to visit with an old copy of his notebook, only the letters were a different style of unreadable than the unreadable letters Benedetta remembered.

"You asked to see this," the woman who turned out not to be Leonardo's mother said. The woman was dressed like an angel, but Benedetta didn't know what to believe right now. "I'll come back when you're not delirious, though."

In her dreams, Benedetta wandered through a camp full of rusty armored battle cars from Leonardo's drawings, and her son came up to her and said, "I wanted something more for my life, too."

"What happened to you?" Benedetta asked.

"I died almost eight hundred years from now," her son said.

Benedetta woke up, sweating. She realized that everyone she'd loved was dead. Since only luck had kept her alive, she felt like she could be dead at any moment.

The people in the future put tubes up her nose and hollow needles in her arms. Benedetta couldn't move her arms to wipe away the tears. "You're crying," Joe said.

"They're all dead."

"Yeah, and you're not in great shape yourself."

"Why did I get this sick?"

"Probably something that evolved after you died. Diseases that people now have natural immunities to."

"Can I get this sick again?"

"We're working on some things that will help you, we think."

Benedetta felt as though she'd been beaten from inside. "At first, I was going on pure energy from the idea of being in the future."

"*Adrenaline*," Joe said. "It's something the body produces when it needs energy. Glands over the kidneys."

Benedetta almost said, I bet Leonardo knew about them from dissections, but thinking that brought a wave of sadness. Everyone is dead. "Leonardo died famous, didn't he?"

"There's a legend that he died in the arms of the French king."

"The one who killed us? I'm strapped down. Please let me loose."

"You were thrashing around when you were feverish."

"I had a strange dream about my son. It was so easy for babies to die, but he lived. And he looked like a strong boy last time I saw him."

"What happened to him?"

"I sent him to my mother. Camps in real war weren't safe for a child. But maybe you could have brought him with me? Can we go back and get him? I saw Emelio die, really dead."

"I don't think it's possible to save your son," Joe said. He started unfastening the restraints. "If you have a relapse, I'll be pissed. I'm sort of getting attached to you."

"Explain germ theory to me again. And how come you don't bring tiny animals into the Archives?"

"We do decontamination procedures. Or we just work with puppets and projections."

"I wouldn't have found you out if you'd just been a puppet."

"You've taught us to improve our techniques," Joe said. "We're going to try to bring up someone from closer to our time and just tell him what happened."

Biometric Illusions

The Archives halls looped back on themselves. Benedetta walked everywhere she could, not testing doors, just seeing what reaction her captors might have to her curiosity. She knew they had cameras that captured light far better than anything Leonardo had imagined.

Did the future people watch her for entertainment, just as men watched dog fights and bear jousts in her day? She felt angry about not knowing more about the tools that manipulated this time: computers, cameras, and time machines. Her lips formed the sounds, but her lungs didn't put breath to them. She wanted to be able to use the tool herself.

"Are you one of the programmers or one of the programmed?" a tall man asked from the door of one of the rooms. He was trusted enough to have an open door, but Benedetta had never seen him before. They hadn't asked her to help with him, then. Maybe he was close enough to their time to understand all this.

The man wore a wool suit cut almost but not quite like the modern clothes that Joe and others wore. Benedetta liked the cut, but didn't know if the suit was special, since the man wore it with both irony and confidence. The man had short blond hair and a tiny mustache, trimmed, not flowing long. If his skin hadn't been so pasty and saggy, and his gut were a bit smaller, he could pose for a god in Ivar's world, Benedetta thought. He was drinking something hot from a cup.

"What do you mean? Are you new here?"

"I was invented yesterday if you don't believe the crap about time travel. When do you think you come from?"

"Almost 1500, from Lombardy," Benedetta said. The question was oddly phrased. *Think* I came from?"

"I think I came from just before the beginning of the plague years, but I could be a subroutine running on a computer that is running a game about time travel. We could be parts of a computer program."

Benedetta hoped the man knew more about computers than she'd been told. "You know about computers? Teach me about them. Most people are in their illusion rooms, with the doors closed. Why is your door open? Why don't you walk around like I do?"

"They're trying to convince me I'm not a computer program, I think, so they opened my door today. I refuse to go out and explore until they give me my own network hookup. So, what did you see in your Lombardy, or were you locked up in a nunnery the whole time?"

"I was a camp wife. My family knew Leonardo da Vinci."

He seemed amused. "A real Lombardian camp follower who knew Leonardo da Vinci? Gee, these archivists are real people collectors, aren't they? I know why I'm here. They recreate odd people from all over the past."

Benedetta said, "You would have died in your own time, would have disappeared, I think. Nobody cared about finding the body. They fish for people with the time machine."

"I fell down the steps, I think. Don't remember anything other than it had started snowing and my wife and children were out for the weekend. Now, I'm here. Either I fell down the steps on an icy day and died in the middle of East Falls, or I'm a self-aware subroutine in a computer who thinks he was a human who died three hundred years ago. Which is more logical to you? Time machine? Computer game?"

Benedetta thought both, or neither. "Tell me about computers and the cameras," Benedetta said. "Your time had them?"

The man looked through—not at—Benedetta, his mind busy with memories of his own time, Benedetta realized. She missed Milan all over again, watching this man miss his time, day before yesterday as far as he could remember. The man said, "Yes, I knew something about computers. I herded cats. And at night, I stalked them."

"What do cats have to do with computers?" Benedetta said. Herding cats was impossible. Stalking them amused some creatures.

"We managers thought of the programmers as cats—petty, spiteful little things always going off in strange directions, thinking that the department revolved around them. We may be dead, you know, and just subroutines in a gaming program running on a computer. Programmers." He sighed. "Maybe it's a distributed program."

Benedetta didn't understand what he was talking about and this frustrated her quite a lot because she had some idea that he didn't quite know what he was talking about either. "Was this the afterlife you expected?" Benedetta asked.

"Sort of. The god programmer avatars make up comfortable lies about where we are. The future. I get to skip the plague years. Go, me."

"I believe they're real. I bit one of them," Benedetta said.

"You believe this is all really time travel and that my name was ... let's say, Fluffy, when I was alive."

"I don't believe your name was really Fluffy," Benedetta said, "but I believe they brought us to the future."

"Have you seen people walking around on screens?"

"That's just the modern example of a camera obscura," Benedetta said. "They told me the computer was like an abacus, only with tiny mechanical fingers and links to the screens, and what the camera saw could be piped in instructions to the screens. It's all dots. I need to learn more."

"I just have to deal with what appears to be my new world without worrying too much about the nature of it. Right? Except that if this *is* the future, my wife died thinking I'd abandoned her. I may have been an aging brat, but I loved my wife and my children."

"Why don't they let you access the computers?" Benedetta asked.

"I could find a way into any machine, cracking them or socially engineering my way in. Pyrophore.ogoense.net, xs4all.nl, Berkeley.edu, I had access on them all. I used computers circling the globe. I'd kept my real identity hidden for years from the net cops. But when Joe's people picked me out of the snow, I had my wallet in my pocket, so they knew who I was. Or they invented me after this old net character, the famous Fluffy, and I'm a subroutine in a computer game, a self-aware avatar, and I only think I was also a man named Jonah Kirkpatrick."

Perhaps he did believe he had been scooped from the past because he was famous for something he did then. Or they had invented a computer character based on him. Benedetta said, "Maybe they're afraid you'd just fuck with them."

"You don't think they recreate people at random, do you? You're not typical of Lombardian females. We're part of a game." The man paused and then said, "It should have been easy to give me my family rather than someone like you, but then that's part of the game, isn't it? Or I really am three hundred years in the future, my family thinking that I'd abandoned them. Which would you rather believe?"

Benedetta said, "It doesn't matter if this is real or not. It is the reality we have."

"Fuckheads. Trapped in the future with a Leonardo da Vinci groupie." The man stood up and paced in tight circles for a while, then reached into a box for a bottle. Benedetta smelled beer. She wanted some. The man who called himself Fluffy said, "You want a beer, too?"

She nodded.

The man handed Benedetta a beer and said, "You could call me Jonah if you don't like to call me Fluffy."

"Jonah," Benedetta said.

"I can wiggle out of the machine dream, I think."

"The cameras could be catching all of this," Benedetta said.

The man pointed his left middle finger in the air—*a fig on them*—drinking beer right-handed. "If we're not parts of a computer program, we're museum pieces. That's worse."

"And there is still plague outside," Benedetta said.

"Hell, I probably saw the first of it," Jonah said. "I didn't die from it." His speech became more precise the more he drank. The man scribbled down something and said, "If this isn't just a program inside a machine, maybe they got careless and trusting. Who knows?"

Benedetta refused the next beer and watched the man drink two more of them. The man finally said, "Oh, go away now. Control. Alt. Delete. Reboot yourself." He slipped her the piece of paper as he pushed her forehead with three fingers.

"Your afterlife is much harder to escape than mine," Benedetta said. "If you believe this is an illusion, then believing it's not an illusion could also be an illusion. Me, I'd have to know more about computers before I could say whether I believed you or not."

"What brought you here?"

"I was left for dead in a battlefield."

"It's an excellent little subroutine, isn't it, the beer hack. I don't think I'm here by accident, or else I goofed when I assumed they knew who I was."

Benedetta left the man drunk in his memories of a past he could be delusional about, read his slip of paper, which said, *I could get you out of this machine dream if it's real and the security cameras aren't monitored live. I can put you behind a mask.* She ate the paper and found Joe. "I met a guy today, blond, tall, speaks a kind of English, who's from near the plague years. Is he crazy? You can't just keep him here drunk."

Joe said, "Yes, we brought him three days ago, drunk and half frozen, with a concussion. We don't know if he's bullshitting us or if he does think he's inside a computer as part of a game. I think he's bullshitting us now."

"What did you tell him he'd been reborn into?"

"We didn't try to fake him out at all. He invented this crap all on his own. We'd heard that was a common twenty-first century belief among computer people. After they died, their brains would be scanned and their information would run on a machine. But it's not what's happening. If this were virtual reality, things would streak if you turned your head fast. And we'd need lots of hardware to run Philadelphia, much less the rest of the world. You're confused? You believe we tried to fake him out by telling him he was a subroutine running on a gaming server? We have learned something from you."

"Whatever. I need to learn more about computers."

"We're going to teach you, just . . ."

"I don't like being ignorant of the major tools of the time I'm in."

"Computers are very complex. Most of us use them more than we understand them, even now."

Benedetta wondered if Joe was exaggerating the difficulties. Perhaps Jonah would be willing to teach her more.

Back with Jonah the next day, Benedetta said, "I've been outside. It's not patterns in a machine. Joe said if it were patterns in a machine, things would streak when you moved your head fast."

"Everything streaked when I was alive. Maybe I was never alive."

Benedetta said, "You're alive and drunk."

"You're not real," Jonah said. "They made you up out of Leonardo's notebooks." Jonah took one of the empty bottles and put it to one of his eyes and twirled it around in his fingers. "See, blur and streaking. Oh, I like having met you. The Time Team knows I think I need company, whatever I am. And you'd be beautiful if you didn't look so much like you thought all the time."

"Okay, I'll see you later." Benedetta began to think that the man was putting on an act and that the mask he'd promised her would be real.

The man said, "They did make me an excellent suit."

Benedetta said. "I like it. Future clothes."

"Are the monitoring camera pictures in color or black-and-white?"

Benedetta said, "Some are black-and-white." She tried to remember where the black-and-white monitors were, what their cameras were pointed at.

"They don't let *me* see the monitoring screens," Jonah said. "They really should let me play with their system. Depriving me of computers is cruel and unusual punishment, even if I am just an avatar in a game program."

"You know what's the best argument for you not being a character in an imaginary game?" Benedetta said. "If this wasn't real, they could easily give you fake computer access and let you pretend to hack it."

"They could give me a real computer that only pretends to be connected to their network, too. Is it necessary for me to believe this is real? I don't want to believe I'm three hundred years in the future."

"I guess it's not," Benedetta said. "You can be crazy if you want to be."

"So these cameras work in black-and-white and in color. Hmm. I need to get out and exercise, don't I? Biometrics recognition could be useful. I'm being silly. Am I sounding insane?"

"Yes, you're sounding nuts." She suspected he was deliberately sounding nuts.

"I'm closer to their real time, only three hundred years away. It's like breathing down their necks, I suspect, especially if civilization collapsed after the plagues and they've just rebuilt. I might even know more than they know. That is, if I'm really in the future and not just in a program. I could have living kin out there. The Time Team can all blow me. Don't you miss people you know?"

"From the last things I remember about my past, I expected to be dead." People who might have remembered her would expect her to be dead, not alive after they were all less than skeletons.

Jonah asked, "How does someone die in a modern American city slipping on ice? Disappearing after slipping on ice? Doesn't this sound suspicious to you?"

Benedetta said, "They said that they can only get people who disappeared. Sometimes, they can't get people they think they can get. They only get people they can get."

The man stood up and walked up and down in his room. Then he said, "The program makes you go away now. I need to think. Or think I think." He looked baggier than usual, tired and frustrated.

Benedetta left.

Jonah passed her a mask a day later, wrapped in a shirt and pants. He yammered about open-source servers and running code and consensus while she looked at it, covering it with her body and holding the pants around it so the cameras couldn't see it easily. It was a mix of soap and paper, padded in the back with more paper, which almost looked like Joe. *Why is this going to work? How is this going to work?* Benedetta stared at it. She could tell it wasn't Joe, surely anyone watching would know it wasn't Joe. The face wouldn't move. She wrapped it back in the shirt and pants. Jonah dipped his finger in a mix of water and gruel and wrote on his plate, *Joe's biometrics. If the door doesn't open, try slipping the bolt,* and slipped Benedetta a stiff piece of what she'd learned was plastic. Benedetta realized that Jonah would rather risk her with the security system than himself. A test. Well, without this future, they'd both be dead, she bled out, he frozen to death.

Benedetta was going to pretend to be Joe behind a mask made of soap. She wanted to know what Jonah meant by biometrics. What could they do to her if they caught her? Keep her locked up for the rest of her life? They were already doing that.

That night, the cameras were waiting. Benedetta changed into the shirt and pants. Jonah was crazy, but she slid the mask on her face and began walking down the white corridors with the doors to various people from various pasts. There was a faint glow in the corridors, barely enough to see her way. She saw a camera swivel and didn't look up at it. Benedetta's face was sweating beneath the soap mask. Jonah had reinforced it with thin paper. Strips of birch bark would have been better. Benedetta wondered if the shoes she had on would be a problem. They were soft, not hard-soled like Joe's shoes. She also wondered if Jonah was joking with her. How funny was this? The soap face would get soft from her sweat and droop. What was she going to do when she got out? Whore?

Another camera swiveled. Benedetta turned her masked face to it, briefly. This felt like a masquerade, like being in Milan, sneaking masked through the streets, with messages from the French offering Leonardo his safety if Il Moro fell.

Benedetta found a door with a camera over it. The camera turned toward her face and moved down, then up. It fixed on her face. Just as Benedetta thought she should run away, the door opened. Benedetta looked at the space beyond the door. It looked like a box trap without a baited stick to bring down the door behind her. There was a space and another door.

Benedetta walked into the space to see if she could get beyond the next door. What were they going to do to her for trying to escape anyway? She stepped through the door and it closed behind her. She saw a bench and beyond that a tiled floor with a curb of raised tiles and a metal drain in the floor. When she stepped across the raised tiles, water poured down on her. The mask felt slippery. She moved through the water, holding the mask to her face with her fingers, certain her breasts were showing through the wet shirt, hoping she wasn't distorting the mask.

Another tile curb. She stepped over that and wind blew at her. She wondered if she was supposed to leave her clothes behind on the bench, if there were more clothes beyond the shower. The mask was slippery under her fingers, but the air was drying it except where water had leaked behind it, through some hair that she hadn't pulled out of the way when she put the mask on. *I should be more careful next time.*

The next door resisted her. She took the card out and slid it between the door and the doorframe. *I'm being a lockpick.* The door bolt slid back but as she opened the door, a noise began. She saw glass, a night with vague shadows and lights beyond that, and ran into the room with the windows to the outside. There was another bench in the room with windows, not bolted down, she discovered. As she heaved, the bench swung up through the air. Benedetta wheeled to throw it at the windows, hoping they were real, hoping they were glass that could break and not a future material that would refuse to smash, or an illusion on a screen.

She heard people in the room behind her. The windows shattered, but not like glass shatters. Still, Benedetta managed to get through the windows as people ran into the room. She landed on a yew and wondered at them planting bow wood even now, as she rolled under it and began creeping forward under the plants. She saw a short iron fence across an open space. She could get across and over that. *And hide where?*

Someone came through the window behind her, so she went through the yews and ran for the fence. A man came at her from the side. She shoved the man, fearing that they would hunt her harder if she hurt him. Then she pulled off the soap-and-paper mask and threw it at the man who seemed shocked momentarily as the soapy thing smacked into his face.

Benedetta ran for the fence, touched it. The fence snatched at her with chills and pain, but she vaulted over it despite the shock, and kept running.

"Lock on her and dart her," she heard a voice say.

"We don't have the smart gun," another voice said.

"I thought she ripped off someone's face," the first voice said.

"Try now," the second voice said. Benedetta threw herself down and rolled. Maybe these darts were smart but she'd try to evade them as though they were ordinary crossbow bolts. She found a space between buildings and ran in.

An animal like a rat but not a rat, bigger than a cat, stared at her and hissed. The creature's presence meant there was at least one other way out of where she'd run. But was it big enough for her? She ran down a space between the rows of buildings. Dogs began barking, so she looked for space out, farther away from the Archives. She went out one unlocked gate into a massed collection of metal-and-glass things on wheels, then farther, across the street with metal rails, and then back into an alley that looked more like the cities she was used to, only with strange stone underfoot. A crowd of people was leaving a building. Some of them were women in pants and shirts. Benedetta slowed down and walked in the middle of the group as though she'd just left the building with them. She wondered briefly what her face looked like, and what they thought about her clothes being soaked with water, her hands slimy with soap.

Two of what she thought were pregnant women turned out to be men with beards and mustaches.

"What happened to you?" one of the group asked.

"I got wet," Benedetta said.

"Where are you from?"

"Lombardy. Milan." Benedetta could tell she didn't sound like them. "I'm staying with a friend here."

"That's in Italy, isn't it? In quarantine long?" the man said.

"Ages," Benedetta said. So there was travel between places despite the plagues.

"You find what you wanted at the club?"

"No," Benedetta said. The man wasn't reacting to her as though she was a woman. Okay, Leonardo's kind, then. Some liked women, some didn't, but they weren't going to try to hump her while she was sore from fighting the fence and running. She saw another alley and decided to hide there. A man put his hand on her. "I need dry clothes. I need to get back to my friends' house."

The man said cheerfully, "You weren't in the bar at all, were you?"

"No, actually not. I ran to hide in the crowd leaving. A crazy ex-boyfriend is chasing me."

"Yeah, right," the man said. One of the pregnant-looking men came over to him.

"Are you really from Lombardy? Archives reported someone missing. And there's no travel between here and Milan at this point."

Benedetta felt trapped. "Yes. I was from Lombardy many centuries ago. I was trapped at the Archives. Are you going to turn me in?"

"Should I? Is there a reward? You need to get out of those wet clothes, dear."

"I was going to look for a nice dry ..." What, a stable? They didn't have horses in these days.

"Some of us have been really rather curious about what's going on with the Archives. And how many centuries precisely back?"

They all love the past in this future, Benedetta thought. "Leonardo da Vinci's time."

The man said, "I know someone about your size. I know a lawyer, too. You can't be held against your will except for medical reasons or unless you've been arrested for a crime."

Benedetta didn't tell him that the Archives claimed to be holding her for medical reasons, even though she'd survived one exposure to the future. If she didn't catch more diseases of this future, she wanted to be a future person, not a slave of the Archives. "My name is Benedetta," she said, holding out her hand until she realized how soapy and wet it was.

The man said, "I'm Mike. Pleased to meet you. How did you learn English?"

"First from English mercenaries, then from the people in the Archives."

"Yeah. I'm kind of curious about those Archives. I haven't heard of anyone escaping before you, though. The Archives has been trying to justify what they're doing to the city council for a couple of years now." They turned a corner.

Benedetta wondered if she needed to run again, if there was a reward for her. She looked at her hands under one of the lights. They were a little blistered where the fence tech bit her. Electricity. "I suspect I'm the first."

"You've got a right to as much freedom as anyone else," Mike said, "however you ended up in Philadelphia."

"Even if it kills me," Benedetta said. Her hands were really hurting now.

"Why would it do that?"

"I'm not used to your diseases," Benedetta said. "I've been exposed to some of them already and recovered, but I didn't show antibodies for all of them."

"Oh, shit," Mike said. "I know people who'd want to help you, but I really don't want you to die on me."

"If I think I'm dying, I'll find a private place away from you."

"Don't be melodramatic. Here's home," Mike said, sticking a piece of plastic in a slot in a door. "You can't make us sick, can you?"

"I don't think so," Benedetta said, "but syphilis was spreading just before I thought I died."

"Look, I appreciate that you told me that you'd escaped from the Archives. I really don't know what's best for you at this point, but if you're not used to our diseases, you probably should go back there. You didn't do anything stupid or violent when you left, did you?"

"No," Benedetta said, meaning *no* to going back as well as denying that she'd done anything stupid. She wished she hadn't come with the man now. After the energy of the escape faded, she hurt more from the science fence. She looked around the man's space in the building and realized how little she knew. The man switched on a light.

Benedetta wondered if the man would call the Archives as soon as she was asleep, but sleep was wrapping itself around her.

"I need to talk to my husband about this," Mike said, "but I'll give you a change of clothes. Take a shower. The bathroom is down there." Mike pointed to a door at the end of the hall.

Benedetta went into the bathroom and stared at the shower. If it worked like the Archives' showers, she should be able to get it to work. She tentatively turned a knob, then the other knob to bring in the heated water. She was falling asleep standing under the water.

Mike's husband with a big belly brought in clothes and said, "I really think you need to go back to the Archives."

"No. Are you pregnant?"

"Yes. This must be a real change for you. We need all the good genes we can get, and I wanted to have a child with Mike. I'm Albert."

Benedetta wondered how the child came out, but didn't really want to know all the details. She shuddered.

"Can we talk about this after I get some food and sleep?" Benedetta said. "Or are you going to tell the Archives I'm here when I'm asleep so I can wake up in chains?"

"Would they really do that to you?" Albert said. "The Archivists don't seem like mean people, just secretive."

"I don't know. I haven't escaped before," Benedetta said, way too tired now for fine distinctions.

The next day, she woke up feeling fine and decided she'd gotten all the diseases she was going to get the first time she was out. Mike fixed her breakfast and said, "If you know how to read English, there's a computer here. You can read while we're out or get help if you get sick."

"I'm not sick."

"Maybe you won't get sick," Mike said. "But we've had some weird problems in the past, including some man-made viruses."

"I think they were exaggerating to make me afraid of moving out."

"They can't just hold you against your will anyway. Maybe you should talk to a lawyer? And maybe there are no diseases left for you to catch."

"What could I give a lawyer to make speaking for me in court worth his while?" Benedetta asked. People like her never had lawyers do anything good for them.

"Publicity," Mike said. "I know just the person."

Mike showed Benedetta how to work a washing machine, before the two men went to work. Benedetta stripped naked then and washed all her clothes, standing in front of the dryer for the warmth. She wondered if she would be allowed men's clothes here, or if she would have to find a smock and gown somewhere before she could go out. She's only worn men's clothes out at night and then rarely. Being naked felt more normal.

Men who loved men were open here. Men could have babies. She felt a pang for Leonardo and his difficulties with Salai. Pity he hadn't been brought forward. Leonardo could have found someone so much better than Salai, in this future.

When Mike got back, he helped Benedetta call a lawyer and then they took a walk around the neighborhood. Mike even introduced her to some women. One of them was sniffling with a cold. Benedetta thought it funny that the future had both lawyers and head colds still.

She continued to be well the next day when she went to talk to the lawyer, but she wasn't after that.

Not a God's Hall

Ivar washed his face before he argued with Joe. He did this to make Joe wait. Now that Ivar understood his room in the Archives to be man-made and not a god's hall, he wanted to move as a man among other men and women, and make his way among these strangers. His beard was growing thicker, a man's beard, staying damp after he dried his face with a towel. The future had good towels, but his beard was stronger.

"We're keeping you here for your own good," Joe said, standing a bit over arm's length away from Ivar. "We have sicknesses out there that don't hurt us anymore but which could still kill you. This Archives section is a set of interlocking buildings that stops the particles that cause illness. We're trying to keep your life safe."

Like jail, Ivar thought. "I haven't seen the sky since I was brought here."

"If you hadn't been brought here, you wouldn't be seeing at all."

"I might have been in Valhalla," Ivar said. Did these people believe that men died to nothing?

"We tried that. You didn't seem that happy with it."

Ivar started to say, *but your Valhalla was a lie,* but wondered if the Valhalla of the priests was no less false. Still, these weren't words that would get him out of this place. "In Norway, a time this light would be summer. I could smell hayfields." Here they burned something called electricity with wires sealed in glass bottles some places and in tubes other places to make the light that went on like summer sunlight all the time.

"Dealing with people really foreign to your ways of thinking can be hard on your mind. You need to learn more about our time. Benedetta was uniquely ready to accept what she saw. She knew people in her past who could imagine a future like ours. Beyond the different life ways, you could be crippled in your balls from sickness."

Ivar felt insulted. "If she was so uniquely ready to accept what she saw, why didn't you let her come and go as she wished?" They walked out to his dinner. Some woman came in and jabbered at Joe in their tongue. *So they wanted to scare me with threats of impotence.* "You future people can come and go as you wish."

"If you're seventeen now, we should be able to teach you more about our world before you are an adult," Joe said.

The woman said, "We can get parental rights over you."

More insults. Ivar would keep his face from showing his thoughts. Even if he'd died to Loki's Hall, and couldn't escape the trickster, he would leave this place for a place with stars and sun. Maybe Loki's stars and sun ate light and spewed it here. If they thought him a child, he would trick them into not guarding him well. He needed the Lombardian woman to become a friend for him. "Where is Benedetta? Why can't she talk to me, can someone else teach me these things?"

The two of them looked at each other. Benedetta wasn't under their control now, Ivar realized. He wondered how Benedetta had managed this.

"There's someone we could introduce you to, but he doesn't speak Norse," the woman said. "We'd like to trade you some freedom for keeping an eye on him. We'll start with teaching you the English we use. You'll pick up a lot about our ways that way." The woman's lips moved strangely, and her words weren't quite coming from her throat. Ivar touched her, but his hand didn't go through her. "Your lips are not where your words are coming from."

Joe said, "She's wearing a machine to shift her speech to your speech. Funny, Benedetta didn't say anything about spotting that when we had this conversation with her."

Ivar said, "You are all settled from England in this country?" They wanted him to be a spy.

"Long story," Joe said.

"Some English spoke Norse speech," Ivar said.

The woman said, "They did, but the language changed. We've got a teaching machine that should help you, but all this will take time."

Ivar bowed his head as much to hide his anger as in agreement. He would agree to their game for now. Until he learned their language, he would be a dumb man traveling on their roads. "Are any of my people left? Does anyone speak as I do?"

"Modern Icelandic is as close as any language. We did a *diff* on how you spoke compared to it and worked closer to your language. We compared the way people spoke Icelandic with the printed versions of Icelandic from the twelfth century and the way you were speaking. Modern Icelandic is close. Just that not much survived because of Reykjavik *airport,* airship landing port."

Airships? What was a fucking *airport*? The words were coming from Joe's mouth but not at a normal speed. "You don't really know what you're speaking, do you? Like a slave thinking in his mother tongue and using some Norse words."

"I know what I'm talking about. I just have a *translation computer* to assist me in talking to you."

Ivar said, "You could use your own words and explain them."

The woman said, "Yes, we could, but you still wouldn't have words for what you're seeing. You need a contemporary language to understand this world."

Ivar wondered if he could get to the sea and find a ship, and then he could get to Iceland, where people spoke as he did. "Please start teaching me this language, then."

"And you do need company," Joe said. "We will let you out if you help us."

Ivar thought black hate at the man. Maybe he could talk the Lombardian woman into coming back for him. She really spoke Norse language, not having a wax-looking thing at the throat talk for her or getting whispers from a thing in her ear.

Ivar knew that the quickest way to teach a slave the Norse tongue was to not use any of the slave's language. Once he could say, "English only," he refused to reply to any of them in any other language. Joe then spoke to him only in English. Ivar wanted to learn some phrases to use on women, and with pantomime, he learned them. Joe burst out laughing at him a couple of times, but Ivar didn't hit him. Joe's lack of fear was odd enough to make Ivar careful of him.

"Remember we did save your life," Joe said periodically. Ivar knew some would feel that made him their man forever. He, however, wished they'd saved him for his own time.

But I need exercise," Ivar said in English the next time Joe visited him, some weeks after the lessons began. "I'm picking up good English. You thought I was dumb, didn't you? Being a Viking? You think we're all berserkers?"

"I didn't assume anything. Really."

But Joe did seem surprised that Ivar was picking on the modern languages so quickly. Desperation made a man a quick learner. Ivar found himself pacing in circles when he talked to Joe, as he was doing now.

Joe said. "We don't allow a man to solve a problem with force. That's why we aren't sure you can adjust, adapt, to our ways."

Ivar just smiled back at him. "Now I know English some, I could be allowed to move about more free."

"We're going to teach you to read both English and Norse. I'd like your opinion on *Egil's Saga*."

"I heard of a guy older than me who fled to Iceland, Egil Skall-grimsson. He was a mean one. He got a saga about him?"

"I suppose the twentieth century can't be judged by the surviving movies, either."

"I'm not like Egil. You'd have told me if I'd been in a saga, right?" He smiled at Joe. *I'm not in the sagas; I'm just a young innocent man.*

"You have a sense of humor, I think."

"I have wit," Ivar said, "but I need exercise. I want to learn to ride a bicycle." Ivar would have preferred a motorcycle from what Benedetta told him of them, but she didn't think they could be used inside the Archives building.

"How did you decide on bicycles?"

"I've been looking for transportation." Ivar didn't like these questions. *So I can get away without having to rely on anything other than myself* wasn't something Joe needed to know. "I could ride around in the halls."

"We'll let you walk around in the halls," Joe said. "You've been pretty patient with us, I think."

"I have obeyed where appropriate," Ivar said. If they didn't have horses, he'd have to walk to where he could get a boat to Iceland if the bicycle thing wasn't as useful as he thought it could be. *As fast as a horse.*

"You could ride a stationary bike if you just want exercise," Joe said.

Ivar was almost happy. He could walk around and learn more. "What about motorcycles?"

"Benedetta was impressed by the one she saw," Joe said. "We even have some horses. I understand horse racing and fighting were popular with your people."

"How do most people get around?"

"By train, mostly. Some fly."

"Flying magically or are there machines that do that, too?"

"By machines, airplanes. See, you still have a lot to learn."

"And Benedetta didn't?"

"Benedetta also has a lot to learn, but she was more prepared for the future than you were."

They weren't telling him much about Benedetta, other than she wasn't visiting him anymore.

Ivar was walking in the halls when a man came up behind him and said, "Nice program, isn't it?" in English.

"What do you mean?"

"You're in a computer program, don't you know. You even understand me, though I think I hear an accent. You can call me Jonah. We're artificial things that exist inside machines."

"Or I'm a thought in Loki's mind. Why does it matter? I think my thoughts are my own. I'm called Ivar."

"But you haven't been out there." The man was dressed in wool, but not a tunic and pants or leggings. He looked like a drunk.

"I'm told that they're holding me here for my own good in a biological containment facility."

"I think I'm a man from almost the time they were in, and from Philadelphia, only three hundred years before now."

"Do you know who Benedetta is?"

"A Renaissance camp follower who knew Leonardo da Vinci. Come on. How plausible is that? Do you know where Benedetta is now?"

"They haven't told me. I just don't see her anymore."

"I helped her get out, if there is a real out. I think they've got a nice program going here and you and I are subroutines in a computer. You do know what a computer is, don't you? Or am I just confusing you?"

"I think maybe we're both in Loki's mind. We both remember dying, don't we?" Ivar realized this was the man he was supposed to spy on. They'd been allowed to meet now. Ivar wondered what the man had been told about him.

"Actually, I don't remember dying, just blacking out. So, you're a fucking transcendental Viking?"

Ivar wondered if following his gods survived until now. "My grandmother didn't think much of the gods. Were people worshiping Thor and Odin when you were alive?"

"After a lapse of a thousand years," Jonah said. "Turn-of-the-century decadence, like homosexual marriage."

"I think I'm inside Loki's mind. You think you're inside a computer. We should get along just fine, then." Ivar thought the man really did believe he was in the future, but was refusing to let the trickster people know that, for reasons of his own. If he could trade getting out by informing on this Jonah, he'd inform. If Jonah could help him more than the future people, he wouldn't inform.

If Ivar himself was a thought in Loki's mind, then this world was all tricks all the time, but being inside Loki's mind would be different than being a program in a machine that man made. Loki's mind was bigger than humankind's imagination.

The world was never completely what it seemed.

"I've heard it's dangerous out there for us," Jonah said. "Do you believe that? Or does the program end somewhere smaller than the whole city of Philadelphia?"

Ivar asked, "Do you want to stay in here forever?"

"It beats being full dead, doesn't it?"

"Why did you help Benedetta escape?" Ivar would ask how later.

"Always get someone else to go further and see what happens to him. Or her in this case. But have they said anything to you about her? Do you really want to go out there if it would kill you? What if there's no there there?"

Ivar didn't answer for a moment. Then he said, "I'm young and healthy. Does everyone from the past die?"

"How far back before the immune system is so different that a disease that wouldn't kill them would kill you? If this is real, of course. What are the rules of the game if it isn't?"

Jonah made the mask that helped Benedetta escape," Ivar said, sure he wasn't telling the future people anything they didn't already know. "And he says he thinks this is all a computer game." Ivar didn't know if he should tell Joe and his friends that he suspected Jonah knew precisely where he was. Hallucinations of Loki, indeed. Or not. Whether a thought in Loki's mind or as a youth brought to a farther future than the natural passage of time would have given him, Ivar knew he had to act as himself, for himself, and had to conceal who he was from the other actors in this place, whatever it was. Loki would have expected this of him.

"How did he know what would work?" Joe asked.

"I'll try to find out."

Joe said, "We think we know how. The security cameras aren't running on black-and-white now. We've boosted the lighting even if the power collective doesn't like it."

Ivar thought Joe spoke like someone who didn't expect his security cameras to keep the past locked up forever. "What does he want to do?" Joe asked.

"I'll find out," Ivar said. "Jonah is just pretending to believe that he's in a computer program, I think."

"And he's a troll, not a Norse under-the-bridge kind, but someone who likes to goad people into losing their tempers," Joe said.

What do you want to do?" Ivar asked Jonah. "By the way, the security cameras all use color now."

"What I want to do is win this computer game," Jonah said. "And I want to find out what happened after I died, if I really had to die to get here. If this is really the future."

Ivar figured that the future people were monitoring them both, just using him to ask questions. "Has anyone heard from Benedetta?"

"She got off the game board. You expect them to tell us anything?"

The court case was settled," Joe said. He was furious, practically dragging Ivar to Jonah's cubicle. Ivar carried a laptop and cables. The Time Team was finally going to give Jonah what he wanted. Joe had three bottles of distilled liquor in his hands, even more of what Jonah wanted. "She almost died, but her lawyer wants to know what the fuck we were doing holding her against her will. We have to tell all of you what happened, where you are, and then let you leave if you want to, if you're adults. We have to come up with an acclimatization plan for everyone. Ivar, you're not an adult, so this doesn't apply to you."

Jonah said, "What if I don't choose to go?"

Joe said, "We have to take care of you, but we've been doing that. We have to give you citizen's access to all communication systems. Jonah, you're free to use the net, but don't try to hack us. And there's this." He put down each bottle with a flourish, hard, with a pause between each of them.

Jonah looked at the three bottles of liquor and said, "I wanted access, not liquor."

"Oh, you will like the liquor."

"I last remember being drunk enough to fall into this mess, so being drunk now isn't that tempting." He still looked at the bottles as though they'd been missed, though.

"We didn't know who we'd picked up drunk in the snow busy freezing to death but we've learned about you since. You assumed we knew who you were and talked about yourself when you were pretending this was a computer game . . ."

Ivar handed Jonah the laptop. "No wireless?" Jonah said. He looked at the computer carefully. "I'm surprised that people who have computers that don't look that much more advanced than this could invent a time machine."

Ivar noticed that Joe flinched. If they hadn't invented the time machine, who did they steal it from and how? Joe said, "No wireless for you. Can't you see Ivar has cables in his hands? I've got to find the outlet and hook you up."

"You don't sound gracious about this," Jonah said. "Giving me access is such a small favor."

"You've got a lawyer. Thank Benedetta."

"What would I have to pay a lawyer with?" Jonah said.

"Benedetta found an activist. They've got all sorts of subpoenas out. We should have kept all this much more of a secret."

Jonah said, "Keeping secrets is a bit trickier than most people imagine."

"You know this isn't a simulated reality, of course."

"I don't admit anything," Jonah said. He was still looking at the bottles. "So what is there in your future for me to play with?"

"Figure it out for yourself," Joe said. "Ivar?"

"Unless it's against your foster parent rules, I'm going to stay with Jonah awhile."

Joe left them.

Jonah said, "So our artillery girl who knew Leonardo escaped and got a lawyer to kick over this anthill. Neat. But you don't seem any happier?"

"I'm too young to benefit from this legal action," Ivar said. "They're claiming parental rights over me."

"If all this time travel bullshit is true, you're quite a bit older than you look," Jonah said.

"Biologically, I'm not quite of manhood age," Ivar said. "What is manhood age here, anyway?"

"Ask Joe. I'm not from now."

Ivar wondered if people had to swear loyalty to an overlord in these times, or if the country was more like Iceland, with agreements between men with land. "And you can't help me get out?"

"Not if they've changed the security cameras. And now they know I know some tricks, so they'll be watching."

Ivar decided he'd tell Joe that Jonah was now harmless.

System and Time

Months passed while Benedetta worked as a liquor machine atten-
dant in an Eleventh Street bar while studying during her free time
to understand computers, time travel, electrical engines, and radio.
She got a room over the bar, shared a kitchen with the bar's other
staff. They were all saving credit for a row house. Row houses still
came in two rooms up, two rooms down, kitchen a shed in the rear,
a design that was old when Benedetta had last lived in one.

All her memories of Leonardo couldn't stop Benedetta from feeling naïve all over again. She'd sued to get out of the Archives, but
she missed Jonah and even Ivar. Being scooped up-time isolated her
among people who took the future for granted, and nobody spun
by hand.

Even though she doubted she'd have known Jonah or have liked
Ivar in what she thought of now as her first life, they were the only
people she knew who could understand both the future and the
past in the way she did.

The future ran on almost imaginary machines, but the people who
made and used them seemed spoiled compared to people who'd
lived through Renaissance wars and plagues. The future people took
their marvels for granted and complained over trifles.

Benedetta applied for a visit to the Archives, to see her friends.

Joe met her at the front entrance to the Archives, still angry at her
escape. He'd thought that he was helping her, and the Time Team

had saved her life. "Hello, Benedetta. Are you coming back or just trying to visit?"

"Visit, Joe. I'm not property; neither are the others."

"Don't tempt them to risk their lives."

Benedetta shrugged. They all might have died centuries ago, but they didn't. The Time Team didn't own them.

"We would have let you out eventually."

"Probably, Joe, but I'm not used to boredom. Can I see Jonah and Ivar?" She had a legal paper in her pocket, to force Joe if she needed to.

Joe looked like he wished he could keep them all apart, but he called Jonah and Ivar to ask if they wanted to see Benedetta. They said yes on one call, so they were spending time together. Benedetta thought an alliance between the two of them had been predictable.

"The Time Team holds the position that since Ivar is a minor, we're serving in the parental oversight role for him, so he can't leave freely."

Benedetta went through the decontamination showers and put on a Time Team uniform. Joe came out just a few minutes later and led her down a corridor behind a door that had to be unlocked. She hadn't gotten through it when she was last there. They went up a flight of stairs to a small suite of rooms filled with computers and bicycles on stands. Foils and fencing gear, which hadn't been invented when Benedetta was in Italy, hung on the wall. The rooms smelled of male sweat. Ivar was lunging forward with his foil against a mechanical target about five inches round, which moved up and down on a chrome post. It also appeared to be able to shift sideways on a pantograph that was scratched shiny from near hits. Jonah was drinking something that steamed in his cup and looking at a computer screen.

Neither of them spoke to her right away. Then Jonah said, "There's a future out there and you came back here to visit."

Ivar stopped fencing with the mechanical target and put the point of the foil against the floor, leaning on it slightly until it bowed. Benedetta knew his body remembered a stiffer sword. Ivar straightened himself slightly so that the foil unbowed, but he still looked as though he was leaning against it. He smiled slightly.

"I wanted to see some people who came from the same kind of world I came from."

"I didn't come from your world," Jonah said. "I came from a world like the one you're uncomfortable with."

"Oh, really," Benedetta said. "Did men have children with men in your time?"

Ivar said, "I bet they could have. Or it's a computer program." He began stabbing at the target again.

Jonah said, "Neither of you understand anything about this future, do you?"

"That's why Benedetta came back to see me," Ivar said. "We're both motivated to figure it out. You think everything is a game."

Jonah said, "Life. Computer program. It's always a game, Ivar. You can play from the white side. You can play from the black side. Or you can be a wild card. Games are reality. You can't take anything that seriously except winning."

Benedetta wondered if Jonah even believed that. His obsessions were getting tiresome. Benedetta said, "I want to help people make the transition if they can."

Jonah said, "If this is real, my family could still be in Philadelphia."

Benedetta wanted to see Jonah quit playing. "I miss Emelio. And Gregorio. I know Emelio is dead, but I don't know about Gregorio. I could have people in this time, too, but tracing them would be ever so much harder." She remembered the last time she has seen Gregorio, her mother holding him back as she left.

"If we're not being lied to, all the people we loved are dead," Jonah said. "So let's see who lived." He put his fingers on the keyboard, and then touched a place where the keys were spread a bit. "Ergonomic, but no brain jack. I feel cheated."

He moved his hands and one of the icons on the screen expanded. "I'm looking for programs that would connect me to an external network. I can receive some broadcasts now, but I can't go out." His fingers moved again. "I can't believe they're really using some of these old protocols, or is this just for me?"

Benedetta saw a picture of herself, on her back, with tubes in her nose and bruises under her eyes. Jonah said, "You looked really pissed."

Benedetta said, "Some of the diseases made me hallucinate. The doctors told me there was no permanent damage."

"So they're not kidding about the dangers then? You knew that and you got a court order to allow us out anyway."

"I lived. Nobody makes you leave."

"Maybe I won't."

Benedetta stopped to think about whether she'd told Jonah about her earlier illness, after Joe allowed her to see the city streets and the woman on a motorcycle. She probably hadn't. "Didn't they explain when they told you about the future? Your rights?"

"They let me think I was in a computer program, remember?"

"Joe said that you thought all that without prompting. They brought you in after us. They tried to pretend I was in Purgatory, but that just seemed so unlikely," Benedetta said. "And Ivar was supposed to believe he was in Valhalla."

"Why?"

"For our own good, they said."

"What precisely are our rights here? You've worked with a lawyer, been in their courts."

"Basically, they don't know precisely if we're citizens or not, but my lawyer is working on getting full Philadelphia citizenship for all of us. The Archives didn't know what to do with us after we tell them about the past as we remember it. They thought it was kinder for us not to know they saved our lives by making everyone we cared about become very dead. Not that they killed the past. The past just died when we left it." She was thinking about Emelio and Gregorio now.

"Or we're programs in a computer who think we were human beings?"

"Was that the common idea of the afterlife in the time you're from?" Ivar said.

"No."

Benedetta laughed. "You tricked yourself. We're here. We're real."

"Oh, please, they bring people up from the past. How plausible is that?"

"How plausible is that they fuck up and have an angel with a cut on his finger when they're trying to fake me out that I'm in Purgatory?"

"It's a very complex game."

Ivar said, "Troll."

Jonah said, "I don't know who's trolling who."

"Troll," Ivar said again. They'd been arguing like this for months, Benedetta realized. She was surprised Ivar hadn't just whacked Jonah.

"Of course, the physics look just like reality," Jonah said. "I guess I could just go along and think it's real."

Benedetta said, "You know it's real."

"I don't know anything," Ivar said. He came over to them and, still holding his sword, watched Benedetta move on the screen through her first court appearance. "If it's real, I could die, but we all will die eventually."

Jonah said, "If it's not real, we could live forever, remembering and yearning for imaginary objects we think were people we used to love."

"For me that would be another Hell," said Benedetta.

Jonah said, "Better that than a future where I'm a stranger who's lost everyone he cared for and who will die alone."

Benedetta realized that Jonah would have preferred to be a program in a computer rather than a flesh man who'd die alone in a strange time. She almost could believe he was right. Being in a computer program now seemed more sensible than time travel. But reality, in her experience of it, was never sensible. "Even Leonardo never drew utterly true to life," she said. "Machines that draw would still be coming from either camera obscuras or from people, right?"

"You don't have a clue about what a computer is, or what a program is, but you are trying to tell me that this is really the future and we're not programs. Sheesh."

"Even if it is a computer, it's the future," Benedetta said, angry with him for pointing out that she accepted what she saw on faith.

"Unless your memories of Leonardo and mine of my family are part of the game, we could be in my own time. Nothing is three hundred years further advanced except the idea that a time machine brought us here. Wherever and whenever here is."

Benedetta tried to remember if she'd heard a word for machines that looked like men. "You could be a simulated man, a robot. If I cut you, will I see gears?"

"And if Ivar or I die, is the game going to be restarted?"

"I don't know why you're both arguing this," Ivar said. "I'm going to assume I got here through a time machine and that I'm in the future, just like they told me, and that we're protected by filters and equipment of various kinds from the diseases beyond the Archives. A lot of the future people died off from various plagues before we got here. And these assholes didn't make the time machine. The future dumped it on them for some reason. Joe thinks there may be more than one future until something happens that makes one future possible and the other not. Like different religions—the gods die when humans don't believe in them. We pick among possible futures. Time forks."

"And that would also be a good way to run a computer game," Jonah said. "Consider the plague. Philadelphia would be easier to simulate with fewer people."

Ivar said, "That's your afterlife fantasy, not mine."

Jonah didn't speak for a moment, and then laughed. He said, "Wow, I must have made it easy for them. For you, they've got to come up with a fake Purgatory that matches your expectations, for Ivar, they've got to have Valkyries and a hall full of heroes. For me, they just keep me in a room and have two improbable people come in to talk to me. I invented my own afterlife. And if they just scooped me up at random ... I couldn't imagine that I wasn't here for a purpose." He poured himself some of the liquor and drank it, then another glass.

Benedetta saw Ivar's eyes narrow and then widen as his lips thinned. Ivar had seen men doing this after a battle, as she had. Benedetta said, "They knew you like to get drunk. They knew something about you ..."

"I told them who I was, because I was sure they knew and that was why I was recreated, saved, whatever," he said. "They didn't know anything about you?"

"They were surprised that I knew Leonardo da Vinci," Benedetta said.

"How real was this surprise?"

"Very," Benedetta said.

Jonah looked at her for a few moments, the empty glass in his hand paused just under his chin. "What are the odds that some Lombardian female met Leonardo da Vinci and ended up here?"

"Ivar never met anyone special. I bet you never met anyone special."

"Ivar's our consensual hallucination. Ever consider how little data he's based on?"

"No, I'm the most real one here," Ivar said. "There's more to me than I've told you."

"You're programmed to say that," Jonah said.

Benedetta didn't believe Jonah was convinced that he was just a program in a computer. She looked at Ivar and shook her head slightly. Jonah said, "Oh, fuck you. Fill in the blanks with Leonardo da Vinci. Did he really try to fly or not? Do you know anything for sure?"

"He wanted very badly to fly. He used my son to test a descending sail." Benedetta sketched the sail's triangular shape in the air. "Made of gummed linen to catch the air."

"Oh, a parachute," Jonah said.

Milan, 1496, Dream of Flying in War Time

Caterina died. The funeral was small. Benedetta thought of her mother then, how casually she had let her go off with Julia. But life had been good, perhaps surprisingly so. Leonardo allowed Benedetta to visit his studio as long as she brought Gregorio. One day, while Salai teased Gregorio with the flying toys, Leonardo talked about a man flying through the air, carried by a giant version of the flying toy. Benedetta watched Salai sharply, to make sure that he didn't pinch her son. Salai said, "I'm a bit too big to fly in a toy. Why don't you take this child?"

Leonardo looked at Benedetta as if this sounded like a good idea.

Salai continued, "And if he died, you could dissect him."

"I won't let Gregorio fly in the machine."

"But I want to fly in the machine," her son said. Benedetta remembered how she wanted to go off with the army.

"We'll do it over the moat," Leonardo said. "Or over a lake. The boy can swim, can't he?"

"Why haven't you had more children?" Salai asked. "Emelio not up to it?"

Benedetta didn't answer him. Emelio and she had worked out a way with lemons and washes that appeared to be keeping them from having more children during these times. No bronze equestrian statue for Il Moro; no more children for people who'd end up fighting sooner or later and could die. Benedetta had nursed Gregorio as long as possible, but he was refusing to be a baby now.

"I can swim."

"You can't swim."

Leonardo said, "I can put floats on him, and fins." He pulled out an older notebook and flipped through until he found the drawing he was looking for. "It will be fun for him, and safe."

"Have you ever made these gloves? Or this?" Benedetta pointed at the drawing of something below, which looked like more swimming gear of some kind.

Leonardo looked annoyed. Salai said, "We can run a pair of the swimming fins up in no time. The flying machines might take longer."

"We can start with the linen descending sail. If we climb to the roof of the castle alongside the tower, no one will be able to see us from the watch lantern."

Benedetta didn't want to know why they were supposed to do this in secret. She heard about Leonardo talking to an old dying woman, then packing her body up and taking it away to dissect.

"Why not use Salai?" she said.

"I want to," Gregorio said.

"You'll wear bladders. We'll do this over the moat."

Leonardo drew more in his notebook. "We'll do this at night."

"Why not over a lake somewhere?"

"First I want to test the descending sail. The boy is small."

Leonardo set up a scale and weighed Gregorio against heaps of weights, then bent over his paper, adding what it took to balance Gregorio on the beam. He looked up and smiled. "Much easier than if he was a full grown man." Leonardo sent Salai out to buy linen and gum arabic.

Benedetta didn't like this but Gregorio seemed determined to hang under the descending kite. The thing would be heavy, with yards of gummed linen falling into the water after him. Gregorio would be under it when it hit the water. "Can you make sure he can get out of it in time?" Benedetta imagined Gregorio trapped in the linen and wanted to tell Leonardo they couldn't do this, but Gregorio wanted to and Leonardo said it was safe.

"We could make it so that he holds on to it, then swings away to drop into the water off to the side first."

They were carrying pieces of the descending sail to the roof. Benedetta carried the gummed linen. It alone weighed as much as Gregó, who was carrying the cords and ropes. Leonardo and Salai carried the poles. They hid the parts for the descending sail where the people watching from the lantern couldn't see them. Over the next couple of days, Leonardo and Salai put the sail together, with Benedetta observing anxiously. This was very foolish. Would Salai use this descending sail to kill Gregorio, or would Salai have to test it if Gregó, lighter and more willing, is not around?

Leonardo, Salai, and Benedetta built the contraption and tied it down so it didn't sail off by itself in the wind. It felt like it weighed about twice what Gregorio weighed, but Leonardo said it couldn't be that heavy. Gregorio would sit on it and then jump forward so he didn't tangle himself in it when it landed. Benedetta wondered if the thing wouldn't just go straight down, if it would hold air with all the gum on the linen, if she shouldn't run with Gregorio and hide. Leonardo could talk to people who were dying and cut them up to see their guts later. A failure would be almost as good as a success for Leonardo and he could autopsy Gregó's corpse besides.

Turn around, turn around.

On a cloudy night, they went back up to the top of the castle, with small lamps shielded on one side.

Leonardo was smiling a strange smile, curving up his lip corners, testing each connection of the wooden frame. "A man can ride this down without injury," Leonardo said. "Truly." His eyes glittered, and he seemed younger than he should have.

After they put it together, the contraption was as high and as wide as the heights of four men, like a field tent. Benedetta couldn't see how the watch in the lantern could miss it, but the castle roof had irregularities to hide such a thing. Leonardo had rigged a crane earlier so they could drop the descending sail right over the moat. "He'll go into the moat," Leonardo said. The night was dank and overcast. The linen almost seemed like it was glowing.

"Will the falling sail fit into the moat?"

Leonardo said, "The moat is wide enough."

Salai said, "Actually, if the thing couldn't fit into the moat and the little boy could, it might be better."

Gregorio stared down into the moat. Benedetta thought that at five years now, he was beginning to be useful, but now she was going to lose him. She looked over at Salai who was looking at Leonardo. Perhaps Salai was thinking that if Gregorio could grow up to be his rival for Leonardo's affections, Salai should booby-trap this descending sail and kill him now.

Leonardo looked at Gregorio and then at the descending sail. "We'll test it now."

"Or just test it without my son."

Gregó said, "But I want to."

Leonardo said, "I've tried smaller models with weights. It's safe."

Benedetta wondered if he cared. "Why don't you do it yourself?"

"I'll ride in it next. There's no wind. It's a good night to try."

The descending sail was heavy, and it took the two men with Benedetta's help to lift it to the crane. Leonardo had a hook fastened, which would release the descending sail when he pulled a cord threaded through pulleys on the crane. Gregorio got in the seat and held on to the side ropes as they lifted him. Even this part seemed fun to him. He was grinning. *My son is brave.* That mattered in a gunnery family.

"It's perfectly safe," Leonardo said to her. Salai wasn't saying anything, just looking tremendously jealous right now.

"Let me go down so I can get him out of the water fast," Benedetta said. She looked up at Gregorio sitting on the seat under the sail. "I'll throw a rock in the moat. You should be able to hear that if you can't see it. But wait for me to get down."

She went back down the stairs, thinking about just leaving and having them not set Gregorio falling under the sail. But they'd do it anyway and she couldn't save Gregorio if she wasn't there. She got to the moat and looked up. The beige linen tent of the sail was huge against the sky, and almost gleaming. There must be a moon out above the clouds. She tossed a stone in the moat.

And the descending sail worked, kept Gregorio from falling like a stone into the moat. For an instant, he was floating through the air like a feather, laughing and laughing.

The whole contraption seemed to crash down and collapse on top of Gregorio as he, then it, hit the water.

Benedetta waited a moment to see if he was free of the falling wood and fabric, didn't see him, and stripped her clothes to dive in the moat herself. Most women drowned because of fabric dragging them down. Her son was covered in fabric.

No, he was floating. Benedetta rolled him over and began dragging him back through the water. The damn frame must have hit him on the head. By the time she got to the edge of the moat, Leonardo and Salai were there with ropes to help her out.

Leonardo didn't react to her nakedness. He rolled Gregorio face-up and breathed into his mouth. "What happened?" Salai asked.

"He jumped free but not far enough. The frame hit him."

Gregorio sputtered and sat up. He felt his head. "I should have jumped out of the swing farther."

"You're not going to do that again," Benedetta said.

"But it was fun, except for getting hit in the head."

Benedetta was putting on her clothes over her wet skin. Salai was watching her. "No, you're not going to do that again," she said to Gregorio.

"We can try the glider in the mountains," Leonardo said. "It will be even more fun."

Gregorio threw up, and then said, "It was wonderful. I was floating in the air. I'll jump farther next time."

"There's not going to be a next time," Benedetta said.

"Perhaps you don't need to come back for more visits," Leonardo said. "You like looking at my engineering speculations, but you don't want to risk your son on seeing them built to work."

"Is using my son for your experiments the only reason you put up with me coming here?" Leonardo didn't have to answer. Benedetta knew the answer was *yes* as soon as she heard her words aloud.

"But I want to," Gregorio said. "And Salai doesn't want to."

"Man should fly," Leonardo said.

"You should fly. You fucking fall in a moat followed by a man's weight or more of linen and wood."

Gregorio looked very disappointed. Benedetta thought of the fighting to come, which everyone predicted. Perhaps now she should foster him out to country people or send him home to her mother to save him from all the messes he could get into—the war, testing flying machines for Leonardo.

Salai said, "Mothers always spoil things for their sons."

Leonardo said, "Stop it."

Benedetta did want to see more of the drawings, but then knew that she wanted to keep Gregorio safe more. But she couldn't even feel good about that. Gregorio liked visiting Leonardo's studio, the secrets under the floorboards that Salai showed him, the various peacocks, dogs, and men wandering in and out. The studio almost lifted out of Milan fueled with fine talk.

She took Gregorio's hand and walked away.

The Past of the Future

"So you blew off Leonardo da Vinci over the safety of some brat who's been dead for centuries now despite you," Jonah said after Benedetta stopped talking. "Or that's where the research ended, with proof that Leonardo's parachute could work, at least until it hit the ground? They tested the design in my day from a hot-air balloon. If you'd cooperated with Leonardo, we might have had the future a lot sooner."

"I'd like to know what happened to my son." Benedetta wondered if these people still had church records.

Jonah said, "He died. My wife and children died. Everyone I knew then is dead. Same for you, only they've been dead longer."

Ivar said, "My people have been dead the longest. That is if you believe we're not computer avatars."

"If we're just computer-game avatars, and they're trolling us into thinking we're people from the past, we can't play it any way other than their way," Jonah said. He was quite drunk now, holding his hands to his eyebrows and temples and rubbing. "We're either in the machine, or we're in the future. Trapped in the unfamiliar, either way. How good are you at dealing with the unfamiliar?"

"Very," Benedetta said.

"But not enough to let your son play with it."

"I don't want to talk about my son again."

"Hey, are the diseases out there fast or what?"

Benedetta remembered her hallucinations, which had come over her the next day or so after being outside. "I think the diseases can be fast or slow. One of them made some people sterile."

"If this is a life I can live, then why should I risk dying out there?"

Ivar said, "It's a damn nonlife if you ask me. I want to go out."

Jonah said, "Funny to think of being here. So they'll take care of us for life if we choose."

"Yes, but many people brought forward in time don't live long," Benedetta said.

"Gee," Jonah said. "Why do they bother then?"

"For the same reason that Leonardo wanted my son to test his descending sail. Because ..."

"Ah, yes, the because-it's-cool factor." Jonah waved one of his hands through the air in an infinity sign, and then dropped it heavily. "And because they can. I can empathize. They're hacking time." Jonah stood up and paced in a tight circle. Ivar looked at him, then at Benedetta, then back at Jonah, a slight smile on his face. Jonah continued, "But I'm an anachronism and I'm not the one hacking anything."

Benedetta said, "They didn't invent the time machines. Someone further in the future appears to have sent them backward."

Ivar said, "Joe seems to wonder about the future's motivations for giving them a time machine now. Rather late for that, considering."

"Oh? So they're the script kiddies of time-hacking. But, still, where does that leave me?"

"You came from closer to their time now than I did. Shouldn't this be less of a shock to you?"

"Why? You're from a time that believed in magic. So you get magically transported into the future. Big deal. No cognitive dissonance whatsoever. I have to consider the most plausible mechanism and there isn't any. Really."

"People who are from further back in the past tend to die the quickest."

Ivar said, "Loki will keep me from dying."

"Cognitive shock for me. For Ivar, it's just another gig in real magic."

"But most of the people from the past don't go outside. There they die of real diseases," Benedetta said.

"And my pretty little fuckhead, do you even really understand any of this bright fucking future that snatched us away from what was in the past? I could have survived falling on ice."

Benedetta said, "My impression is that most of us would have died in the past."

"Why do you believe any of this?" Jonah started pacing again, small, wobbling loops.

"Because I guess I trust Joe," Benedetta said.

Ivar said, "I trust Joe, too. He's been talking to me a lot."

Benedetta wondered if Joe really understood what seventeen-year-olds were capable of in the days of edged weapons and famine.

Jonah stopped pacing and held on to the pole of Ivar's fencing target. "They're curious, so they pick us up out of time, pump us for info about the past, and then we live out the remainder of our poor undereducated misinformed lives in genteel jail cells, until we die, quickly, out of boredom and terminal irrelevance."

"I'm not going to die that way," Ivar said.

"Why do you think not, Mr. The-Norse-Trickster-God-Helps-Me?"

"We can help each other," Ivar said. "We can get out and make the future ours."

"How? Benedetta ran out into germs just waiting to nail someone with an antiquated immune system. I don't know that mine's much better, but yours is likely to be worse."

"I survived," Benedetta said.

"As far as you know. Some diseases take a long time to incubate. I've been reading some of their sites, at least I think that's what I've been doing, and some of these diseases sterilize you, only you won't know for decades."

"Sterilize?"

"Keep you from having children."

"I wasn't all that fertile ever," Benedetta said.

"And who in her right mind would want to get pregnant and raise a child in an archive cell?"

Benedetta said. "I don't want Ivar or you to die quickly."

Still holding on to the pole, Jonah leaned toward Ivar, "Do you want out, Ivar?"

"No, I want to curl up and die in this stupid time trap, why do you ask? I'm stuck here until I'm of age."

Benedetta said, "I wish Leonardo could have been brought to the future. He and Salai would have been just accepted here. They could have had children."

Jonah said, "So ass bandits can marry but everyone gets diseases. Tell me. What kind of people did you see out there?"

"It's just like Italy. They've got all sorts of people. Africans and mulattoes even."

"How nice to know it didn't change that much. Now, do I want to go outside and meet people and maybe die of diseases, or do I want to stay in here and drink myself to death? Which would you choose?"

"Outside."

Ivar said, "I'm going outside to change this place."

"Damn right. But should I hack my way out, or see what a lawyer comes up with?"

"Technically, you're free to go anytime."

"Oh?"

Benedetta thought about her job at the bar. "But what would you do once you got out? What will you do for a living, for food?"

"I doubt seriously that they've done away with currency and accounting, or that their computer programs are utterly intelligent agents. If you were bold enough to go outside and Ivar is bold enough to want to go outside, I should go outside, too."

"Ivar and I were soldiers. We're used to having to improvise. You were, what, something like a notary?"

"I did sums for banks, to put it in terms that might be familiar to you. I was into usury. It's an old Russian dilemma—if you could stay in one place for eternity and not die, would you accept it? Only if I don't get out of here, I think I'll die of boredom, and this isn't eternal life unless it *is* a computer program."

Benedetta decided Jonah was being melodramatic and self-pitying. Being older than she and from her own future didn't make him saner or nicer. "I want to see Ivar get out sooner than his twenty-first year."

"You could be my guardians. Can you ask your lawyer for this?" Ivar said.

Jonah said, "You know if there were more of us, this might not feel so bad. Certainly, if Joe could hack time machines ..."

Ivar said, "Troll," and flicked his eyes toward the ceiling, meaning *They're listening to us.*

Benedetta wondered if the future could hold lots of people who'd almost died in their pasts. All of the people she'd met so far would have died without the future's medicine, but the future wasn't giving them all the medicine they needed to move completely into the future. "The past is their foreign lands."

"This future is all connected by the net but each city and region is physically isolated. The plagues made cowards of them," Ivar said. "Men in my day traveled to England, to Greenland, to the land of the Slavs."

Benedetta realized that Joe underestimated Ivar and didn't think the young Viking would be able to use what he'd explained to him. However, Joe might have preferred to leave Jonah tangled in his delusion about the computer game, but he wasn't inhumane enough to leave Jonah isolated.

Jonah said, "I'm still wondering if I should go out or not."

Ivar asked, "Are you afraid?"

"I'd rather be a computer program, compared to some of the history that I know about. Maybe, Ivar, at your age, dying fast beats risking boredom. Living in this future could be quite an adventure for you. But if you left, I'd have to go out or spend the rest of my life talking to Joe."

Benedetta decided she really didn't care what Jonah decided. "I'll ask if I can be Ivar's guardian."

Ivar said, "I'm sure Joe would do anything you like, Mistress Benedetta."

Jonah said, "Consider making him an emancipated minor, if that's still an option in these times."

Ivar said, "Why didn't you mention that earlier, fuckhead?"

Nobody expected a Viking with a lawyer

Ivar's lawyer sat down with Ivar and Benedetta to explain what he'd been doing for the time travelers. He was an eager, jovial man in a three-piece suit. "You could have come out at any time," he told Benedetta. Over the protests of some of the medical researchers, he'd gotten Ivar a full set of inoculations for modern diseases.

Benedetta wondered if the real reason the past people hadn't been inoculated and vaccinated against the diseases wasn't that the vaccines and inoculations might be as deadly to them as the diseases that had developed since their times, but that researches wanted to see what immunities they had naturally, wanted a clearer picture of the past diseases.

She did have a minor relapse when they gave her some of the inoculations, but Ivar was very sick for a week.

"Funny," Ivar said when she came to see him as soon as he was better. "I came close to dying of the cure." He sounded different, as though he was learning to speak Future better than she. He was wearing a suit like his lawyer's, but with a narrow silk cravat.

"Did Jonah leave the Archives, too?"

Ivar said, with a nasty little smile, "No, I think he wants to be safe. Died in his time of slipping on ice and he wants to be safe."

"We're soldiers. He isn't," Benedetta said.

Ivar made a face at her. His lawyer looked, for once, slightly nervous.

Of the other five people who also came out of the Archives at this time, three died. Both survivors had been wanderers: a poet named Villon from fifteenth-century France and an American slave who'd been born in Africa.

"Villon has already gotten a job teaching creative writing," Ivar's lawyer said to Benedetta. "I think you might enjoy meeting him if you speak French from that period. He's almost your contemporary, born 1431, disappeared 1463 while traveling."

"I met him," Ivar said. "Pretentious churl."

"Villon was quick to pick up English, a very bright man," the lawyer said. "He loves it now. The slave, an older woman, wants to move back to the Archives."

"So most of them, it wouldn't be safe for them to come out," Benedetta said. "Can we go back in? Would I have to have a job there to live there again?"

Ivar said, "Why in the world would you want to work for them?"

"I want to talk to Jonah."

"Why?" Ivar asked. "To persuade him to take a chance on dying rather than living in a tiny little room pretending to be a confused computer program?"

"Yes," Benedetta said. "And because you're scary, and I'd like a friend here."

"I'm scary. What do you mean by that, bitch?"

"Ivar, easy," his lawyer said.

"Women in this time aren't afraid of me," Ivar said.

Benedetta found herself flushing and hoped they would mistake it for a blush. Ivar's lawyer smiled jovially. Benedetta wanted to put a knife in one of the lawyer's kidneys for a second, then said, "Ivar's people sacrificed women to their dead warriors."

"The women slaves volunteered," Ivar said. "There was much honor in doing so."

Ivar's lawyer looked a bit uneasy for a moment, and then said, "We don't do things like that now. We don't have enough people to spare."

"I know how to behave in different places," Ivar said.

"Really," Benedetta said. "How, by conquering them and enslaving them?"

Ivar looked young and defenseless for a moment. The lawyer chuckled. Benedetta felt mean. "I'm sorry. I like Joe."

"Yeah, don't let me stop you then. Okay, I want to go out and see the streets paved with crushed old houses," Ivar said. "Now that I'd know what I'm seeing."

"Just looks like a stone street with one giant long block without any spaces or joints. It's only impressive if you know it was made of crushed houses." Benedetta thought Ivar was jealous of her for getting to walk around in the future during the day before he did. The Archives weren't really the future but anterooms of the past.

Ivar said, "We might need Jonah to join us. Loki has plans for this time."

The lawyer said, "Loki is the Norse trickster god, isn't he? You believe in him?"

Ivar said, "I don't really believe in him, but he's an interesting proposition as a god."

7

A Future in Broad Daylight

Ivar didn't know why he had to have tiny hollow steel rods dripping fluid into his blood, but he *was* feeling better. The doctors of this time had first saved him from drowning, and now were saving him from the future fevers they caused while trying to save him from future fevers. He still didn't know if he was grateful or not, or if any of the fluids dripping into his blood were more than magical tokens. Sometimes trying to figure things out made his head hurt.

The Norns visited him while the fever was at its worst, watching him with cold eyes while they spun men's life threads. One of them looked like Benedetta, and Ivar wondered if all this was a dream, again. The Norns' visit did appear to come from the fever, but this all could be a dream inside a dream.

Jonah could be Loki, then. He certainly behaved like a trickster.

The world when he was alive had followed the rules until the end. The rule of now was that he had to have tiny hollow steel rods in his arms and hands to live, so Ivar was as patient with these people as any man could be. The people tending him, not all women, called him a good patient, considering what he'd been through.

After about a week, Ivar was walking around, not as patient as he had been, feeling better but hating that his body was sluggish. He guessed that the people in this future would not approve of his going off rowing and practicing sword fighting. Out of sheer boredom, he asked about exercise.

They took him to a place with a treadmill. Ivar wondered if they knew the insult, but they appeared to be as friendly as before. "What does it work?" Ivar asked.

"The treadmill? Your legs."

"If it's still a treadmill, what does the mill part do? Grind grain? Full cloth?"

"No, it's just for exercise. Here." The woman showing him the exercise room in the hospital moved a plastic lever and the treadmill began moving.

Ivar thought this was funny. "Oh, it gives me power."

"Well, you have to keep up with it."

Over the next week, Ivar learned how to keep up with the treadmill at several speeds and inclines. This treadmill imitated hills, even.

And one man was willing to use a strange sort of sword with him, all covered in plastic foam but heavy enough. Ivar was chagrined to find the man used his sword in ways that Ivar had never learned. A god's dream could be like this.

Ivar decided that if the gods or Norns sent him beyond the Archives, then he had to get to know this place better. Being chosen for a god's dream would be good; being alive in a future world he didn't understand ... Ivar could manage either. The real world was happenstance chiseled by deeds.

But the god's dream would be easier if he was the hero. That was the trick with being a god's dream. Which god was dreaming him?

Even if Ivar was Loki's dream, Ivar realized human deeds couldn't change that. The future fed him better than at any other time in his life except for feasts and fall slaughter. And he more than recovered his strength on the strange machines in the gym. The women began to smile at him and slide their fingers through their hair, and flash their palms at him. Some things hadn't changed.

Doctors gave him a vaccination for the pox, which swelled up in one place and itched and left a scar, but just one. They had small versions of diseases, which appeared to block the larger versions.

He was amused that they had things to put over a man's cock to keep the seed from impregnating women. "But it's also good against disease." Ivar never heard of getting a disease from women except sore throats. Those came from the tongue, not from the cock. "The women you meet will have condoms, even if you don't."

Ivar found a young woman to show him how to put on the silly skin to see if it caught all his seed.

Time to see Philadelphia. Ivar wanted to know more about the present than Benedetta, who'd been in the future longer than he had and from a past that could imagine this future. Or so she claimed. He wished Jonah were here with him. Ivar swore he would bring Jonah out from the Archives if he could. Surely, being from a time nearer the plague years, he could survive the diseases better.

But Ivar didn't want to go near the Archives. If he was here now, he didn't want to go back to where he was a prisoner. The people of Philadelphia had many sorts of þing, and one was a neighborhood council. The council was going to assign him work.

By now, Ivar understood that Philadelphia didn't send its young men on summer raids and trading expeditions. Benedetta's friend Mike wanted to sew costumes that Ivar might have worn a thousand years before; Ivar wanted to look like the future natives. People didn't tell strangers much. At least, they didn't a thousand years ago.

But Ivar found that telling women he was from over a thousand years ago worked very well. Actually, more like fifteen hundred, but that just didn't sound as impressive, and one thousand, five hundred was too clumsy. "I'm from over a thousand years ago" impressed the women in just the right way.

Everyone in Mike's neighborhood knew he was from the Archives. The present people believed that history before the twentieth-century machines and the twenty-first-century plagues had been a smooth and unbroken series of constant wars and starvation, neither of which they'd had enough recent experience with to see as real. But history had ruptured many times in the past, too. Ivar's world broke when one man decided to become king of all Norway, and had probably broken a couple of times since and would rupture a couple times more before the Bifrost stopped life on Earth.

The story of humans ran in a wheel. The man in the wheel could only guess how large the whole wheel was. Things had been bad, better, and then worse, now better again. That was life.

He went into a room that had windows made of colored glass set in lead bars—or what looked like windows made of colored glass set in lead bars. All the adults and children in the community he was living in came in to the meeting. The headmen and their women sat in non-remarkable chairs behind a table on a platform, facing everyone else who was sitting in equal chairs, just not on a platform behind the table of rank. The meaning of high and low hadn't changed.

People's politics felt familiar enough. The computer screens and cameras were of this age. Ivar saw them as a domestic magic he didn't need to master, although Benedetta said they were the looms, smithies, and guns of this time. Computers were the fire of the time, Ivar thought. People didn't need to know how fire worked to warm themselves with it.

"Ivar, we think you might enjoy going on salvage operations," one of the men on the platform said. Ivar remembered the fake Odin, high tables from his past. He wondered if he could turn down this offer.

"Why?" he asked.

"Because you could get out and be physically active, and perhaps salvage would teach you about the times you find yourself in. It's useful work."

Ivar knew that slaves did all sorts of useful work. "Will you continue to teach me about this time?"

"Learning is part of life," one of the women said.

"I want to learn to write and read your English," Ivar said. Benedetta could read before she was scooped into this time. He had only known Norse letters.

"It will happen," the woman said.

Ivar sat through the rest of the meeting that was about who got garden plots and how many pumps the community had for water, and whether or not they could bargain with the Falls for more electricity, and how well the trains were running, and the price of hydrogen compared to the price of cleaned coal gas. As with þing from Ivar's past, the community voted. Unlike all the þing Ivar had been to as a boy, women and older children voted with the men.

After the voting, the þing sat in silence for a while, then a woman spoke, "I'd like to thank Ivar and Benedetta for giving us the opportunity to help them."

"We owe the past," another person said. "Some of it was bad, but we've lived beyond those parts."

Everyone looked at Ivar and nodded. After the general meeting closed, everyone began talking to their neighbors about the crops, the Amish problems, and the state of the rails beyond Harrisburg.

Ivar felt that he had been slighted, but not enough to challenge the þing over it.

The four men on the salvage team looked like rough men, big chests and square faces. One was a red-haired man with freckles. They looked over Ivar's body as he hadn't had it looked at since he learned how to wield a sword and a shield. A dark brown man had a broken fingertip that went sideways. Ivar realized he hadn't seen broken hands here before and that they'd been common when he first lived. The two other adult men had dark hair and almost fair skins, the oldest dark with gray at the temples and a bald patch at the crown. A boy hung back behind the grown men. He also had black hair and the same skin, sunburned. The three looked like a family: grandfather, son, and grandson, stoutly built, the boy showing signs of a bull chest already.

"I'm Bert," the red-haired man said. "You're used to work?"

"I'm willing to work." Ivar wondered if Bert was Irish and if he'd remember what the Vikings had done to his people.

"It's not city work," the dark man said. "I'm Bryce. The father, son, and grandson are Taylor, Joe, and Chip Giorno." The three nodded but didn't say more. The boy was a couple of years younger than Ivar.

The salvage team took a train as far as the power lines were working, then switched to a human-powered railcar that reminded Ivar of a land-going ship, mainly because he was helping to make it go, only by pedaling rather than rowing. They went through country where people had been. Foundations of buildings stuck up through the fields where a strange giant reed was growing. Ivar asked what it was. The answer was, "Corn," but it wasn't like what Ivar heard of as corn. Cattle were larger, but not auroch-size. Ivar missed seeing horses, then spotted two giant horses pulling a wagon.

"The horses are larger than Norse horses," Ivar said. "But some things never change. Horses pull plows."

"Horses came back as draft animals after we decided that oil and gasoline were more valuable for other things. Now people are building steam tractors. There's a lot of coal left."

Ivar thought of coal as something to burn for heat outside. Coal fires killed people when burned on a hearth inside. He thought seeing the country would make him feel less foreign, but everything was slightly to tremendously off what he'd known in his own time. Those fifteen hundred years gapped like a crevasse, now.

A double trailer truck with odd, colored tires almost as high as Ivar's chest and an iron cylinder across the back of the first bed was waiting for them. The men who'd been pedaling the railcar got in the back of the second bed, which was hooked with a joint like a wagon's, only in metal, not leather and wood, to the first trailer. Slowly at first, the truck began rolling on its giant tires over broken roads where most of the paving had been removed. It rolled like a ship over waves in some spots, the different sections of the truck flexing, the big tires showing cuts in places where broken wrecks had snagged them. One tire was blue; three were a dirty red; the others were brown-mud colored. Ivar remembered hearing that Philadelphia streets were paved with crushed suburban houses and ground rubber car-tires, whatever those were. This road had a coating of gravel and rocks on it. They came to buildings that looked like a smaller Philadelphia, only empty and frost-broken. In the past, men had pulled the asphalt pavement off the parking lots to build walls around some of the buildings. Those were crumbling now. The truck rode over a low place in a wall and pulled up to a large building without windows. *Some kind of fortress?*

"We've heard this was a collocation facility back in the day," the red-haired Bert said to Ivar. "If it hasn't been looted already, we should have some good salvage. The grid didn't die here until about fifty years after the first major sickness."

"If looters found it, the building would have been broken open already," the grandfather Giorno said, rubbing his bald spot.

They circled the building and didn't see any obvious holes.

The building's doors were still closed. "Damn, we might even score a generator," the grandson said. He and his father took crowbars to the door. "We don't have to worry about Trenton folks here, do we?"

Ivar picked up a shiny ax with two close points on one side and a blunt wedge blade on the other and began whacking the metal door. The father and son stopped prying the door with the crowbar as Ivar beat a hole in the door with the ax, levering metal away with the two points, breaking metal with the blade. He noticed the ax handle wasn't wood but something like amber—plastic, which threw off one whack, but he got into his rhythm again.

"Don't wreck it so we can't open it when we get in," Bert said.

"He's not neat, but he's thorough," the black man said.

"If it's an electric door, it ain't going anywhere, anyhow," the middle-aged Giorno said. He stood by his son, both holding crowbars, the points against their boots, and the shafts in their hands at waist level.

Ivar stopped and panted a moment, then said, "Well, I'll make it big enough to carry stuff out with, then."

"I can tell you there won't be a generator," Bert said, "but there's probably a UPS inside."

"The batteries will be long gone," Bryce the black-skinned man said.

Ivar went back to work on the door, a bit pissed that they were letting him do all the hard work. But it felt good to use his body and the ax.

Ivar stepped through the hole he'd chopped. The others followed him with electric lights. The leader handed him a light that he could make work by squeezing it. Dust patches of rotten cloth and some bones sat by the next door. Ivar wondered if the man had died defending the building from the copper looters. Bryce began checking around the door jam. "Another electric door." Then he swung his light to a window that was still intact. "Gee, we might come out of here with some serious copper, too." Ivar let other people break the glass out of the window. He was a bit winded from breaking the door. *Not getting enough play with an ax these days.*

Then Ivar looked around and knew that computers were the forges, guns, and powers of these days if they'd been so protected. Men had died for these machines.

Beyond the glass were cages made of woven heavy wire, with another dead man's clothes and bones by a box that was open to show green, corroded copper bars. Ivar bowed his head to honor their deaths, and then stared at the machines in cages going back into the darkness, a huge hall of stacks and stacks of computers. The men they'd seen died to protect the machines he and his new people were taking. The barricades hadn't protected them in the end. Something else had driven the attackers off. Ivar wondered if that something was gone after three hundred years. Bert brought in snips for the wires, but Chip said, "Ivar and I can climb over and get down, then open the cages from the inside."

"They put computers in cages?" Ivar asked, realizing obviously he could see that they did. He was still stunned that men died protecting computers as though they were treasure.

"And they had people watching to make sure people couldn't climb over like we're going to do. And some of them were in cabinets." Chip swung his light. The beam settled on a group of metal boxes. "They cut loose the halon. They weren't supposed to have halon by the time of this facility."

"So that killed the two guys?" one of the other men said.

"Um, possibly. Or the halon cut loose later when something malfunctioned. Since it wasn't looted for copper, let's see about finding the main routers," Bert said. "And let's be sure to get the fiber."

The fiber wasn't anything Ivar knew as fiber, but was more smooth, coated cable with protruding glass. *Oh, that's the fiber—it's glass spun thin,* he realized.

Bryce said, "Most of our network is radio, but fiber and copper are nice when a city or something smaller than a city wants its privacy. This is a very nice find."

"Maybe the Viking is lucky for us," the old man Taylor Giorno said.

"I had the luck of not drowning," Ivar said, "and I've come to the future." He almost said something about escaping the Archives and finding people who helped him stay free of the Time Team, but wasn't sure he should be rude about the people who'd saved his life, even if they had planned to keep him trapped until he died. *Oh, fuck it.* "And I had help from a man almost of this time in getting out of the Archives. Maybe of the time of these machines. He begged them for a networked computer." Ivar wasn't quite sure what a networked computer was, but remembered Jonah asking for one.

"Oh," the leader said. "We thought all the people they brought forward were from preelectric times."

"Not Jonah. He thought he was actually living as a program in a computer for a while. Or said he did."

Bert frowned slightly. "That guy might be useful to the present if he really knew a lot about computers. Did they have screwdrivers in your time?"

"Do I look like a carpenter?" Ivar said. He didn't want to admit that his people built only with nails.

"No, you look like an ax murderer," Bert said, as though some ancestor touched him with memories of the Vikings. "I'll show you what to do. The big cage in back is probably the telco cage. We inherited the stuff at 401 North Broad. People kept that facility going all through the plagues. We get stuff for the 401 North Broad group and they tell us what to bring back."

Ivar climbed over the largest cage in the back and dropped down between rows of machines. The men slid an oilcan and wrench under the edge of the cage. Ivar soaked the door lock with thin oil, then took the wrench to the round knurled knob and broke it free of three hundred years of rust and corrosion. The door slid back.

"Bring our crash cart in," Bryce said. The crash cart had a charged battery and terminal with a keyboard. "If we're lucky, one of the hard drives will actually spin up after three hundred years."

"And throw off the media like those guys' flesh is dust," Bert said. "Just pull the boards and memory and let's get out of here."

"There's a bunch of lead in the big UPS."

Ivar didn't understand what they were talking about. He paced around the cage looking at the rows of metal- and plastic-covered boxes with wires hanging off the back, mostly rotted to green scales. Occasional monitors were glassy black behind the dust. This was treasure that dragons would hoard, if the future had dragons.

"What we'd really like to find is a working CD drive and media kit disks," Bert said. "Or good solid state drives."

"Gold and lead," the grandfather Giorno said. "Flash isn't necessarily stable. Better to salvage the gold than go for data."

Ivar saw something wrapped in what he'd learned was plastic. The outer layer of the plastic had rotted, but there were several layers of it. He pulled the plastic package out and unwrapped it. Inside was a set of plastic cards. Bert saw what Ivar had found, and came over. "Media cards, no moving parts at all. Wrapped in plastic." Bert pulled out fresher-looking plastic and quickly resealed them in that. "Sometimes the flash cards have something more than bits of gold in them. If not, the breaker yard crew can boil them for the gold."

Ivar kept moving through the heaps of junk around the machines, then learned how to pull the memory chips, tipped with gold.

They found a cart whose wheels hadn't rotted off and loaded it with chips and motherboards. Bert called on his cell phone for another truck, and asked the team to start dismantling the racks the machines had been in. "We can always use aluminum," he said.

Ivar had never seen aluminum before—it was almost as soft as lead but amazingly much lighter, somewhere between lead and silver in color.

The ends of the copper wires were corroded, but Ivar scraped off the plastic and found some copper still good beyond the corrosion. The first truck was full; the second truck arrived.

"We can get the plastic stuff later. It will take a while to get all this to the breaker yards. The breaker yards have to be downriver from our water but under Philadelphia control," Bert told Ivar. "We boil the gold off the chips with acid."

Ivar felt as though he was in the company of magicians. "This is all like a dragon's hoard."

"It is science, not magic," Bryce said.

Ivar was chagrined that he was not controlling his face better. Everyone scrambled for places in the truck beds and made nests in the chips and rolls of cable. The truck went out into the country filled with fields and walks of rotten asphalt, then pulled onto a main road where the asphalt looked fresh. Ivar could see the city to his left across acres of marsh. A ferry took the truck across the Schuylkill, where it entered the Delaware. They drove off the ferry to the breaker yards.

Broken computers, bicycles, ancient automobiles, and other junk were piled hundreds of feet high outside old industrial buildings. Around the heaps, steam and smoke rose from hundreds of small fires where people reclaimed gold and lead by boiling chips in acid for gold or melting lead off boards at temperatures that left the gold solidly behind. The people doing the work wore masks with double snouts and goggles.

Bryce said, "Reverse plating is the safer way to recover gold."

"Still need acid in the end, but that's better than cyanide-based recovery systems," Bert replied.

Ivar wondered if Christians had seen such sights to inspire their hot Hell.

The youngest Giorno, said, "We try not to pollute too much, but gold and lead have a number of uses."

"What do we do next?" Ivar said.

"We unload the truck and go home," Bert said. "I'll pick you up another day when we go back for the other stuff."

The aluminum went on another truck; the computer components went into the recycling piles. After the salvage men from Ivar's neighborhood off-loaded the second truck, the first truck drove them to yet another railhead, where a train was waiting. Ivar began to get a sense of Philadelphia the city, between two rivers, with good farmland at its back, bigger than any city he'd ever heard of before. He was beginning to make sense of Philadelphia as a human place.

But he felt he'd seen way too many people on this day. Thousands and thousands of them rode the train returning them to Center City. He wanted badly to get out to a farm, ride even one of those giant horses.

"Tired?" Bert asked him.

Ivar wanted to conceal what he was thinking, but decided to trust this man. "Overwhelmed. So many people."

"Philly's back up to about half a million, but that's a sixth of what it was three hundred and fifty, four hundred years back."

"Plague hit."

"Plagues, craziness, small wars over this and that. People stopping having children was the big one."

"Small wars over what?"

"Network equipment. Had to keep that running or we sank back ... um, what we think of as the Dark Ages, though it was probably just your everyday life in the past. You know the place we salvaged today. You think they dug up their parking lots and built defense walls for nothing?"

"Do you still have small wars?" Ivar said, wondering if he could find a place with an army.

"Not with weapons you'd understand," Bert said, "and not lately in any real sense."

Ivar wanted to see Jonah again. He knew more about these machines.

"Tomorrow we'll be going back to the site we scavenged today," Bert said. "Don't wear yourself out whacking doors next time."

Ivar was distracted by a very small wisp of blue mist that seemed to have an eye staring through it. Was this the future—or a future—looking at him? If Joe was right, Ivar could be making a switch from one future to another now, just by thinking.

He would learn as much as he could.

Bert treated Ivar as a son and kept explaining things to him. Ivar was both greatful and embarrassed.

"We don't teach things formally as they did in the past," Bert said. "We bring the children up to know things. If they're good at something their community doesn't know how to do well, we find them people who'll work with them."

Ivar didn't know many families that did things differently. A whole way of dealing with children had come and gone again since he was a young boy.

After a couple of days of physical work with the salvage team, Bert didn't come to pick Ivar up, but a woman came to take Ivar to a computer data salvage center. "We lost so much when the past was busy reinventing its systems every few years," she said. "Now, except for people researching computers, we keep the same designs for decades. We're trying to copy everything we find onto pressed CD-ROM or DVD format. Anything on iron oxides from the past tends to be gone. And a lot of the programs weren't kept in printed source code, or they were lost. Some people set up caches of information in microfiche. Those are the best finds. Low information density, but it's a lot harder to damage. Finding the caches is the trick, then figuring out the decoding. We still go through all the CDs we find, looking for surviving text strings."

Ivar nodded as though he understood what the fuck she was talking about. Ivar wanted to learn how to read English, not just recognize when there were designs on the screen that might be useful. "How do I tell if it's a useful pattern or not?"

"You can't read?"

"I can't read your language."

"Could you read anything?"

"I could read the letters used in our language."

The woman thought for a moment and said, "I don't have time to teach you. We'll have to find something else for you to do."

"I want to learn to read and write English."

"Someone has to have the time assigned to teach you. Or we find a teaching program," the woman said. "Still, run some checks. You can see when there's anything left at all. I'll tell you what to look for."

Stick disc or card in the appropriate reader, see if there's anything on it, repeat until something throws a design on the screen.

Ivar put one of the disks into the computer's extended plastic tongue, and then pushed the button to make it retract. The woman bent over the keyboard and typed on it. "I've bound keys to some commands. Push this key and you'll mount the CD-ROM drive. Then this key, and you'll be in the CD-ROM. Push *l* and *s* to see if the computer can read the basic directories."

Ivar pushed the first two keys, then the *l* and the *s* keys. Nothing showed up.

"Dead disk. Try another one until you see anything show up after the *ls* command."

There was a huge stack of rescued disks. Ivar hated the bound keys, not knowing what he was doing, not finding anything for a half-morning while other people made little orgasmic cries of discovery. Finally, he got a message from a gold-colored disk with no printing on it, just hand-inked markings.

The woman came over and said, "JPEGs. That will be copies of photographs." She didn't sound as excited as Ivar thought she would be. "Porn, from the titles, I suspect."

"What's porn?" Ivar asked.

For an answer, the woman loaded a program on another computer, typed on the computer Ivar was using, and then typed more into the computer with the program. "I copied it to my machine." A dressed woman with a naked cock and balls erect across her face popped up on the screen. The woman on the screen was staring out at Ivar, at any person who looked at this.

"That's actually a fairly interesting photograph," the woman said. "Mostly, porn is a naked woman diddling herself or being fucked."

Ivar felt that looking at this was both silly and something he wanted to do more of. They didn't have slaves for sex in these days, so they could only look at pictures if the women refused them. So sad.

"You want to see more?" the woman asked.

"We had slaves for this," Ivar said.

"I've heard you aren't finding us now-time women completely

rude to you." The woman grinned. Ivar realized the women now were as gossipy among themselves as ever.

Ivar said, "I don't understand you now-time women."

"We need more people, so everyone encourages the women who can have children to have them. We all raise the children. It's hard to want children and not be able to have them." She sounded like this was her personal problem. "Especially when men can have them."

Ivar shuddered at the idea of men bearing children and didn't want to know right now how that was done. "So one of the plagues is still with you?" Maybe one of their plagues gave men wombs.

"It's not as bad as it was. The people most susceptible to it died out, but since the only symptoms are infertility, it's harder to track than the diseases that cause more melodramatic symptoms like hallucinations and high fevers."

"If I had the melodramatic diseases, does that mean I didn't get the seed-killing one?"

"Don't know. Don't care really. I'm just a salvage tech." She seemed more like a man than a woman, but then being barren would have made her less a woman.

"We people from the past are a sort of salvage, too, I think," Ivar said.

"I think so. We're immune to your diseases, but you people aren't necessarily completely immune to our new diseases. But if you survive, you'd be adding both a knowledge of the past and genetic diversity, maybe even better immune systems."

Ivar remembered that the time-travel machines weren't invented in this present but appeared to have come from the future.

And there had been an eye watching him from that blue cloud.

8

Seals & Photographs

Jonah wanted to leave the Archives, just not right away. *Stay here and die of boredom. Go out and die of some disease that didn't exist three hundred years ago. Decisions, decisions.*

He wanted company from his time, not the deep past. The future seemed closer than the Italian Renaissance as seen through a camp follower's eyes. He'd known the tools that this present still used, but the culture was more alien than he would have expected, with its paranoid collectivism. And he just wanted to be with Benedetta, but the flirtation required a decent respect for the families both had lost. But did she feel her losses as keenly? Her people were longer dead and in another country. His descendants might still be in Philadelphia or at least surviving somewhere. Kirkpatricks survived the Black Death in the fourteenth century and had spread from Scotland to Hong Kong in his time.

Until Jonah entered the real future, he could imagine his family continuing on, remembering him, and perhaps hating him for abandoning them. He amused himself by imagining his explanations to his great-grandchildren about what happened. He'd almost died going out in a snowstorm for something he couldn't remember now. Probably he went out for cigarettes, beer, or fireworks, or to use a neighbor's computer for an untraceable prank.

Once he entered the real future, he could find out whether he had descendants or not.

Born in Texas, reared in Oregon, Jonah Kirkpatrick had moved to

Philadelphia three hundred and some years ago, with memories of house and street that now were older than most of old Philadelphia when he lived there. Seeing the house as a ruin or as a rehabilitated historical collection piece would make that missing three hundred some years all too real.

But these future people didn't know any of my aliases or what I'd done online. He'd given himself up thinking they knew already, a mistake he'd never made in the past when he was testing the limits of various parts of the network, seeing if the machines running INN for net news would crack under stress. One of his adversaries who wrote parts of the code he tried to break had called him the best beta-tester of server software out there.

Three hundred years in the future, his net reputation still had been waiting, but he was the one who pinned his net persona to his real-life identity. He'd slipped in the snow going out to do something that must have seemed urgent at the time, and didn't freeze to death and leave a skeleton wearing too few clothes for the weather to be discovered curled up against the back of a house much later.

Chance alone appeared to have dragged him out of a minor role in the history of network games to this future.

Time to meet his new future.

"I choose to leave," Jonah told the Archives staff after a weekend of solitary brooding with a case of beer. They gave him a lawyer's number and a packed suitcase.

"You can come back; you'll just have to go through the decontamination room first," Joe told him. "University City says they'll take you in. They're curious about you."

"Do I have any choice?"

"You're free to find another neighborhood, but this one wants you. You have more to learn than you realize."

Bunch of Quaker Commie intellectuals, no doubt. Or young hackers who want to reconstruct the past the way it should have been.

Two English professors who specialized in late twentieth-century poetry picked him up from the Archives. The man and woman did dress as Jonah imagined futuristic liberals would: very comfortable leather shoes with thick plastic soles that looked moderately compressible, slubby-weave linen shirts with bone buttons, and matching pants and long skirt in earth tones. He didn't know if they were trying to look like twentieth-century college professors or if certain types of college professors hadn't changed their styles of dress since 2005. Both of them had moderately curly hair down over their ears and were within an inch of each other's heights, the woman being both slightly taller and slightly skinnier. The man introduced both of them to Jonah, though. "I'm Riymend Pilma and this is my colleague, Herrit Thamas."

Herrit said, "I believe you were a Meower. We've been wondering for years about the connection between the L=A=N=G=U=A=G=E poets and the Usenet Meowers." They led him to a private car that ran on the streetcar rails and was electric. "Can you understand us?" She did have a funny accent, but Jonah understood it. He then realized that what the Archives people had spoken to them was a dead dialect. This was the real twenty-fourth-century English.

And Jonah didn't know who the fuck the language poets were. The woman had punched the air with her finger between the letters she'd spelled out. He tried to remember what other people might have told him about any connection to other forms of performance art. One of the Meowers had been a classics professor. Jonah mentally shrugged. If he was the only surviving Meower, what he said wasn't going to hurt or expose anyone else these days. But he needed the professors to feed him a few more clues.

Trolling was always a good distraction from life problems. He could troll now to distract himself from being lost in the future. All the people he cared about died thinking that he'd abandoned them. "I don't remember all the details. Couple of decades I wasn't involved, you know."

"Was Charles Bernstein a Meower?"

"He was the one who ran the Meow Server," Jonah said, happy to have a proper name to add to the Meow legend. Pity he couldn't share this moment with the other Meowers. But he needed to know more about this Bernstein character.

"We've had some people argue that Bernstein and the Meowers' Usenet Performance Art were separate movements, because there's no evidence that our Charles Bernstein ever posted to Usenet. There weren't even that many other Charles Bernsteins posting. None showed any interest in our Bernstein's concerns. On the contrary, the Meowers tended to be conservative politically, but debauchers online, sort of the Hellfire Club of their day."

Jonah wondered how they even knew about Usenet. Most people in his own time hadn't, which was why he could play so hard with it. If five hundred people couldn't get their messages posted on a given day because his toys broke Usenet, what was that compared to falling down icy stairs into the future? "How did you know about Usenet?"

"People kept updating the Deja-slash-Google archives into new media throughout the plague years. It's our best record of those times. Computer scientists are using the Deja-slash-Google files to reconstruct other electronic media formats. We have some L=A=N=G=U=A=G=E MP3s—one of someone who hacked someone else's Web site. Do you remember, 'Your Louisiana troll ass is owned in alt.hackers.malicious, troll?' Or was that before or after your time?"

Jonah giggled. He wondered if their only other records from the late twentieth century were various masters' theses photocopied on 100-percent cotton paper and saved because nobody ever read them until all the better records were trashed by UV light and pulp paper. "I suppose you got the archives with even the x-no-archived posts in them."

"Of course. We were very grateful to have the records of many technological citizens of that day."

"Usenet was always filled with obsessos." Jonah wished he hadn't assumed he had been brought forward in time because of who he'd been online and hadn't outed himself. Oh, well. "Bernstein knew what he was doing. He never posted as himself and he always pretended to be a classics professor."

"Raoul? Bernstein was Raoul Xemblionsky?"

"Of course." Unfortunately, this troll was going to get tedious with the poetry bullshit, and didn't appear to have any immediate mean twists.

"We believe we have a copy of one of the bots you used." The tone was slightly frosty.

Jonah suspected that canceling Usenet posts was like chipping bits off the Rosetta Stone, as far as these people were concerned. "The bot we used for the Poetry Festival in 1996?"

"No, the bot you used in August 1998 to crash servers worldwide with control-message floods," Riymend said.

Herrit asked, "Bernstein wasn't involved in that, was he?"

Jonah almost said, *of course,* but knew that enough references on Usenet pointed to the night on the Meow server when two Meowers beat him up for siding with HipCrime, the man who actually wrote NewsAgent, the program that fucked with Usenet. "No, and I didn't know that some kid was using NewsAgent to do the same thing from the Pittsburgh Public Library public-access computers."

"We have so much to ask you," the woman said.

The man steered the car off the rails into a parking building. The car rolled into an elevator that took it up to a railed slot. Some parts of the future actually did seem futuristic. "You use public power and private cars?"

"The grid is there. Hooking onto the power supply is easy enough. The car also has an engine and battery, what you would have called a hybrid."

"Where are we?"

"Clothes depot. Factory and sales, for West Philadelphia."

"I hope I'm not supposed to make them myself," Jonah said. He was feeling tired now, probably the onset of one of their plagues, or just a cold.

The two people looked at each other. "You probably had specialists skills in your day. We tend to do a little of everything, even in University City."

"Mind if we call you Fluffy?" Riymend asked.

Jonah suddenly realized how silly so much of that had been. "Call me Jonah. Jonah Kirkpatrick. I was an accountant in real life."

The two professors looked at each other as though they thought he was really trolling now. Jonah didn't know what it would take to convince them he was who he said he was. They showed him samples of clothes he could get from the computerized cutters and put together, or have the assembling done in trade.

"Putting together clothes is fun," Riymend said. "Really. The machines practically sew them for you."

"Who weaves the cloth?" Jonah asked.

"We do all the weaving here by machine these days," Herrit said.

While Riymend measured Jonah and fed the measurements into the computer, Jonah wondered how much of this they reinvented after being complete little handcrafters had bored them into reconstructing automated factories.

The computer then showed Jonah a range of garments: pants, suits, tops. He picked something that looked like a plain shirt, jacket, and pants, then selected the fabrics—linen for the shirt and a tropical-weight wool for the suit, then underwear, which did appear to come completely finished from knitting machines. He ordered five of each in different colors, wondering if the linen was real linen or some artificial fabric textured to look like linen. "Do you have tailors in this time?"

"A few. We don't use them, ourselves," Riymend said.

"And what about shoes?" Jonah said.

"We have shoemakers. They make shoes that last years with resoling, so it's a sensible use of human energy."

They went up to the cutting floor and found the packages of cloth for Jonah's clothes. A number of people were working at sewing machines and sergers. One serger was unoccupied, so Herrit took the shirt material to it. "Linen tends to unravel if it's not serged," she said.

"Real linen?" Jonah asked.

"We can't grow cotton locally. Most of the current cotton-growing areas are disease-free now, but we got in the habit of growing linen, since we could get it without traveling if we had to quarantine other zones, or when we were under quarantine."

She finished the first shirt rather quickly. Jonah tried it on. The fit was good, the lines very functional, and the arms seemed to be less constructed than he remembered from his own time.

Riymend taught Jonah how to sew on the serger so he could make at least one pair of his own pants. The machine seemed to lock onto lines printed on the fabric and follow them with minimal guidance from the operator. Why not just completely mechanize the operation? This future sweated too earnestly.

"Are you feeling okay?" Herrit asked.

"No, not really."

"You might die on us, but the University City group is working on medical tech that might keep you going better if you come down with some of the more awful stuff."

But Jonah didn't feel more awful than a vague, achy feeling that settled briefly in his balls, and then wandered up and down his body. He just didn't feel like trolling these people anymore for about three days.

Sterility, that's what I caught.

They invited him to meals, which he took with the group, listening to them talk about reconstruction of other archives and work on computer salvage. Ivar had made a reputation for himself already, breaking an old collocation-facility door with a fire ax and hauling out most of a row of racks on his shoulders. The crazy Viking kid seemed to have found his niche in the future and exploited being exotic quite nicely with the ladies.

"And there's an Italian chick who was an artillery man's mistress, wife, camp follower, something, who knew Leonardo da Vinci." Now, that would distract them. "I helped her get out," Jonah said before he realized he didn't want to explain a whole lot about that now.

They didn't seem impressed. Perhaps knowing Leonardo was unexceptional in this future. Everyone in Milan and Florence who came forward into this future probably claimed to have known Leonardo. One of the younger guys at the table asked, "What is the thing you find the most unique about our time?"

"That it's got these past people in it after all the dieback and diseases." The future perversely blended summer camp and occupational therapy and was just too earnest, but Jonah wasn't going to say that. He wondered where he could get an all-wool, tailored suit that he wouldn't have to sew himself. "I wonder if any of my children lived to have descendants."

"We'll find your descendants if they're still here. We have DNA banks so we can attempt to steer people toward good matings, keep the survivors inbreeding judiciously."

When the rest of the past shows up here, it will walk all the fuck over these people. The future was wide open to people like Ivar or the Italian girl who'd left a child to die in the past when she joined a war that should have killed her. "What's remarkable about this future is that you don't have overcrowding and all the artificial food and gyrocopters, but you're not butt-simple primitives, either."

"We decided to make everyone as competent as possible, in case there are more plagues."

Jonah knew what he had been good at—looking at accounting databases and finding information the company he was auditing didn't think it was telling him. He probed systems for profit as well as fun. The future people didn't seem ruthless enough to have survived the twenty-first century as he remembered it. But they had, and he would have died in a snowstorm without them.

In a week, the University City team had names and an address for him in East Falls, near where he used to live, but on the river. According to the historical plaque at 30th Street Station, the trains still followed the ancient track beds, now on their tenth generation of rails, with new pantographs and recycled copper wire stripped from the suburbs. The train went through farmland above ground, with a small town where Temple University had been, then to East Falls. Riymend went with him.

The hospital buildings still stood. They'd closed in his lifetime, and then reopened during the plague years. Jonah wondered if one of them was still for the insane. He'd rarely taken the train in his real life—*strange to think of the past as the real life, is the future the unreal one? Could I really be an avatar in some complex simulation?*

The train stopped at East Falls Station's most recent iteration, inside a building that had been a quarantine point. The doors to the outside weren't levered sealed shut these days, but Jonah saw the plastic gaskets and door bars where they had in the past. The gaskets were grimy and probably wouldn't work now.

A man and a woman were waiting in the station. Jonah realized one of them was kin, and tried to guess if it was the man or the woman. "Did the house end up being the ancestral family house?" Jonah asked. "The stone colonial off Henry Avenue?"

"The ruins are still there," the woman said, sounding vaguely familiar and very alien at the same time. "I'm your descendant, six or so generations removed."

"Okay. I'm Jonah Kirkpatrick."

The man with his great-something-granddaughter told Riymend, "You can go now. We'll bring him back to you later."

Jonah's granddaughter, six or so generations removed, said, "We're going to talk to our ancestor in private."

Riymend looked as though a research project was stolen from him, then said, "Please make a full report of what you discuss, of course."

"Of course," the woman who still hadn't introduced herself said. Jonah knew a fake promise when he heard it.

Riymend stayed in the train station as the three of them walked away. "I'm Lizevidda," the woman said.

"I'm Mitt," the man said. "I'm also kin, but not from your immediate line. We've been waiting for you for a while. There are some guys from one of the futures who told us you would be showing up in this continuum."

"One of the futures?" Jonah asked. So, beyond the earnest social communitarians were alternatives, he thought.

Lizevidda said, "We've seen them stay stable for about a year—so maybe they're the future."

"Why were they waiting for me?"

"Let's get inside," Lizevidda said. "They will be thinking you can help them."

Jonah was getting an odd, familiar feeling, the feeling he'd gotten when someone had just handed him a really good program for screwing up networks. Not that he didn't enjoy screwing up networks from time to time, when sysadmins got complaisant, but having that rep follow him for over three hundred years turned the reputation into something a wee bit claustrophobic.

They walked down the hill by the ruins of the cathedral to the Schuylkill River at the river stairs, which Jonah remembered as being there in his day, but not used, and certainly not flanked by a kayak-and-scull rental. The water also seemed different. It was faster.

"The river's different," he said.

"Yes, there's no dam at Fairmont these days. Someone decided to blow it up during the early plague years because mosquitoes carried disease vectors. Someone remembered that the Falls of the Schuylkill had been particularly healthy before the Fairmont dam was built. Having the river running faster helped."

They walked a few blocks west to a house with a city lot–size garden between it and the river. At least his descendants looked prosperous for these times, with a freestanding house and garden. But if 80 percent of the population died back, even Philadelphia would have land to spare. The house was built of ceramics, wood, and fused glass, with a greenhouse roof on the top floor. The door had the same sort of seals that Jonah had noticed at the train station, but clean, with a door-seal bar that looked well maintained. "You're self-sustaining here?"

"Yes, a turbine in the river generates our electricity. And we've got about a thousand square feet under cultivation on the top floor. As long as the central grid doesn't go down or someone doesn't mess with our turbine, we can seal ourselves up for a couple of months. Haven't had to do that this century, but we can lock down better than the Archives."

"I hope so," Jonah said mildly. "But isn't the greenhouse roof fragile?"

"No," Lizevidda said, without explaining. Just inside the front door was a foyer with a desk, coat racks, two armchairs, a small sofa, an open door to a small but complete bathroom, and a second door with seals. Lizevidda picked up a remote from the desk and pushed a code to open the second door. They went through that to a decontamination room with showers, but didn't use those and went on to the main living area.

"This is a private house?" Jonah asked.

"It's the Kirkpatrick river place for your various kin."

"I thought the whole society was utterly egalitarian."

Lizevidda said, "We built our house. We don't share it. That's allowed. We just can't get help."

Jonah followed them to the basement filled with a faint whir that sounded like a computer. A blue light opened in one corner and a man said, "We've been waiting for you."

"What is this?" Jonah asked. "Who are you?"

"The future," Lizevidda said.

"Maybe the real one," Mitt said. "There's no time like it."

Jonah remembered what he'd read about branching time lines. Mitt and Lizevidda said the future branched. "You mean this isn't the real future now?"

"You're in my past," the man said. "And we watched you help that Viking kid and the Lombardian woman get the far past to invade the past you're in now so we could get to this present, which is the real edge of all the possible times we know about."

Jonah thought, *Cut to the chase.* "So I don't have any free will."

"No," the man said. "But we have to help you."

Lizevidda said, "Ever wondered why you bothered with all the silly stuff you bothered with?"

"What silly stuff?" Jonah said. These people were giving him a long day in less than two hours.

"Newsgrouping floods, taking over other people's computers through back orifices, jousting with people who could really embarrass you at work."

"I thought it was fun at the time," Jonah said.

"It was your destiny preparing you for what you did, or will do," the man in the blue-light patch said.

"Okay." Jonah decided that he didn't want to ask the man how he fared through all this.

"The Viking and the Italian woman are a cute couple, aren't they?" the blue-lit man said.

"They don't even like each other," Jonah said.

"They will," Mitt said.

"We'd just give you more time machines, but the past doesn't let us operate quite like that."

"You don't get any free will, either. Good," Jonah said. This sounded more and more like some kind of computer game, or someone was trolling him and would pay for it.

"We are stagnating now, genetically, emotionally," Lizevidda said. "Learning three or four trades may have been useful when we were still fighting plagues, but we haven't had a serious plague in years. Humans need structure, hierarchy, and leadership. But people now fear that someone will take advantage of them if they're not eternally perfect paranoids."

"I knew people who would have thought this system was Utopia," Jonah said. He was glad to see that his descendants hadn't fallen for übercontrol freakdom of "we all do everything."

"I can't imagine one of us being one of them," Lizevidda said.

"You're going to help bring up a lot of people from your past," the man in the blue light said, "so the twenty-fourth century present there ends up the future I'm in."

"This sounds dangerous," Jonah said. He would do it to get back at this silly present for all the boredom he'd suffered before he decided to take his chances outside the archives, but he wasn't going to just agree to be helpful right away.

Of course, he could be a computer program deluded about being a man, but the other alternative didn't have any more room for free will, either, and he hadn't been told how this ended.

Or even if he survived for very much longer. But he would have died, or thought he would have died, if he hadn't been brought to this time, or programmed into this computer, whichever was the real case.

"Forward," he said. "To the future."

"Whichever one that works," Lizevidda said.

"You need to persuade Benedetta to work with you," the man in the blue light said. He said something to the others, which had the rhythms of English but wasn't. They spoke back. Jonah tried to remember where he'd heard that dialect before. He hadn't. The future present he was in spoke differently, but he could understand it, since the people he first spoke with here were making an effort to match his dialect more at first and then had drifted into speaking their own dialect with its different vowels. Herrit was a morphed form of *Harriett.* Riymend had been *Raymond* when he came from. "What language are you speaking?"

"I think it's what evolved out of English and Welsh," the man said. "Owen Glendower was quite the political organizer."

When was Owen Glendower quite the political organizer? Jonah had a funny feeling that the historical Owen Glendower's future as a political organizer hadn't happened yet. "Shakespeare made fun of Glendower, a crazy Welshman trying to call up spirits to fight the English."

"We had a lot of trouble steering Glendower in the right direction. He's about as stubborn a Celt as we've dealt with. You're another one."

Jonah almost said, *I haven't given you any trouble yet,* but decided to keep his mouth shut. "So I assume that everyone who disappeared without a trace in history ended up in the future. Ends up. Whatever."

"Probably not everyone," the man said. "Sometimes time seems to just lock down and not let you have things happen."

Lizevidda said, "Where time was flexible, it moves people through. Sometimes, though, the past won't budge."

So the past has a mind of its own. "What was my mission that I've accomplished? Can I assume I can't help doing it regardless?"

The man looked like he was about to say something, but decided against it just as his lips began to move. The blue patch of light he was in went out.

"We can explain further," Lizevidda said.

"You're going to steal the time machine at the archives and enlarge the portal space," Mitt said.

"There's no suspense or fun if you know I did it successfully."

"Just because that future says you did it successfully, doesn't mean it will be easy. Or that we were talking to the permanent real future."

Jonah wondered if there was more to this than he'd been told. Like if he failed and got killed trying, did a new version of him start trying from the same level a few seconds later?

Is this game completely internally consistent and are there any real bugs?

Jonah wanted to find Benedetta. She'd be better for the gig than that Viking kid, even if she ended up with the Viking kid in the end.

Maybe these future people only hoped they were time's leading edge, and were lying to him about what he had to do.

If the future of now was the ultimate player in these time-travel games, the present was caught in the middle between a past that was invading them and a future that wanted them invaded. If what he'd seen wasn't the real future, who knew what would happen next? Jonah decided if the future had many branches, he had free will.

Boredom Attacks

In a South Philly townhouse she shared with two women from her work group, Benedetta found herself trying to reinvent Milan with the closest things she could find to the bright glazed Milanese pottery, which she bought from shops that carried old things. She filled vases with fresh flowers shipped in on the bullet trains that were beginning to run between Florida—so appropriate a name—and Philadelphia. And she shopped online for things shipped in from the Amish country and farther, and saved up credit for a walnut chest built like her cheaper wood chest in Milan.

Her roommates were kind, and Benedetta stayed in touch with the men who'd given her a bed her first night out of the Archives, but she found herself wishing she was not split between the past and her-present future.

Every Thursday, Benedetta went back to the Archives. The people left there were too frightened to leave, too primitive to want to leave, or insane. But she found herself drawn to the primitive and the frightened.

"Do you want to join our team?" Joe asked, saying that in the tone of a man who wants the answer to be *I want to stay with you.*

"No. Thursdays are enough."

Both the visits to the scared primitives and the house decoration began to make Benedetta as cranky as too much spinning had made her as a girl. How was distributing food and beer, cleaning houses, and making clothes so different from the life she'd fled as a child? Now what came next?

But Benedetta wasn't sure where to go in the future—to Ivar, to Jonah from just before the plagues, or to stay with her work group in South Philadelphia, where most of the people, female and male, bore children. Technology made them all urban craftspeople, complete with gardens in back of their houses. They had the same gossiping nature of the craftspeople back in Milan, always knowing what had happened, though perhaps less malicious about their gossip.

Joe said, "But you could stay in the work group you're in now, of course."

"Well, of course," Benedetta said. This week, she was trying the kind of silk clothes Milanese ladies had worn in 1489. Next week, she'd try something different from the Web sellers—dog skin, kits for interactive lace, and shoes that molded to their wearer's feet. Benedetta wondered what interactive lace could be.

Interactive lace kits turned out to be interactive bobbins and a board that jacked little pin-size posts up and down, the bobbins changing patterns depending on board angle, on which pins were in or out, and perhaps at random. Chinese made them and sent them to America by automated boats. Benedetta wondered if this place she was in, despite the time machines, was a backwater.

So, she was bored.

Then Jonah showed up again, just to see her, he said. The little Viking brat hadn't done that.

Jonah was cold, and that alone made Benedetta miss the men in her past, the winter coldness on a man's skin when he kissed her. This kiss was on her forehead, though. "I'd like to visit the Archives for a few days," he said. "You think that could be arranged?"

"I visit there on Thursdays," Benedetta said.

"So I've heard," Jonah said. "I missed you, Benedetta. Why do you go back?"

He was lying, but Benedetta knew that she'd be involved in trickery with the man. He'd proved himself good at tricks with the soap mask that got her beyond the security cameras. She asked, "Why would you want to stay there a few days?"

"Don't you ever feel confused by the present? Or want to see the machine that brought you here?"

"Joe wants me to join their work group."

"Maybe they'd take me instead."

"Joe doesn't have the hots for you," Benedetta said.

"Even after you bit him and ran away."

Benedetta realized she'd always needed someone to take her away from boredom. *I suppose I should be more introspective and worry about this trait, but I'm more interested in seeing what Jonah needs me to help him with.*

When Benedetta showed up with Jonah the next Thursday, Joe said, "You all have the legal right to walk out. He doesn't have a legal right to walk back in."

Jonah said, "I need a refuge from the future."

Joe said, "Bullshit. You need a refuge from your drinking."

Benedetta could almost taste Joe's hand between her teeth again. "Why are you being so harsh with him? I visit every Thursday."

"I don't want you in and out," Joe said to Jonah. "I don't trust you. I'd have left you believing you were a program until you died."

"Today, I believe I'm a creature of free will. Who knows what I'll believe tomorrow. I want to visit again."

"I saved your life. You stole my research people from me."

Jonah said, "You saved our lives with some mysterious godlike machines that you still don't understand."

Joe stopped talking. Jonah stood on the balls of his feet, swaying very slightly. Benedetta wondered which one of them would punch the other.

"I've been talking to someone who says he lives in the real future," Jonah said. "Do you want to learn more? Let me stay here a few days."

"We'll let you know. Benedetta, what do you know about this?"

"First time I'd heard of actual contact with people further up in the future."

The rest of the day Benedetta spent walking around the cold city with Jonah, who began the walk with an introduction. "Let me introduce myself more formally. I'm not drunk right now. I'm Jonah Kirkpatrick. I was married. I miss my family as if they disappeared last year. And I'm still not convinced this isn't some sort of simulation, but it's a marvelously complex simulation in any case. If the futures fork and aren't just one future until we do something, then I have free will. You do, too."

"I miss people, too," Benedetta said. "Why are twenty-fourth-century people so complex in some ways and so easy to fool in others? Would that be something you'd get with being avatars of a game program in a machine?"

"You'd have to know way more about computers than even Leonardo could have imagined, to understand why I could believe we were simulations. But simulations could have free will. I've been told I'm destined to do what I do. I think I'm being trolled."

"The future says it saw you do things?"

"Yes. And another thing. I miss you."

"Aw. What did you miss?"

"I'll have to think about it." He led her to a streetcar and they rode in silence to the house where his descendants lived.

His descendants were worried. The people from the future had disappeared. "We made a wrong decision somewhere and their future didn't happen, or forked."

"That's fucked," Jonah said, and giggled. "So they weren't the leading edge of our future after all."

"Who disappeared?"

"People who were going to explain how we were going to steal a time machine and change things to bring about their future," Lizevidda said.

"It is just a game," Jonah said.

"So, what's stopping us from stealing the machine and bringing back people from the past on our own?" Benedetta said. She didn't trust plans someone in any future had for her, but there were plenty of people who deserved this time more than its present residents. "Maybe I can bring back my son."

"What about your husband?"

"I saw him die. I don't think people other people saw die ..." Benedetta didn't want to think about that anymore. "My son could have disappeared to here."

"I don't ... I don't know. We don't have any guides from the future, now," Jonah said.

His great-granddaughter many times removed said, "Maybe another future will reach back."

Mitt said, "Any future thinks it's going to be The True Future. We did deal with a completely different future once. They tried to trick us into an attack on the city council. We knew we didn't have the forces for that."

"So we just go on our nerve," Jonah said, wondering how many people they did have supporting them.

"The machines have been stolen in at least one time line, by you, Benedetta, and maybe the Viking guy."

"This game is wicked," Jonah said.

Lizevidda and Mitt looked at each other and sighed. "It's not a game," Mitt said.

Benedetta was tired of listening to arguments over which future, what game. "Who cares?" she said. "I want to see if I can find my son and bring other people I want out of the past."

"That's what screwed their future up, I bet," Lizevidda said. "They want us to bring up some leaders. You're just looking for your son and people like you."

Benedetta said, "All we need to do is build a fake model of the machine and take the real one out. Just like I got out of the Archives with a fake Joe face."

"Made of soap," Jonah said.

"Why didn't these future people just tell you how to build a time machine?" Benedetta asked.

"It's not part of the game," Jonah said.

"The time machine is from yet another different future," Lizevidda said. "Probability lines are screwy."

"All we need to do is get a machine, take it apart, analyze how it works, and build more of them," Benedetta said.

"It's not that simple," Jonah said.

"We're craft-culture people—okay, you're not, but I am. This is not a big one, as you say."

"Do you know how the computer works? You'd have to take it apart to the molecular level to reverse-engineer it," Jonah said.

"There were a lot of smart people in the recent past. We can find someone to help once we've stolen a model," Lizevidda said. "We might have to keep them quarantined here. Or we can work with another city."

Benedetta thought about Leonardo, what he'd have given to be living in such times. "What do we need to take a time machine apart down to the molecular level?" She didn't really know what the molecular level was, but these people could certainly tie themselves into verbal knots if left to their own devices.

"A future that will let us do that," Mitt said.

"Let's make it," Benedetta said, happy to have something to look forward to other than days tending the weakest-minded of the temporal refugees or gardening and running clothes-making machines. Stealing, reverse-engineering, bringing in other people from the past to shake up this time and make a different future, that was more interesting. "We can do this. We obviously did it once before."

"I don't think you were quite the same," Mitt said.

"Obviously, she wasn't Benedetta that future was expecting. They disappeared just after ..."

"It could have nothing to do with her. Perhaps the wrong butterfly died," Jonah said. "Or time lines aren't constant. Or it's really a computer simulation, just like I said." He smiled at them.

The blue haze appeared again, this time with different faces in it. "We finally reached you. Benedetta, good to meet you. We thought we were cut off in a parallel time line, where you died. So, now we are your future. What happens next is that you need to find an atomic-force microscope and do a layer-by-layer analysis of the chips controlling the quantum fold ..." The rest of what the man said sounded like gibberish.

Jonah said, "Ignore the man in the blue haze."

Benedetta said, "Did I rescue my child?"

The face disappeared. Mitt said, "We'll try to talk to them a bit later to see if they've got a future worth losing free will over. Or we'll make them go away somehow."

"What happens to them when they disappear like that?" Benedetta asked.

"Maybe they dropped the connection. Maybe they aren't our true future," Lizevidda said.

Jonah said, "An atomic-force microscope would be a very cool toy."

Lizevidda asked, "They had them in your day?"

"Even had open-source software for them."

Benedetta wondered what in the world an atomic-force microscope could be. They needed to find one so she could use it and figure out what it did and how it worked.

"It would be simpler just to steal the time machine and start fishing around the twenty-first century for people with high-tech skills who've disappeared," Jonah said. "There's no paradox involved if they disappeared, right?"

"I'd rather figure it out for myself," Benedetta said. "If I can control the machine, I can get people I want here." The Italian Renaissance was a high point of human creativity and intelligence, Benedetta thought. What would be the point of bringing in someone from nearer to now? The people of this time didn't invent the time machine and didn't make copies of it either.

"Did anyone try to make a copy of it?" Jonah asked.

"There's only one," Lizevidda said. "If you deconstruct it and can't put it back together and can't build a new one, you can't get any more people from the past."

"Why do you want people from the past?" Jonah asked.

"Genetic diversity, to study what was lost, and just because," Mitt said. "We all agree on that one, collectivists and people who want a more dynamic social order."

" 'Just because' has always worked for me, but I think we should steal the machine and see if it works for us first, then take it apart," Jonah said. "Just because."

"If there's a small discontinuity black-hole feature in the machine, taking the machine apart would be interesting. If it's just a matter of circuits, people should have been able to make time machines by now," Mitt said.

"Of course, if we're all just characters in a computer game, releasing a captive discontinuity would simply reset the game," Jonah said.

"Depends on the size and containment," Mitt said.

Benedetta decided that she and Ivar would be a better team for stealing the time machine than these people. If it could be carried with a hand truck or a small forklift, she and Ivar already knew how to be physically sneaky. These people could work much with language, but they'd never had to be physically devious.

First, she had to go back and look at the time machine and see what the size of the damn thing was. Better to do that without either Ivar or Jonah along. "I think I need to talk to Joe."

"Why?" Lizevidda asked.

"Have any of you actually seen the time machine?"

"Good point," Jonah said. "If there's not really a time machine, and it's all just another computer game with delusional subprocesses that think they have lives ..."

"Jonah, don't fuck with me," Mitt said. "Benedetta, you're right. We could be talking about stealing something that would break if it wasn't super-cooled."

"Or something that's about the size of Leonardo's horse," Benedetta said. "We'd need a truck for that."

"It would be kinda cool if we did rescue Leonardo's horse," Jonah said. "Who cares about people? Save the art."

"First, we need access to a time machine," Benedetta said. She liked Leonardo's horse well enough, but the French had shot it to bits after Milan fell. But most of all, she really wanted to save people from her own time—if not her son, then someone like her. Hundreds of camp followers just disappeared in history.

Jonah and Benedetta arranged to meet Ivar on Mantua Bridge. Mantua, an odd name for a neighborhood that never appeared to have any Italians in it, Benedetta thought. Spring was bringing out some early leaves, but the day was too cold for most walkers. Some of the houses were ancient, with vines all around them. One old building that looked like a stone castle was covered with small machines that crawled over it, repointing the mortar.

From a distance, Benedetta didn't recognize Ivar standing on Mantua Bridge on the art museum side. He'd changed his clothes for the future and wore a long black overcoat, wool pants, and a hat that covered his blond hair. When he moved and waved, she recognized him and met him in the middle of the bridge. Jonah walked behind them, looking around through binoculars as though he was watching birds, checking for parabolic microphones.

In Ivar's Norse, Benedetta said, "We want to steal the time machine, reverse-engineer it, and bring more past people into the future."

Ivar stopped walking forward. "Why? Not too many of us, so people can like us. Lots of new people moving in would make the people of this time tense. We'd be bumpkins moving into the cities. Being unique has its advantages, especially with women."

Behind them, Jonah said, "He doesn't sound happy."

"I'm not," Ivar said in English. "Why do you need me in this mess?"

"Isn't there anyone you'd like to bring up-time?"

"No. I like this life."

"Well, I suppose it is an improvement over being beaten up by your Irish slaves," Jonah said.

"Fuck you," Ivar said. He started to turn around.

"The technical challenge doesn't interest you?"

"I thought I was dead. I'm not dead, just ahead in time from everyone I used to know. If we bring in others, I won't be unique. And being unique gets me laid here, without having to buy a slave or get married or hire a whore. I'm learning neat things. Programming, networking. We'll be the immigrants with bad accents and no skills if a lot of us come in."

Jonah said, "But you could learn even more neat things."

"What was it like for refugees in your time?" Ivar asked. "Jonah, Benedetta." Ivar started walking toward Jonah.

"It depended," Jonah said. "If they were clever and learned English and didn't try to pretend that some dirtbag country that couldn't support them was really their true homeland to which all their spare money must return, they did well. We won't have that problem. The past can't use our credit. The old country is literally old."

"I like being unique."

Benedetta didn't want to have the two men really quarreling with each other. "Ivar, you're not going to talk to anyone about what we've asked you about, are you?"

She wondered if she had bed skills enough to make him forget these other women, if it would come to that. *I never was so cold-minded in my other life.* But she caught Ivar looking at her as if she were an older sister, not a potential bed partner. *Okay, fuck off.*

"I have not sworn my word of honor to anyone here," Ivar said in Norse. "Not you. Not them. Not even my work folks."

"There's nobody you miss, at all?"

"Don't ask me." Ivar looked down at the river below them for a while. "Yeah, I miss my m ... some people, but I've grown up since then. You and Jonah came from the past as adults. You were a mother. He was a father. I wasn't wed yet. My beard came in fully after I was here. I've even grown some. This time is where I became a man. I love this time now. It's even more fantastic than what I'd heard about Iceland."

Whatever had driven Ivar's family to flee Norway, he'd broken with his past when he got on the ship headed over the horizon.

"We're not trying to break this time. We're talking about adding more people to it, people who disappeared in history, to add to the population the diseases reduced."

"Jonah, why would you want to do this?" Ivar asked. "Strangers are treated badly if there are many of them. They have to deny who they were or they have to live in their own communities after they finish whatever scrap work the people born in the community give them."

Benedetta suspected that Ivar was right. If huge numbers of past people came into this time, they'd be less welcome than the handful who had moved out of the Archives.

Jonah said, "I miss the world I was in. Admittedly, it was superior to yours."

Ivar said, "You know, if you're going to steal the machine, you don't want to go in and ask permission to see it, then come back later and steal it. Ask permission to see it and steal it right then and there, have a large van waiting. If it's bigger than a van, you can't steal it anyway."

"Would you help us?"

"This would make outlaws of us. You know that."

"Not necessarily," Jonah said. "Depends on who we bring in from the past. I think it's time they had some new old ideas. This perfectly paranoid egalitarian society is making them way too brittle for their own good. They could be helped by a good troll."

Ivar said, "I don't believe in trolls, much less good ones."

Benedetta realized Ivar had understood the word *troll* literally. Jonah sighed. Benedetta wondered if having a woman in the mix created tension between them. But she wasn't going to abandon the first real excitement she'd found since running away from the Archives.

"Will you tell Joe what we're planning?"

"No. I'm not an informer," Ivar said. He stood for a minute, looking up the Schuylkill. "I don't think my people would be unhappy if they had some twenty-first-century help with what they're salvaging. And the people of the breaker yard have their own uses for things."

Now that was an angle Benedetta hadn't thought of.

Jonah said, "And the time machine is a very cool techno toy, isn't it? Would the salvage community want it?"

"I'd have to talk to them, and I don't know who might be willing to inform on us. Do you want me to risk that?"

"Steal first, then talk," Benedetta said, "if you don't know where all their loyalties lie."

Ivar said, "I was thinking of stealing from the Archives as if I were thinking of stealing from my host in my own culture. But taking from people who tricked me and lied to me might not be really like stealing from my hosts."

"We helped you escape them."

"Yes, I haven't forgotten that," Ivar said. "But the Archives saved my life."

"They fished and happened to catch you," Benedetta said. "You owe them your honor for that?"

"I owe my honor to the community I work with now."

"What would they want?"

Ivar shrugged. "I don't know. I'll have to think about this. My life here is good, but I'm certainly not going to be famous for eons because of it." They walked off the bridge into West Philly. Benedetta thought about going back to the Archives but it seemed like a convent or monastery now, a place to leave inconvenient people. A museum of people, some of whom still believed they were dead and in a peculiar form of Hell.

Jonah himself had a bit of that madness in him, or perhaps he was correct and this was all a play inside a computer, or they all were the future's version of puppets.

Whatever, she still had to deal with the plot.

"Come visit me," Jonah said. "We've got a lot more to catch up on." He sounded lonely.

Ivar found a bicycle and unlocked it and said, "I've got work and a woman who wants to meet me from my profile online."

"Oh, my God, they still have computer dating," Jonah said.

"People tend to marry outside their communities," Ivar said. "The men say that the community women are too much like sisters. I'm hot because the women and I didn't see each other with mothers' milk on our lips. Jonah, you should get out more."

"That's all right," Jonah said. "Benedetta?"

"Okay." She wondered if Jonah still felt married to his now-long-dead wife. She had seen Emelio die. He was her man, though they'd never married in church, and she felt like a widow when she thought of him.

Ivar got on his bicycle and rode away. Jonah said, "Fuckhead and a bonehead. He's not going to work with us."

"Pity I didn't sleep with him before he got loose in the twenty-fourth century."

"You would have done that?"

"Not really. His kind murders women slaves to accompany their dead in funeral pyres, so he's not really my idea of a great bedmate, and he looks at me as though I were his older sister."

"Hadn't they stopped sacrificing humans by your time? Hadn't they become Christians well before the fifteenth century?"

"He's not from then. You weren't surprised by this time. The only reason I wasn't surprised was that I'd seen Leonardo's drawings. So what's still like your time? What has changed?"

"The tech is more or less the same from my time to now, with some improvements. As for the politics, the worst combination of tree-huggers and collectivists won. But they do appear to be paranoid enough about each other to actually make an almost egalitarian society more or less work. They don't appear to have delusions about innate human goodness, which makes them bearable."

Benedetta thought the social order in the twenty-fourth century wasn't that different from a Swiss pike unit's order.

"I need to get drunk," Jonah said. "I'm tired of being a perfect sober paranoid."

"Can we trust our friend?" Benedetta said, not saying anything directly in case they were being overheard in these more crowded streets.

"He needs to come up with his own twist to the idea to justify what he wants to do. Looting and pillaging and raping are his genetic heritage."

"That is a bigoted statement."

"You've spent too much time with the liberals, my dear."

"I'm really annoyed that he thinks I'm too old for him."

"Well, he is a stupid little boy, then." Jonah walked up to a building that looked like some future people had heard rumors of castles and put round towers on the corners, then decorated the whole thing with cutwork done in wood. Jonah noticed her glance traveling slowly over the wooden trim under the roof and around the windows. "It's Victorian revival. Most of the original Victorian stuff was not quite this goofy, but with laser saws and fake wood, you can do quite ornate bargeboards."

"Fake wood?"

"Yes, you think anyone would have the time to keep the wood in good condition in these short-handed times?"

Benedetta thought that Jonah had brought her to his room for sex, but he quickly began drinking and seemed only to need her to listen to him. She remembered Emelio and Carlo talking and talking after a battle, with Julia and herself listening, even when they'd been in the battle with the men themselves.

"And in the end, what was it all about?"

"Male pride," Benedetta said, having not paid all that much attention to the story about people she had never heard of and didn't know.

Jonah laughed. "But some of them were women. Women flaming each other was almost as good as a chick fight in real life. Better. You could imagine better bodies for them than they had, hair-pulling and nipple-biting."

Benedetta remembered some women-on-women fights in her day. The men had never tried to stop them. She asked Jonah, "Why, really, do you want to steal the time machine?"

"Because . . ."

"Tell me, really."

"I know that my family went on without me and died in history, so yeah, I'm not as motivated as you are to find the disappeared. You can hope that they didn't just disappear because they died and nobody buried them, or that someone used them for target practice or weapons testing. Maybe the mob didn't bother to know who the poor fucked-up starving bastard caught stealing in the market was? Maybe your mom gelded your son and sold him to musicians? Maybe he entered the priesthood and took a new name and died documented and completely gone?"

Jonah hadn't told her why he wanted to do this at all, just goaded her to distract her from her question. "That's not an answer. Why would you want to bring people in out of the past to this time?"

"Why would I? I just want to annoy that Joe bastard."

Neither Ivar nor Jonah was a man she'd trust at her back in a real battle. She even wondered if they'd have been golden for the side that didn't have them. Maybe she should try to figure out how to operate the time machine herself, in secret, and go fishing through time for people she cared about without either of them.

Jonah put down his glass and said, "Perhaps I want to make you happy."

"I don't believe that," Benedetta said.

"I realize we don't really look like reliable allies. A drunk old troll like me; a Viking-gone-twenty-fourth-century-slick-boy like Ivar. But if you can't put the machine under one arm and walk out with it, you're going to need help."

"I know," Benedetta said.

"You don't have to sound so utterly despairing when you say that. We're both more reliable than you may realize."

"You're drunk."

"So? You think I can't be reliable while drunk?"

"Why would you want to help me?"

"Because I want to shake these silly people out of their silly fantasy that they've solved the human condition finally."

Benedetta didn't say how much she liked the way the future had arranged its social order. Maybe she needed to buy a motorcycle and get her excitement legally.

"And if we don't do something, the game will restart anyway," Jonah said.

"You really don't believe that, do you?"

"You don't really know for sure that it's not a computer game."

"Computer games don't get mosquito bites, either, do they?"

"If it was programmed in, they could. You know, there are some futures where you've already obviously stolen the machine," Jonah said.

"Do those futures exist? Could they be fantasies projected on that blue fog?"

"Steal, don't steal. Trust or don't trust. It's that simple." Jonah made a move as though he was thinking of trying to seduce her, but he flopped back into the chair, staring at the air as if waiting for blue fog with faces and voices that would tell him what to do next. He was too drunk for his cock to work.

Benedetta realized she did want to sleep with someone. And she'd thought that died with Emelio, but widows didn't gain their reputations as hot and easy for nothing. "Steal. Don't trust."

"Only a person from as low a background as yours could say such a thing." Jonah's brain was still getting residual alcohol from what he'd put in his gut. "Trust has nothing to do with it. You certainly can't make more time machines without lots of help. You can't fig-ure out how to use a time machine on your own. You haven't a clue about the theory behind them, have you? Camp-following cunt."

He was raging because he was impotently drunk. Benedetta said, "But all I would need then would be Ivar."

"Fuck the Viking. Or don't fuck the Viking. Fuck Joe. Get him to help you look in the past for your son."

"I don't like the idea of having some people in this present control who has a chance for more life and who doesn't."

"I feel exactly the same way. It's not just freedom of speech. It's freedom to live again."

Benedetta accepted that as true. "More people should have that chance. It's that simple for me."

Back in the Time Track

Ivar left Jonah and Benedetta at the Mantua Bridge and rode his bicycle down by houses that were either four hundred years old or fakes of houses that old. Some were fakes of a future that never arrived.

What could his salvage community do with a time machine? He knew that stealing wasn't considered honorable now, but salvage hadn't always been peaceful in the past, since some sites were battle wrecks.

His memory threw up images of a raid he'd been on when he was about twelve years old. He remembered being scared then, but the mental pictures were exciting, not terrifying like when he remembered the raid without recalling the events in his mind's eye. The fear seemed separate from memories of the raid. Thought and Memory, Odin's two ravens. He'd never thought about that before, how odd it was, but a lot of his memories seemed to be not quite what he thought and felt about the events when he recalled them by name and not the mind's eye, up to the drowning and the visions of Odin when he thought he was dead.

Shivering in the boat, vaguely seasick, he'd rowed with the older men while listening to them talk about the Danish market town the leader wanted them to loot. Some spoke for the raid. Others said the townspeople were likely to fight back, but they all agreed to let the leaders decide. The leaders of the two boats wanted the raid for loot and glory.

All together, they walked the boats through shallow water and hauled them half up on the sand. Ivar followed his brother, wondering about two ship-fulls of men attacking a whole town.

His brother said, "Let Aki go in first."

In the twenty-fourth century, Ivar read *Egil's Saga* and wondered if the Aki he'd known at twelve had been the same as the Aki who went raiding with Egil of the saga. He remembered stories of Egil who traveled throughout the Viking world, from England to Iceland and from Denmark into Finland. So Aki and Egil made names beyond their lives, more than a thousand years of sagas repeated and printed and discussed among bookmen.

Had Egil merely claimed to have been on Aki's raid?

As sheer feeling, the raid was terrifying; as memory of sights and sounds, it was exciting. Time changed his memories, and his mind split the fear from the story. Thought and Memory.

Now, again, a raid. Yes, no? Ivar felt that the time machine would be good salvage, but doubted his work team would want to raid their own city's people. Perhaps he could say that they found another time machine, lie about where this one came from.

He didn't think he could reverse-engineer a time machine without more modern help than from a woman who had known Leonardo da Vinci and a crazy man pretending to be a troll who believed he might be a character in a computer game.

They could make a great stealing team, though. Benedetta could distract guards, and the belief that nothing was real could make Jonah fearless beyond what he might be willing to risk if he believed this was real life.

Ivar doubted that Jonah really believed he was a subprogram in a computer game. And would Benedetta be willing to flash a tit?

Ivar also realized that if he went from not interested to wanting to lead the stealing team, both would suspect him of being treacherous. Too sudden a change of mind was suspect in any age.

First, he needed to start visiting the Archives, get the guards used to seeing him. Benedetta was the only one who still had free access to the Archives, but perhaps Joe would trust Ivar more than Jonah. Ivar could play naïve if he needed to.

So, can I come see you again?" he asked Benedetta by telephone. Telephones still amused him. They weren't as efficient as either talking person-to-person or sending letters by computer. He could almost hear what was clipped out of the voice that wasn't needed for the sounds to be clear-meaning. He didn't want Benedetta to see what his body was also saying. His uncles had given him some practice in holding lies on the spine and not showing them in the face, but he'd not quite mastered self-control when the slaves took over the ship.

Benedetta said, "I don't think they're holding tremendous grudges over your leaving, but Joe doesn't tell me everything."

Ivar said, "Couldn't I go with you on your next Thursday?"

Benedetta called back to tell Ivar that Joe, who'd been hesitant to let Jonah back in at all, said he'd be perfectly happy to see Ivar again. So Joe didn't think of him as a trickster. Ivar smiled, even though Benedetta couldn't see it.

Joe reminded Ivar that he would have to go through decontamination before he could walk around the Archives again. Ivar found a tiny location device that could be radio-activated and built it into a hollow coin. He wondered what the Archives people would do to him if they found the coin.

Ivar wondered if Joe made decontamination special for him, with the stinging solutions abraded in with stiff brushes, and the lung and nose douche. The coins in his pockets were irradiated; his ID card and house keys washed with alcohol and scrubbed with soap, then washed with alcohol again. He wondered if the location device would be broken. He transferred the coins to the pockets of the white clean-room suit they gave him.

"You could leave your pocket change, keys, and ID in a locker," Joe said. "We all get decontaminated like that when we come in." He didn't look perfectly happy to see Ivar.

"No, I'll keep them with me." Ivar felt embarrassed that he'd ever fallen for their Odin trick. The religious awe was in his head, not in the room with holograms. He hadn't remembered how he'd felt that first day waking before now, and he hated having been tricked and felt immune to awe forever after.

The Gods are inside us, his grandmother said from memory.

The computer game is inside Jonah, he told the memory, *and you've been dead for centuries, old woman.*

Except he carried his past inside, Ivar realized. Only the present changed the past, redefined it with new words.

His past had been only a couple generations deep. Now he was reaching back centuries, and the reach could only get better if he had a time machine to fish the past.

"So, are you bringing people forward still?"

Joe said, "We've put the machine away until some of the legal issues get straightened out. Perhaps the past is better left where it is. Most of you died."

"All of us would have been dead by now without it."

"You want to see it?"

Ivar wondered if this was a trick question, a test, but why not speak the truth as much as possible. "Yes. I'd really like to see it." He almost expected Joe to ask if he'd come to steal it from them, but Joe simply motioned for him to follow. Benedetta came with them.

Joe led them to a back freight elevator that looked older than the rest of the building. They went down two levels and got out. Fluorescent bulbs lighted the corridor and there weren't any cameras visible. Ivar didn't know if that meant they didn't have security in the subbasement or if they assumed the security at ground level would be enough. He also wondered if there were other tunnels from earlier buildings here, some way to break into the Archives from below—old subterranean train lines. The scavengers must know.

Covered with dust and spider webs, the overhead light tubes looked old. They passed an open door to a room full of bicycles half-fallen to rust. Ivar remembered seeing the sea-corroded and ancient ship nails that would have been new in his day. These bicycles looked almost as ancient. The next room was full of terminals and computers. "All the machines we could find that would read data on old medium. All we've found so far was transferred to new media, but your group still finds things we've missed. We especially like finding caches of microfilm."

"I've done some data recovery," Ivar said, not mentioning that he had also learned a machine language and routing protocols. They were in a section that was whitewashed, lit by the long tubes, a bit cleaner. Joe unlocked a door and swung it inward. Ivar stepped inside.

Ten feet long, almost half again as wide, the time machine was cowled in brushed stainless steel. On top at the front was an exposed flat-screen monitor and a panel that slid back to show a keyboard and controls. Joe touched the machine in another place, and a second, larger panel from the middle to the rear rotated down into the machine, showing a gurney inside. The gurney rode on bars that could extend it out of the machine into the past. Ivar wondered if they'd cleaned the machine between rescues or if the machine cleaned itself. He'd been wet and drowning. Benedetta had been bloody.

He had been here, unconscious with his last memories of drowning. But one gurney at a time wouldn't work for bringing in groups of people. He wondered about getting a gate people could run through, if they could be persuaded to do that. "So how does it work?"

"We can see what we can get on the screen, and then we try to make a scoop. Sometimes, the machine just blocks, and the person dies. Sometimes, we get someone on the gurney."

"Is there anything special about the gurney?" Ivar asked. "Can people travel back to the past?"

"Not as far as we know. But this traveled to here and the gurney and the scoop arms appear to be able to go backward in a blue space that's sort of an overlap of the past and the present. We think."

Ivar remembered an eye looking out of blue fog. Jonah the Troll claimed to have talked to men in blue fogs. "So that's how I got here. Can we try to bring someone up?"

"We've stopped doing rescues since you got your lawyers to free whomever wanted to leave. Lots of people died, since their immune systems weren't capable of dealing even with our vaccines."

"Or they died because everything they knew and loved had died centuries earlier," Benedetta said.

Ivar realized she was also seeing the machine that had trawled her out of the past for the first time. "So, I couldn't go back?"

"We've tried to send someone back, but it doesn't appear to be possible. Maybe there would be someone whom the past could absorb, but why should we want to go there?"

"To really see what the past was like," Ivar said, but he realized there was no one past, that each person knew different things, went different places, and made his own meaning of his life. All humans split thought from memory.

The machine was too big to steal single-handedly.

Joe said, "We use the present to see the past, even if we can talk to people from the past."

"No way out of the present, then," Ivar said. He put his hand lightly on the steel shell and wondered how this thing worked. He found the catch to close the shell over the gurney. It was a curved lever on a pivot pin that didn't look that different from what could be made in his past, recessed in a scooped-in place on the shell. The instruments were still exposed. "Does it have its own power source?"

"Appears to," Joe said. He looked from Benedetta to Ivar and back.

Ivar realized the Archives couldn't move the thing quickly. They should steal it before Joe wondered more about his interest in it. *I'm asking too many questions,* he thought. "So Jonah was the last," Ivar said.

"I don't regret saving you, but I don't think saving people from the past served us as well in our research as we'd hoped."

Ivar hummed, and then said, "It's been an adventure." If this machine could be modified to bring in more people from the past, he could give this time an even bigger adventure.

Originally, he'd planned to get them used to his coming and going at the Archives, but perhaps what he really needed to do was a quick snatch, through a tunnel if one was near and useable. What he'd need would be a mole tractor.

Ivar felt a bit dizzy for a second, going from lapstrake ships to artificially driven battering rams in the time of one pulse. These people had given him a new life. Perhaps he should be more grateful, he thought as he pulled the coin with the location beacon out of his clean-room suit pocket.

But stealing this machine was a challenge, just as learning how to make a new time machine would be. He moved his fingers over the toggles that exposed the controls and the gurney again. He touched the gurney, thinking about lying there half-dead, and tucked the coin into the sheets on the gurney. Sleight of hand. He patted the gurney again, then closed the gurney cover and turned back to the instrument panel.

Joe moved as though to stop him. Ivar looked at the controls and wanted to play with them, too, but Joe's body said that if Ivar touched the controls again, Joe would tackle him. Ivar grinned and moved his hands in the air over the controls.

Joe closed the panel.

When Ivar stepped back from the machine, Joe said, "The screen shows the location in the past. There are some presets, but you can go looking through time if you can extrapolate the space-time coordinates. You can even look at other solar systems, but everything out there that's not Earth appears to be lifeless."

Benedetta said, "If there are presets, then the machine compensates for the ongoing movement of Earth."

This was going to be a very complex piece of machinery to reverse-engineer, Ivar thought. Give up. Be happy in this time.

No. He wanted a slave girl to burn with him on his funeral pyre. He didn't want to die alone in this future even though he preferred to be the only Norseman in the present.

Plus, reverse-engineering the machine would be a fabulous technical challenge. More toys to play with. More things to learn. He could become very famous.

All who came from the past forward in time would change or die. Learning new things had changed him.

"You think we should use the machine to rescue people, without worrying about what they can or can't teach us about the past?"

"Yes," Ivar said.

"Some of us are tempted to do that," Joe said. "I'm not. I worked too closely with the people we did save. The real successful adaptations were rare."

Ivar would ask Benedetta to find those who wanted to save people from the past. He said, "Am I one of your successes or one of your failures?"

"You're one of the very few who still live outside the Archives. I'm thinking about the people who came forward and died anyway, of culture shock, of the diseases they didn't have immunity to, of terminal homesickness."

"We who survived were wanderers in our own times," Benedetta said.

"Not socialized to local norms," Joe said. "So people who fit into their times were more likely to die here, and asocial people would be more likely to survive. Do you want us to bring in more asocial people?"

"Do you think I'm asocial?" Benedetta asked.

"Not you, in particular, but ..."

Joe is thinking of Jonah and me. Ivar kept his face still. "I've seen the machine. We can go now."

Going out was simple. They didn't count the coins in his pockets as he took off the clean-room suit and pulled on his street clothes, and transferred his ID, keys, and coins from one set of pockets to the other. Ivar felt as though a Norn's hand had touched him, cold and inhuman. He didn't believe in the Norns, but whatever that cold feeling was, time pivoted on the hinges of eternity. He was the pin in one hinge.

A machine to rescue another machine—that's what he needed now. And he needed a place to spend a few months, if it took a few months, to understand the time machine.

Doomed to do it.

He walked the streets outside the Archives where the old Mint used to be, listening at grates for creeks that were now running in ancient sewer tubes.

The people in the recycling flats in South Philadelphia rented machines without asking too many questions. Ivar didn't know what a mole tractor could cost to rent, but Jonah knew a man who might have the money. First, Ivar needed a quote, so he went down on his bicycle to where scavengers used acids to pan gold out of old computer chips.

A girl by a fire burning in an oil barrel said, "Go talk to Mr. Wythe. He's in the shack with the faired bent in front." She pointed up beyond the trash she was going through to a building about two hundred yards away. Ivar saw a blue-shelled recumbent bicycle, like a tiny plane without wings, just the lower quarter of the spoked wheels showing under the fairing. It leaned against a board-and-batten hut that could have been from any time.

As Ivar pedaled his own bike on rough paths cut through the heaps of salvage and junk, a man came out of the hut and watched Ivar approaching as though the girl had passed the word on. The man was thin, tall, and slightly bald. His hands were shoved in his pants pockets. Ivar reached the cleared ground around the hut, stopped a respectful distance from the man, and said, "Mr. Wythe? You have a mole tractor I could talk to you about?"

"What would a salvage techie who leaves the dirty work to us want with a mole tractor?"

"Bit of salvage."

"Well, yes, but can I get my machine back after you do the bit of salvage, or should I sell it to you?"

Ivar thought about trying to steal the mole tractor, but the man knew him, and the salvage yard people were allies with his collective. "Probably sell it to me, and I'll try to sell it back to you."

Mr. Wythe smiled very slightly, deepening the faint lines in his face, then said, "Three 2003 to 2006 model antique faired bents and a Stradivarius violin. In advance, of course. I suppose you'd want a stealth mole tractor."

"I'll have to see what I can do," Ivar said, wondering if there was a cheaper way to steal the time machine. Jonah's friends should be willing to find those things, though, if they were connected enough to have a separate house by the river. Mr. Wythe nodded and watched Ivar leave. His hands had never left his pockets.

They all met at the house by the river that Jonah's descendants Lizevidda and Mitt owned. After Ivar explained his plan and the cost for the mole tractor, Lizevidda murmured, "A Stradivarius violin. I think there were some in New Jersey, if they weren't destroyed in riots."

"Can we fake this?" Mitt asked. "The 2006 faired bents won't be difficult. We can have those built and fake a badge."

"Would a junkman know?" Jonah asked.

"Mr. Wythe would," Lizevidda said. "Getting a Stradivarius isn't utterly impossible but it's close to it. However, could you steal the time machine any other way?"

Mitt said, "We're not getting contacts from any future right now."

Benedetta said, "I can't really believe that we ended time."

Jonah said, "Maybe we ended the possibility of the futures being able to contact the past?"

Lizevidda said, "We've gone weeks before without contact."

"But we're planning such significant things," Mitt said.

Ivar wondered if the future was too undecided right now to help them. "Maybe none of the alternatives last that long until we act?"

When they went down in the basement, though, there was a violin with a note waiting for them.

The note advised them to not bring in any of the Knights Templar.

"Is it possible? Someone can send things back to the past," Ivar said.

"The time machine itself came from the future," Benedetta said. "So, obviously some people can send things back to the past. Why wouldn't they want to bring in the Knights Templar? They got hammered for no good reason in my past."

Ivar looked at the violin. "Okay." Ivar wondered if Mr. Wythe had his messages from men appearing in blue fogs and asked for the violin to see if they also had up-time contacts. How many people were agents for various futures wishing to keep their home futures going?

Mr. Wythe looked at the violin in Ivar's hands and smiled so deeply that his eyes looked like wolf eyes. He reached out with both hands for the violin and took it inside the hut, shutting the door before Ivar could follow him in. Ten minutes later, Ivar heard fiddle music coming from the hut. Mr. Wythe came back out in fifteen minutes with the smile still tight on his face. "I don't know where you got it, but it's four hundred years older than it's supposed to be. And it plays just like a Strad."

"We found it in a basement," Ivar said.

"We've found some interesting things in basements, too," Mr.

Wythe said. "You forged the bents, of course, but I'll take them anyway. There's always a market for a good forged recumbent bicycle. You're going to need a lesson on the tractor." The man tossed Ivar a key ring with a plastic fob and some metal keys on it. "If you use the fuel cell when you shouldn't, you'll suffocate yourself, but the electric motor has limits, too. You need a map of the city tunnels to anywhere in particular?"

"Would you throw that in free?"

"Of course not. I'd like to know what you're doing. The future is investing in you if it leaves you Strads in basements. A few weeks ago, one of the kids found a couple of computers in the middle of one of the junk heaps. The kids dismantled one of them and salvaged the gold before someone realized they'd never seen media like that before. I booted up the second machine. It worked. There's a message for you on it. It's biologically locked, which I suppose I could have hacked, but if I didn't get that done right, I could destroy the message. You let me see this message to you, too, and I'll give you a sewer-and-tunnel map. I think I'm supposed to see the message. I can't resist history, now can I?"

Ivar followed Mr. Wythe into his shack, which was full of jewelry and icons made from computer chips and parts. The man turned on a very neat laptop. The screen displayed a message: *Turn on the camera.* Ivar looked for a camera and saw a tiny lens in the top lid of the machine. The screen displayed a camera icon, then cycled back to the message *Turn on the camera.* When the camera icon came up again, Ivar touched it, and pointed the tiny lens his way.

The machine's screen read, *If you're Ivar, please put your hand against the screen.* A hand appeared on the screen. Ivar put his hand on it. The machine flashed once, then the screen read, *Okay, you can ask the man you're with if he is willing to help for a few more artifacts. We have a reason to believe he will.*

Mr. Wythe laughed.

Ivar said, "It's one-way communication. I wonder why they can't send people through."

"Because they can't or they would have," the junkyard man said. "I wonder what was on the other machine now."

Ivar wondered if the future people casting artifacts back in time had good aim, or if they'd sent redundant computers with messages for him, other Stradivariuses that got lost in the wrong basements.

The screen said, *You need to consider how much you want the times changed. Rescue whom you can of the Knights Templar. Download these instructions.*

"Who the fuck are the Knights Templar?" Ivar said. "The other folks said don't rescue any of them."

"Guys who learned the hard way about the rights of kings and the loyalty of popes and the power of pain and behavior mod," Mr. Wythe said. "I guess you Vikings weren't paying attention then."

"I may not have been born then," Ivar said.

"Who held Jerusalem in your day?"

"Bunch of monotheistic fuckheads, does it matter?"

"Yeah, these guys were a bit later than you. They were accused of the usual vile sins and misdemeanors that got people to stop thinking and start burning."

"We only burned people after we killed them, and they had to agree to it," Ivar said. "It was to honor their lord. The folks who sent us the violin didn't want us to rescue any Knights Templar."

"The violin is worth more than the computer," the junkyard man said. "But there's more of a message for you."

"Software for an atomic-force microscope." Ivar realized this implied that he did master the time machine by taking it apart molecule by molecule to understand it.

"Old software," Mr. Wythe said. "It's from just before the plague years. Open source."

"Do you want to help us?" Ivar said, realizing that the man probably knew by now what he was after.

"What are you going to do?"

"Salvage people from the past," Ivar said. "As many as possible."

"The Knights Templar had a few members who disappeared. You guys have to disappear in the past to end up here, don't you?"

"Yes, and be almost dead, too, I think." Ivar realized that bringing in scores of mortally wounded people could be a problem.

"People in this time don't like hard work particularly. I suspect I could use some people from the past to work here. Let's see what sort of people you rescue."

Ivar wasn't sure he wanted to sell slaves to the junkyard man, but he didn't want to drag his own salvage community into what was obviously going to piss off people who didn't want the past invading their tidy present. He owed the Archives his life, but they'd lied to him about where they'd brought him, and tried to keep him captive. That would justify stealing the time machine as long as he didn't hurt any of the Archivists.

But the present was tidy and full of girls.

"You need to see how to keep from suffocating yourself when you're using the tunneling scoops," the junkyard man said. "It's not going to give you miles and miles of tunneling capacity, but it will do a little rock-ramming."

The mole tractor was about twenty-five feet long and looked very used, with dirt on the digging blades and along the scooped-out sides where the dirt went when it was thrown behind the machine. It sat on treads that looked like plastic. The front window was thick glass or something modern like glass, and had been cleaned up recently. The whole front of the machine and the treads looked vaguely fluid, cleaner than the rest of the machine. Ivar wondered if he should have gotten a bigger one, or if he could have hired a crew from the junkyard who'd have been willing to break into the Archives from above. But that would give the Archivists a chance to destroy the time machine if they guessed what he was coming in after. He'd have to either drag the time machine behind him or assume that the scoop was not part of the driving device and lop it off before loading the rest of the machine in the mole tractor's cabin.

Best to take the whole thing. He couldn't go back for parts later.

The small plastic fob on the key ring opened the doors remotely. They slid back and he and the junkyard man climbed into the machine. The floor of the cabin was littered with fast-food wrappers. "As you can see, it's been used," the man said.

Ivar nodded. He saw on the steering column where the fob fit, inserted it, turned it, and heard a motor start.

"Look over the instrument panel before you do anything more," the man said. "And find the pedals on the floor, but don't push anything yet."

Ivar looked at the panel. One read-out was an obvious speedometer. Another display looked like it might be the angle of the machine front to back. On the floor were three pedals. The steering wheel felt loose in his hands.

"You steer right and left with the pedals. You push up and down on the steering wheel for digging angle. Center pedal gives you range of speeds. There's nothing fast. Push the pedal down one click."

The machine began to crawl forward silently. Mr. Wythe said, "You're on the electric motor now. It's very quiet. This one was used in raids between New Jersey and New York City. Nothing Philadelphia knew about."

Ivar steered it a bit to the right and a bit to the left. "More speed, bring us up to a trash mound." Ivar pointed the machine at the nearest trash mound. The inclination device showed that the machine was rising in front.

"Now flip the toggle switches on the bottom of the panel and lift the wheel slightly."

They began digging into the trash mound. Cans and plastic disintegrated into multicolored shards. Glass bottles seemed to liquefy. Then there was no light. The man bent toward the control panel and hit two toggle switches, and there was a glowing edge of squirming junk turning into dust at the window, with fractured shadows and glints off dead motherboards, glass, and plastic beyond that.

"If you tunneled all the way down, you'd reach the plague years, so don't. Bring it back up."

"The junk of the plague years?" Ivar asked.

"Yes, this is a very old dumping ground. There are probably bodies below us."

Ivar asked, "What about air? You were going to explain how not to suffocate."

"You can carry about twenty-four hours worth of compressed air. The salvage team you work with should have an air compressor. I'll show you the tanks when we stop. The nose of this thing sends out ultrasonic waves, like the kind of saw surgeons used to cut through casts . . . well, you wouldn't know about that, or tooth-cleaning applications. Okay, and the cabin is insulated from them, and the treads and front of the tractor are plastic so they don't crumble either. The scoops carry the broken-up stuff away. It's very neat. New York City. They're ahead of Philly in tech, I think."

Ivar wondered if the mole tractor would break the time machine as well as the wall in front of it, and how much noise the Archivists could hear as he broke through to the room where the time machine was waiting. "Can you turn off the shock waves?"

"Yeah, here." The man reached back over for the toggle switches he'd told Ivar to flip earlier. "This one is for the shock; that one is for the scoops. You want a manual for this?"

"Yes, if you can just throw it in without asking for another violin," Ivar said.

"Hell, to save you driving it off the lot, I'll get a tractor trailer to deliver it to wherever you want. Some people up-time really like you, and I can see why having you as a friend might be useful, or at least amusing."

"You wouldn't happen to have a map of the old train and subway tunnels from the twenty-first century, would you?"

"I'll leave that in the cab. Just tell me where to deliver it."

Ivar gave the junkyard man directions to Jonah's descendants' house on the Schuylkill near the ancient low bridge.

The best place in is the tunnels of the old PATCO High Speed lines," Mitt said, pointing to the map that had come with the mole tractor. "That will get you to between Vine and Race before the Ben Franklin Bridge checkpoint. The end of the tunnel is blocked off. We could probably create a diversion and drop you in at the train tunnel. Short run from there to the PATCO tunnel, if that hasn't been filled with rubble."

Ivar hadn't realized Mitt and Lizevidda had a group, but obviously, he didn't know everything, or anything, just that future people knew his name.

Jonah and Ivar went in disguised as a network repair crew, and lowered the mole tractor from the tractor-trailer down into a service tube. Jonah said, "Very good graphics, you know."

"You're trolling." He wasn't going to tell Jonah that his future friends wanted the Knights Templar brought up-time.

"If we die and pop up back at the Archives to start trying to escape again, you'll know I was right. But we might not remember we'd played the game before."

"We're not going to die. We're going to steal the time machine. Lots of people in the future seem to think I'm going to get away with it."

Jonah laughed. "All the futures want to be *the* future."

Ivar turned on the front lights and turned on the ultrasonics to start paring away at one of the tunnel walls, carefully going over the cables. The dust settled below and Ivar inched onto it, and then angled down slightly.

"You sure this isn't making a hellacious amount of racket?" Jonah said. "Or that someone's not picking up the breach in the wall?"

"Obviously not," Ivar said. "Or the distraction is good enough." He thought about going for more speed, but that would probably draw attention.

"Want me to get out and push?" Jonah asked.

"I'll turn on the scoop screws when we've got fifty yards to go. The treads seem to pull material to the rear themselves."

"So how fast can this thing go on land? Because we're not going to be able to crawl back the way we came."

Ivar said, "We'll dive into the river and go up the Schuylkill, but there's going to be a switch for the machine. Mitt's got a transfer planned."

"I trust you have a snorkel for this thing."

"Compressed air."

"I brought something better, Viking." Jonah pulled out a small machine gun. "I just found it in a public toilet, so one of our friends from some damned future or another thinks we'll need it."

"You don't know about guns."

"Well, neither do you."

Ivar saw blobs of blue in front of his machine as he cut through the wall to the PATCO High Speed line tunnel. Faces watched him, disappeared and reappeared, the blobs merged into a solid blue of futures waiting for him to rescue one of them. He wished they'd go away so he could see what he was cutting. Then he broke through and was in the tunnel, which had debris and stone-drips in it. Crunch, crackle. He sped up a bit. The blue blobs swirled to his rear.

"Ah, the people who watch this video game," Jonah said.

Ivar didn't bother to reply. He turned on the remote for the locator's transmitter, began reading from his handheld where the time machine was. It wasn't moving. It was closer than he'd expected, on the near side of the old Mint site. He maneuvered the tractor around, cutting a radius beyond the tunnel and then going forward. The time machine still wasn't moving.

The blue blobs of indeterminate times evaporated. "Game over," Jonah said.

"*We're* still moving," Ivar said.

Jonah rubbed his fingers over the small machine gun, and then waved one hand by his eyes. "No streaks, good tactile qualities. The resolution is excellent."

Ivar said, "Better you believe it's a video game than you scream with fear." Jonah's video-game crap annoyed him.

"Like you did when the slaves threw you off the boat."

"I jumped to avoid dying at thralls' hands."

"Well, I guess that got you to the next level anyway."

"Shut up now. We're going into cutting." The noise of the scoop screws would drown out talk even if Jonah wouldn't shut the fuck up.

Ivar cut through the debris, soil, and foundations of buildings that had long since disappeared above ground. The mole tractor jerked slightly when it hit the first wall between him and the time machine. Ivar put the machine into fast forward and shoved the nose into the surface in front of him, seeing it explode from the shock waves plus the sheer weight of the machine. They broke into the room where the time machine was. Joe and four armed men were waiting for them, while another group was starting to load the time machine on a trailer attached to a front loader, getting ready to hide it.

The room filled up with blue blobs. Ivar said to Jonah, "Okay, we both pop out now and tell them that we're better armed than they are."

Jonah and Ivar popped the hatches and came out. Another small machine gun dropped out of one of the blobs. Ivar caught it. The men with Joe hadn't pulled their own weapons.

Joe said, "Fuckhead."

Ivar said, "You can let us have the machine. Or nobody gets out of here alive."

Joe said, "If anyone wanted you to have a time machine, they could have given you one. The real future doesn't want you to have a time machine. Only the rogue alternatives are helping you."

"I don't care what you think, Joe. Step away."

Joe lifted a wrench and started to smash it down on the time machine. One of the small blobs grabbed his hand.

"Shit," Joe said, looking at his hand inside the blob. "They can't do that."

Ivar smiled, thinking about machine guns and violins showing up in toilets and basements.

"We've had some of the futures talking to us," Jonah said. "Now, go back." He waved the gun at them.

"You can't get away with this," Joe said.

"We already have," Ivar said.

"You think you're going to get away with the machine in that." Joe pointed to the mole tractor with his free hand.

The blobs were swarming around the room, maneuvering between Ivar and Jonah and the armed men. A voice came out of one of them, "Step back, gentlemen. The machine is going with the mole-tractor operatives."

"Video games shouldn't deliver deus ex machina resolutions," Jonah said. "This is unsporting."

"Jonah, beware of Merovingian women with guns," the voice said.

"Oh, steal the damn thing, then," Joe said.

One of the armed men said, "We can handle this."

One of the time blobs said, "In seventy-nine out of a hundred and seven time lines, they succeed. You win in the rest."

"Okay, we're supporting one of the losing time lines. I can't just shoot you, Ivar. I'm not sure what this is about."

"You can't shoot us," Ivar said. "You'd lose your hand." He didn't know this, but acting as if he did seemed to be the right thing.

Joe said, "But you'd be happy to kill me."

"If you tried to stop me, I'd do it but I wouldn't feel happy about it."

One of the armed men was listening to an earpiece that seemed to be telling him something that wasn't to his liking. He moved his throat slightly. Ivar remembered something about microphones that picked up throat movements that whispering people could make, or even people making the throat-and-tongue movements of talk without even a whisper. Ivar shifted his gun in the man's direction, but the man said, "We'll stand down. We'll get you later in at least half the futures."

Ivar said, "Okay." He looked at the time machine and pulled his locator coin out of it, stepped on it, and then said, "If we throw out some compressed air, I think we can fit it in here."

It was a very tight fit, but the time machine was mostly shell and not that hard to lift. The blue blobs filled the room, some winking in as others winked out, then Ivar backed the machine out the way he came but turned toward the Ben Franklin Bridge and dropped into the Delaware. Some of Mitt's friends met him at the bottom with air tanks and a small submarine. They took the time machine out. Ivar set the mole tractor's course with his handheld, and he and Jonah swam up to a small powerboat and went as far up the Schuylkill as they could, then just walked back to Mitt and Lizevidda's house as other people in clothes like theirs took the boat away.

"We'll get the machine to Three Mile Island," Mitt told him. "The residual radiation is contained but people are superstitious about it; nobody will bother you there."

"You're going to get help," Lizevidda said. "From New York. We've been talking to Mr. Wythe about it."

Brain Berserking Molecule by Molecule

Mitt and Lizevidda gave Jonah a handheld and tiny one-time cipher chips, which they'd gotten from their smuggling connections. Jonah understood that Mitt and Lizevidda smuggled and sold something banned from now-time Philadelphia, but he hadn't asked because he didn't want to know details.

As much running as Jonah had done online, he'd never physically had to leave the place where he'd lived. Now, with his two accomplices from the past and a stolen time machine, he was running around Amish country full of people who'd been inbreeding since the seventeenth-century. Life was weird.

The three of them set up a lab in one of the control rooms at long-abandoned Three Mile Island and set a generator in the river. Ivar disappeared for two days and came back with a pedicab and three fairly contemporary atomic-force microscopes. Jonah suspected Mr. Wythe at the junk heap had helped with those.

Ivar didn't explain where he'd been, just wiped the sweat off his face and dragged one of the cases into the control room that had been gutted of useful things about a hundred years earlier. "Get the other two, why don't you," he said to Jonah.

If they hadn't been outlaws, the work would have been really tedious.

Jonah worried that the two past people would be eager to do something, anything, rather than work out the huge puzzle the time machine presented. But Ivar suggested that they begin by making sure the time machine's hull was the same sort of stainless steel familiar to them and not part of the workings of the machine.

Ten feet long, four feet diameter, times pi 3.141592 equals roughly twelve feet around, which amounted to a huge number of two-by-two-centimeter areas to scan, destructively, to make maps that would help to move atoms in other stainless steel to look just like it.

Jonah said, "Let's go time-fishing with it first."

"We need more machines, fast," Ivar said. "We can set up one microscope to scan and the other two to manipulate."

Ivar had some older scripts for writing letters molecule by molecule. Jonah hoped there was a script for disassembling and reconstructing the machine hull. They had the axle; now they just had to reinvent the wheel.

The next day, Mr. Wythe showed up with a young man and a somewhat older woman. They spoke a different dialect of English, which Jonah understood easier than the one the Philadelphians spoke. "We understand the time machine is now in your hands. We're interested in having one of our own," the woman said. She appeared to be the young man's minder, the agent in charge of making sure the young man came home.

"In New York?" Jonah asked.

"We admit to being not from around here," the woman said.

According to what Jonah understood of current city-states politics, people not from around here weren't supposed to be in the area at all.

"Do you have anything we need?" Jonah said.

The young man said, "Tool fabrication works. We've been in touch with Switzerland. Putting a machine together with an atomic-force microscope is probably not necessary. I also know I know more physics than any of you." He had wiry black hair and somewhat protruding gray eyes. Looks like a geek, Jonah thought.

"We don't know that it isn't necessary," Ivar said. "Didn't you get your New York City mole tractor back, Mr. Wythe?"

Mr. Wythe said, "I would appreciate you taking these two young people in. I've done a lot for you, Ivar."

"The more minds the shallower the problem," the woman said.

"The more lips the weaker the security," Jonah said. Maybe she wasn't just the young man's minder.

But she turned out to know no more about physics than Jonah did, just had better communication devices, which he saw her use from time to time.

The two from New York weren't the only people throwing themselves into outlawry to get enough information to make their own time machines. Philadelphia's University City sent an engineer, an older man who had practical objections to the more hair-up-the-butt ideas the New York kid came up with. Another young physicist from West Philly, a part-Chinese, part-everything-else kid who called himself Lucius, showed up the day after the engineer. Jonah knew that meant everyone who had an interest knew where the time machine was—so much for hiding out in a decommissioned atomic-energy plant.

Ivar and Benedetta kept up with the now-time people. Jonah saw the skull work bring them together and felt jealous, cynical about it all, and excluded.

The truce would last until the machine could be reconstructed, Jonah thought. Then the New Yorkers would try to destroy or trick the others and race back to where their true loyalties lay, to make more machines and bring in migrants from the old country, save that the old country of this present was truly the *old* country. New York had always been more open to immigrants than Philadelphia.

For now, hacking the time machine brought the five technically minded people together. Jonah and the New York boy's minder only watched.

Ivar and the two other young male geeks his age spent their spare time skateboarding on a ramp they'd built and kept extending as they found more wood and angle iron inside one of the cooling towers. They were as active physically as they were mentally. Jonah was glad to see that Benedetta wasn't one of the skateboarders. He could stand with her and remind her, "We're grownups. They're kids."

"I'm closer in age to Ivar than I am to you," Benedetta said. "But I've got enough scars and I don't want to get any on my face."

Lucius from University City broke his nose when he missed a ramp. But in the morning, he was back with a late-model version of a micrometer, going over the overt circuits in the time machine, charting a 3-D graphic of the energies in the machine.

They decided to sample the hull rather than take it completely apart. Ivar seemed miffed, but had been right to suspect the hull of contributing to the time-traveling effects. The New York physicist kid found anomalies in how electricity moved across the hull, and he and Ivar spent two days with finer and finer probes, using cautious micro jolts across centimeters, then millimeters of the hull, tracing the places where the hull wasn't normal stainless steel at all but had gold circuits in patches, with glass molecules isolating the circuits from the stainless steel. The gold traces went through to connect to other patches of circuitry.

The engineer got to work tracing each long gold strand to the next set of circuitry. By the end of the week, Benedetta was mapping the strands connecting the patches while the guys worked on learning as much as they could about the microcircuits before using the atomic-force microscope.

"Is location important?" the New Yorker wondered.

"Let's assume for the sake of our sanity right now that it is," Benedetta said. "Duplicate it exactly."

Lucius said, "Let's assume for the sake of our sanity that it isn't. The dimensions of the machine would be absolutely inflexible if the surface geometry was. You're thinking like a traditional Chinese metallurgist shaman from the 1200s. To get steel, follow the exact procedures that got you steel the last time, even if half the steps aren't necessary and the carbon source could be improved."

"I don't think so," Benedetta said.

Ivar said, "Both ways, to be safe."

The kid from New York City said, "How flexible is inflexible? If we're off by a couple of molecules, will that matter?"

Two maps—one flexible, the other as inflexible as possible. After making that decision, the three young guys hit the skateboard ramps hard, the blue round of sky and the slits around the bottom lighting the shadowy guts of the cooling tower. They turned on arc lights and continued skating until midnight. Jonah and the New York boy's minder stayed up, not willing to leave the three in the other's presence. The woman seemed to have decided that Jonah was Philadelphia's spook. He didn't explain that his faction wanted to subvert Philadelphia more than she could imagine.

"So, we're all playing nice until they've got a working duplicate of the machine," Jonah said around the time he noticed the boys were getting sloppy on their skateboard ramps.

"You think?" the woman said.

"Or you could sabotage the work before they get a working machine, if that's what you want. That's what the Archives people probably want."

"I'm only concerned about his safety. Minds like that . . ."

"He could cut his own deals. Ivar and Benedetta could, too, I imagine."

"This skateboarding . . ." she said.

Jonah sensed he wasn't going to get any more out of her tonight. "You want Ivar and Benedetta?"

"They seem bright enough, but they're not really well educated. My young friend is really well educated. The West Philly University City kid, I'd like to see him come back with us. I want to get them to stop skateboarding now before they hurt themselves." She walked out toward the ramp.

"You and I want to go to sleep," Jonah said. "They're fine." He remembered what it was like to be hyped with adrenaline, working all night, going out for fireworks and seeing the arcs of light thrown by gunpowder through the sky, hearing the hiss of fuses, the bangs that had neighbors' dogs barking. He missed fireworks more than he could imagine.

Two women snuck in one late afternoon, watching the skateboarding in the cooling tower. Jonah and the woman from New York caught them. "Why are you here?" They seemed too young to be trained agents or science geeks.

"We're here because we've heard that some guys have built the coolest skateboard ramp. And we heard right."

Ivar, coming down shirtless, his hair and beard flying, flickered through the slotted light at the bottom of the ramp and came flying up to them like a Norse godling. The girls grinned and grinned and palm-flashed and fingered their hair.

"Where are you from?" the woman from New York asked.

"We're local."

Jonah expected the woman to throttle them on the spot, but she shuddered once and said, "I need to talk to your parents."

The New York woman went off for half a day and came back with fresh produce and an obvious understanding that the girls needed to stay away from the dangerous boys.

"How did you do that?" Jonah asked. "Are the locals friendly?"

"I told their parents the boys were in quarantine as people who'd been exposed to time travelers. They'd heard about time travelers but weren't sure they believed all the news out of Philadelphia. And I got the locals who aren't Amish to take a gift of a couple of tractors and a hydrogen fuel plant. I'll do them favors. They'll do us favors. They're simple people. We're going to be here awhile, you know. The work would go faster if we had a larger team, more tools ..."

"Philadelphia might not allow that, Miss ... ah ..." Jonah said

The New York woman, who still dodged questions about her name, shrugged.

"Just invent me a name you can remember," Jonah said.

"Alice," the woman said. "I'll be Alice for you."

"Pleased to meet you. I'm Jonah Kirkpatrick."

"I understand you shut down net connectivity for Croatia for a couple of days back in the 1990s."

"Net cop."

Ivar and the New York science kid went beyond skateboarding to fencing with wooden swords after reaching impasses in their work with the time machine.

Alice didn't find out they'd been fencing until her charge came back in with bruises on his ribs. Ivar wasn't the best skateboarder of the three, but he was the one who'd practiced with wooden swords in his past life.

"Alice, you're a woman. You don't understand men's play," Ivar said.

"Give me one of your swords," Alice said.

"I don't practice with women," Ivar said.

"Yeah, pussy," Alice said. Jonah wanted to watch this one. She was going to let a mad-on reveal herself as a professional fighter. The other guys were standing around grinning.

Ivar looked at them and said, "She's a woman. Should I do this?"

"Oh, yeah, man, Ivar," Lucius said.

"She's here to make sure I get back home safely," the science kid from New York said.

Alice said, "Not that you had to tell this one." Her head jerked toward Jonah.

"So, you want to have a bout with me," Ivar said.

"Better with me than with him," the woman said.

Ivar's eyes moved from her head to her feet, slowing down at her breasts and crotch. Jonah knew a mature person who was nicer than he was should stop this, because whoever won, the loser would hold a grudge. But he wasn't nice enough.

Benedetta came out and said, "Ivar, I'm going to be jealous if you fight her." She smiled as though she were joking, but put her palm on his shoulder and squeezed slowly.

Spoilsport, Jonah thought. "Why don't you two women fight?" He didn't know if that would egg them on or reduce the tension, but he could live with either result.

"Oh, fuck off, Jonah," Alice said. Ivar looked at the New Yorker whose ribs he'd been bruising earlier.

Trying to sound like a young boy, Jonah asked, "Can I fuck off with you?"

Alice laughed. "Okay, I don't want to have you hurting each other with wooden swords unless you're wearing padding."

Ivar said, "People who learn in padding don't learn to fear the blade."

Alice said, "Why in the world would anyone want to learn to fight seriously with swords in this day and age?"

"Because the past is coming back," Benedetta said.

Jonah wondered if Alice was there to make sure the past stayed the past. But the past was never simply the past. And now, how many cards still weren't on the table?

Alice said, "The past will pick up handguns as quickly as they learn what the advantages are."

Ivar said, "A more elegant weapon from more civilized times," as though he was quoting something. Jonah realized he was quoting a twentieth-century movie.

The next morning, the kids were swarming over the time machine again, cutting out sections of the hull-mounted circuitry and putting it section-by-section under atomic-force microscopes. Jonah and Alice watched them. Alice said, "That's why they were so antsy last night, they'd decided to cut the machine up. If they can't hack it, they've broken it."

"You think we need more people on the project now?" Jonah said.

"More would be nice if I could trust them. Benedetta and Ivar just want to go back and find more people like them. Simple motivation. You, I don't know. We shouldn't be that different from your own time."

"You're quite a lot different, at least in Philadelphia."

"New York isn't like Philadelphia. Never has been. You'd be more comfortable there. Would you like to come back with me?"

"Perhaps." Jonah didn't tell her she might be wrong about Ivar's motives. Ivar was Loki's boy, Jonah thought, and a great troll of twenty-fourth-century folks. He realized that Alice had been planning to kill the others. Jonah didn't know how. He wondered if she was making him a genuine offer, and found time to back up the data the boys and Benedetta had gathered so far.

The day after the boys cut up the hull, Mr. Wythe rode up in a faired recumbent pulling a large, low-slung bike trailer. He opened the trailer's gull-wing doors and said, "Some equipment you might find useful, hot from Switzerland. Someone's perimeter-watch bots might need replacing."

Alice turned an amusing beet-red. Jonah thought Mr. Wythe had a touch of Loki in him, too. Alice said, "What's in this for you?"

"A time machine," Mr. Wythe said. "Aren't we all interested in making more of them?"

"Why can't the future people just give us more?"

"Obviously, it didn't happen that way," Mr. Wythe said.

The boys were oohing and aahing over the kit in Mr. Wythe's trailer. He had some replacement tips for the atomic-force microscopes, plus a couple of ounces of gold and borosilicate, and two large computers with a bucketful of what looked like loose flash-memory cards. Jonah wondered how many more of those he'd need to smuggle out the plans. Redundancy, redundancy, redundancy.

And trophies, he thought as he pocketed about a dozen of them. Our lives don't have to be in a computer to be a game.

A month passed, then two more months. Jonah wondered if the guys were faking the lack of progress. He mentioned his suspicion to Alice, who said, "They're taking the machine apart one layer of molecules at a time. You expect this to go fast?"

No, but Jonah was getting very bored in the country. He wished he had stayed in an advisory role for all this, so he could return to

Philadelphia now, find something to do that was loud, noisy, and drunk. "Can't they script it?"

"There's absolutely no reason to expect that this will work. The Archives didn't consider the hull an active surface. Now we might be the ones missing something." Alice looked at him and said, "You need something to do? I'm surprised you haven't figured out how to make mischief already."

"Why does everyone have that impression of me? I was a good father, a hard worker. Just blew off steam on Usenet. It's not like anyone needed it."

"I've got a stash of Roman candles," Alice said. "I believe they were illegal in your day, but you shot them off anyhow."

"Okay, I like fireworks, too," Jonah said. "I'd like to play with your candles."

"Don't shoot them at anyone," Alice said.

That night, they all went down to a sandbar and drank good local beer while Jonah shot Roman candles into the air, shooting them all off. When he finished, he felt vaguely foolish, as though he'd jerked off in public. Not enough. And Alice was humoring him. He wanted to go back to the house by the Schuylkill and hack the Philadelphia network and tease Joe, or just find a job he could do in these times and then go trolling again. Find some people to play against each other.

Alice said, "You could come to New York with us."

"You don't even like me," Jonah said.

"I feel sorry for you," she said. "If you'd come from closer to our time or from further in the past, I think you'd have known what you were up against."

"You're a ball-breaking dyke. I don't need your pity."

"You're drunk. The fireworks didn't make you happier, either."

"Not when …" He wanted to say that fireworks should be an illicit thrill, not something some security bitch gave him to distract him from how utterly bored he was and how she was going to try to kill him later if he didn't agree to come with her to New York.

"The Italian woman is involved in the project. It's annoying to see her catering to the males ..."

"You are a dyke."

"You are a product of your age, my three-hundred–and-some-forty-six-year-old friend."

Jonah decided he needed to get away from this before the beer had him saying stupid things like, *Why do you care? You're going to kill us all if you can, you bitch.* He shrugged and went off to listen to what the wireless net could pull down in these times, which was more than he'd expected. He decided he was too drunk to contact Mitt and Lizevidda.

Next day, the boys began building the first duplicate hull. They found that the interior components were socketed, and decided to see if they'd gotten the hull right first.

Mr. Wythe brought them a couple of stainless steel hulls as close as possible to the dimensions of the time-machine hull. "One for practice," he said. "Two for luck. And here's the special stuff you asked for." Mr. Wythe pulled out two small cases that looked like walnuts. He opened one, and light appeared to sink into it. Jonah reached out for the second case and found that the walnut-size things weighed more than ten pounds. He almost dropped it. Then he noticed that Mr. Wythe's hand muscles were almost quivering. Jonah set the case back in the bike trailer and saw the trailer shift slightly from the weight.

"We found the trick," Ivar said.

"We think," the New Yorker said.

"What the fuck are they?" Jonah asked. "And how did you get them?"

Lucius said, "Appears to be a space-time discontinuity. Black holes that small and that light aren't supposed to exist."

"Where did you get them?" Alice asked.

"The Swiss," Mr. Wythe said. "It's always from the Swiss."

"How do we get more of them?" Alice asked.

"You ask me about it later," Mr. Wythe said.

"You can grow them if you feed them the right energy," the New Yorker said.

Jonah snuck out into the woods and found the handheld where he'd stashed it. Thinking that he'd been neglecting his descendants, he loaded the handheld with his second one-time cipher disc in the tiny slit in the handheld and began typing the message in. The chip would scramble the message. All Alice might know is that he contacted someone. *No blue fog for the last three days,* he entered. *Mr. Wythe has been very helpful. We have space-time discontinuities to try. I'll let you know when we're ready to test. We'll need help getting out of here.*

He waited for a reply, but didn't get one. He destroyed the chip and went back into the woods to hide his handheld again, in a different place this time, with a thread pulled from his pants over the place to let him know if anyone had found it before he used it again. He copied data from the computers the boys had been using and hid the chips in the woods. *Spare backups,* he thought.

The boys wore masks and gloves as they built their circuits and then installed the space-time discontinuity in the hull. After three weeks, they'd finished.

Jonah snuck off again and set the next one-time chip up: *Tomorrow, we're testing. They're not telling me what the target is.*

Carefully, Ivar moved what they figured were the navigational controls from the first time machine that had been pared down to plain stainless steel to what they hoped would be the second. Benedetta and Ivar looked from one machine to the other.

Ivar said, "Mr. Wythe wants to be with us when we try it the first time." He grinned.

Alice said, "You don't need to wait for Mr. Wythe. Let's try it now."

Jonah said, "My friends also have some interest in this."

"If it works, Mr. Wythe and your friends can see it the second time," Alice said. She looked tense. *Kind of outnumbered here, Ms. Time Cop,* Jonah thought.

Ivar smiled like he didn't really care, and set up the machine for its trial.

The machine hummed and made blue fog in front, then the gurney extended and pulled back with Mr. Wythe. "Suspected you would try it without me," he said as he got off the gurney. "The boys promised me my own machine."

"You're armed, aren't you?" Alice said. "With something I shouldn't fuck with."

"I get along fine with the New York people," Mr. Wythe said, "but I do want a time machine of my very own. I wasn't sure whether our understanding would hold up to New York's perceived interests."

Ivar nodded to Jonah. Jonah hoped that nod meant *I'll make a distraction and you download everything onto those chips you pocketed.* Downloading the chips looked like the only way he was going to be able to deliver anything to his faction.

Ms. Alice didn't know Norse, Jonah thought as Benedetta began screaming, almost distracting him. Ivar swung around to help her, and all the attention left the machine. Jonah went to the main work computer, not the computer standing by the machine, and fed his pocketed flash cards into the machine, hoping that Ivar gave him Unix copy commands to work with and that all the data was on this machine as well as the one by the time machine, and if he couldn't get this data, they could work out the last of it from the chips he'd already made.

He'd just put the fourth chip in his pocket when he realized he was done and those chips held a lot more than a couple of giga-bytes per card. Still the size of postage stamps and twice as thick as a business card … yippee. He moved them to a small pouch and then stuck the pouch inside his pants. Later, he could tape the cards under his balls.

He put another data chip in as he heard things settle down be-hind him, and stood waiting for Alice. He wanted her to think she'd caught him before he copied things. Good, good, good, good. Alice's hand pulled his away from the keyboard and ejected the chip. She smiled at him. "Benedetta appears to have had the vapors over see-ing the machine work."

"Maybe she knew all this would fall apart and we'd be at each other's throats the instant we got a working machine."

"Or something." She made a fast dab for his pockets, and found two more data cards. They were empty, of course.

"Okay, Jonah. You think the data would have fit on just three cards?"

Jonah said, "I'd have used compression if it hadn't. You know, we're just game tokens."

"Don't pull that computer-games crap on me, Jonah. I know you know that's not so."

"Live-action role-playing, my dear," Jonah said.

"Like paintball?" Alice said. "But with real weapons?"

"We're pawns in the up-time games."

"You think?"

"We had up-time help in stealing the machine in the first place. Whatever you do, it had already happened in some time-stream or another."

"Our free will makes the future."

Jonah said, "We got help and advice from the future."

"Yeah. What advice?"

"Rescue the Knights Templar. Whatever we do, don't rescue the Knights Templar."

Alice laughed. "So the future contradicts itself."

"The futures are in conflict. We both have allies beyond now."

Alice shrugged.

"Are you still going to try to kill us and get away with the plans?"

"Why would I kill you? I don't know enough about the people behind you to know what sort of enemies I might be making if I did that."

"Ivar and Benedetta, then. I don't know enough to be dangerous."

"Ivar's got Mr. Wythe behind him. Mr. Wythe has been a friend to friends. Not that I like leaving plans in any stranger's hands, but ..."

"Maybe someone from a blue cloud can advise you," Jonah said.

"Mr. Wythe is arranging for me to leave in fifteen minutes, with my boy and as much machinery as we can take with us."

"Before the University City crowd can react?"

"The University City crowd went home already."

"Gone? We were supposed to test the non-determinate circuitry tomorrow."

"They've got the plans. They can do that at home."

Jonah wondered if Ivar and Benedetta could do more on their own. "Well, you slick clever now-time people."

Alice seemed less pleased. "Benedetta appears to have thrown a distraction for them. I'm seriously tempted to shoot the bitch out of sheer frustration."

"I know the feeling," Jonah said. "Benedetta doesn't put out for anyone."

"They had an airplane waiting on the river."

"Couldn't you shoot them down?"

"The University City makes for a bad enemy," Alice said. "They'd have killed me and taken the boy if Mr. Wythe hadn't arrived."

When Alice, the boy from New York, and Mr. Wythe had gone, Jonah noticed that all the machines and computers were gone, too, but that there was one space-time discontinuity left in its walnut-size wrapper, drinking down all the light it could get when Jonah opened the case. He closed the case and put the heavy little container back in a safe place. If anyone came back for it, they wouldn't find it.

The next day, Ivar slept late and so soundly that Jonah feared the others had drugged him before they left. Benedetta said, "I can't find the space-time discontinuity."

"It's safe," Jonah said. "Let's make sure nobody comes back for it before we start working again."

"We need to get out of here, now," Benedetta said. "People can be expendable after they've served their purpose."

"That's nicely cynical," Jonah said. Being a mercenary's camp wife taught her well. "How much of this time-machine shit do you understand?"

"If you've got the circuit plans, we'll be okay. I don't want to think we did all that work for other people."

"I noticed we'd been cleaned out after Alice and her charge left. At least they didn't kill us."

"Not yet. What about your connections? Your descendants?"

"What did I tell you about them?"

"Gee, Jonah, you should remember that."

"Whom do you work for?" Jonah asked her.

"Every person caught between death and some weird future who won't have to die if we bring them up-time."

"I've never been sentimental about people who had bad luck. And if I'd been them and known who I was, I wouldn't have rescued me."

"Ivar wants to test it the other way, but all the computers are gone."

"I saved the data."

"So did I," Benedetta said. "But redundancy is good."

"I'd say let's go back to my descendants' house unless we'd make things too hot for them."

"When Ivar wakes up," Benedetta said. "You know anything about how to treat berserkers after they wake up?"

"They were working awfully hard on all that, weren't they?"

"He said it felt like a berserk toward the end."

"Sugar water, vitamin C, and cocaine."

"What?"

"I was joking about the cocaine, but see if there's mint anywhere around here, or dandelion greens. Make some warm water with sugar in it. Is he going to feel betrayed that he didn't get to go with the others?"

"I asked him to stay with me. He got proof of concept."

"How much of that did you actually understand?"

Benedetta smiled like a Renaissance Madonna, not speaking for a moment. "More than they realized."

Jonah hoped Ivar had squirreled away something. If he didn't, they had no tools, one space-time discontinuity, and two sets of plans. Then Jonah wondered why he cared. He wanted to get back to the house on the Schuylkill, to be with his descendants, and to just get really drunk and bawl over his lost world.

Ivar woke up and stumbled out to piss, then started looking through the supplies they still had left and grabbed the cocoa mix.

Jonah stopped to wonder how they imported cocoa these days, then realized Florida was now warm enough to grow it. Ivar heated water in the microwave and drank two cups of cocoa, then sat there, staring at a wall that had been full of monitoring instruments in the days when Three Mile Island had been an active power-plant.

Jonah said, "Unless you made extra parts, they've cleaned us out."

"I don't fucking care," Ivar said. His voice was deeper than it had been before, or more hoarse. "We got a set of plans if you took advantage of our diversion. Have you gotten in touch with your people?"

"Not yet."

"Do it. We need to get out of here … as soon as I can."

"You pulled a berserk?"

"I feel like I did the brain equivalent. It was wonderful to work with those two." He looked at Benedetta slightly, as though apologizing for not considering her one of the real work team. Jonah didn't see her face shift at all.

They heard what Jonah realized were helicopter motors in the background. "Anyone you're expecting?" Ivar said, his voice still deeper than it had been.

"If they've got infrared search tools, we're fucked," Benedetta said. Jonah looked at Ivar as though he'd expected him to be the one who said that.

"Let's hope they don't," Ivar said. "I've got a few things to take with us."

"You made duplicates?"

"I'm not stupid," Ivar said. "Mr. Wythe had to use me to get things he wanted, but he could have taken us with him when he left if he'd wanted. So he considered me expendable. Fuck him."

Jonah got the space-time discontinuity from where he'd hidden it and put it in a cloth sack. He wished he had something that would insulate their body heat. Che Guevara and his friends had been tracked in Bolivia by satellite and infrared detectors as early as the 1960s.

The river was cold. Jonah wondered if the space-time discontinuity could stand getting wet. He pulled out his handheld, loaded a one-time chip, and explained things as they hid under a tangle of fallen trees.

The handheld advised him to turn it off and move at least fifty yards away now.

"Fucking radio-location devices," Jonah said. The helicopters sat in the air almost over them.

"If we move now, they've got us, whoever they are," Benedetta said.

Ivar was shivering, but he pulled them back in the water. "If we can get by York Haven, we're okay. The river's real narrow there."

"Let's stay somewhere until dark," Benedetta said.

Jonah said, "It doesn't matter. Let's surrender to them."

"That doesn't work the way you think it does," Benedetta said. Ivar nodded.

They knew warfare conventions from the eras of city-states better than he did, Jonah thought. "Maybe someone will send us another submarine."

"Move *now*," Ivar said, and they let the river sweep them along, ducking under water as much as possible. The helicopters started dropping depth charges.

"Out of the water, now," Jonah said.

They hauled up with their gear onto a sand bank just before York Haven and covered themselves as best they could. They heard the explosions in the river as the helicopters dropped charges.

Whoever those people were, they were mean. Jonah tried not to breathe and wished he were the same temperature as the logs they were hiding under. And he wondered about Ivar and hypothermia after a berserker-level energy spurt that had gone on for three and a half months. The helicopters danced around one another like malignant dragonflies, then moved on, dropping explosives down the river. Jonah doubted it was over and felt abandoned by his descendants, but then perhaps the family had never forgiven him for going out drunk in a snowstorm.

"If they go too far down," Ivar whispered, "the Baltimoreans will gun them down."

"They won't be that stupid," Benedetta said. "And they've probably made a deal with Baltimore. Otherwise, they'd have to cross Philadelphia's air space."

The helicopters came back up the river, sweeping the banks with searchlight and gunfire. Jonah wondered what the locals had been told, how dangerous he and these two kids from the past must be.

Ivar and Benedetta went under logs before one of the helicopters moved across the river to strafe the island where they were hiding. Jonah watched the bullets splash the river, almost ready to just die, then his body jerked him under another log.

"Fuckhead," Ivar whispered when the helicopter had moved on.

"They'll burn the driftwood next," Benedetta said. "Back in the river."

Jonah said, "They're going to run out of fuel and ammo."

"Before you and Benedetta run out of adrenaline?"

"Can we use the space-time discontinuity as a weapon?" Jonah asked.

"No, that's what they're after," Benedetta said.

"We could just ..." Jonah knew that they couldn't just give up the space-time discontinuity, not in this time line.

He wished the cavalry or what passed for cavalry in these days would arrive. The helicopters flew off, but were obviously going to be back with more ways to kill them as fast as they could refuel and reload.

"Move now," Ivar said. "Time to steal something and head overland."

They found a motorcycle and a bicycle. "We can't split up," Jonah said. They were abandoning him. His descendants hadn't come to help him.

"We're too obvious if we don't," Ivar said. He looked at the rider's seat and sighed. By now, he was quite exhausted. He got on the pillion and wrapped his arms around Benedetta's waist when she stepped over the frame. They were both muddy and bruised. "Move," Ivar said.

Jonah moved his memory chips to somewhere more comfortable than against his balls, amazed that they hadn't fallen off earlier, and then proceeded to pedal just off, west, in any direction, toward what he hoped would be Philadelphia, only the wrong side of the Schuylkill. He'd never stolen a bicycle before.

Pretending to just be an ordinary tourist from Philadelphia, Jonah rode to Marietta to join the shoppers on their own bicycles, then found his way to Lancaster, moving as close as he could to various horse-drawn Amish carriages and other bicyclists, trying to make sure that if the helicopters found him and came gunning, other people would die, too.

Jonah hoped they hadn't been after him in particular.

The Trickster and Friends

Benedetta decided that stealing horses would have worked better than trying to ride this motorcycle, as she turned the handlebars to get the gears to work. She'd read about motorcycles but hadn't actually driven one. Things meshed. The machine started, moved forward. Benedetta twisted the gears and got a speed so fast that the wind whipped water from her eyes. Leaning, not twisting the handlebar, she turned the bike. She steered away from places where houses began to appear, moving into farmland. After a half-hour, she found an empty shed and pulled in out of sight for a while. She asked Ivar, "Who was trying to kill us? And why?"

"New York wants regional hegemony. They want to control the Delaware. But the New Yorkers got a little data corruption. I encrypted the data. But this is too quick for them to be trying to kill us over that."

"Ivar. After all Mr. Wythe did for you."

"The little twerp underestimated me. Not Mr. Wythe, the science kid who wouldn't tell us his name."

Damn, but at least they hadn't blown off Jonah's people. "Can you make that good for Mr. Wythe, at least?"

"Maybe."

"You guys pissed me off, too, by treating me as just an assistant who didn't understand what was going on. Alice pointed that out."

"Did you let her eat you for that bit of obvious observation? You didn't contribute as much as we did."

What was that to Ivar? "I hate this machine."

"We need to find Jonah." Ivar pulled out a handheld and said, "He's headed for Lancaster."

"If you can track him that way, they can track him, too."

"Well, I don't think so unless they're sweeping all the frequencies, but if it is so, we have to get to him before they do, don't we? He's got the only space-time discontinuity in our control until we get set up to breed more of them with coherent microwaves. But we'll need some lathed magnet hulls first."

She realized that the machine was much faster than horses and that if they hadn't had to turn around for Jonah, they'd have been at the Schuylkill in another hour or so.

"Okay, fuck."

Ivar was sucking on a thermos he'd brought from Three Mile Island, probably cocoa and milk. Benedetta was hungry and thirsty, too, but she realized he had been working harder than she'd been. He had encrypted the computer data. All the copies? No, the University City people had gotten out before she'd thrown her fit and so probably had working designs as well as one of the space-time discontinuities.

"You do know how to reverse the data encryption, don't you?"

"Of course. You use the rot13'ed text of Odin's *Prayer in Norse*, transliterated by me into the English alphabet as the decryption key. Then you pull out the junk data I put in, which you could do if you transliterated Norse the way I do and knew where the word breaks would have been if I'd put in word breaks. Quick and dirty."

For a second, Benedetta thought that sounded too easy to break, then she realized she didn't know how much of this Ivar had done or what the Norse text looked like or how it had been distributed in the data.

Ivar said, "I think Jonah's right about this being a game for someone, with us as counters. Let's get going."

"Into a town on a stolen motorcycle?"

"I'll claim I had no idea it was stolen. You're the one driving it."

"Oh, you fuck," Benedetta said. She started the motorcycle and began moving down the road.

Behind them, they heard the *whomp-whomp* of a helicopter, then an explosion about where the barn had been. Benedetta gunned the motorcycle when she heard the patter of bullets on the pavement behind them. But then something swooshed overhead and she heard a larger explosion. Benedetta stopped the motorcycle and looked back to see a black smudge where the helicopter had been, and bits falling out of the sky, and the other helicopters fleeing the area to the south.

"We were right about the deal with Baltimore to get refueled," Ivar said. "We don't have to worry about New York for a while, now. Philadelphia has surface-to-air missile defenses and someone's made sure they're using them for us."

Okay if you say so. Benedetta got the motorcycle moving again. Ivar used his handheld again and said, "Lancaster is that way."

"You love this shit, don't you?"

"As long as the guys attacking me die or suffer," Ivar said.

Benedetta passed a couple of buggies and got them into Lancaster, whose streets were crowded with buggies, farm carts, and people on bicycles. Except for the bicycles, the town looked like any market city in Northern Italy in her day. Maybe more glass, Benedetta thought, and yeah, the cloth is subtly wrong. And the buggies are too nice for peasants. And wrong. Benedetta thought about what was causing her sense of cognitive dissonance and realized carriage wheels in her day didn't have thin steel spokes like bicycle wheels.

Jonah was at the train station. He'd abandoned the bicycle. "My family's coming to pick me up. Go away."

"Did they tell you to tell us that?" Ivar asked.

"Philadelphia isn't after us. The helicopters were from New York. Ivar encrypted and salted their data with garbage text, but they probably didn't know that when they sent the helicopters." Benedetta wondered if Ivar had done that as a bargaining chip.

"Is my data worthless, then?"

"No, it's an easy fix. I'll tell Mr. Wythe how to fix it when we've got a couple more machines built ourselves."

"My legs are killing me. I haven't had this much exercise since … since …"

"Poor baby. If people in your time had been in better shape physically, you wouldn't have had such problems with the plagues," Ivar said.

"Don't fuck with me. You nearly got us killed."

"If they'd known about the data corruption before they sent helicopters after us, they'd have wanted me alive to tell them how to fix it. They were planning to kill us all along after they got their stuff out. I didn't know if it was New York or Philadelphia until someone took down a helicopter with a surface-to-air missile. Hard to drive down enemy roads with a surface-to-air missile carriage, so that had to be from Philly, and the helicopters are New York out of Baltimore, having cut some kind of deal there."

The city-state politics made perfect sense to Benedetta. Baltimore and New York were Philadelphia's natural rivals and that made them natural allies.

"We'll all go back to your family's house," Ivar said. "If Mr. Wythe can talk to the New Yorkers still, I'll tell them how to fix their data if they promise to leave us alone. Not that I trust their promises."

Benedetta pulled out a Philadelphia barter-credits card she'd tucked away and went to see if the local vendors would honor it. She had a few hours of housework on it. A vendor who also ran a booth at one of the urban markets took it and gave her a couple of soft pretzels and three iced teas for two hours of cleaning. Eating one of the pretzels, she walked back with the iced tea. Her heart was still beating faster than normal. She handed Ivar and Jonah teas and gave Jonah the other pretzel, then handed Ivar what she hadn't eaten of hers.

She wondered if the train station would take barter cards when the Philadelphia train pulled in. Jonah's family, Mitt and Lizevidda, came down the stairs, and they all waited while the train loaded up with produce for the city.

When they got on the train, Lizevidda opened a picnic basket and gave them all sandwiches and more iced tea. Benedetta ate, thinking the train's gentle swaying was more comfortable than trying to sleep in a cart lurching across rutted roads. She fell asleep against Ivar's shoulder, woke up to stumble onto another train and then in and out of a car. Lizevidda led her to a bedroom in the house by the river. Benedetta took off her clothes, crawled under the top sheet of the bed built of padding over springs, and felt her spine relax, supported by the springs under the padding. She hadn't slept in so soft a bed ever. Thinking about how it must be made woke her up a bit. Finally, she drifted off to sleep, feeling somewhat safe for now.

When she woke up, she found that now-time clothes in her size had been laid out on the dresser. She took a shower, happy to have nice hot water again after living in the camp for months, even though she'd lived without running hot water until she almost died in the past. Then she walked out toward the voices she heard. Everyone was hashing out whether Ivar had been brilliant or very bad to fuck with New York's copy of the research data.

The two people from University City they'd worked with were there. Mr. Wythe was supposed to show up, but he'd apparently been detained as a suspected agent for New York.

"We had good relations with him," Mitt said, "and this makes him look bad."

"Tea or coffee?" Lizevidda asked Benedetta, who shrugged. Neither had been anything she'd drunk as a child. She decided on coffee.

"Why did you steal plans early, and the discontinuity?" Ivar asked the University City people.

"We wanted to get out before New York did. Looks like a wise choice, now," the older engineer said. "You'd have fucked with our data, too, but we made backups like you did."

Ivar smiled slightly.

"We've got to make right with New York," Lizevidda said. "We don't need to make them that big an enemy."

"They were trying to kill us," Benedetta said. "They plan to take Philly over eventually. Before they found out Ivar salted the data with Norse and used the Rune Prayer to encrypt it, if they've figured that out yet."

"We got their agent busted," Mitt said. "One of their helicopters downed. Men died."

"They were trying to kill us." Benedetta remembered Leonardo in Milan, going away with the French. What was Milan to Leonardo? What were they to Mitt, Lizevidda, and Jonah? What was Philadelphia, even?

"Okay, how does the key go?" the engineer asked.

Ivar scribbled a bit on paper, and paused to say, "After you use the key, go through the code looking for this. In English, it starts with this:

> Wounded I hung on a wind-swept gallows
> For nine long nights,
> Pierced by a spear, pledged to Odin,
> Offered, myself to myself
> The wisest know not from whence spring
> The roots of that ancient rood

And ends with this:

> Know how to cut them, know how to read them,
> Know how to stain them, know how to prove them,
> Know how to evoke them, know how to score them,
> Know how to send them, know how to send them.

He chanted in Norse then as he wrote the rest of the poem out in runes, then in his transliteration with some thorns still in the text. Benedetta felt a chill to her bones, not sure why. Ivar blended his Old Norse childhood with the manhood of a scientist in now-time, and that Old Norse childhood was more alien to her times than this now-time was.

Lizevidda asked, "Are you saying you worked through pain to the knowledge you have now?"

Ivar smiled a quick smile again, turned up the corners of his mouth. Benedetta thought about what Ivar had just told them about whom he'd sacrifice himself to—himself. She smiled slightly. Ivar sent everyone his message. They just needed to pay attention to why he used those words.

"I think we need to see if Philadelphia wants New York to have the key and info on finding the corruptions," the engineer said.

"Perhaps they should run the experiment first and see how people fleeing the past for their time manage," Jonah said.

"We're too comfortable these days," Mitt said. "The human spirit has been corrupted."

"We're still negotiating to have the city forget what Jonah, Benedetta, and Ivar did," the engineer said. "People could have been seriously hurt when they stole the time machine."

"We had all time on our side," Ivar said.

The engineer said, "There's always a chance that New York can re-create the work. They know how it was reverse-engineered. We're leaving. We've had our own problems with security."

Ivar looked like he was going to miss his science playmate Lucius, Benedetta thought. The two University City people walked out of the room, going to the train station. She was stuck here, not quite sure she liked the company.

"We ought to give New York the way to clean up the data," Jonah said. "They'll be grateful to us. They're going to figure out how to clean up the code anyway."

Benedetta said, "The more people have guns and gunpowder, the less valuable any one artillery person is. The more machines we get working, the less anyone's particular knowledge of them matters."

Everyone nodded thoughtfully, and then remained quiet in their thoughts on the wonderfully upholstered chairs and couches with all the springs built in and with fabric that looked like people still spun line flax and wove linen.

"Nice chairs," Benedetta said.

"Real linen," Jonah said. "Hardly saw much of that in my day. Everyone now wears it."

"We grew it, spun it, and wove it right here," Lizevidda said. "The springs came from the metalworkers' community in Fishtown."

"Next we need to fabricate the circuits and ..." Benedetta began to say.

"No, next we need to feed energy into our space-time discontinuity and get more of those," Ivar said. "We do that with coherent microwaves."

"A microwave laser," Mitt said.

"No, actually, first we need to lathe some round magnets, thread them, so we have containers for the discontinuities," Ivar said. "Then we microwave the one we have."

Mitt carefully brought out the walnut-size case and looked at it. "You're sure?"

"That was in the instructions for me on the computer from the future," Ivar said. "So far, that future hasn't lied to me."

Benedetta had a sudden vision of the space-time discontinuity exploding. A good way to lure them into doing something lethal was to give them good advice up to a point. But if they wanted more machines, they needed more discontinuities.

Jonah looked at her and said, "And are you thinking what I'm thinking?"

"Um, about it being a live-action role-playing game?"

"Um, yes."

"Yes."

"I infected you with my memes," Jonah said.

"That should make you happy," Benedetta said.

After two days spent lathing little containers for space-time discontinuities, Benedetta realized machine-guided lathing might as well be spinning. Lizevidda also wanted Benedetta to work around the house and help with the garden to pay for being rescued and to earn her keep. Benedetta wondered if she'd traded companionship on somewhat tedious jobs for being a house servant to someone who wanted her family to be the Sforzas of Philadelphia. She was grateful for being saved from the New Yorkers, to a certain extent, but what she wanted from time rescue was different from what the Kirkpatricks wanted. They wanted people who could help them gain power. Benedetta didn't want to help them.

The lathing, at least, would be done when they had twenty magnetic containers for the baby space-time discontinuities. As soon as Benedetta had finished five of the hulls, Ivar whisked them off and started using his special microwave laser to make more of them. Benedetta wanted to see how this was done. Even more, she wanted to do it herself and understand how to make more space-time discontinuities. She knew that wasn't the plan, but she went into Ivar's workroom anyway and memorized what the equipment looked like, then photographed it with a small digital camera she'd found in Lizevidda's room. It was easy enough to get the camera that was watching her in the room to loop data. She took out the digital card (standardization was so nice) and put the camera back again, looping the signal for a few moments.

Maybe I'm telling them just how smart I am, Benedetta thought. She wanted her own information to trade if she had to.

About a day later and with twenty fissioned-off space-time discontinuities trying to suck down all the local photons, Ivar told Benedetta to go down to the main living room. The others were already there. He went to the basement and loaded a dumbwaiter. He came back up, brought the dumbwaiter up, and opened it as if he had found gold or a weapons cache. One by one, he pulled out steel plates with circuitry that ended in bosses and plugs. He took gold wires out with alligator clips and sockets at the ends and attached them to the steel plates. He laid the plates and wires out in a grid that had neither the same curvature nor the same dimensions of the original time machine. He pointed to a spot about ten feet from where he'd put a space-time discontinuity in the circuit and said, "If it works, it will go blue there." He slowly turned a rheostat. *For dramatic effect, the prick,* Benedetta thought.

When the rheostat was halfway twisted to full power, the air turned blue.

Benedetta said, "Going for anyone in particular?" Ivar looked vaguely hurt at her tone for half a second. *He's trying to impress me,* she thought.

"Proof of concept," Ivar said. "We don't need the hull, but we don't have any way to scoop people up. They have to move into the flux."

"Most people of my time would have to have the devil at their backs to go into that," Benedetta said.

Mitt, Lizevidda, and Jonah didn't move for a few moments, looking at the blue fading from the air as Ivar slowly and almost as dramatically turned the power off.

Benedetta wondered if she could just walk out of here, go back to the Archives, apologize profusely to Joe, and work with the University City people. Ivar looked at her as though wondering why she wasn't more excited. She looked quickly at the others, but they were still looking at Ivar or the place where the blue had been.

A future got back in touch with them that afternoon. They wanted to talk to Benedetta, alone. Mitt and Lizevidda fussed, but the man in the blue flux insisted. Everyone else left the room. Benedetta stood facing him, knowing before he spoke that he had bad news for her. "Your son died with witnesses," the man said, speaking slowly. Benedetta realized he was speaking in the hill dialect that her father had spoken. "So don't go there. We know that this won't kill your interest in the project."

So this is a project, Benedetta thought. She wondered if her son was dead in all possible pasts or if they'd done things that . . . no, it was the future that had alternatives. The past was braided into one thing. She tried to frame her thoughts with the shreds of the dialect she remembered. "I don't like these people," she said, meaning Mitt and Lizevidda.

"You and Ivar can get away from them and use the machine to actually save people who deserve to be saved, for their own purposes, not to serve others. Philadelphia is worth defending, too."

"Big job," Benedetta said. "We don't have access to raw materials except through these now-time people." She didn't ask if she was free to walk away from Mitt and Lizevidda. She hadn't tested it, but she still had her lawyer's number—unless they kept her from all communications. Damn, they could do that, except for this.

"We'll change that," the man in the blue flux said. "We've got ..."—he switched to the English she knew—"... coordinates"—then switched back—"... to some people who share languages with you and Ivar. They really need your help."

Benedetta wondered who these people might be. The man faded away, leaving her a little gold flower with four petals, on a chain. They could get materials through. Benedetta put the necklace on under her blouse and called the others in.

"He wanted to tell me my son died with witnesses," she said, genuinely grieving but also happy to have some way to explain why he had to talk to her in private.

"Coordinates?" Lizevidda said. They had, of course, been listening, could probably figure out soon what-all had been said.

One time line wanted some Knights Templar rescued; one didn't. Were the Templars going to support the Kirkpatricks or Benedetta's dream of saving as many people as possible and adding them to the ongoing community without breaking it?

The king of France and the pope had betrayed the Templars. They'd been tortured into admitting to anything the torturers wanted them to admit. Let's bring them in, Benedetta decided. She and Ivar didn't discuss it, but Benedetta knew that they were going to do a secret rescue sometime.

Ivar came to Benedetta's room and showed her keys to the house so they could get out to the grounds that night. He had a backpack on his back. In the moonlight by the river, they laid out the lines and circuits. Ivar looked into the flux and told Benedetta to call them in French, to tell them to come running. She saw men and called them. Two of them held back, but began screaming as other men came up behind them. Benedetta's body squirmed with its memories of stab wounds. Twenty men dressed in rags came through the blue flux. The men behind them stopped and crossed themselves. Benedetta wished she knew who'd deserved stabbing.

One of the men looked as though he'd recently escaped torture, one hand dangling. All of them were bearded and dressed in wool tunics. One supporting the wounded man still wore a white tunic with a red cross on it. Even dirty, the white almost glowed in the moonlight. Benedetta expected Mitt, Lizevidda, and Jonah to come rushing out of the house.

The men began babbling about witchcraft and magic until Benedetta told them that they'd been saved by science. She wasn't sure her French and theirs were close enough, but they did understand her and stood trembling, looking at their senior member, a man who looked more Italian than French.

"We don't know why it was important to bring you forward, but we believe you would have died if you'd stayed," Ivar said in Norse. "Tell them that," he said to Benedetta.

"I already did," she said.

"Well, let's get them in the house, then," Ivar said, smiling his Loki smile again.

"Just like that," Benedetta said. "We got the Knights Templar, didn't we?"

"They're hungry, curious, and have swords," Ivar said.

"And no experience with modern weapons at all," Benedetta said. She told the knights in French, "Follow me," and they walked behind her into the Kirkpatrick house, not getting too close to her. They thought women were unclean, she remembered from some lore about these people, which might have been true or might have been lies their enemies spread about them to keep the survivors from finding refuge.

She had to admire them for not utterly freaking out as they faced a refrigerator, a gas stove, and a microwave. Ivar grumbled in Norse about Christians. They kept looking at one of the older men to figure out what to do. He said to Benedetta, "Please put the bread down for us and let us get it."

"You're not allowed to touch women." The rumors had it that they had sex with each other. This wasn't going to be a problem in these times. However, if they tried to bring their flavor of Christianity to now-time, then things could get pretty tedious. Maybe the future that advised them not to rescue Templars knew what it was talking about.

"Thank you," the older man said. He tried Lombardian on her and she nodded that he'd guessed right. "We're going to feel a little safer if we find you respect our rule. We moved into the future? How far? By what means?"

"Yes, um, it's about fifteen hundred years from his time," she said, pointing at Ivar, "and about eight hundred years from mine. You guys were maybe two hundred years before me. Early 1300s. I was born in the early 1470s."

"And Jerusalem?"

The Kirkpatricks showed up, furious but aware that they were outnumbered, at this point. Lizevidda still pulled a gun. One of the Templars seemed to know it was a bad thing.

"The fucking Templars. You had to bring in the fucking Templars," Mitt said. He put his hand on Lizevidda's arm, moved the gun down. Benedetta didn't think the Templars had a clue about guns, but wasn't sure. She did suspect that if something happened to one of them, the others would cut everyone down with their swords.

The knights picked up the word *Templars* and tensed.

"Oh, give them breakfast and then get them out of here," Mitt said.

"We're going with them," Ivar said. "And we're taking my stuff. You can find someone to make a copy for you."

"You can't threaten us like that," Mitt said. "I'll hand you over to the city council."

Jonah laughed. He said, "I suspect he can threaten you like that. He's the golden boy of the future that is winning now."

"This is so stupid," Lizevidda said. "After all we did to save you two."

"You locked them in last night?" Mitt said.

"Do you think I'm stupid?"

Ivar smiled his trickster smile again and pulled a key card from his shirt. "I fixored it, as Jonah would have said. Do you think I'm stupid?"

The head Templar said, in Latin that was close to Italian, to the others, "Eat, we can discuss our options later. Don't put your swords away." He looked at Benedetta and realized she understood what he said, so, he switched to another language. Arabic, she realized, but she only knew a few words of that. She noticed that he wasn't armed with a sword. Priest of the Templars?

Weapons, languages, and a possible grudge against established authority, how useful. She almost felt Loki's presence in her own life.

"We need to use a working phone," she said to Mitt, who looked from her to the Templars, especially to their swords, and handed her a cell phone.

Benedetta pulled her lawyer's card out and explained the situation, and asked him to find out if there were any charges outstanding against her and Ivar for stealing the time machine.

Whatever she and Ivar might have to face, the Templars didn't need to get into the mess she and Ivar might be in.

"Lawyer," she said in French, then repeated "lawyer" in Italian, curious about what languages they knew. "Lawyer" in English got some terms in various other languages back.

"I have a lot to ask you," their apparent spokesman said.

"We've got to find a place for you to stay and something for you to do," Benedetta said. "It's going to be a major change, but you've got each other, so it won't be as rough for you as it was for me when I came up-time alone. You might be sick for a while." Some of them would die, but all of them would have died if they had stayed.

Ivar and Benedetta walked out with the Knights Templar and their staff. Benedetta didn't want more of the sort of past where the peasants toiled under the orders of people who called themselves dukes after being peasants two generations earlier themselves. She wanted even less to put her trust in the old families, and the Kirkpatricks were like that even in now-time.

"My name is Pierre de Bologna," the Templar who seemed most in charge said. "The Church I'd served all my life did this to me. Fuck the pope." With his good hand, he pulled back the sleeves of his tunic to show badly healed burns on his wrists above his broken fingers. "We were all tortured. No sleep. We agreed to whatever they said, but none of it was true." He wanted her to believe him. A thousand years had passed, but he had just been tortured. "They accused me of fucking men. I have been celibate against all desires."

"I'm sorry," Benedetta said, thinking of how many more people had been tortured without someone from the future snatching them to safety.

"Why did you save us?"

"Someone up-time, in our future, thought it was a good idea. I think it is. You're gifted in languages, fighters, and you're used to moving from Outremer to France, de Bologna. And you know Lombardy."

"We lost Jerusalem. We lost Acre. We left Ruad in the end, last place off the coast of Outremer. Then with those losses still raw, we were accused of heresy, of betraying our oaths. I thought when we began that we could explain ourselves and that the pope would rescue us. The accusations took on a life beyond the truth. What happened?"

Benedetta thought that the order had been abolished and their leaders burned at the stake, but didn't want to tell the man that until he was a bit more adapted to the present. He wasn't stupid and understood what her silence meant. Before she could lie, he said, "Obviously, nothing good."

"We knew that the pope had abandoned us, so we came for you, Father," one of the armed men said. "We needed your skill at logic and argument."

"Some of the same lies told against the Cathars were the lies told against us. I'm sorry I believed those." He paused and looked out the train window at what they were passing, then said, "This really isn't magic? Is there a branch of our order here?"

Benedetta said, "No, to both questions."

"Whom do I serve now? My church made me a liar. I am so sorry. I perjured myself to stop the pain. They broke my writing hand."

"We can fix your hand. Help us save whom we can of the past. Reinvent your church if you must."

They got off the train at City Hall and walked over to the Archives, which had agreed to put the knights and their men up until they'd had their vaccinations and lived or died. Benedetta went as their translator. Ivar brought his toys in and built the Archives another time machine, a penance they probably didn't want but it allowed them to save face.

Her lawyer said, "You were lucky that nobody was killed when you stole the time machine."

Benedetta thought about the people who'd been trying to kill them from the New York City helicopter that Philadelphia's Defense Community had shot down.

The priest, Pierre de Bologna, asked her to have dinner with him after he'd been in the Archives for a few days. One of the young sergeants served them, to guard, Benedetta suspected, against her being alone with Pierre. The young man brought out candles, as Pierre said, "I want to sit a few moments in the light I'm used to."

Benedetta nodded. Her body tensed at the candlelight at first, then relaxed. The body had memories for things. "Fire doesn't bother you?"

"I wasn't burned by candles," Father Pierre said. "Does it bother you for any reason?"

"I wouldn't want to go back in time, but there's a part of me that trusts candles better than the electric lights. And a part that doesn't."

"What providence brought us here?"

"Father, I'm not a believer. I wasn't in my past life, either."

"I'm not sure what I believe in now, but there's a spirit that made us, even if we don't understand it. And you rescued us."

"The people who guided us to you must have had a reason."

"Can your time machine rescue anyone?"

"If there are legends of people disappearing into blue clouds, that's probably going to have been us."

He smiled at the skewed tenses. "Would it be God's work to rescue everyone we could?"

Benedetta said, "The now-time people might not like that, but it would be good human work."

Pierre stared at the candle for a while as the young man brought in small roasted birds. Benedetta recognized partridges. "How did you get partridges?"

"I asked," Pierre said. "Your friend Joe speaks Italian and Latin, badly."

"I haven't had partridges since we poached them between Milan and Montferrat."

"You were a soldier's woman." Pierre and Joe had talked quite a bit, then.

"Yes, I was, and not married in the Church, either, Father, though we were pretty much faithful to each other. I saw him die. My son also died in the past. Let me ask you, Father, if we could rescue Saracens with this time machine, would you still want to bring them to now-time?"

"Joe said that there are paradoxes involved, and that sometimes, the machine appeared to be blocked. If we can rescue people, we must." He smiled at her. Another trickster? Except for Jonah, Benedetta hadn't found people who were subtler than she was. This one was from further back than she but didn't rely on her alone for explanations. She wondered what else Joe had told him.

"You were tortured a few weeks ago; you were tortured a few centuries ago and everyone else you knew has been dead for a very long time," she said.

"And you think I'm feeling for any others who may be facing torture throughout all time? Yes, I do."

"We can't possibly save them all," Benedetta said. "And my question is: whom do we not save?"

"I knew Saracens. They are not as monstrous as our propaganda." He smiled slightly, eyes unfocused but full of flame reflections.

"What if the now-time people try to stop this?"

"Joe sees that people brought up in groups are less likely to just curl up and die. And the vaccines are better now than when you first came up. Some of us died, but we would have all died if we hadn't come up in time."

Benedetta finished her partridge and sat there, thinking hard about city-states she'd known, about how strangers were treated. "Now-time Philadelphia has communal government, even more so than in our time."

"I was much heartened that someone finally figured out how to make that work. It always fell apart and the people ended up bringing in a hired ruffian to rule them."

"Like Sforza." Benedetta tried to remember when the great-grandfather Sforza went from being peasant weaver to military leader. After this man's time, in 1360s. "Were there Angevin kings in Naples in your day?"

"Very messy, the Angevins in Naples. So, how long did they last?"

"Robert was a good king, I've heard the old men say. Then there was Queen Joanna who hanged her husband when he interfered with her reign. Not with her own hands, of course, and she wasn't there when it happened. Still her husband's people sacked the city after the pope refused to punish her. Everyone was fighting over it when I came up-time, and had been for a while. The French claimed Naples, but the French were claiming everything." She remembered that Byzantium fell to the Turks before she was born but didn't know if a man who'd sailed defeated from Jerusalem needed to know that.

"Joe told me that the Turks took Byzantium in 1453."

"Spain threw out the last of the Moors during the time we were fighting the French."

" 'Next year in Jerusalem,' " he said, as though quoting someone.

"Do you still hate the Saracen? So many people did," Benedetta said. "Some worked with them."

Father Pierre leaned back and threw his hands out sideways. "So long ago, this was. Should I hate Saracens eleven hundred years after Saladin died? I didn't hate them all then."

"We Italians remember for a long time," Benedetta said. "I'm glad I'm not pure Italian. Father spoke German from his family."

"I will miss Rome," Father Pierre said. "I shouldn't have been in France."

"God's work," the young man said. Benedetta was almost surprised to hear him.

Pierre laughed, which seemed to shock the young man. Then he leaned forward and asked Benedetta, "Did you ever get to Rome?"

"Sorry, no, but I was often in Milan."

"Rome reminded me that not all men in the past believed as I did and still they made beautiful things. And I now realize that not all men in this time believe as I do. But I haven't seen beautiful things here."

"They're more inventors of comforts rather than things of beauty," Benedetta said. "I'm happy to be comfortable, but I do miss the art." She realized Father Pierre wouldn't know who Leonardo da Vinci was.

"Imagine a future with the past's beauty and the present time's fabrications."

"Using past people to remake the present?"

"Precisely." Pierre's eyes gleamed.

Benedetta didn't tell him that first, all people from the past changed when they interacted with the future. What they'd learn in now-time would restructure their past memories. And second, probably most important, their conversation this evening had no doubt been bugged.

But for now, they'd gossip in the candlelight about Italy. She poured herself another glass of wine before the young man could serve her.

The future is an extension of now, but it would be better if we make it what we want it to be.

Just Family

The Kirkpatricks lost that game, Jonah thought one morning after the city council took away Ivar, Benedetta, the Templars, and all the time toys. He stayed on with the Kirkpatricks and kin. Sitting on a bench in the river garden, he watched people riding by on horses. Were they from now-time, the past, or even the future? He was feeling old now in his fifties. A flotilla of red, blue, and yellow kayaks came by, people laughing. He knew they were not laughing at him. Or for him.

Mitt and Lizevidda had talked about calling in their lawyers to get back the time toys. Jonah wondered if they knew how difficult recreating the old days they thought had existed for them would be. In his day, those days were a perpetually receding past—the Elizabethans, the early Christian Barbarian Age, when everyone was in the right social position and respected those with power over them, and when those who needed to rule got to. When people knew IQ was absolutely hereditary and white.

In China, those who killed off others to become emperors had the Mandate of Heaven. Those who failed in their rebellions died. Heaven was fickle, not like the divinely anointed kings of the Europeans.

Jonah pressed the air in front of him—control, alt, delete. Reboot. He laughed at the very idea. This game couldn't be rebooted, couldn't be halted, and he would not be reborn if he died again. He got up and started weeding the garden.

No blue flux full of people from the future visited the Kirkpatricks. Weeks, then months passed. He heard of court battles and people coming from the past speaking Welsh, dialects of Italian, and setting up small farms in the Northern Liberties. Six centuries later, Billie Penn's dream of a green city full of gardens and small farms became reality.

Jonah also remembered William Faulkner's "The past isn't over. It isn't even the past."

At dinner one night, he said to Lizevidda and Mitt, "These people were the losers of the struggles of their days."

"For the most part," Mitt said. "Ivar's been running rogue sites. And he refuses to cooperate with me."

"Strange behavior for a slaver," Jonah said.

"Indeed. He offered me a machine of my own."

"Why didn't you take it?" Jonah said.

"I'm not a techie. We'd need an operator. Ivar just laughed at that. You'd know more about rogue electronic gear than I do. Could you run a machine if you got one?"

For a moment, Jonah fantasized about hacking Ivar's rogue sites and diverting the people to the Kirkpatrick house. He giggled. *All your blue are belong to us.* "Sorry, I thought of how Ivar's face would look if we hijacked his blue flux." He didn't want to explain the ancient joke.

"Whoops, we now have all these time losers to deal with," Mitt said. "I want to find out how to bring up people who could help us reestablish a dynamic order."

Jonah decided that would be a real problem, grabbing a random handful of people and trying to get useful work out of them. The Southern Kirkpatricks had done that in the 1830s, but they'd been buying field hands, not strategic thinkers. Grab a few warlords and chiefs and teach them all English and get them to fight for your side.

Right. "I honestly don't know how to hack his machines, so take him up on his offer."

"And if he keeps running rogue machines, I can always blackmail him."

"If this goes on too long, those people will be a presence in Philadelphia," Lizevidda said.

"Time's losers, brought to life in your city by the Archives, which still have ties to all the other archives in Atlanta, Baltimore, and Washington," Mitt said. "We can work with that. We can start rumors that Federal Union forces want to take over the cities by flooding them with people from the past."

Jonah wondered if the now-time natives would get pissed enough to stop time-rescues before the past completely took over now-time. But then, what sort of people did now-time get when it rescued those who'd follow voices to run into a blue cloud rather than turn to die fighting on familiar ground?

Odd sorts. Strange attractors.

Jonah wondered if his descendants were idiots or if they had some way to pull this off. They smuggled goods, thus the connection with Mr. Wythe, the money, the house that wasn't bothered because they provided services that people wanted but didn't want to admit to in public. Plus leaving the Kirkpatricks alone was easy, since they had been taking care of themselves, not calling on the city council or any of the many subdivisions of Philadelphia to help them. But few successful smugglers managed to do more than protect themselves. And if the city needed to, it could take the house in less than an hour.

Getting shot at had been scary and he didn't want it to happen again real soon. He said, "I miss the kids."

"Your kids?" Lizevidda asked.

"Ivar and Benedetta. Cute couple."

"I don't miss them at all. I wish I'd known how utterly manipulative and dishonest they were going to be," Lizevidda said.

Mitt said, "They looked after what they thought were their interests. We have to look after ours. I was surprised at Ivar, though. I thought he would have sided with us."

"Ivar wouldn't have worked for you," Jonah said. "He works for the greater glory of Ivar."

"So we're rivals then, since we work for the greater glory of the Kirkpatricks," Lizevidda said.

"So, with Mr. Wythe under surveillance, how are you getting in cigarettes, silk, and bootleg videos?" Jonah asked. That was a bit rude of him. He wasn't supposed to have noticed that his descendants were involved in smuggling with Mr. Wythe. But since there were no investment banks and stock markets, their income wasn't coming from their third-floor light garden unless they had pot there. And since pot appeared to be legal now, that wasn't exactly a cash crop.

Mitt said, "If the city councils want to be hypocrites, we have no problem with making money from the hypocrisy. Are you complaining?"

"I see nothing wrong with tweaking a bunch of silly collectivists," Jonah said. "If you can tweak them. No fun being tweaked."

"You stayed with us and not with them. We'd like you to spread some rumors for us, get a feel for the mood in various city groups."

Much of success in life was bluff, Jonah thought. The rest was accounting. "Okay, which rabble am I going to rouse?"

"We thought the salvage crews would be a place to start."

"Are they losing jobs for muscle-boys because of the past people?" Jonah asked. "Or do they feel that Ivar fucked them over?"

"We'd like you to talk to them," Mitt said. Jonah suspected Mitt was squeamish about talking to roughnecks. Effete aristocrats were useless.

"You could also work with the queers," Jonah said. "The people from the past aren't going to be so queer-tolerant."

Mitt looked at Jonah as though he'd completely lost his mind. Lizevidda said, "They sympathize with all victims, past and present. And there is no 'queers' now, either."

Jonah said, "I suspect if they harvest enough almost-dead people from Christian Europe, they'll get bigots."

"Start with the salvage crews," Lizevidda said. "Or think of people who'd be threatened by large groups of unskilled people from the past."

"You don't have unskilled people in now-time," Jonah said.

"You haven't seen the salvage crews," Lizevidda said. "We've worked with these people before, so you can start here. They've never had the scale of operation that Mr. Wythe has, but they've been useful in the past."

Jonah wished he had a car so he could drive down to where the airport had been, but he didn't, so he made the trek by public train and electric bus. The train was full of people dressed in surcoats and tights, or long linen gowns, but most talked in now-time accents. The European past had become fashionable, the way black style had become fashionable at various times in the twentieth-century. Next week, they could be dressed in kimonos or Chinese Mao tunics. Very American to cut up cultures and wear the colorful bits, Jonah thought, glad to see some things hadn't changed in over three hundred years. English would also scarf up vocabulary and idioms and mutate again. Maybe the language would bring back case endings on objective nouns?

He got on the bus with a number of people who looked like they'd tried to find something now-time to wear and figured these were the real folks from the past, but not all of them were dressed in computer-cut-and-sewn linen. He looked at his wrist for the address of the people he was trying to find, wondering if this was the crew that Ivar had worked for, or if they knew people on that crew. *Earnest political work with sweaty people is not what I'm really good at,* Jonah thought.

When he saw the mixed crew—black men, Italian toughs, and some Chinese kids in Mao pajamas—he knew that he should start with recent aristocratic arrivals who'd want to agitate for special privileges, but then they'd be in competition with the Kirkpatricks.

"Some friends wanted me to talk to you," Jonah said. Maybe the Chinese kids would like to be capitalists. "Mitt and Lizevidda."

"The kids here would like some tobacco. We've been trying to explain that it's bad for them," one of the Italian toughs said.

Things had gotten that bad, Jonah thought. He hadn't intended to help with the financial side of the operation, but why not. "I'll see what I can do. This working well for you, having people from the past competing with you?"

One of the black men snorted. The three generations of Italian toughs grinned. The other black man said, "We all fled shit some time or another."

One of the Chinese kids said, in three-hundred-year-old English, "some of us were to the left of Mao and some were to the right." Another kid spoke in Chinese. "He was with the Boxers, before my time," the Chinese kid who could speak English said.

The second black man said, "I can barely understand that, but they both understand work."

Jonah wished he spoke Chinese, but didn't think he was going to get anywhere with them. "Lots of genetic diversity."

"Yeah," said the guy who appeared to be the leader. "Bringing people from the past is a lot like salvage work. Ivar, that Viking kid, was good at salvage when he worked for us. We were rather fond of him. If you know him, tell him to drop by and see us sometime."

They'd like to buy some cigarettes, but otherwise, they're okay with having more help," Jonah said, not telling his descendants that the salvage people were now half time-fugitives, or their sympathizers. "I was thinking about agitating among the past people who are more like us. Get them to want their privileges back."

"If you can find them," Mitt said. "Or work stirring up trouble between the different religious factions."

Jonah knew Mitt had no idea how messy that could get. But if the aristocrats preferred life with electronics to being almost killed once and having to risk their lives for privileges again, they wouldn't agitate against this collectivist sludge. Stirring up old religious passions would probably destabilize things quite nicely. Only most of these people had been on the losing side of religious passions. Jonah told himself to stop being negative before he actually found some religious fanatics.

Jonah had to ride a bicycle into Center City. Life. Here. Now. The sun was shining. People rode their horses and bicycles along the river. Other people were netting geese and wringing their necks. Closer to the city, he saw construction cranes—no, actually deconstruction cranes—moving chunks of dead multistory condos out of the way, hauling it off on flatcars to open up Penn's city. People were building new small houses clustered together along the river, surrounded by their gardens. Peasants, all of them, Jonah thought, but very much better armed than peasants had been centuries earlier.

He went looking for Benedetta and found her in South Philadelphia with the Templar leader, talking Italian at a sidewalk café, smiling at a child who was blowing bubbles, and listening to music on a pod. Everyone looked deliriously happy. Benedetta smiled at him, smiled at the Templar. She picked up some plate that was glazed in bright reds and blues, almost overdone. "Jonah, would you have imagined all this when we were outlaws?"

The Templar leader smiled as though he'd heard the story many times already, probably with Benedetta as the heroine.

"I'm still having trouble believing all this exists," Jonah said. "Seems like a dream that will end badly eventually."

The Templar man said, "Ivar says much the same thing. He plans to go to Iceland next summer when he gathers more of his people."

"How are they getting there?" Jonah said.

"Probably flying," Benedetta said. "Rome is using Iceland and Newfoundland as quarantine points for flights to New York and Philadelphia."

"Not going to row over? What's the fun in getting to Iceland if you're not going the old-fashioned way?" He had hoped Ivar would help him put a boot to this happiness, but, no, Ivar was going to finally get to Iceland.

"Iceland's a lot warmer than it was when he was a boy, and larger. But it's still the place where the spreading ocean rift zone is above sea level. Pierre, did the baking team get your order yet?"

Jonah thought there was something wrong with a fifteenth-century Italian camp follower knowing about tectonic-plate geology.

"The world was so much older than I realized," Pierre-the-past-Templar said, speaking English with a double accent, past dialect and past Italian. "Yes, we're fine on the hosts."

Still Catholic, Jonah thought, smiling.

"People love the familiar rituals. They've had to accept so much change. It's nice to give them some consistent comfort, don't you think?"

Jonah said, "But what if your familiar ritual was flogging your slaves?"

Pierre said, "Most of the people here were running from people like that. Even our Saracens."

"Your Saracens," Jonah said before realizing that Pierre probably was one of the few people who could speak more than one or two languages.

"I learned Arabic in Outremer. While our dealings with the Saracens were not heretical or treasonous, we did have to deal with them."

Benedetta said, "It's the future, Jonah. We're all getting beyond what we think we remember from before. Memory is treacherous sometimes. People are happy to be alive, to have another chance in a different world. Food in their bellies. Sex that doesn't give them clap or the pox or get them hanged. Babies to hug that live beyond their first year."

"Do you tell them they're pawns in a game played by the far future that we don't really understand fully?"

"We make the future," Pierre said. "What we do now."

"You think? You haven't seen fifty different possible futures grabbing for your attention and help, flickering in and out of existence."

"That was then," Benedetta said. "We settled the future in more ways than one."

No talking to them now. Jonah walked away without ordering and found a place that sold pizza, and didn't know if pizza-selling survived from his day to this or if this was yet another archaic fad or if they'd rescued some people from some tiny wreckage in the past, which managed to not be noticed in the twentieth-century. It was Louisiana pizza. The red-haired girl who sold it to him recognized his twentieth-century accent and said, "The people who really appreciate now-time are us past folks."

"Philadelphians always bitched about Philadelphia," Jonah said. "Some things never change."

"Pizza," the past girl said. "Last thing I remember, I'm drowning in a hurricane and then I'm here and I see a Louisiana pizza place and I start selling pizza again."

Where is Loki's man when you need him? Jonah walked down the street, eating pizza, trying to not let the street stalls full of lace, furs, and wildly decorated pottery distract him too much. South Philly was just one neighborhood, full of immigrants who had always had a tradition of grabbing mudbugs and calling them crayfish or treating garlic rice stew with cheese as a delicacy.

Move on, Jonah thought, and find a neighborhood full of Scots, Swiss, or Germans, people who understood predestination. He walked eating his pizza with the mudbugs on top and ended up in Society Hill, where some of the houses were on their fifth century and the others were replicas of those. Surely these people understood tradition, but then he noticed that most of the pregnant people looked male. He turned down toward the river on Walnut and went to where Society Hill Towers had been. They'd been deconstructed and the land they'd stood on was being used for multistory greenhouses.

Where the Ritz Theatres had been, there was a new theater, still called the Ritz, but it wasn't showing movies. He bought a ticket and watched actors and actresses doing *Hamlet.* Had any of them been in the original production? They hadn't gotten much of an audience, but this was the matinee. They were going through the play faster than Jonah had ever seen the play done, so some of them were from a time when this was entertainment, not high culture. He noticed the more sinister bits better that way, the implication that the Ghost was demonkind. Or maybe that had been this cast's interpretation.

In the end, Hamlet paid for listening to the Ghost. That hadn't been the interpretation in Jonah's time.

He went backstage to talk to the actors and found out that men had, as in the original productions, done the women's parts. "Are you from this time or the time of the play?"

"Some of us are from Shakespeare's time. Great fucking playwright he was, even if his company wouldn't hire us. Too old to stay boys with Jonson and not quite ripe enough for the King's Men. Others wanted to find out how to play the old way. We're doing the Scottish play next week with the original dances at the end, then *Antony and Cleopatra* as a comedy with teeth."

"Okay." Society Hill was entertained by the time-rescue cases. He couldn't agitate here.

Maybe he should just sink into now-time, accept that it worked for more people than it didn't. But the complacency made his troll teeth itch. Paradise couldn't be paradise without the snake.

Philadelphia had combined its surviving genes and was inbred enough now that families had children in a range of hues. Racism as an irritant was out. And whatever shit he stirred against the past could make his own life difficult, not that Mitt or Lizevidda cared. He stopped in the street near Market and Broad, where Billy Penn still stood over the city, the high buildings gone again, City Hall still its reproduction-baroque self. He wondered if Mitt and Lizevidda didn't care, or if they'd decided to keep their own hands clean if the past brought its bigotries and malice into now-time without doing anything to lift now-time out of the collectivist sludge.

Jonah considered the happy pizza-seller and wondered if now-time was going to fill up with stone-crazy people who'd run to a blue cloud. He went to City Hall Station and got a train back to East Falls, but didn't walk straight back to the house on the river. He wanted to see where he used to live again and walked up Midvale to the library and then up Warren. The houses were now a mix of old and new, with more space between them than in his day, gardens in those spaces. Every house had a greenhouse. A deer popped its head up from chewing on hostas and looked at him, one ear turned toward him, one flicking to the sides, then the ears switched duties. "Dumb deer," Jonah said. "The hunters are coming."

The deer stamped its front hoof and slunk back toward the shrubbery. Jonah kept walking and came up to his house, which still stood there, looking four hundred years old but with a new roof. The stairs he must have fallen down were still there, with a freshly built stone wall up beside them instead of the black-painted iron railing he'd had. The granite wall looked nicer than the iron-pipe railing had looked.

He wanted to go inside and see his family there and find out none of this happened. He'd teased them to screaming at times; he'd loved them dearly and they probably thought he'd abandoned them. And whatever his descendants knew in now-time, he could never go back and assure his wife and children that he hadn't abandoned them. If he'd died, it would have been better.

Then he wondered if he really believed that. He had disappeared in a snowstorm. Would they have necessarily assumed he'd abandoned them? He sat down on the bottom steps for a moment, trying to remember what the storm had been like, what he'd said to his wife before he went out. He had snuck out, but now he couldn't remember why. He could look up the census records, find out whether his wife had stayed in the house, what happened to the children, but he wondered if he wasn't having this attack of nostalgia because he was tired, and got up before someone came to find out why he was sitting there crying, and he walked back to the river house.

Mitt looked at Jonah when he walked in, a questioning, concerned look. Jonah said, "I went by the old house before I came back."

"I didn't know if you wanted to see that again or not. Some people claimed it for rehabilitation about six months ago. From the past, didn't think you'd want to hear that. How did your day go?"

"Not well. The salvage crew remembers Ivar with considerable fondness. The Italians and Cajuns love each other's cooking. Everyone is so happy they didn't die that they're not fighting each other over anything that almost killed them in the past."

"I suspect they'll get over that," Mitt said.

"Has it occurred to you that a whole lot of these people are going to be crazy? Whoever in their right mind would run into a blue cloud to save themselves from whomever was chasing them?"

"The colorblind," Mitt said, smiling slightly. "Anyone really desperate, I suppose. Hide in the fog, not really thinking of the color."

"Maybe we should agitate among the Predestinarians," Jonah said. "Stir up some religious passions about interfering with the course of history."

"The people rescued are going to believe they were predestined to be rescued," Mitt said. "Now-time Philadelphians don't tend to be your kind of religious. You think you can grow a beard and agitate among the Amish?"

"The past peasants will be competing with them as farmers."

"Lots of luck," Mitt said. "We hired a string quartet and invited some friends over, so fix yourself something to eat and join us."

"Is it a now-time string quartet or is it a past-time string quartet?"

"It's a student string quartet from the music academy. I don't know if they're all from now or not, but probably. It's a cheap string quartet."

Jonah heated up some goose stew in the microwave, and went up to take a shower and change before joining the party. When he came down, he saw Mr. Wythe sitting with some strangers in now-time clothes—two women in silk pants and two men wearing tailored wool garb. If the silk was real, Jonah wondered if someone had kept that many silk worms or if the silk was imported. The string quartet wore black, not the black suits and cocktail dresses he'd remembered musicians wearing, but black jumpsuits almost like Japanese puppeteers wore when they manipulated their nearly life-size puppets. *Bunraku* theater—he'd seen it once in New York. It was still funny to think he couldn't just get in his car and drive to New York for a day.

The musicians were supposed to be invisible, leaving the music floating in the air. Jonah looked at them anyway—a woman playing the cello, another woman and a man playing the violins, and a second man playing the viola. The music was older than he was.

Hearing Mozart again made him feel unglued in time. He sighed and sat down beside Mr. Wythe. They all just listened to the music. When the musicians finished, the cellist brought around a tray of drinks. Jonah said to Mr. Wythe, "I hope we didn't cause you much grief."

"You weren't the cause of it," Mr. Wythe said. "They're playing my Stradivarius. The other violin and the viola are two of Axelrod's instruments that we salvaged from New Jersey. There was almost a war fought over those. And now we rescue people."

"I saw someone who went from selling pizza in the twenty-first century to selling pizza now. She's utterly as content as a dairy cow would be to go from a twentieth-century milking machine to a now-time milking machine."

"Ivar's done so much it feels like we've always had Ivar bringing people up from the past. A force of time, our Ivar."

"I don't think he's shown you much gratitude. He's said that he doesn't trust you and will pay you back for those helicopters nearly killing us." Jonah felt a thrill in lying to Mr. Wythe.

The music started again, a string quartet by a composer Jonah didn't recognize, from after his time.

Mr. Wythe didn't stay afterward. Jonah wondered if Mr. Wythe, despite what he'd said, still considered Jonah to have been part of his problems.

Lizevidda led the musicians to the kitchen. Mitt and the other guests stayed in the music room while Lizevidda dealt with food and paid the musicians. When she came out, the guests who were still there thanked her for the entertainment. She smiled and sighed as though she'd worn herself out playing.

"This must continue and expand," one of the men said.

"We hope," Mitt said.

"You're also a Kirkpatrick?" one of the men said to Jonah.

"Yes."

"Good family. They've forgotten about good families these days."

"There were good black families in Mount Airy," another man said. "Free blacks from before the American Revolution. Good stock. I think some of the Kirkpatricks married some of those families."

Oh, my. Jonah looked more closely at Lizevidda and Mitt.

"Whoever survived and managed to hold on to land was good family," Mitt said. "Land and steelworking tools and crew mattered for a long time after the worst of the plagues."

"Having a good chunk of electronic gear didn't hurt either," the first man said. "Wythe is a good example of that."

"Man has everything in that junk heap of his," the second man said.

Mr. Wythe could rescue people who didn't want to run and hide in blue fog but who were too near dead to squirm away from the gurney, yet he couldn't rescue them by the losing army-full. Probably couldn't use them by the losing army-full, either. Jonah wondered what New York was up to, if he could talk his way into New York. *All of us have time machines now, so why still be mad at me,* he thought. "Other than Mr. Wythe, do you have contacts in New York?"

Silent pause. Everyone else began talking about Mozart and the musicians, which of them would move on to the Symphony, how expensive keeping the Kimmel going had been with all that glass.

Then the guests made their excuses and left. Jonah, Mitt, and Lizevidda went out to see them to their pedicabs. Jonah wondered if these were private or public pedicabs. Private pedicabs would be almost like having a sedan chair, just not requiring so many people. He wondered if sedan chairs would ever come back. A certain elegance had passed out of the world in the nineteenth century—and sedan chairs didn't require even as much pavement as a pedicab. Jonah had heard that British Kirkpatricks had employed chairmen, but that the public chairmen were as rude and presumptuous as taxi drivers had been later.

After the guests left, Jonah asked, while they were still outside, "Was I rude to ask about New York?"

"It's a sore point and we're not sure the place isn't bugged now by the City Council."

"Perhaps if you're making money from a hypocritical chink in the system, you'd be just as well off letting things continue as they have been," Jonah said.

"An influx of people who aren't used to the intricate emotional manipulations of the current system will force a change. We might not have to do anything if we're patient."

"Do you honestly believe people from the past don't feel intricate emotional manipulations by their communities already?"

"I'd like to stay one step ahead of any changes," Mitt said. "And I'd like to guide changes in a useful direction. A lot of very talented people are wasted on community-maintenance chores. I doubt Ivar likes cutting and sewing his own clothes, or preparing his own food."

Jonah suspected that Viking men who went off for months in the winter hunting booty, and who had a reputation for being cleaner than the local Anglo-Saxons in the Danelaw, probably knew their ways around needles, to repair both clothes and sails. "Don't know. Benedetta probably thinks not having to spin every inch of thread she wears is utterly wonderful."

"Talented people are being wasted," Mitt repeated. This seemed to be the slogan of people like Mitt, Jonah thought. Mitt wanted to let the people who love making and selling pizza make more of it for people who preferred investing in new technology companies.

While the statement made sense, it sounded like a slogan when Jonah heard it the second time. But unlike the egalitarians, he didn't believe that everyone had even remotely the same talents. Were the people who thought they deserved to have other people sew their clothes and grow their food really superior? "I think you've underestimated the ability of most people to find present life too comfortable to fight."

Mitt said, "Surely, the present makes some miserable by forcing them to be more than naturally accomplished."

"Well, that is a completely different take on it. I just have to find people who feel they've been forced to become too smart."

Mitt and Lizevidda stared at Jonah for a second. Lizevidda said, "It's late and we've had alcohol."

If the stupid hadn't rebelled against all the training they got to be multiskilled, either the system had some slack built into it or the plagues had killed off the stupid.

The next day, Jonah looked for Ivar.

A New Man of Now-time

Ivar stood with his back to the sun, outside the building where he and his had set up a Time Station, warming himself after the cold deaths he'd just seen in the past, the people he couldn't get out.

Walking, Jonah shuffled like an old man in the hands of grandchildren waiting to be his heirs. Jonah stopped for a moment, his hand over his eyes, squinting. "Jonah. What are you up to these days?" Ivar had heard that Jonah was looking up old friends, and one of the old connections, Mr. Wythe, had been talking about meeting with Jonah again.

"Doing good. Doing good," Jonah said. Either Jonah was doing well, or Jonah was doing things Jonah considered good, regardless of the opinions of others. Ivar understood that kind of doing good deeds. He'd done his own kind of good himself. Jonah asked, with a more personal tone to his voice, "See much of Benedetta?"

"Some. I don't speak any language she, the Templar, and their Saracen don't have covered."

"Saracen?"

"Yeah, with out-and-out pagans like me around, a Saracen is practically a coreligionist to the Templar. They both speak Latin and Arabic."

"Did they know each other before?"

"Haven't asked. The Saracen is black-skinned, really black-skinned, not like the locals who are darker than most. Do you know what a Moor would be?"

"Someone who's really pissed off to hear that Islam never retook Spain."

"No, this one doesn't care. Didn't appear to have cared then. He was a musician there, stringed stuff, took to computers like he'd been born to come up-time and believes that. Yammers about Pythagoras. You know who that'd have been?"

"Guy who believed that tuning music instruments said something about how the world worked at some musical level."

"Sounds like our guy studied him in the original Greek. Learned programming languages in a couple of months, says Benedetta. I could use him, but he doesn't speak any languages I know yet."

"You're going to Iceland?"

"Yep. Iceland can use people, so they've hired me to come over, with the city's permission. They still speak Norse there, just weird Norse. And you? Want to come with me?"

"Maybe. I want to know if you're still Loki's man and if you'd like to change things in now-time."

"Not the way you'd like to change things, I suspect. I've got my fame. Only from the inside, fame feels like just living well."

"You're getting soft in now-time."

"I was just a kid in my old time, okay, and just wanted to be a warrior because that meant something then. Now, I can say *warrior*, and people ask if I mean gladiator or guided-missile expert or pilot."

"They have gladiators here?"

"We brought some in from a shipwreck near Pompeii during Vesuvius's eruption. They're showing some of the local kids how to do it. Blows off steam, looks real, and it entertains people. I've gotten in the ring with some of them."

"Nobody needs to use a sword or pike to get his way in now-time."

"Not in the old sense of getting your friends on boats to get some other folk's girls and goodies. We did use trickery and a bit of force to get the time machine, but more trickery than force. That was a fun time, Jonah."

"But there are other ways to get your way."

"I know, Jonah. You and I have stolen bicycles together. What's your plan for mischief, and why do you need me to help you?"

"Why do you assume I'm up to mischief?"

"If you're not up to mischief, why not?"

"It's not precisely mischief."

"Bullshit, Jonah, you don't have anything challenging to do so you look for mischief. I'm not the troll."

"And you?"

"Come with me. We've got a fix on a major battle."

"What kind of challenge is rescuing people who were on the losing side?"

"Some of them were on the losing side with an earthquake, floods, fires. Jonah, I've heard these arguments before. You're the best case for someone getting rescued who was a waste of skin, to be honest."

"I helped Benedetta escape."

"Well, yeah, and she wouldn't have stayed out except for now-time lawyers. We wouldn't have gotten our pardons without now-time people. You go out with us and you do so damn little while we're breaking the machine that the other folks were speculating whose agent you were. Maybe we got shot at because of that." Ivar stopped talking for a second, and looked away from Jonah, then back at him. "Okay, probably not."

"I think we can make changes in this society that would make it a better place for us."

"For us?"

"For people who aren't interested in spending the rest of their lives running computer programs that make their clothes."

"Most people only operate the machines that make their clothes. Relatively few people run the machines, much less write the programs. But enough of those people exist in now-time that being the computer programmer and systems operator isn't a full-time job, much less an overtime job, for anyone. The programmers and computer guys do enough of it to stay sharp and not so much of it that they can't do other things."

"And aren't you going to tell me that I was just a script kiddy on top of that?"

"You can accuse yourself of that by what you do. Anyone who had been a programmer would have been more involved in the work we did at Three Mile Island."

"You ungrateful fuckhead."

"Why should I be grateful to you?"

Jonah shut up for a moment. Ivar remembered the days when they were in the Archives together. Jonah said, "I helped you practice English."

"An old dialect. I learned now-time English from other people." Ivar wished Jonah would retain his dignity on this one and go away, even if he went away a foe. He had made a better life after Jonah, but he remembered Jonah with more fondness than he'd expected. He was being harsh to the man, and they had been company for each other once, when now-time was still strange to them both.

"Can we restart this? How are you doing?"

"We're working a long battle. Most of the time, people died. Sometimes, I can bring people through."

"Any particular battle?"

"Stamford Bridge is what the English called it. Also, Gate Fulford."

"Rescuing your people."

"Anyone we can get." Ivar thought Jonah's problem was that he craved sensation that didn't cost him much. Jonah could have all the action he wanted if he had less fear of risks, but he was an old man now.

"I'd like to watch."

That, also, was Jonah's way. "Okay, let's go see whom we can't save today. I'll show you what frustration is."

"Benedetta shows me what frustration is."

Ivar didn't let himself answer that one, but crooked a finger and waggled it to tell Jonah to follow him. Back inside, where blue flux connected them to England, Stamford Bridge, early morning, 25 September 1066. "The English have armor. The Norse men do not."

The horses were pony-size compared to modern horses in Philadelphia, the giant jumping horses used in games in the park or the plow horses of the Amish. The flux shrank to a pinpoint, making a reflection of the scene upside-down behind them. He heard Jonah gasp, seeing that for the first time. "Camera obscura effect. What it means is that we're almost completely shut down at those coordinates."

"The light is from the past."

"Well, duh," Ivar said. He hadn't seen this particular set of slashing and throat-cutting before, but what he couldn't save didn't interest him. He moved the fine adjustments, couple of minutes this way, half a kilometer that. The future was a fog on the Derwent, upstream from the bridge. Ivar looked for people who might have disappeared in history, people who spoke his mother tongue, even if they were now Christians. Everyone knew that most of the Norse men became Christians to save their countries from Crusades. "I want them. I want them out." He realized he spoke that in Norse.

"Nobody like you here?"

"So far, no. At first, I liked being the only Norseman. Now, I'd like to have some company who spoke my tongue."

"Even if you get them out, will they be like you?"

"Ninety percent died. Surely I can save some of them." *No, you can't save any of them* appeared to be a possible answer, but Ivar wasn't going to give up without sweeping as much as possible.

"Do you care that much about saving lives or is this a problem to be solved?"

Ivar almost hit Jonah, then thought about what he'd said, and the tone of Jonah's voice, which had been soft, not mocking, not that humans who followed troll ways couldn't fake concern. "Both probably. First, a problem to be solved."

"What do you do with them if you can get them out?"

"Talk to them. Hope they don't go crazy on the spot. Hope they want to make their ways in now-time. All men. The women are up in Orkney."

"Were up in Orkney," Jonah said.

"I need to concentrate," Ivar said.

"When you came here, you didn't know words like *concentrate*. They're Latinate."

"Fix my mind to its work, then," Ivar said. He found a man running and maneuvered the flux, but it went into a pinpoint again. Jonah turned to watch the past light on the wall behind them play out the scene again.

"Slit his throat, they did. Why did your people piss other people off so much?"

Ivar thought Jonah wanted to be thrashed, but moved the time flux again. "England belonged to Norway's king."

"You want to bring those passions back to now-time?"

"Jonah, what passions do *you* want to bring to now-time?"

"I don't believe the old fights stayed in the past. I think they've always been here. People are just being hypocritical for the sake of soft lives."

"Your little group of lawbreakers looks like a bunch of smugglers pretending to be the heirs of the industrial empire. They're tolerated because they're entertaining. Now-time needs some elegant bad people and has them right where they want them. Your family and Mr. Wythe are gossip fodder. Now-time tolerates the Kirkpatricks and the Wythes, but they're not going to allow them to have power."

"And you were different, a bunch of thieves pretending to be warriors."

Ivar turned and looked Jonah hard enough in the eye that Jonah backed away from him. "Obviously, we were entertaining as legends after we were gone as a people. And what one set of Norse men lost, another won. In 1066."

Forty-five hundred men dead. Ivar started the calculations for Uppsala, but kept working on Stamford Bridge.

They got out one badly wounded boy who died before they could stop the bleeding, one Englishwoman who appeared to be lost, and an Englishman. Ivar realized he'd swept through the battleground twice now. The Englishman and woman didn't speak English that Jonah knew; theirs was closer to Norse. They would go straight to the Archives.

"And another day, another two living people who don't speak your language rescued."

"If we could save them in droves, it might be a problem for now-time, but we can't. No reason to make a political issue over rescuing whom we can."

Ivar used the one-person scoop to check a few Merovingian or Germanic period crossroads for adulteresses buried alive, and found two corpses and a live girl. He said, "Now this is a hobby of mine.

I've mapped several bog ways where bodies have been found. The girls got staked or buried alive for betraying their marriage vows, so we have to pull them out if we spot them, since they can't run. They tend to be hysterically grateful for being rescued, even if you can't understand what they're saying. Most of them were strangled completely dead first."

Jonah looked at the shivering, gasping girl who looked like she was about fifteen, and said, "Can I take her home?"

"She needs to be deloused and dewormed first," Ivar said.

Jonah said, "Glad to see that your attitude about women hasn't changed."

"I want to be buried properly when I do die," Ivar said. "With a companion who volunteers to accompany me."

"Still pagan at heart."

"I don't know if it's that, or just wanting company in the pyre. Death is still very lonely."

"Get cremated in the city's crematorium. You'll have plenty of company from the freezer to the fires."

"If I save them, don't I get to take one of them with me later?" Ivar knew that Jonah was right, though. The machine working out the coordinates for Uppsala beeped; he switched from Stamford Bridge, 26 September 1066, to Uppsala 1087.

"Where are we now?"

"Looking for a day with an army," Ivar said. "Uppsala, the Christians are attacking." Ivar was thinking in Norse now, translating into English. "These were the last of them who honored the old way until nine hundred years later." He'd met men who still honored the old gods, but was wary of them. "There's a well here. My coreligionists would immerse men in it. If they disappeared, the gods had answered their prayers. If the men just died, not."

"So you brought those men to now-time?"

"We can always get them, now, next week. I'd like to save people from this battle today."

"You can always save people from this battle tomorrow, kid. It's getting late here."

Ivar considered what Jonah said. If he had saved them, they'd be as much saved tomorrow as they would be today or next year. He was tired, but he wanted to see Old Uppsala before he went to sleep. He found the night lit by the moon. He looked out at the grave fields, the temples that seemed to be modeled on temples seen in foreign lands, and the old timber longhouses, one longer than the others, the king's house. The trees this time didn't have bodies hanging in them, perhaps never had had as many as the Christians claimed. How much of any of that was real? "I don't really want to bring it all back," he told Jonah. "I love my now-time toys."

"But are there people who do want to bring it back?"

Ivar had met some contemporary Asatru. "They think they do." He decided he was tired of Jonah's company at this point. "If you want to come by when we sweep Uppsala tomorrow, you'd be welcome, but I am tired now. As you said, we can save them tomorrow." Ivar would invite some of the now-time Asatru to join them in sweeping Uppsala.

"Cattle die,
Kindred die,
We ourselves also die;
But the fair fame
Never dies
Of him who has earned it."

Ivar found the now-time Asatru weird, but recognized that they revered him as the Time Master. He wondered what they'd have said to his grandmother, who said all the gods were inside men's heads. But human minds had room for the gods inside them. After his studies turned under Odin's Rune Lay, and he experienced the pain and thrill of getting knowledge through self-sacrifice, Ivar realized that gods were a way to focus the mind. Pain purified knowledge. Sacrifice justified actions.

Two of the Asatru snuck in from New York to see Old Uppsala. One was a man who called himself Ketil Trout, a name from the past he'd claimed as his own, and a woman who called herself Thora Lacecuff. Ivar wondered why they felt dishonored by the names they'd gotten from their parents, but finding any old name and using it without blood connection seemed to be common enough. Thora wore on her cuffs the froth of thread wrongly called lace, not laces to close the cuffs against winter—not that they had strong winters here. Ivar couldn't explain to these eager strangers that who he was depended on kin telling him the lore of his family. He was Ivar Sigtryggson, son of Sigtrygg Godfredsson. A man whose fame burned bright lived in memories beyond his father's father.

Generations from now, he would be Ivar, Lord of Time. He said, "Today, we will save whom we can from the last battle of Uppsala."

They were dressed in clothes they'd copied from painting and museum relics, plus his descriptions.

Then Jonah came in, and Ivar felt deflated. He looked from the people whose faces glowed with some religious joy he didn't quite understand to Jonah, whose expression was impish. Troll-kind in human form. The religious joy in those faces had descended from the Christian mysticism, not the pragmatic bargaining between man and his choice of god. And for the Norsemen, Fimbulvetr, the winter of winters, brought Ragnarok, the destruction of this world and the rebirth of another. The end was tragedy with slight hope. The men fighting for the gods knew, as the gods knew, that they'd lose. Christianity had offered more than a cold end and a handful of survivors at the margins of a final war.

The past died; the few escaped to now-time.

Ketil Trout said, "We want to be heathens again."

Jonah said, "You haven't a clue what that means, or what it could mean."

Ketil Trout said, "Ivar, why is this insulting man here?"

"He's an old friend. I've brought you here to show you Uppsala, to help me with rescues of those who speak Norse. You've learned Norse."

Thora Lacecuff said, "We need instruction in how to hold a proper blót."

"You can't hold the strongest form of blót," Ivar said. "The city council frowns on human sacrifice."

"Just a technicality," Jonah said.

Ivar said, "Who plays with Loki now, troll boy?"

They found the battle at Uppsala. Obviously, the historical record was scant, because neither side wished to talk about blue clouds sweeping men up from both sides. The Christians and pagans still fought after they came forward in time until Ivar dropped a net over them and motioned for his crew to inject them with sedatives.

"Modern medicines are so fast-acting," Ivar said.

"You saved Christians?" Thora Lacecuff said.

Ivar said, "Kind of hard to sort them out when they're fighting each other." He found some Norsewomen running and dropped flux in front of them. Some of them swerved, some of them ran into the future paying way too much attention to what was behind them.

"We could sacrifice a Christian," Ketil Trout said.

"In New York, they allow you to sacrifice men?" Ivar asked, sure they were too in awe of him to recognize the sarcasm. Jonah, however, got the tone and winked at him.

Back and forth across Old Uppsala. Tales of human sacrifice appeared to have been rather exaggerated, but Ivar was able to pull a few guys out of wells before they stopped for the night.

Jonah said, "You ought to ask what the prayers were for and see if you can grant them."

"'Shit, mother, get me out of this well' was what the poor goofs they threw in the well were praying," Ivar said. "We did."

"You fulfilled some prophecies, I suspect, with the saving of your coreligionists at Uppsala," Ketil Trout said, his voice full of awe. Ivar resisted the urge to kick him in the butt, and sat down to dinner. His crew folk brought in a couple of the Swedes, freshly inoculated and filled with antibiotics. The dialect wasn't quite the Norse Ivar knew, but they worked out how to talk to each other. The now-time Asatru looked just so jealous, but Ivar was more interested in who'd ended up king of Norway and what happened to the Icelandic settlers than he was in playing heathen hero to some people who didn't know how marvelous their own time and ideas were. The lamb tasted like lamb to them all, with good beer and bread. Ivar could explain computers later. This rescue washed away the bitter frustration of his losses at Stamford Bridge.

One of the Swedish women asked Ivar what gods brought them here, and when he told her that he brought them here with machines that used millions of very tiny winches, she said, "You're probably lying, but the lamb and bread are good, and I'm happy not to have been raped or enslaved or forced to lie about Jesus saving me."

Thora Lacecuff asked, "What did she say?"

Aren't you supposed to know Norse? Ivar thought. "She said the lamb and bread are good," he said, wondering if the now-time people could understand what a shock this was going to be to the Swedes when they realized all the implications of what had happened.

Ivar waited until his acolytes had left, then invited Jonah to join him in a bar.

"Are most days like yesterday, or are most days like today?" Jonah asked after they got mead from the dispensing machines and found a quiet table.

"Most days aren't even like yesterday," Ivar said. "Ninety-nine percent of everyone we see died." Five thousand years ago, most of the land was practically empty except for seacoast areas in China. So who was going to disappear? If it had been common, people would have remarked on it in records. He'd gone back to the Mount Toba eruption of more than seventy thousand years ago and tried to save any survivors after that. Nada.

Jonah said, "I'm glad we can't import millions of unskilled peasants into now-time."

"We can't even import hundreds of people who were heroic enough to become gods." Ivar didn't tell Jonah, but one of the things he'd learned from digging in time was that the poem Ketil Trout had recited that night wasn't true longer than a couple of generations in most cases. Egil lived on because memory was committed to words. Thousands of equally bold and aggressive men vanished from the world and time.

"So sometimes, you save an adulterous cunt or two."

"Adulterous women ... they are good for something, no?" Ivar said.

"Is this culture, the ways of now-time, going to be able to absorb all the past people you bring it?"

"I don't think we see the same now-time, Jonah. And the past we're fishing in isn't one thing."

"They're more like each other than they are like now-time," Jonah said.

"You can only say that because you came from close to now-time. People believe fewer different forces these days. The forces they believe in are more reliable at accomplishing real tasks. Plug in a metal halide lamp in midwinter, don't sacrifice, and wait for the sun to get over its sulk. It will come back more and more each day regardless of what you do."

"But maybe we've lost things that are important to know."

"My acolytes want me to save a religion that told us all gods and their enemies would perish but 'Life' and 'Eager for Life' would survive, two humans who hid rather than fought in Ragnarok. This is the post-Ragnarok world and we jumped through the world's last destruction."

"We Christians killed that world."

Ivar laughed. "I learned most of my religion from now-time data-bases. My understanding of my own religion was much less sophisticated. Or more so, given my grandmother. Gods are thoughts who get force from living in human minds."

"And those people expect you to revive Asatru?" Jonah laughed back.

"People can believe amazing things," Ivar said. "If you talk to enough people from enough different times, you'd figure that one out."

"Aren't you encouraging it?"

"What man kicks away those who think he's wise?" Ivar said. "But yeah, I do mess with their minds sometimes."

"The way people live now is so restricted," Jonah said.

Ivar wondered about the time before the plagues. By the standards of his past, now-time was pretty amazing. "Compared to what?"

"Compared to how the powerful lived when I was alive."

"Were you powerful?"

Jonah said, "I lived better than people do now, and was better educated than most in my time."

"You don't carry yourself like a man who was powerful. Is that why you played network tricks?"

"Power is relative."

"Power is getting fed, laid, and kept warm, and having fame and respect from those who matter to you," Ivar said, not quite sure he believed that. "Three hundred years ago, humanity lost a huge chunk of its population. The plague years might as well have been Ragnarok. The survivors did what they felt was necessary to keep from losing the tech they had, because they believed that without it they would descend to what they considered savagery. What they saved kept them fed, laid, warm, and gained them the respect of their neighbors. They wagered that those who survived could do more than the past authorities had believed average people could do. They won the wager, as crippled as this city might look to you."

"Maybe only the smart survived," Jonah said.

"Or only the cooperative survived," Ivar said, but he didn't completely believe that either. "Though that's also probably not the entire story. We can't know the entire story."

"So, why do you go fishing in the past for people?"

"Because it's a challenge. Because of what I learn."

"You don't have some need to save people?"

"That's for Benedetta and Pierre. Saving people."

"They want to convert people to Catholicism?"

"Nope. They believe that if we can save people, we should. But they're not working the machines; they specialize in talking to people afterward. China goes back to save Han from drowning. I go looking for the Norse. I don't know what New York goes looking for."

"How did you find out about China?"

"They bought a machine from your friends the smugglers. And then they needed some advice, both on the machines and on how to deal with people who'd been recovered."

"Man. Whoever sold the Chinese a time machine was stupid."

"You think it's dangerous for them to repopulate?"

"Exceedingly. Who sold the machine, my people or Mr. Wythe?"

"Probably Mr. Wythe, but your people are his people, or he is your people's man. Why do you say the Han are dangerous? We were the peril of the North in our day. People prayed that we stay home."

"You know, some of the very nasty technology, the atomic bombs and the missiles, must have survived."

"If it wasn't used during the plague years, why in the world would that war tech be used now?" Ivar was aware that he was drunk and had talked more to Jonah than he'd thought was wise.

"Because we're recovering from the plague years?"

"People are valuable now," Ivar said. "All of us."

"Not if the Chinese save a billion of their own people."

"If they do, they did. Now-time stays in the current time track."

"Where does now-time go?"

"To bed, now. You should ask your people why they sold the device to the Chinese without helping them with the programs to make an operational machine. I didn't give them anything they couldn't have figured out for themselves, but they were promised more."

"You don't know that they would have figured it out without you. Mr. Wythe wouldn't cheat people."

"Mr. Wythe is a smuggler and exploits the people he has rescued before he sold his machine to the Chinese. You know you can't know precisely what the Chinese needed to know. You didn't master the machine when we worked out its secrets." Ivar realized he'd lapsed into Norse and decided not to translate the last two sentences.

"Eventually, you'll get bored with fishing through time."

"I expect I will."

"Then what?"

"A farm in Bucks County, with a couple of women and farm machines. I'll have lots of sons." Ivar grinned at Jonah, sure that the city man had no conception of why a farm with modern machines and greenhouses instead of surly slaves and a winter full of whey-pickled meat and salty cheese would be so marvelous.

"Bah. Peasant. I thought you were a warrior."

"Farmer. We went to Iceland to be free farmers, not king's men."

"That was fifteen hundred years ago."

"A thousand years of sleeping through a nightmare." Ivar thought about the Norns who spun men's lives, and giggled at the idea of one of them spinning and spinning his to run over a thousand years, the ball of thread bigger than a house.

"You don't believe in your old gods. And you edit your past. Fifteen hundred years."

"Little parables. Learning requires sacrificing yourself to yourself even if you aren't Odin. Do you need a pedicab to get home? It's late." Ivar pulled out his phone and called James, a friend who was a pedicab driver—he'd been an English chairman in Bath before Ivar rescued him from drowning.

Ivar looked at the drink containers and knew he hadn't had any whiskey, just the mead. Jonah was, Ivar realized, much drunker than he was. They didn't say anything more to each other until the pedicab arrived, then the usual "Glad to see you again, come back. Sure. We should talk more often." Jonah looked happy to have a British English-speaking cabbie. The cabman looked worried. Did he fear a drunk's vomit in his cab?

"Fuckhead," Ivar said at Jonah's disappearing back.

Stir up trouble? Yes. No. With Jonah?

Mr. Wythe showed up the next day as if Jonah had relayed the Chinese business to his family and friends. Or not. Ivar waited to hear what Mr. Wythe was going to bring up. He'd come in his own transportation, because Ivar's circle of pedicab men hadn't phoned to let him know Mr. Wythe had been spotted. "Ah, Mr. Wythe," Ivar said.

"I'd like to hire you to rescue Owen Glendower as soon as possible."

"I know where he is. I know we will get him, so I figured I'd wait for a while. He's going to come up, why right now?"

"I want him as a personal favor."

Do I owe you a favor? Ivar thought. "Why do we need a Welsh rabble-rouser, or are you collecting people to go with your musical instruments and rides?"

"He speaks English close to Shakespeare's time and we know he's coming up."

"Eventually," Ivar said. "I thought you were here about Shanghai."

"The Chinese?"

"Yeah, someone sold them a time machine and suggested they get in touch with me when they couldn't work things out."

"Why would you think I was the one who sold them a machine?"

"You, New York City, us, the Kirkpatricks. Somebody. We didn't, or they'd have gotten the full instruction set." Some now-time people thought past people were simple, obviously not having read any of the sagas. "Was I supposed to get motivated to do something to fight the Eastern menace or something? They seem like saner people than most Europeans of my day. Why did you cheat them?"

"Well, I don't trust the Kirkpatricks. I didn't sell the Chinese a time machine. I only collect European relics."

"Do the Kirkpatricks trust Jonah?"

"They want him to do some rabble-rousing for them, but his legend was more that he created his own messes rather than organized. And they were pretty anarchic."

"As opposed to Owen Glendower?"

"We know he shows up eventually and organizes."

Ivar said, "You can go get him. You've got a one-man scoop and I'm sure you can do larger field-generation work." Mr. Wythe had lied to him about who sold the time machine to the Chinese, Ivar realized, or he would have gotten Owen Glendower out himself.

"I can't work the machine now. Someone must have infected the computer with a worm."

Or Mr. Wythe didn't have a time machine now because he had sold his to the Chinese. "Why do you want me connected with this? I don't speak his English or Welsh, so I need to get someone involved in this who can talk to him. In the 1400s." Ivar tried to remember if Benedetta knew English before she learned it in now-time. "So, it's not going to be a secret scoop. Benedetta and Pierre work with the city council."

"I can speak Welsh."

"Your name is close to Norse. You're not Welsh if that's a family name, so what's your game?"

"Must it all be plots?"

"If you're not plotting, let's wait until some of the plots have died down."

"What plots?"

"Jonah has been going everywhere looking for people who might be unhappy with now-time—me, you, Benedetta, a pizza seller. He's trying to be subtle about it, but Benedetta called me after he looked her up for a chat."

"My mother's people are Welsh. I want Old Wales back."

"Look, for me to be mystical about the Norse gods when I was seven made sense. I didn't have a computer, databases, libraries, comparative religious studies, or any language other than our dialect of Norse. For you to be craving so much of the past is just crazy. Violins, bicycles, crazy Welsh mystics."

"Owen Glendower wasn't a crazy mystic."

"Someone from the future said he'd be a great organizer in now-time. Do you even remember if that was someone from a future that evaporated or from the main-line future? I sure don't. 'Bring the Templars. Don't bring the Templars.' Whatever we did, we destroyed whole alternatives, people who existed in an alternative future that's either completely evaporated, as if it never was, or completely cut off from our time line. Would I even know if we disappeared? It would be like before I was born in this life, split between times. I can remember the past, but I've shaped those memories through what I've learned since. I can't remember my birth—though I was alive then. Bet you can't either."

"No."

"So, if we do something that cuts off a time line, was there any reality to the people in that time line?"

"I don't know."

"Why Glendower?"

"I've been promised stuff."

"And you can't tell them you sold your time machine to China."

Mr. Wythe didn't deny it this time, just shut his mouth and tightened his jaw.

"What did you get for my time machine?"

"Passage out if I need it. Vaccines, computer chips. Real silk. Bales and bales of it. I was going to trade the operating instructions for passage out."

"They must be seriously into rescue."

"They were the hardest hit of any continent."

"Oh. Why was Jonah so upset?"

"He sees them as a threat from his own time."

"They looked less Asian than Lucius from University City, so they must have bred with any survivors in Australia. And their politics can't possibly be the same now, either. Nobody's have stayed the same."

"Can you help me bring Glendower forward? As a personal favor."

"Can you make sure someone dies with me and burns when I die?"

Mr. Wythe looked shocked.

"Why should you be shocked? Everyone dies. Make it painless for the girl. I won't mind that."

"I can promise, but if death is death, you'll never know if I did it or not."

Ivar realized that was the truth and laughed a bit. "I don't know why going to the pyre alone bothers me. And I don't find going to the flames with everyone else who died that day in Philadelphia a suitable replacement as a comfort."

"I'll do this for you if your girl wants to die with you."

"We always had slaves choose to go. I have no kin to do this for me. And I don't know if you'll really do this."

"Only if the girl is willing."

Why not give him Glendower even if he was lying and would try to persuade the Chinese to rescue him despite trying to hold them up with the operating instructions. They'd have figured those out anyway. Philadelphia was happy to have Ivar speed their progress for some considerations that no one explained to Ivar.

"I'll bring you Glendower. Want any others?"

"Enough to attend to him properly."

"He'll be happier." Ivar wanted to go see the Swedes now, even if the language they spoke wasn't quite what he'd spoken as a child.

"I imagine you're the best one to talk about that. Thank you. We need color in this life."

"I'm not enough color?"

"You've assimilated, all except that last wish. Seeing you three years ago, then seeing you now, you've really changed. It probably was gradual for you."

"Perhaps I also grew up."

"You grew up here."

"I should ask something from you that's more now-time, I suppose."

"Old men go back to what they were as children."

"Will I live that long?"

"I think you will. You deserve to be an old man eventually. When can I get Glendower?"

"They make a strict accounting of people I bring forward now. Does that work for you? You couldn't take him home immediately. He'd have to go through orientation."

"Can you do it another way? I want to steer clear of the city council."

"I've got some stuff packed up. I'll put his coordinates on my handheld."

"Are they that concerned about who gets brought up-time?"

"They want to know who's coming up and I've been asked not to bring in any stone-hearted killers."

"Could you?"

"Stone-hearted killers? No, I wouldn't. Why do you want me to do this without the city knowing?"

"Oh, an old man's whim. And I'll promise to see you laid out properly and burned with a dead girl if it's my son or daughter helping. I'm amoral enough to honor that. You know anyone else who'd agree to this?"

"Maybe Jonah, but he'd say he would and then wouldn't. And I don't expect he will outlive me." Ivar now liked the idea of tricking the city council at least one more time.

He went to his locker and got his time-gear pack, and then leaned over the main computer and downloaded Owen Glendower's last known location in time and space into his handheld.

That night, he joined Mr. Wythe in a carriage pulled by real horses. The carriage had enough room for them plus three or four Welshmen. One or two more could ride on the top behind the driver.

"We get a number of horses, too, from time to time, but mostly they shy away from the flux." Ivar remembered getting, four months ago, a blind horse, whose rider had tried desperately to turn the horse away from the fog.

He called James and told him to leave the cab behind. "Where are we going?" he asked Mr. Wythe.

"The junkyard seems as good a place as any."

"Predictable. If some notice my gear is gone and people have noticed that I've been talking to you, that's the first place they'll check. What about up in the Wissahickon Park?"

Mr. Wythe nodded, and Ivar told the chairman to meet them there. Bath chairmen spoke a number of dialects of English, he'd found. Maybe not Welsh-accented London late–Middle English, but they'd have to see.

"He's educated," Mr. Wythe said.

Ivar nodded. Glendower was educated in laws that weren't used, in languages that had mutated since he was a boy, and that happened even in his own time. The English tried to portray Glendower as a Welsh mystic, a throwback to the pre-Christian Celtic times. Nobody who spent seven years in the Inns of Court as a boy was going to be that mystic.

Ivar said, "He's an old man. What kind of political organizing can he do that Benedetta and Pierre aren't already doing?"

"I'm more interested in who he was than what he could do in now-time," Mr. Wythe said.

Ivar wondered if Mr. Wythe would ever give him his first name, but felt it would be rude to ask. His chairman caught up to them and paced along beside the horses.

"Damn," Mr. Wythe said. "That man's fast."

"He was a chairman. In Bath, 1680s."

They turned up Forbidden Drive, which had been widened for coaches again after four hundred years, and drove up beyond the Valley Green Inn, which claimed to be over five hundred years old but looked like it had been rebuilt far oftener than the historical signs admitted. In the dark, Ivar spread the circuit plates and attached the wires, then began fishing for 1413, Wales. "I can go back and pull a lot of people out from the Battle of Shrewsbury if he needs friends."

Mr. Wythe was smiling. "I don't think it will be necessary."

Ivar got a fix on Snowdonia, and moved the flux up to a point where the trees stopped and a jumbled mess of rocks began. Mr. Wythe said, "It was all growing up in rhododendron before the plague."

Ivar thought it looked like Norway, just with more trees. The men on the track were running. Mr. Wythe said, "I can speak to them."

"Go for it," Ivar said, and he swung the flux uphill from the men. Mr. Wythe began yelling at them in what must have been Welsh. Ivar wondered if it was the right Welsh, or if border lords who learned English to advance themselves politically knew Welsh.

But they came running through the flux, six of them. *Something is wrong,* Ivar thought, before one of Glendower's men flattened him, and another put a sword against his cabman's neck.

"I take it you needed help you trusted to steal another of my machines," Ivar said, lying on his back with a cudgel in his face. "Fuckhead. Don't sell this one."

"Would you have just given me one?" Mr. Wythe asked.

"No," Ivar said. "Don't hurt James. James, stand down."

"I can take them."

"Not with a sword at your throat. Not worth it."

"Welsh mollies."

"That's an old insult I've only heard in the compound form," Mr. Wythe said. "Mollycoddlers."

"That, too," James said.

"James, calm down. Mr. Wythe, tell your little mob to let us go."

"You're not going to report me."

"Fuck you," Ivar said. "You know I can't."

"Precisely."

Ivar worked in his pocket slowly so the guy with the cudgel wouldn't smash him, fearing a knife. He showed Mr. Wythe his handheld. Mr. Wythe said, "Dead man switch?"

"GPS. We put some satellites back up. Set them in space about five minutes past now-time, geosynchronous orbit. And some other stuff I'm not going to tell you about."

The Welsh had never seen a handheld before. Since it didn't look like a blade, they hadn't seen it as a weapon.

Ivar cursed himself for not being more suspicious of Mr. Wythe, but fortune preserved a bit of suspicion in him. "Let James go."

Mr. Wythe said something in Welsh and the swordsman shoved James away. James didn't stagger, which seemed to have disconcerted the little gang a bit. Owen Glendower was the older man with them, obviously.

"You speak English, Glendower?" Ivar said in the oldest English he knew.

"Yes," Glendower said. The accent sounded strange.

"Did your Welsh-speaking friend explain where you were and when?"

"When?" Glendower looked around and spotted street lamps and frowned slightly. He looked back at both Mr. Wythe and Ivar. *Been running for your life too much to think lately, Glendower,* Ivar thought.

"Around nine hundred years later, and an ocean away."

"Witchcraft," one of the other men said. So, not all the men around Glendower were Welsh peasants who couldn't speak English. The man crossed himself. Ivar felt disgusted. More Christians.

"Keep the cudgel in his face," Mr. Wythe said. "He fears wood."

"I'm fucking outnumbered. And I didn't bring a gun."

James coughed slightly, but Mr. Wythe pulled his gun before James could pull his. The sword went back to James's throat. Mr. Wythe said, "Keep the cudgel on him. Tie the other one up. Pack up those things." He pointed at the circuit plates, the battery pack, and the wires.

James cursed them for being Catholic Welsh bastards.

"Pity you didn't learn Welsh," Ivar said.

"They couldn't afford Bath in my day," James said. "Not even as chairmen. Had to own your own chair."

Still energized from whatever had them running in Snowdonia, the Welshmen packed everything up and then tied Ivar with the checkreins from the horse harness.

Everyone knew that Ivar and James would be out of their bonds rather quickly, but Mr. Wythe probably had more surprises for the Welshmen when he transferred all this to something less obvious than a coach.

Ivar and James got back to Ivar's rooms sometime very late. Ivar was almost amused by Mr. Wythe's little game, but he knew the son of a bitch wasn't going to burn a girl for him when he died. He'd get Mr. Wythe for this.

From what he'd seen of Glendower, however, Mr. Wythe wasn't going to have a pet Welsh prince for all that long, either.

Wales in Secret

Mr. Wythe had stolen another time machine from Ivar and wanted Jonah to help him. Jonah wondered what his family wanted him to do.

"Yes, we wanted to buy that first time machine," Mitt said, "but he sold it to the Chinese. We knew that. What else have you learned?"

Jonah was somewhat miffed that Ivar, not his family, had told him Mr. Wythe had been dealing with the Chinese. "He had some people beat Ivar up over it, but Ivar doesn't think I had anything to do with it."

"I trust that you didn't have anything to do with it," Lizevidda said.

Jonah tried to put the facts he had in sequence. "Was that why Mr. Wythe was over for the party a few weeks ago?"

"We wanted to know why he'd stopped bringing people forward."

"The city council wants all newcomers to be registered, is what Ivar told me. They are processed through the Archives, free to go after things are explained to them in whatever language they understand."

"Why does the city council need to know who precisely is in Philadelphia?" Mitt asked. Jonah was aware that Mitt really knew the answer: New York didn't always have friendly intentions toward Philadelphia; people could come forward from five minutes in the past as well as thousands of years earlier; and communities needed additional services if their populations expanded. Beyond the practical reasons, the city council didn't want to see people brought in privately, in case anyone was going to try to revive slavery by not telling people what precisely had happened to them. The Archives had been just a bit too sneaky with the city, so the city wasn't going to allow anything like that again.

Mitt and Lizevidda wanted land beyond the farmlands that Philadelphia had either controlled or influenced for centuries. They hadn't explained much to Jonah, but he figured they wanted to import some people to work the land for them, maybe set up some light manufacturing, without any pesky civil-rights issues.

The three of them stopped talking for a moment. "What do you want me to do?"

"Find out what Mr. Wythe is up to. Ivar's pissed at him," Mitt said. "We'll see about helping if he's doing something useful."

"So, we need to New York, even, if necessary," Lizevidda said.

"But we'll handle that," Mitt said, looking hard at Lizevidda. Jonah tried to show the right level of concern. Talking to Mr. Wythe about what he was up to was busy work. He would talk to Mr. Wythe, though.

"Are you still looking for ways to disrupt now-time's social order?" Neither of them answered him.

But, since he liked staying with his descendants, he'd see what Mr. Wythe was up to. "Do you have Mr. Wythe's phone number?"

Jonah had some calls from Ivar, but didn't answer them, since he didn't know what revenge Ivar might be cooking for Mr. Wythe. Viking fought duels, didn't they? And raped their prisoners, men as well as women. *Not right now, Ivar,* Jonah thought as he went to see Mr. Wythe. He erased Ivar's message, not wanting to walk into Mr.

Wythe's compound with anything from Ivar. He thought a second more and erased Ivar's contact information from his database. He thought about a secure delete, but Mr. Wythe probably would have found absolutely no traces of Ivar in Jonah's handheld to be more suspicious. *Walk right in, sit right down,* Jonah thought. What did Mr. Wythe think he knew?

The junk heap was as large as ever, but the people boiling the gold out of the old computers looked like dwarves compared to most now-time people. Ivar was of people who'd been considered giants for their time, and he was about five-eight, shorter than Jonah. These people were shorter yet, dark-haired and dressed in embroidered wool that looked too fancy for the work they were doing. Ah, Mr. Wythe, did you get permission to be setting these people to this work?

Two men stopped him with bill pikes, talking to each other in yet another language that had been abruptly yanked from oblivion, no doubt. "Go 'way," one said.

"I'm here to see Mr. Wythe," Jonah said. "Mr. Wythe asked to see me."

A third man came up with a camera. Mr. Wythe obviously told them he was expecting Jonah. The first two men pulled their pikes upright. The pikes had a faintly Oriental look: long, tapered blades on the ends of long poles. Jonah followed the man with the camera.

"Let Rhys search you. I'll want to look at your phone, check for bugs."

Rhys was the man with the camera. He grinned at Jonah and said, "All the clods."

Jonah figured this meant "All the clothes." Rhys was Welsh, but Jonah wasn't sure when his accent had been current.

"You like it here?"

Rhys ran a scanner over Jonah's body, looking for radio waves, no doubt. He looked disappointed that Jonah wasn't transmitting.

After Jonah put his clothes back on, Rhys took him in to see Mr. Wythe in the little board-and-batten shack. Jonah wondered if Mr. Wythe had a better house somewhere else.

"Appears you've got a bunch of Welsh folks here."

"More off in the border country, where you were couple years ago."

"Does Baltimore have any objections?"

"Not since I sold them the time machine Ivar gave me."

"That doesn't appear to be Ivar's story, from what my kin told me. Have you ever considered just keeping one of the machines?"

"Too much demand for them," Mr. Wythe said. "Access to land is more valuable once you've got your population base."

"Welsh?"

"Yep," Mr. Wythe said.

"Owen Glendower?"

"Kind of an older man, like me, a bit older. Cynical after all that, grateful to be alive. Understands who his friends are."

"So what did you want me to do for you?"

"I'd like you to help us keep the city council off our backs. We bred another time-nut from the one we had, using coherent microwaves. So, I need the circuitry for it. The idiots in Shanghai won't help me. They owe me."

Jonah didn't know whether he should walk out of this and go to the city council and leave all the politics and time-jockeying to the people who really cared. But then, who'd take care of him?

"I'm just a script kiddy. I don't know anything."

Mr. Wythe said, "You copied the plans?"

"Yes."

"You gave them to your Kirkpatrick kin. So you can get the plans to me, too."

"Why didn't you analyze one of the machines while you had them?"

"We don't have anyone here really that good," Mr. Wythe said. "I tried."

"You mean a couple of teenagers were brighter than you and your experienced salvage crews."

"Unfortunately, yes. I underestimated Ivar in some ways."

"He's pissed as hell, I've heard."

"He tried to get in touch with you, your handheld says. You appeared not to have answered him. You erased his contact info about a half-hour ago. I thought he'd get over ..."

"... having his machine stolen? You've got to be kidding. He's a Viking heathen. He hated you before this, remember."

"He made me promise to sacrifice a girl and burn her with him when he died. He doesn't trust me?"

"So, what kind of blaze of glory is he planning? Or didn't he notice you were older than he was?"

"I considered the promise more like a test of my ability to accept him than a real promise."

"Had you already sold the machine before you stole it?"

"No. We sold it because we needed land."

"We?"

"The Welsh."

"Are you collecting a lot of mystical now-time yo-yos who want to be neo-primitive?"

"Ah ..."

"Ivar's got a little group of people who want him to tell them how to do blóts. He thinks they're nuts but lots of fun."

"Extrapolating from that, yes, you could guess that we've got a chunk of twenty-first-century neopagan Celtics as well as Welsh Catholics from Glendower's day. We need someone to explain them to us and us to them. I thought perhaps you could help us with that, too. Glendower thinks they're all possessed, when he's not making fun of them."

"Why don't you send them to the city council and the Archives, let them figure out what to do with them?"

"Archives don't care for twenty-first-century people. I get the impression they think your time was full of people too slick and cynical to be grateful for being saved, and way too prone to argue."

"Burn them as heretics."

"I get the impression that would not make up-time happy."

They went back outside and took Mr. Wythe's coach to a coal-burning truck and then rode that to above Harrisburg into the Valley and Ridge geological province. Glendower's men rode out to meet them, bringing horses. Jonah hadn't ridden a horse since he was a child visiting relatives, but maybe riding a horse was like riding a bicycle. And it was a tiny horse.

"We've got a better genetic base here with the twenty-first-century neopagan Celtics, too, and Glendower halfway understands why it might be a good thing."

"What do you want me to do?"

"Persuade your past-time people that it would be in their best interests to pretend to be Christians. Glendower has this thing about the Welsh being the first Christians in Western Europe, forced to conform to a later version of Christianity. I didn't think I'd be hearing about the Synod of Whitby as a mistake when all this began."

"They only had an independent Celtic Christian Church for what, three hundred years. They were pagans for way longer."

"Don't make that argument to Prince Glendower."

"Okay. Is he going to try to convert now-time to Celtic Christianity?"

"I don't think he really believes in any of it, but he really finds the neopagans offensive because they don't treat him like their prince."

"I never understood neopagans when I was alive the first time, so I may not be your man."

The little horse Jonah rode decided that it should be grazing right now, and ducked its head down. Jonah jerked at the bridle and the horse jerked back. One of the escorts laughed as he whacked the pony on the butt with a stick. The pony kicked at the stick, grazed for a while before it decided to get home fast.

Jonah wondered if he'd been given a particularly stubborn pony as a test.

They rode into a place with little round stone huts and a larger stone building with a timber roof—the prince's castle, though it was only two stories without windows, just slits for weapons, on the ground floor. The community was raising pigs and cattle, and had fenced off arable terraces going up from the stream that fed the Susquehanna. They'd found coal somewhere and were running forges and bloomeries to remake scrap iron that they'd collected.

All of Wales's history from the Neolithic to the Iron Age was on display in the valley, Jonah thought. He spotted the twentieth- and twenty-first-century neopagans by their height. Someone had set up a waterwheel and a stone mill. Jonah wasn't sure whether that was medieval technology being revived or the neopagans reinventing the overshot waterwheel.

"It's all very colorful," Jonah said. "I take it all of them find now-time offensive."

"Owen Glendower wants to go to Philadelphia and make sure that they will be allowed to live by their own laws here. New York would like him to be their ally. I'd like to keep Glendower independent of Philadelphia."

"Bet you, the city would be happy to leave them alone if they produced crop surpluses and didn't sell them to Baltimore or New York."

Mr. Wythe didn't say anything as they dismounted and left their horses with grooms. The first floor of Glendower's house was mostly an armory, with weapons even more diverse than the technology Jonah had seen coming into the valley. Someone had rigged big halogen lights over all this, but only three of the bulbs were burning, leaving the space a mix of glare and shadows. Bladed pikes and spears were racked against one wall. Carbon-fiber modern bows were stacked in a corner by the pikes and spears. Jonah spotted a crossbow or two. Tubs of arrows and quarrels were over on another wall. In the center of the room, right under one of the halogens, was a heap of semiautomatic rifles, ammo cases, and a couple of reloading presses. What did the neopagan Celtic woo-woo people think of the armory, Jonah wondered.

"What's the threat? And who got them modern weapons?"

"They will not be conquered again."

"Modern weapons in medieval Welsh hands. Holy fucking shit."

"I don't know what Ivar's got. Or what the city council has."

Jonah almost told Mr. Wythe that he was being paranoid about Ivar, but he remembered Ivar's chanting as he ran the trial of the first duplicate time machine, the archaic feel to that. Ivar wouldn't forget an insult. Still, he decided to lie again. "I think you're being paranoid."

"Prince Glendower doesn't ever want to be outgunned again."

"Did they even have guns then?"

"Cannons. They don't want anyone stopping them from developing this community. They've been led to believe Philadelphia is a threat."

"Seriously, this-level weaponry isn't going to make anyone happy to have them as neighbors. So, why did you bring them here and what do you get out of it?"

"A private army."

"Smugglers with private armies tend to attract way too much attention."

"I can share my resources with your family. That's the other reason I asked you to come here." They walked up to the second floor. Glendower liked electricity. His throne was surrounded by what looked like Christmas-tree lights, all blue. Jonah watched to see what Mr. Wythe did. A brief bow from the waist seemed to be adequate. Jonah bowed, thinking he could play this game. Glendower nodded curtly. He looked ancient and shriveled and very lonely. The English had killed most of his family, his wife and daughters and at least one of his sons. The surviving son refused a pardon until about a decade after the old man disappeared. No surviving family at all. Who was going to lead this community after Glendower died—or was he planning to sire a new family with some neopagan woman and let Mr. Wythe serve as his regent until the new prince was of age?

The plan seemed hopeless to Jonah—like setting up another Wales to fall to the domination of yet another larger power. Maybe they could play Baltimore and New York off against Philadelphia, but they'd tried to play France off against England back in the day, and France had left them dangling.

"We need to assure Philadelphia that we only desire trade with it," Glendower said. "We understand you know one of the people from my time who had contacts with the city council."

Benedetta? Pierre? What was the reputation of the Knights Templar in fourteenth-century Wales? Had to be Benedetta. "I know a priest of the Knights Templar and a woman who's been active in helping time refugees."

Owen Glendower had as good control of his face as Jonah had ever seen in any time, but Jonah knew that Glendower would cheerfully sell out Mr. Wythe if he thought this would protect his people better than the deal he got from Mr. Wythe. "We seek a peaceful solution."

Jonah wondered if Mr. Wythe had been stupid enough to sell them a small tactical nuke. Glendower knew how to sound dispassionately ruthless without saying anything nasty. "Yes, Your Highness." That was right for a prince, wasn't it?

Glendower looked at Mr. Wythe out of the corner of his eyes, a rapid jab of a glance. Yep, he knew Mr. Wythe tricked him into attacking Ivar and his cabman and sold the time machine to Baltimore. Jonah suspected that Glendower wanted more Welsh, real Welsh contemporaries, not the neo-Welsh neopagans, but Mr. Wythe had another deal to cut. And Baltimore had an alliance with New York, probably as a defense against being taken over by Washington, if Washington survived the plague years. The cities that survived seemed to have had good farmland near them—New York had Long Island, Philadelphia had Lancaster and Bucks counties. Both fought over New Jersey. Jonah needed to learn more about city-state politics.

Glendower said, "We shall master the current English and speak to the Philadelphia City Council. I hope that you can arrange this."

Mr. Wythe tried not to look surprised.

"I'll do what I can," Jonah said, wondering if this would be something that would throw now-time's political arrangements into disarray.

"Bring us the woman from our time."

Jonah realized that the speech had been rehearsed in Jonah's own dialect of English. A neo-Welsh type who spoke a dialect of English intermediate between Jonah's and now-time's came up to Jonah and said, "His Highness is serious about this. I don't think it's a good idea, but it's what His Highness wants. I'll go with you to help explain the situation to the city council."

Jonah asked, "How did you get here?"

"New York's time machines. They're trying to find plague survivors who almost died of other things, not going for the pre-plague past beyond the early twenty-first century. We would have died in a sailboat accident. I'm Jack Anderson. You?"

"Jonah Kirkpatrick. I would have frozen to death," Jonah said. "And you came here?"

"My family wasn't interested in living in New York, then or now."

"Neopagans, I presume," Jonah said.

"No, survivalists. Cities are still not good for human beings."

"So you joined the Welsh? You could have joined the Amish." Jonah suspected this character of being a New York agent, because the story sounded so bizarre.

"We're not anti-tech."

"You responsible for the metal halide lights over the armory downstairs?"

"No, we're responsible for the reloading presses. I knew where they were hidden."

Neopagan nuts, survivalist nuts, what next? Jonah figured Owen Glendower had to have been a bit of a survivalist himself. He doubted the city council was going to like having a small private army about fifty miles from the outlands.

Mr. Wythe said, "Benedetta would probably be your best contact. She's running for the city council to represent past time and has served an apprenticeship in government."

"I don't know if Benedetta trusts me."

"I need a safe conduct from City Hall," the survivalist guy who'd been sailing during plague time said. "The prince wants to talk to them but he wants to make sure he can speak as well in this English as he could in the court English of his day."

Mr. Wythe was hanging close to them. Jonah said, "I don't know if I can get you a safe conduct. You want to come in and take your chances. We can try for a safe conduct for the prince." He needed to talk to Jack without Mr. Wythe listening to them. Go to see Ivar first, he thought, and Mr. Wythe would hang back even if he tried to bug them.

As Jonah expected, Mr. Wythe didn't want to see Ivar, and Ivar had technical goodies that swept the bugs off them and fed Mr. Wythe some idle chatter while Jack and Jonah explained the situation to Ivar.

"Ah, why did you come to me?"

"To make sure we could talk without the smuggler listening."

Ivar looked at Jonah as though wondering why Jonah was there then. Jonah shrugged. Ivar said, "Jonah's from another set of smugglers."

"We had to start somewhere," Jack said. "Can you introduce me to the city council or do I need to speak to Benedetta da Milano?"

Ivar said, "Benedetta could probably help. I don't know if she knows your man's English or Welsh, though. Pierre might help."

"I know you'd rather I didn't come along," Jonah said.

Ivar said, "I don't care. Someone has to explain things to Mr. Wythe. Next time I see him, his ass is mine."

"You trust me?"

"You've never pulled crap on me, Jonah, so I'll trust you until you do."

Jonah didn't take that where he could have taken it, but he

wasn't sure how Ivar felt surrendering in an ambush brought about by trickery compared to losing a one-on-one combat. And he had trolled Mr. Wythe into mistrusting Ivar, though the theft would have probably gone down the same without that. Ivar wasn't just going to turn over a time machine to anyone.

They met with Benedetta and explained the situation to her. She wasn't really happy to hear about Welsh colonists that near Philadelphia owing New York and smugglers for help, but thought that she could get them a hearing with the city council.

Two hours later, the city council convened in session to talk to Jack and Jonah. Benedetta, Ivar, and Jonah decided the less Mr. Wythe was mentioned the better.

Jack said, "The prince would like a safe conduct to talk to you."

A somewhat Asian-looking councilman, who was in his thirties, asked, "What, basically, does he want?"

"He wants to build a Welsh colony to the west of Philadelphia and establish trade. The Welsh were cattlemen and later good mechanics and miners."

A councilwoman said, "The Amish will have to be okay with this."

"How's the place to be governed? Royal families rot in time," Benedetta said.

Jack looked like he wanted to argue with that. Jonah wanted to argue with that, too. Good breeding was careful breeding. A family that paid attention to the people they brought into the family could last centuries without becoming feeble. But princes were flattered in ways that might have cost them their good judgment. Nothing better for people than stable rule by someone who worked more for glory and being honored than for looting his subjects with no thought to future generations of his family.

A cynical memory from one of his brothers countered this: *We were just middle-class men educated beyond our stations in life, not really upper class.*

Another person said, "We could let them run such a culture as an experiment. People who don't like our way could see if they'd fit in better in a more hierarchical government."

"Few volunteer to be peasants," the Asian councilman said. Benedetta nodded.

Jack said, "Prince Glendower, at this point, has no heirs." Jonah wondered if Jack's family included any nubile daughters who'd be willing to sleep with an old prince from the past. Someone's family might have those ambitions. He didn't envy Glendower if the old prince wanted to continue his line. Perhaps someone could fake a pedigree if necessary—how gullible was Glendower? Jonah tried to remember whether the Welsh kingships descended through the maternal line or not. Jack continued, "Glendower is prince of Wales by proclamation, not by birth. New Wales would be a meritocracy. Glendower married a woman who was part English and part Welsh. He has no hate for blood or breeding."

Mr. Wythe must have done some coaching, Jonah thought, even if the old smuggler wasn't welcome at this meeting. Selected as prince by his peers sounded better to the city council. Meritocracies were the very soul of how things worked now.

The city council agreed to give Owen Glendower a safe conduct to come before it to propose the founding of an outland community that would be governed by the laws of Hywel Dda.

Jack led the city council to understand that all the Welsh and neopagans had been brought in by Mr. Wythe, who had misled them in ways that he was going to let the prince explain. Jonah looked at Ivar, who looked back at him without giving anything away in his face. Jack hadn't mentioned the New York connection. Jonah wondered if all the neopagans were spies or just some of them.

When they got back to the Welsh encampment, Mr. Wythe appeared to be otherwise engaged. Jonah wondered if Glendower figured that selling out Mr. Wythe would be prudent.

Glendower came into town riding a white horse, dressed in silks, which had to have been smuggled in from China. The silks were brocade and trimmed in fur. The prince wore a gold band on his head, not a crown exactly. He had only changed to silks and horse for the last couple of miles into Center City.

His honor guard had found an old diesel-burning Mercedes and a Land Rover and enough oil to run from the Welsh encampment to Philadelphia. Jonah rode in the car, thinking that he hadn't been in an internal-combustion private car since he found himself in now-time. The horse rode in a trailer until they were at 30th Street Station, then Glendower changed to his silks, not bothering with privacy, though no doubt people from various factions were watching. He had help getting on the horse, which appeared to be used to riding in trailers rather than being ridden by an old man in silk. The horse was a large modern horse, not a tiny medieval one.

The Mercedes crept behind the horse for the trip down Market between Thirtieth Street and City Hall. Jonah wondered what they'd do with the horse when Glendower went in to talk to the city council. Someone would hold it or they'd sacrifice it. Who knew?

Jonah watched Glendower's back from the rear, and the horse swishing its tail in irritation when various children got too close. At City Hall, Glendower dismounted and handed the horse's reins to one of the men who'd ridden in the Mercedes.

Ivar and Benedetta were waiting to show Glendower up to the

council rooms. Jonah followed behind Glendower. He wondered what the city council thought about all the pomp, if they'd expected it.

City council members were wearing clothes that looked like a cross between clerical garb and officers' uniforms in navy blue. Everything was well cut; they made Glendower's silks look tatty.

Glendower nodded to the city council members, looked as if he was expecting bows back. City council members rose for him, but didn't bow.

One of Glendower's men held a white flag with a golden dragon on it beside Glendower. "My lords and ladies of the council, Prince Owen Glendower," the man with the dragon banner said. Glendower stood, legs slightly spread, right arm at his side and his left arm holding his right elbow.

"You have a request for us," one of the councilwomen said.

"We would like an alliance between the City of Philadelphia and our community beyond Harrisburg, which I understand is a property of the City of Philadelphia," Glendower said.

"We understand that you made initial alliances with New York and Baltimore," the somewhat Asian councilman Jonah remembered from the last meeting said. "This wasn't wise, but you may have had bad advice."

Jonah wondered what the city council knew about the Kirkpatrick operation. Not that smuggling was bad, just that untoward allies might be a problem.

"We were snatched from our proper time and did not have any understanding of now-time. We want only to have a community of like-minded people, to trade peacefully with the City of Philadelphia." Glendower looked around the room, his face impassive. He didn't look like the impulsive young man who'd raised the Welsh dragon flag because he felt slighted by the English. He looked like someone who'd figured out the hard way that he was on his own, that Philly was closer than New York and perhaps better armed.

Ivar grinned once and looked at Jonah, who wondered if Ivar was himself in a position to make difficulties for Glendower.

One of the councilwomen said, "The Amish insist on this group staying on the other side of Harrisburg and not interfering with their fields and cattle."

Jonah wondered if the Amish of now-time were still pacifists or how they were going to enforce this.

"We will agree to this," Glendower said. Jonah wondered if most of this was as much show on the council's side as on Glendower's and the whole thing was scripted before Glendower rode into town.

"In the future, you will testify as to what you know about the dealings of the man known to you as Mr. Wythe."

Glendower looked at Ivar again, and Ivar grinned again. Glendower asked, "Has he been captured?"

"Not yet."

"He lied to me. I will testify. We had not been told all the alliances and enemies of this new place."

"Mr. Wythe would have misrepresented them. If you've got mechanics among you, perhaps you would allow your people to work the salvage yards. We can train your people."

Jonah knew the Welsh didn't understand toxic chemicals. Excellent choices—get rid of Mr. Wythe, keep the old-time crews he'd brought forward, and add a bunch of Welshmen.

Glendower said, "We need to ask one of those you'd sent to us a few questions." The council exchanged a few glances, and then one called for a voice vote. They all agreed.

Oh boy, I am getting dragged into this, Jonah realized when Glendower came toward him and asked, "Is this a good deal for us?"

"The work is dangerous, but the hazards can be managed," Jonah told him. "Make sure they allow you to get a time machine and bring more people forward."

Glendower nodded. He turned back to the city council and said, "We wish to get a time machine to add to our numbers. We understand that the work you've asked our people to do is dangerous."

"Do you know where we can find Mr. Wythe?"

Glendower dropped the royal plural. "I don't know." He looked like he remembered the realities of being a pawn in larger games. Time's passing hadn't changed that. He looked back at Jonah, a huge amount of sorrow and mistrust in that glance. *Whom do I belong to?* Jonah thought.

Ivar grinned again, another flash of teeth.

Someone called for order, and then the council went into executive session. Jonah noticed that Benedetta was allowed to stay in the session, but not Ivar.

Glendower said, "Now I put away the flag." He didn't want to let Ivar get too close, Jonah noticed. At lunchtime, Glendower and his honor escort pulled out baskets of smoked trout and walleye, onions, and cheese. Ivar looked like the food was familiar, but so were a couple of the men. Ivar didn't get close to them.

Jonah said, "Ivar, let's have lunch somewhere else."

Glendower said, "No, I want to apologize to him for stealing his time machine. Would you want it back?"

"No, I want Mr. Wythe. You were tricked. Are you good at getting tricked?"

Glendower's face flushed with blood, as did that of the man who'd put his cudgel in Ivar's face months earlier. Ivar smiled and relaxed. Glendower said, "Is this done?"

"I can give you a time machine as long as the city council allows you to have it," Ivar said. "I'm gracious and forgiving. But I want Mr. Wythe before the city council gets him."

Glendower understood that he was being insulted as payback, and seemed to be willing to accept the insults in that light. He looked at Jonah and shrugged. "If I can help you, I'll do it. I don't like people lying to me about who my enemies are."

Ivar said, "Thank you." He reached for one of the smoked trout and a piece of cheese. Glendower seemed to recognize this as feeding social needs, not just hunger. Jonah felt sorry for Mr. Wythe, who would obviously be better off in the city council's hands than in Ivar's. "May I ask a boon from you?" Ivar said, after eating some of Glendower's food.

"I may not be able to grant it," Glendower said.

"I'd like to borrow your cudgel man when I hunt Wythe."

The cudgel man understood what they were saying and grinned widely. He nodded at Glendower, who waved his hand in a scoop from the man toward Ivar. My man is your man, the gesture said. "He didn't like being tricked either," Glendower said.

Jonah wondered if the men intended this discussion to get back to City Hall. He also wondered if Mr. Wythe had some inside tracks that nobody was aware of yet.

After the executive session and everyone's lunch, they went back inside. Glendower told his standard-bearer to leave the dragon flag in the car. As Glendower and his followers came in, Benedetta, sitting behind one of the councilwomen, leaned forward to whisper in her ear.

Jonah felt isolated from both Ivar and Benedetta now, and aware that the survivalist Jack Anderson and his family weren't with Glendower's escort. They were New York's people, then, as Jonah had suspected, and gone home to report they'd lost an ally or two, or were in Philly's Roundhouse waiting for a spy exchange if they did that in these days. Benedetta had become Philadelphia establishment, which probably was what she really wanted all along: to belong to a power clique. Ivar was what Jonah had hoped to be, a person whose ideals couldn't be pinned down. Jonah wondered if he was too old to be a good troll.

Glendower said, "Cheer up, young fellow. You're still alive." He then asked permission to speak to the council again. Once they said yes, he began speaking. "When I came here, I represented Wales in exile, but realized after seeing the city how far away I've brought my people. We want to be educated in your time. I'm not using the royal *we* of a ruler speaking for his nation. I, too, have much to learn here. I wanted to build two universities in Wales when I was in my time. I understand from Jonah Kirkpatrick that the work you would like us to do has some hazards. We will do this work for university education in your time for ten of our young people a year. Of those, three must come back to teach us.

"At this time, none of us share your skills or know much of the science that brought us here, but we see people from further back in the past mastering the skills I want to see my young men and women master. Much of the ways of people is still the same—the small nations then are equal to the small communities now. We are caught between the larger communities that have as much population as whole large nations had in my day. I was rash then to stir Wales to rising and to expect the help of the pope and king of France. So here I am, an old man who has saved some of those who followed him. We want to find a way to become our modern selves without doing violence or denying what and when we came from. Education then was my dream for improving the lives of my people. Education now is critical for bringing my people all the way to now-time as quickly as may seem good to you. Humanity almost died. We want to rebuild humankind, not just a future new Wales. Thank you."

"You'd trade the work for the schooling for your young, then?" the woman who sat in front of Benedetta said. If she knew much about Benedetta and Ivar, she'd know that brains hadn't evolved in several thousand years or maybe even in twenty thousand years. Culture allowed men to survive stupidity.

"Yes," Glendower said.

"What if after they're educated, they want a representative or communitarian government, not a prince?"

"The farm folk need to be educated to know better how to manage their lives. None of us, neither you nor I, has power more than people are willing to give us. That's always been so."

Someone sitting behind another councilman muttered, "Son of a bitch."

The councilman who looked vaguely Asian asked, "Would your people be willing to defend Philadelphia against its enemies if any future negotiations fail?"

"I can pledge for my people as long as I'm prince of the community. If your education cannot hold our loyalty, then you must press your cause in other manners. As you knew when you shot down the helicopter that was trying to kill the people who recreated time machines, a display of arms has a certain effect."

Benedetta's mentor leaned back and talked too quietly for Jonah to make out any of the words. Then she leaned over to the swarthy councilman beside her. Glendower stood watching them. Jonah couldn't figure out whether Glendower had threatened Philadelphia in some slanted way, telling them that if anyone came along with even better arms, then Wales community would be foolish not to switch sides. Or whether Glendower had simply thrown like a girl.

"We'll vote now."

The civilians walked out again. It was about three o'clock. Ivar and Glendower talked about swords, smiths, and horses. Jonah wondered if Ivar had ever had any real experience with bloodshed as a

Viking teenager, or if he'd merely been the boy back at the boats. Glendower sounded like he'd found out that skill couldn't beat numbers except for a short while. Jonah thought Glendower had some things to learn about technology, though.

At four, the city council gave Glendower the dump heaps, five language teachers, and permission to keep a time machine as long as he registered those he saved with Philadelphia.

Glendower bowed to the city council, a bow from the hips with his hands sliding down his legs, an old man's bow. Jonah looked at Ivar and Benedetta. Ivar smiled his little crescent-moon smile with the corners of his lips upturned. Benedetta was too busy talking to her councilwoman mentor to notice Jonah.

The white horse went back in the trailer. Glendower rode in the back seat of the Mercedes with Jonah. "I thought about changing to a suit of now-time clothes tailored as the councilmen's suits were tailored, but thought that would be too obvious. Leaving the banner behind and speaking as the local spoke was the right touch."

Mitt and Lizevidda, who'd been watching on net TV, saw right through all the display. "Kings. Can't trust them at all. They'll sell out their nobility and good families to the peasants in a nanosecond," Lizevidda said.

"He was quick to sell out Mr. Wythe, too," Jonah said, not sure where his loyalties should lie in the future.

A Future Takes Care of Mr. Wythe

Ivar watched the once and future prince of Wales leave. The horse went on a trailer; his loaned cudgel man stayed behind. Ivar didn't know if the man spoke now-time English or something Benedetta or James knew, but he waved his hand in a "follow me" gesture and the man understood.

"Do you speak any English?"

"Little. Tell me who to hit."

"Hit the man who stole from me. Understand?"

The man nodded.

"Now we have to find him," James said.

"That's easy. Some people from one of the futures have told me where he's going to be." He handed James a scrawled map.

"Right bastardly of them," James said, holding the map in his hand, memorizing it, then tucking it in his shirt pocket.

"Can you fit both of us in your pedicab?"

"And make good time, too." James unlocked the cab from the cabstand. The cudgel man got in. Ivar wondered if the man could use something more than a staff, but a nice hardwood cudgel could do a reasonable amount of damage, and the man might not be as good with his reflexes if there was a blade he wasn't used to, on top of his staff.

Ivar wasn't sure he shared Jonah's fear that this was all a game played by the various future times, but didn't know why any future would turn Mr. Wythe over to him. *Fuckheads,* he thought, remembering Jonah's term. Or perhaps they had motives beyond any a ninth-century Viking boy could understand. Mr. Wythe represented all that was treacherous about this time. Ivar felt frustrated being on the outside scrabbling to catch up, both being grateful for his life and resentful of how much he'd lost.

Poor Wythe, if some future really betrayed him. Poor him, if that future was tricking him. He sat rigidly in the pedicab, one hand moving between a gun in a belt holster to a dagger dangling beside it, the other gripping the side of the pedicab.

The cudgel man looked at him nervously. James kept pedaling, cursing anyone who tried to cut him off. They went up Broad Street, then over on Gerard toward the Delaware River. Ivar saw signs that people had been clearing away the old houses and planting crops here. A small boy ran in front of the cab. James swerved, and turned down one of the side streets. Ivar put on a Kevlar vest and pulled his hair back and banded it with sticky tape to keep it out of the way. They turned up Fletcher Street. Ivar put a Kevlar vest on the cudgel man and said, "Back door. Keep from running out." They chained the cab to a streetlight that had long since lost its bulbs, wires, and electronic components. James didn't look happy about leaving it behind, but pulled his pistol out of his fanny pack. Ivar and James made sure they had spare magazines, made sure they had chambers loaded. The three nodded at each other, and then walked quietly through the backyard. Ivar pointed to the door to guard. Then he and James circled around to the front of the house on East Colona.

The houses here all were tiny two-story houses, mostly abandoned. Mr. Wythe had probably found this one when he sent scavengers out. Unlike the others, it had shutters, closed now downstairs. Ivar wondered if he and James were walking into an ambush.

James had a lockpick set and worked on the lock. Ivar touched his dagger. Daggers were useless if Mr. Wythe had a gun, but then guns were useless if Mr. Wythe was crouched behind a solid ironwood stove or cast-iron tub, or even behind a solid piece of furniture or was wearing body armor. Daggers could slice.

Ivar wondered if a troll future had set up an ambush for him rather than for Mr. Wythe. In his memory, Jonah said, "It's all a game." Ivar went in the front door and saw the cudgel man at the opposite end of the building at the backyard door, waiting. Mr. Wythe's house was empty on the first floor, with a clear view front to back through the two rooms, but Ivar heard voices upstairs. A face in blue flux materialized to his left and put its finger to its lips. *Be quiet.* Ivar shrugged, as that was obvious. The face disappeared. Ivar slid his shoes off, walked through the house in stocking feet, slowly twisted the lock knob, and quietly opened the back door. The Welshman came in. Glad that the blue flux had disappeared before the Welshman saw it, Ivar put his finger to his own lips. James held his pistol pointed at the floor, the index finger off the trigger. Someone had trained him, Ivar realized. He held his own gun the same way.

One set of stairs up, with a turn in them, so Ivar couldn't see to the second floor. Windows to the outside where the stairs turned. Ivar didn't trust the stairs not to creak, not to give warning electronically.

"Come up, Ivar," Mr. Wythe called.

Damn. What game was the future playing? He looked at James and the Welshman.

"Why?" Ivar called up.

"The future is waiting."

"A future." Ivar's heart started beating faster.

James said, "A trap?"

Ivar said, "I have no idea."

Then they heard voices again. Mr. Wythe said, "They want me to come down to you, Ivar."

Ivar shrugged. He held his gun pointed halfway between level and at the floor. James raised his gun slightly, too. James looked like he'd used a gun in this way before. Ivar felt good to see that. Cabmen, chairmen—they had money and had to find some way not to be easy targets.

"Come down, then."

"I don't know if I trust them."

"That makes two of us."

"They said they'd save me from you."

"They gave me this street address. I'm here."

"Ah, yeah. I wonder if I'm bait for you."

"In what way?"

"To make their future the real one."

"I've got friends with me. You have any with you?"

"Can we cut a deal?"

James rolled his eyes. The Welshman might not have understood all of this, but he knew what the rolled eyes and the tones were, and giggled.

Ivar said, "You could jump through the window and take your chances with the city council."

"I've got some things you might want."

"Nice asshole."

"Ah, what?"

"I'm not going to kill you. Trust me on that."

"Word of honor?"

Ivar said, "Word of honor."

"Can you help me escape? Are we going to have an official honor duel?"

"Something like that." Ivar looked at James who was grinning. Ivar told himself that he had not sworn anything.

"First blood is enough?"

"Oh, sure," James said. Ivar heard more voices and saw a faint blue. The Welshman started as the blue got thicker.

"Steady," Ivar said. "Steady." He hoped the tone got through if the man didn't understand the words.

The man stared at the blue, then at Ivar and James. He seemed to be wondering, what the fuck is this? Ivar was also wondering.

As Mr. Wythe started down the stairs Ivar couldn't see, one of the faces said, "Put the guns up."

Ivar laughed. "I trust you like I'd trust my last thralls if I saw them again."

Someone said in Norse, "Put the fucking fire sticks away."

"Nobody's saying we can't grab him," James said.

"Ivar said Mr. Wythe's ass was his," the face said.

The Welshman's eyes were huge now. If he weren't holding that stick for dear life, Ivar thought, he'd be crossing himself. Ivar said, "I'm not going to shoot him unless he tries something."

Mr. Wythe stayed just around the bend in the stairs. "Please, Ivar. I'm sorry I tricked you. Jonah told me I couldn't trust you. Can we have a duel and put this behind us?"

Jonah could have done that. Ivar remembered the futures grabbing out to stop people when he stole the time machine. He handed his pistol to James. James put both pistols back in his fanny pack but swung the pack around to his belly. The cudgel man moved to lay his cudgel aside, but Ivar shook his head.

As Mr. Wythe came down the stairs, Ivar went up on the balls of his feet. Out of the corner of his eye, he saw James shift his hips and knees. Boom. They tackled Mr. Wythe, who tried to get his hands free.

"You promised."

The blue fog came back. Several people were watching. "His asshole is yours," a voice said. Ivar realized they expected him to rape

Mr. Wythe. No, they wanted him to rape Mr. Wythe. The fight was giving him an erection. He could.

Mr. Wythe got a hand free and slugged Ivar in the nose. Broken, fix later, Ivar thought. Broken noses bled more than they hurt. The Welshman nailed Mr. Wythe on the wrist—hard—then hit the other hand for good measure. Something cracked.

The blue flux intensified. "They're watching this. Bet they're wagering on it," James said.

Mr. Wythe squirmed around. "I got first blood. It's over. I won."

The voices in the blue flux said, "Rape him, Ivar. He's lying about Jonah setting you up."

Mr. Wythe lunged for Ivar with his teeth, then whipped his head out of the way as the Welshman raised his cudgel again.

"Can you use lubricant?" Mr. Wythe said, in an almost conversational tone of voice. He went limp.

Thinking about all the people expecting this, Ivar went soft. He thought about the girl slave who'd volunteered to die with his kinsman, fucking them all before her throat was slit. He thought about Benedetta, about the first now-time girl he'd bedded. "I'm not that Ivar anymore." He hauled Mr. Wythe to his feet, jerked him once to get his muscles to hold him upright.

"James, call the patrol for Mr. Wythe," Ivar said, blood from his nose still dripping down his neck.

Mr. Wythe said, "I can pay you well if you help me escape. Didn't you promise you'd help me escape? You're going to be making enemies you don't know about."

Ivar shook his head. The men in the blue fog winked out one by one, then the fog held one man.

"Ivar, are you satisfied?" The voice again spoke Norse.

Ivar said, in the same language, "No."

The fog vanished.

James said, "I don't like people who trick people and steal from them. Getting robbed is an occupational hazard in my line of work, and I believe in making people pay for it."

Ivar motioned for the cudgel man to take hold of Mr. Wythe, who seemed almost ready to faint. Ivar reached up for his nose. Still bleeding.

James said, "Might want to put some flexible straws up when we get you back home, sir. We didn't have those for prizefighters in my day, but I've helped afterward with dogs and men both."

The watch came in a van. They knew who Mr. Wythe was, knew who Ivar was, and didn't ask about how Ivar found Mr. Wythe. Mr. Wythe seemed tiny and old as the watch took him away in chains. They asked Ivar if he needed to go to a clinic, but Ivar shook his head gingerly no. He wanted to be with James and the cudgel man for a while.

I destroyed a mean future, Ivar thought, *by refusing to live up to their expectations.* He didn't want to believe in alternative futures where he followed through.

James and the cudgel man chased off two kids who were trying to saw through the cab's chain. Then James pulled out a blanket and wrapped Ivar in it. The cudgel man seemed slightly disappointed about something. Ivar thought he should feel vindicated or at least better, but he didn't.

"Putting him in gaol was proper revenge," James said.

"Terrific," Ivar said. The cudgel man went home with them and curled up on a blanket beside Ivar's bed while James tended to Ivar's nose.

"I can take him back to his lord in the morning after we've all eaten. I'll need something for doing that, though, if he needs a cab all the way."

Ivar waved his hand around, not talking as James pushed and pulled at his nose before he taped splints on either side of it.

"Now-time medicine couldn't have done you better," James said.

"If gold chunks would be of use to you, I've got a couple. And I can provision you in the morning. Or you could take the train out with him and call the Welsh community to come and get him."

Ivar felt dizzy, lying on the bed. James shut the door behind him. Even asleep, the Welshman gripped his cudgel. Ivar unloaded his gun and put the clips up. He was glad he was flying to Iceland in a few days—away from all this.

Before he and James could get the Welshman back to his master, Benedetta and Pierre showed up, asking him if he would make a deposition against Mr. Wythe before he left for Iceland. The bulk of the evidence was coming from the Kirkpatricks, who'd turned council evidence. New York was even offering some information in trade for more commerce between the two cities.

James said, "I'll fix breakfast for us. You go out with them."

Benedetta and Pierre took Ivar to a restaurant that served various porridges for people from various times. Ivar realized that he missed Benedetta and wondered if she'd been avoiding him. Neither would have approved of the rape if he'd done that, but possibly both would have felt quick, harsh physical punishment was better than being behind bars for months or years.

Pierre said, "What happened to your nose? Have you had medical attention?"

"Mr. Wythe. Faces in a blue flux wanted me to rape him."

Benedetta and Pierre looked at each other sharply. Pierre said, "And you couldn't. Could you have ever?"

"In the past, I could have, if I'd stayed there. I don't know."

Benedetta and Pierre spoke in Latin to each other. Ivar resented this, but he'd bruised himself on someone's dream of him as the mad Viking rapist and wasn't in the mood to fuss with them.

"Looking forward to finally arriving in Iceland?" Benedetta said.

"Yes. No matter how many years have passed, something of my people must have survived in the culture there."

"You think?" Pierre said.

"I keep meeting people here who worship the old gods," Ivar said.

"No continuity," Pierre said. "Not really."

Benedetta said, "We want to have someone make sure New York isn't still influencing our Welsh friends."

"Send the neopagans away. I'm not sure what I think now of my neo-Asatru who snuck in from New York to hear Norse lore from me. Blóts. Sacrifice. They haven't tried to reach me since Glendower swore allegiance to Philadelphia."

"You didn't tell us about that earlier. They were sneaking in? Why did you trust them? Do you trust Jonah?" Benedetta sounded almost exasperated with Ivar, which made him feel lonely.

"No. Do you trust me?"

"What would have become of you if you had gotten to Iceland in your past, Ivar? You're gifted in skills we can use now. I don't think they had a place for a computer programmer, much less a time tech, then," Pierre said.

"So the Norns send me to Iceland now. They can use my skills now."

"Seventeen families survived the plague years in Reykjavik. Couple dozen more people here and there. Some Eskimos left Greenland and ended up there," Benedetta said. "They're inbred as hell even with the Eskimo blood. Yes, they want more genetic material, but they'd be better off abandoning Iceland and joining a community with a wider genetic base."

"Tell me, why does Philadelphia still let me bring people forward?"

Benedetta said, "We argue about that in the city council all the time. Some of us believe that we should save anyone we can."

"My position," Pierre said.

Benedetta said, "I understand the morality of that position, but I'm beginning to see some problems with bringing too many people in too fast."

"Sometimes, we can't save anyone," Ivar said. "We can see them and they just die. We can't help them and we can't give them quick deaths to put them out of their pain."

"We have to try to save them," Pierre said.

"Priest, you don't watch what I watch, day after day."

"But you save people anyway."

"It's a puzzle for me, but today, I'm tired. I think I destroyed a future that wanted me to rape Mr. Wythe, which wanted me to be their fantasy Viking. I'm tired of being people's fantasy Viking."

"You're not my fantasy Viking," Benedetta said.

Ivar shrugged. He wondered what loyalties he owed any of them, to Benedetta for getting him out of the Archives, to Jonah for getting Benedetta out. Pierre owed him for saving him, but Pierre probably gave his god all the credit. "You seem to be doing well, Benedetta. Now-time made use of your skills better than your own time did, didn't it?"

"We're all better off," Pierre said.

Ivar said, "Not dead, which was the alternative. Do you still believe in your god?"

Pierre said, "I don't know if I believe in the same way. Do you believe in your gods?"

"As metaphors, as ways to focus the mind," Ivar said. "But they were that for my grandmother even in my time."

"The future that betrayed Mr. Wythe was one of the reality bubbles off in the fringes," Pierre said. Ivar realized Pierre's faith didn't quite know how to factor in disappearing alternatives in various timelines. Ceasing to be wasn't like dying. Suddenly, the fame you thought you were leaving to the memories of your people evaporated with people who'd ceased being, without even a whimper, much less Ragnarok. The universe proved to be a cold place with small temporary lumps of fusion reactions circled by planets too hot or too cold for life. The one known exception existed in bubbles of alternatives that actions and even thoughts pricked into nonexistence one by one.

His people's vision seemed closer to the real than Pierre's, but the real was even bleaker than the most pessimistic Norse skalds imagined. Human futures were boxed possibilities that events obliterated or released. Everyone who wasn't obliterated by a time change died anyway.

"Send us messages from Iceland," Benedetta said. "I want to see more of you and Jonah. Now has been good for me, but I keep thinking about you two, and the days at Three Mile Island."

"The months at Three Mile Island," Ivar said. "Skateboards and atomic-force microscopes—I was younger then than I'd been on the ship going to Iceland."

"Better fed, healthier, and more mentally stimulated," Pierre said. "I've also felt younger, even if the torture did permanent damage."

Benedetta said, "I've felt that I finally found a place that works for me, only I'd like someone to share it with."

Ivar looked at Pierre and wondered why he'd failed to set up housekeeping with Benedetta, then saw how Pierre was looking at him. Oh. Then he said to Benedetta, "You're not asking, are you?"

"Ah, not really, just thinking out loud. You look sad, Ivar."

"Sort of. What is the city council going to do to Mr. Wythe?"

"Rusticate him without his toys," Pierre said. "He'll be tagged and watched by those satellites you put up in orbit. If he tries to play games with New York again, we'll know. We don't trust New York, but all through this, New York and Philadelphia keep the network up between them."

"What had Mr. Wythe been smuggling?"

"The usual: cigarettes, coffee, tea, silk, other drugs, plus he was selling gold and technology to New York and China, not just the time machines. Breach of quarantine laws," Benedetta said.

"Who gets his stuff?" Ivar asked.

"We've already given some of it to the Welsh. They're happy to have it. We're talking to China about importing silk legally now that they've got the robot ships going."

"What happened to François Villon?" Ivar remembered Villon as a foppish poet who had disappeared in France after pissing off some rich people, or after getting involved in too many tavern brawls, and popped up in a Time Team scoop about the same time he was rescued.

"Penn gave him tenure," Pierre said as though he disapproved.

"Sympathetic female undergraduates and graduate students will make him happy whenever he is," Benedetta said.

Pierre said, "Are you flying to Iceland?"

"Yes. Thank the city council for giving me permission."

"They'd dropped off the net at the plague times and nobody knew what had happened for two centuries," Benedetta said.

Ivar said, "I'm looking forward to some people whose ancestors lived as I did."

"They were lucky they listened to the Greenlanders this time," Benedetta said.

"And the world kept Björk for them," Ivar said.

"What?" Pierre asked.

"A singer from the twenty-first century. Jonah remembered some things about her, played her songs to me, as a joke, I think."

"They asked us to send your DNA," Benedetta said. "We have bad news and good news. Bad news is that your family wasn't one of their surviving genetic lines. Good news is that they're looking forward to harvesting your sperm." She looked almost pleased for him.

"They can harvest my sperm all they want if the girls are pretty," Ivar said.

Iceland at last. He'd heard about glaciers and hot springs and volcanoes, as a boy, but hadn't quite imagined how that would look until he'd seen photographs taken centuries later. Björk's singing, though, made him feel a connection between the Iceland he'd never arrived at and Iceland at least three centuries before now-time. Or maybe he just liked her elfin face.

The plane took off from Philadelphia and flew to Newfoundland, which had been Vineland. Ivar waited in quarantine for six days with the people who were going through to Europe. When the blood titer test showed him with adequate antibodies and clear of new diseases, he got a window seat for the flight across to Iceland and watched the coast of Greenland below him. Threads of green cutting up into the ice were the only green he could see, but the water had boats on it. Hard to tell from the air how big they must be. The plane crossed water again. Then he could see Iceland from the west, green and brown and fields and rocks.

Flying across the fields, the plane began to sink down toward what looked to be ordinary runways. Ivar wondered how they'd been maintained for three centuries, but realized when the plane touched down that the pavement under the plane's wheels wasn't as smooth as the pavement under the plane at Gander had been.

After another week of quarantine and testing by the Icelanders, everyone else would be flying on to Europe. Ivar was free to leave the containment area.

A man dressed in a tunic and pants greeted Ivar, "Ivar Sigtryggson. I'm Birningr Steinarsson. Welcome to Iceland. We're about an hour from Reykjavik by track." Birningr was speaking Norse; not quite the way Ivar remembered it, but Norse.

"Did you learn that for me or does everyone speak as you do?" Ivar said.

"Some changes for you, but I think you'll master it quickly."

They embraced. *Iceland. Norse.* "You want something to eat?"

"Do you still have skyr?" Ivar said.

"Yes, we make it with both sheep and cow milk," Birningr said. "You'll still need to go through testing. I know we got samples from you earlier from Philadelphia City, but we'd like to test for ourselves. Fifteen hundred years, we could have mutated."

Ivar followed Birningr through the airport lab. He suspected that the Icelanders were trying to relearn recombinant DNA cloning, or invent it for the first time if it hadn't been invented before the plagues came.

After a technician took blood and cheek cell samples, Birningr led Ivar to the airport restaurant. The people who sold food were mixed: blonds and brunets. Some brunets had gray eyes; some of the blonds had eyes with an almost Asian fold.

"Genes are sorting themselves out," Birningr said. "The lethal recessives killed what the plagues didn't, but we got some solid outcrossing from Eskimos who came here."

"Why didn't you bring more of us from Norway?" Ivar asked.

"They wouldn't come here or let us go there. Closed the cities up and killed anyone who might bring more diseases. We went back to medieval tech during the first plague years. You'd have felt right at home. Dropped off the net until the Eskimos showed up with electronic gear."

Skyr was packaged in little glass bottles. "Historically, it was put up in plastic tubs," Birningr said.

"Historically, it was put up in wooden tubs," Ivar said. "Why glass?" He found a tray and added a plate of what looked like sheep's-head jam and some flat bread.

"Easier to make low-tech glass than low-tech plastic," Birningr said. "Glass is easier to recycle."

"So you want me to help you with a time machine?"

"Yes, we'd like to save those who should be ours—the Greenlanders, people who would have drowned at sea."

"Who's financing this?" Ivar said. A tiny group of people who had barely survived by farming for the last three centuries wasn't going to have serious funding for biotech.

"It's a trial for the former Norse countries. They're between the Central Europe network and Russia, again. We're part of the Norse Federation again. The Island, Iceland, sometimes runs its own show and sometimes doesn't."

Ivar thought that some things never changed. The skyr tasted like skyr, only colder than any skyr he'd had as a child, and fresher.

"We think you'll like the Island," Birningr said. "We've got you on leave from Philadelphia, but you can apply for landed status after the leave period ends. Bet you haven't had whey-pickled food in ages."

Ivar was looking at the women walking around the airport cafeteria. Birningr noticed and said, "We're always looking for fresh blood, especially if it's Norse or Celtic."

"Thralls' blood?"

Birningr sighed and didn't say anything.

"Sorry. I would have been killed by some Irish thralls we'd captured if the Archives hadn't saved me."

"That's okay. Genetically, we're the same, though. Palaearctic genetic movements were interesting. Greenlanders were even kin to some of us through their mothers' lines, which implies that not all Norse women starved to death when the Little Ice Age froze the Norse out there."

"I want to see Iceland. I heard stories about mountains that smoked, hot water springs." Ivar took a breath. "We had glaciers in Norway, though, so I'd seen those before. But not mountains that smoked."

"Volcanoes," Birningr said, using the English word. "They give and they take."

Birningr's car appeared to burn hydrogen. The road to Reykjavik passed through rock fields and patches of grazed land. The Island looked nothing like Norway's steep hills. Red deer and horses grazed among the sheep. "The whales are back," Birningr said, pointing to the sea beyond the road. Ivar saw a dark back roll down. "They're happy we've died back, but now we eat them again."

"And seals? Do people still preserve flippers?"

"Yes, but I think that stopped for a while in the early twenty-first century."

Houses showed up on either side of the road to Reykjavik. Some of them were stone bermed with earth. They looked ancient, but no less ancient than the houses made of cement block and corrugated iron. The houses dropped away from the road for a while—plague barricade, perhaps—and then as they came over a low hill, Ivar saw a huge stone building with a narrow pyramid high above all others. The town looked like some parts of Philadelphia but with more space between the houses. The roofs were red on many of the buildings, and fir trees filled the gaps between them. Iceland, at least Reykjavik, was as modern as Philadelphia.

They drove out beyond the center of the town and Birningr

showed Ivar to his room in the local science institute. He was on a top floor, under one of the red roofs overlooking the huge stone building and the mountains beyond the town. "Hallgrim's Church," Birningr said. "Impressive, isn't it?"

"So Christians won here."

Birningr shrugged. "People who gathered together a lot to pray spread diseases, so a lot of Christians died. But the building was worth saving. It's late twentieth century, poured concrete. A bitch to keep repaired in a cold country."

The houses were colorful below it, all yellows, reds, and blues, brighter than those colors had been in Ivar's day, so Iceland had been importing paints from somewhere.

"Tomorrow, I'll show you more of Reykjavik, but I imagine you're tired from your trip, so I'll show you to your room now."

After Birningr left, Ivar lay down on the bed, which was built in the same way as his Philadelphia now-time bed. All his people whom he'd known as a child fifteen hundred years ago were still dead. Iceland had a flavor of his past, but the fragments of that past made him realize how much he'd lost, more than living in Philadelphia did.

Summer in Iceland—the sun refused to set, as it had refused to set in the north of Norway fifteen hundred years earlier. Ivar found the controls that drew down lightproof shutters on the windows and turned out the room lights. Next door, he heard two men talking in Chinese. They knocked on his door and asked in bad Norse if he could stop the light. He got up to help them with their window shutters.

They also spoke English. Ivar wondered what they were doing at this science institute and if he'd be reported back to the city council if he spent much time with them.

"Working on time travel, eh," one of them said.

"Perhaps," Ivar said. "Are you from China?"

"Vancouver," they both said. "We have always had many contacts with Asia in Vancouver."

Ivar tried to remember where Vancouver was—Pacific Coast of North America. The Pacific Coast was another world to the Philadelphians.

"Iceland very much looks like Vancouver," one of them said, "but with fewer trees."

"Norway with fewer mountains," Ivar said. "Good night."

"Good night."

Ivar went back to his room, realizing that he didn't really know enough about the political divisions and alliances of his present. But he hadn't seen any blue flux, so the future was being quiet for now, which was fine with him.

In the morning, Birningr took Ivar and the two Canadians around Reykjavik, explaining that all of them would be working together to bring more people to Scandinavia. Norse land, Ivar thought, was now all one again, with cities in alliances with other cities that shared similar dialects. Birningr spoke English. They passed some greenhouses. Birningr said, "Geothermal heat. Without greenhouses, we don't know how we would have eaten through the lean years."

Ivar realized the times the Icelanders thought were like medieval times hadn't been like the times he'd known. "How did you melt sand in those days?"

"Peat fires if we had to, turning it into something like coke first. We tried not to break greenhouse windows," Birningr said. They were speaking in English. Ivar could barely understand the language spoken around him, and wondered if they moved toward the Old Norse tongue or away from it, or both, over the years.

The Chinese Canadians seemed fascinated by the geothermal pipes and radiators. Ivar felt more isolated by the small similarities to his childhood than by the now-time Scandinavian wireless network crossing from Finland and Denmark to Iceland. The languages would converge again.

Tour of the city done, they all returned to the science institute. Ivar suspected that Iceland did the time imports so the rest of Scandinavia could isolate the experimenters in case the past brought plagues again.

Ivar had brought his basic kit and the programs for calculating the path the planet took through time. The institute had copies of the circuits and two discontinuities in iron shells.

The Chinese Canadians and he worked well together. They asked him whom Philadelphia was rescuing and whom New York was rescuing, which he answered in generalities and evasions, even about New York, although they had tried to kill him. He asked them if they knew why China was still referred to as China when the rest of the world had broken up into city-states, and they said they thought of Shanghai as China, but they knew Beijing and a couple of other cities from radio connections.

At night, they went drinking in stripper bars, where the naked women on the stage could not be fucked and weren't slaves and laughed back at the men as equals. Men stripped, too.

But horses were still horses. Ivar and Birningr rented two Icelandic horses whose gait was as old as forever, going smooth and fast to Thingvellir, where, in year 1000 in the Christian calendar, the nation of Iceland lost its religion. A little over two hundred years later, the Island lost its independence to Norway, and then Denmark took Norway.

The Island still moved against the seas around it. The geological forces that gave it the hot springs also opened volcanoes where the planet's crust thinned. Norway was a dead place compared to this. Thingvellir wasn't the center of the spreading rift these days, though.

Birningr said, "The chiefs built turf booths and each year brought wool tarps to cover them. Archeologists found traces of them there. And the cliffs served as a sounding board behind Law Rock. The original Althing, where the Gray Goose Laws were settled."

Ivar was thinking. If Iceland's rifts widened by two meters per century, then the Iceland of 898 was three thousand meters narrower than this Iceland. Ivar spread his arms to what he had learned was about a meter and imagined fifteen hundred to two thousand men standing across new-made ground, their fingers touching, meter-to-meter.

"The rift is still active, isn't it?" he said to Birningr.

"Yes, North America on one side and Europe on the other. Metaphor and reality," Birningr said.

"I would have died before Christianity was declared here. And the land has moved three thousand meters since I was a child."

"I wondered if you were praying when you spread your arms like that."

"No, thinking about the distance in time and space, how many men wide. Anyone worship the old gods now? Anyone still eat horse?"

"Well, eating horses, yes, but it's not a religious thing with us. We've just got lots of horses now."

"The food and horses haven't changed in fifteen hundred years, but the women have."

Birningr laughed. "The food is probably more back to what it was. We'd almost killed off the whales in the old days—not your old days, the twenty-first century. Seal flippers in whey had gone out of fashion, too. People wanted Indian takeaway."

"Is your Iceland a reconstruction of what you imagine Iceland was, then?"

"Yeah, the Iceland of the 1990s, and you've probably figured out that we're where Scandinavia puts its experiments. But we're going to repopulate as much as we can with rescued people. We're trying to figure out the social side of that."

"Get very young children," Ivar said. "It would be so much easier with nurslings."

"This isn't really your Iceland, is it?"

"Steal babies and women," Ivar said more lightly, feeling a touch less morbid in reaction to Birningr's sympathy. "It's never going to be easy coming up-time as an adult from a completely different culture."

"I don't think immigrants ever had it easy."

"I don't know if I'm typical or not, but I keep thinking I want to go home—and home is Philadelphia, not Norway, not here." Ivar wondered if that would offend Birningr or make sense to him. "I do like the horses and the food though."

"We have good work for you here, interesting work," Birningr said. "You're famous here."

"I share history with people in Philadelphia in a way that coming here as the historical-curiosity-*slash*—" Ivar cut through the air with his finger to emphasize the slash, "—time-tech-expert from abroad can't give me."

"Over time, this could become home."

"Being reminded every day of what I lost, the language I can almost understand, isn't comforting. I thought it would be."

"You've been picking up more and more of the dialect. Give yourself time. You'll have new friends here soon enough. Time always changes life."

"I'm sorry. I want to go home." Ivar switched back to Norse. "I honor you as a host, Birningr Steinarsson."

"You have done much to help us, Ivar Sigtryggsson."

"You owe my city for the help, Steinarsson."

"We don't forget our friends, Sigtryggsson."

They smiled at each other. "But I did finally make it to Iceland," Ivar said. "And this was worth seeing." He looked around Thingvellir, at the cliffs behind Law Rock, then switched back to English. "I'm glad to be living when I can sweep through vast tracts of time."

"There is that," Birningr said.

Ivar saw a patch of blue flux and an eye watching him. "And there is that," he said, pointing at the flux. "A future is watching us."

"The future is always with us," Birningr said. "One of them suggested that we invite you to Iceland."

Ivar made a face. He realized that this future suggested the invitation before the other future tried to egg him into raping Mr. Wythe. "A man I know in Philadelphia, from the twenty-first century of current reckoning, first thought this was a computer game, then a game played by the futures."

"What if it is? Would that bother you?"

"Yes."

"Because they brought you to Iceland?"

"They would have known I wouldn't fit in here."

"However many futures there might be, can you live differently now?" Birningr asked.

Ivar thought of Odin preparing for a war he knew he would lose. "Maybe we just do what we can."

"We Islanders always made the best of our lives, tapped heat out of fresh lava and lived off the sea when the land wasn't giving. Times change, with or without time travel. Do what you can to improve life, always."

"I would like to come back. Now that I know what to expect."

• • •

As Ivar waited through quarantine at Gander, he understood finally what Birningr had told him. The Philadelphia he'd be going back to wasn't the Philadelphia he had left, either. He wasn't the same man who'd started for Iceland, either fifteen hundred years ago or a couple of months ago.

But he had finally been to Iceland.

Time Changes Again

Philadelphia lawyers decided that the city council had set a precedent when it gave the Welsh their own community. The city council told Benedetta to figure out how to make a maximum number of people happy without making it too obvious that now-time assimilation was the ultimate goal.

Once Mr. Wythe had been rusticated, the council asked Benedetta to see if Jonah would help them deal with the Kirkpatricks after they'd been freed for identifying New York's agents, who were politely and quickly traded for Philadelphia's agents.

"Who, me, what," Jonah said to Benedetta. He promptly moved out of the Kirkpatrick house and went back to University City to work on English dialect changes as mediated through the development of networking.

Benedetta learned strong encryption and set up the council machines to use it. She didn't trust Jonah not to try to pull various computer tricks again, especially since he had access to all the university databases. She couldn't blame him for not wanting to inform on his kin, though. Once, someone tapped the council's servers from West Philly, first through a UPenn machine, then from a machine that hadn't been locked down and which proved to be compromised when Benedetta sent the watch to check.

Benedetta wondered if she should monitor Jonah's online activities even more carefully.

Was he really avoiding his Kirkpatrick kin? The city council mole among the servants the Kirkpatricks had finally been allowed to hire said that he was.

Then the Kirkpatricks abandoned their house and disappeared.

Benedetta wondered what to make of that. Mr. Wythe, at least, hadn't escaped to bigger and better smuggling, at least not in this time line.

Back to work. Most of the time, Benedetta enjoyed helping people find places in Philadelphia or set up communities that could contribute to the local economy, which was rapidly becoming more and more complex.

One of the other city councilmen, Thaddeus, an older man who read even older writings and books about the city, said, "Don't worry about their children. They'll be like the children of every other immigrant group and will want to be just ordinary Philadelphians. Some of us will wring our hands that we've lost something special. Others will claim that all we lost was poverty and ignorance."

Benedetta thought that this would only work if the past people didn't overwhelm now-time. The Amish had stayed the Amish after centuries of being one or two days by horse outside the city, close enough to use the city as a market, far away enough to keep speaking their form of German.

"Why do you feel responsible for them?" Thaddeus asked. "You were just one of the first."

"I helped the team that figured out how to reproduce the time machines."

"Doesn't make you responsible, really. Do you enjoy the work?"

"Most of the time," Benedetta said. "I hate it when the guys are horrified to have to listen to a woman, though."

Today's problem was between two groups of Merovingians. One group of fifteen was women; the other group of seventeen was mostly men. The women wanted protection from the men. The men apparently wanted to have power of life and death over unchaste women. They were squabbling in some language that appeared to be close to Ivar's Norse, but had a priest with them who translated into near Latin for the men. As Benedetta understood the priest, the men thought the women belonged to them. One of the women had learned enough now-time English to yell that the men were lying killers of women.

Benedetta sent for Pierre to check what the priest was saying. These people were from roughly five hundred years before Ivar's time even, but if that was Latin, Pierre could speak to their priest better than she could.

"Colorful little people," Thaddeus said. "Next generation won't understand what this fuss is about at all."

"If the guys and girls can't get together, they're not going to have a Merovingian next generation."

"Ivar used to go hunting for faithless women in bogs," Thaddeus said. "Perhaps we indulged him a bit too much."

"I don't think anyone should die for getting a little on the side," Benedetta said. "I sympathize with those women."

"Depends on why they were unfaithful and why they got caught. Dumb and full of some other man's cum isn't a good combination in any age."

"Still shouldn't die for that," Benedetta said.

"Were you faithful to your husband?"

"Yes, but I was with him almost all the time."

Pierre came in and ended up in an argument with the Merovingian who spoke Latin. He turned and addressed the city council: "They're not really Christian. In Christianity, both men and women are sinners. Just killing the female partner isn't fair."

Benedetta said, "Tell the men that they'll have to find women who agree to marry them. Tell the women that they need to learn to do something productive."

"Not that they couldn't make their livings on their backs if they were taller and cuter," Thaddeus whispered in Benedetta's ear.

"They're just ordinary people caught up in some stupid war that history didn't record, who got magically whisked into some other world that tells them that they can't do something that's obviously very important to them," Benedetta said. "But the women don't want it done to them and don't want to play by those rules anymore." She remembered thinking that she'd come to a future that Leonardo had predicted. Yes and no.

Whatever decision she made here, she'd lose some votes in the next election for councilperson-at-large. The woman who spoke some English was crying. Benedetta wondered if that was for the family she'd lost or because she was afraid she hadn't really escaped her past as she'd first thought.

If Ivar was going to play savior to women who'd thought they'd been murdered because they'd taken a lover, why didn't he take better care of them? Or had he taken enough care of this one that she had some rudiments of English and some idea of what had happened to her and where and when she was? "Pierre, tell them that the place that rescued them does not allow killing people for crimes other than deliberate manslaughter. Other than that, those who agree to live in a community agree to abide by the custom of that community. But just because those women are from their time, roughly, and speak as they speak, the men can't lay claim to them."

Thaddeus said, "What about the women laying claim to the men?"

"That, too. We can try to find their wives and daughters in the past, or women who would be willing to join them. These aren't."

Pierre said, "Neither side is being completely rational about this, but I understand. They're all trying to grab onto something familiar."

"The women aren't," Benedetta said. "We need to get the men a bit more familiar with how the city works before we cut them loose. Their group isn't big enough to be a functioning breeding group."

Benedetta decided she wanted to slow down the movement of the past people into now-time, to deal with them in smaller numbers. She realized she'd moved from seeing now-time as an immigrant to seeing it as a citizen. This was probably hypocritical of her. However, if the past began to overwhelm the present, then people who had never known anything but now-time might be even more concerned and hostile. And now-time was more coherent than the varieties of past cultures that were showing up.

The Merovingians were split up. The women got to join a Quaker weaving group in North Philadelphia; the men were sent down to South Philly, where other groups with Latin-speaking representatives had already been settling.

Jonah called on her phone to arrange a meeting on Mantua Bridge.

Remembering an earlier meeting on Mantua Bridge, Benedetta wondered what tricks Jonah would be up to this time. They walked to the center of the bridge and looked around. He was wearing a long coat, even though it was warm. "None of those damn blue fluxes. Is Ivar working on a way to block them?"

"Ivar has been loaned to Iceland."

"He finally got to arrive there fifteen hundred years late."

"He might be quite happy. I've found Romans to be rather like Italians, even with a two-millennium spread there. We dance; we get drunk; we gossip about the Augustans, the Sforzas, and the Mafia."

"Do you know what happened to my descendants?"

"They disappeared. Kicking and screaming? Mr. Wythe wants a re-trial."

"Oh?"

"Yes, and he claimed the future people tricked him and tried to get Ivar to rape him."

"Yeah, Ivar was determined to get Mr. Wythe. Does the son of a bitch have a first name?"

"Ellard. We think. We're really not sure where Mr. Wythe came from."

Jonah laughed. "Ellard? Well, I wouldn't use that either. Not sure when he came from?"

"Now-time. We can do a sort of pre-and-post-atomic testing and also test for antibodies that would be era-appropriate."

"What about the future? Futures?"

"We don't have samples for those, but he's quite consistent with now-time," Benedetta said. "And you're from when you say you are."

"But if Mr. Wythe was a bad guy from the future, maybe he couldn't get a time machine from there. And maybe they could fake ..."

"Yeah, yeah, or we're all in a computer," Benedetta said. "I don't care when he was from. I don't want him turned loose ever. After he was rusticated, we searched the salvage yard and found more weapons caches beyond what he'd sold the Welsh. Really, we don't need that. New York and Philly did a spy exchange. We're working on dividing up New Jersey without fighting over it, making it easier to visit each other."

"Have you searched the Kirkpatrick house yet?"

"Yes. They stuck to drugs, personal adornment, and stolen art. You know anything about those things?"

"Gee, I'm surprised they didn't smuggle in weapons. They wanted to be the local aristocrats. I'd like to claim the house."

"No, it's forfeited to the city. Is that why they worked with New York?"

Jonah laughed. "No, I don't know anything about that."

Benedetta wondered if Jonah knew about any connections between Mr. Wythe and his now-time kin, but she wasn't going to ask him right now. "You think I should see that Ivar stays in Iceland? He's scheduled to come home and he hasn't asked if he could stay. But he sent me some photographs of fjords and horses."

"Mr. Wythe promised to burn a girl for him when he died." Jonah's face twitched slightly, repressing a smile. "I'd keep an eye on Ivar if I were working for the city. And wouldn't you want company in death? To give your friends a great funeral party?"

Benedetta couldn't believe that Jonah thought this was all funny. So Ivar was still a shit toward captives.

"That's just fucked, Jonah, in any age. But then, he didn't rape Mr. Wythe even though that future was cheering him on. Did you know that at the time?"

"Um, I neither confirm nor deny that I knew that or that the future still talks to me."

"What did Ivar know about the Kirkpatricks?"

"I'm not your snitch. You'll have to ask him yourself, if he doesn't just lie to you. Ivar lied a lot more than you realize. You know about the New York agents who used to visit him, don't you?"

Benedetta wondered if that was a lie and left thinking that Jonah got more out of her than she'd gotten out of him, and didn't know whether he was lying about Ivar or not. She walked home, down by City Hall, down Broad Street, then over on Lombard, then down Eighth.

The Latin speakers hung out at one of the cafés on South Street, which served bread with oil and garlic, chunks of cheese on the side, and wine, something that all of them had eaten in any era where men spoke some dialect of Latin. Benedetta sat down with a computer translator in her right ear and began working on improving her Latin. Pierre, dressed in a Renaissance-style doublet and hose, pulled a chunk of bread through oil and garlic with his gnarled hand, looking amazed to find something so familiar in this electric-powered time. Pierre said, "Ivar wants to see everyone again. Dinner party."

"He didn't stay in Iceland, then." She sat down with them and pulled off a piece of bread herself. "Funny, so many of us find hanging out here easy. It's like time doesn't matter," Benedetta said.

"Old saying from our people, probably older than Roman. 'History is like a river. Civilization is what takes place on the banks.' What I care about now is this ..." He held up bread soaked with the oil-and-garlic mix and popped it in his mouth, then drank some wine and looked at the glass. "... and that. Our people from the Etruscans on understood this. The Christians made it a ritual. The Northerners want to be on History's winning side."

"Not all Northerners. And my father was Northern."

"My dear, I think that's why you're on the city council while I spend as much time as possible looking at Chinese furniture and Impressionist paintings in the museum. The things I missed. Like my clothes?"

"They're from my time, aren't they?"

"I had them copied from a Caravaggio painting."

History had tried its dead-level best to kill both Pierre and her. If technology was part of culture and not part of history, then culture made now-time the place where everyone escaped drowning in History.

"Did Ivar want me to come to his dinner party, too?"

"Yes, and Lucius, the guy from the university who helped us, and some of his Merovingian women friends. You're not close to him?"

"Some of what he believes creeps me out."

"He's a pagan, but now, outside History, I'm not going to convert anyone."

"You seemed to have learned to be sensible in Jerusalem."

"Perhaps too sensible, but that was then." A couple of Latin-speaking men came up to talk to Pierre, and Benedetta wrote out the time and place for Pierre and stuck it in the top of the bright doublet. Pierre, still talking to the men, took the paper and stuck it in a pocket.

"Pockets are anachronistic," Benedetta said.

"We are anachronistic," Pierre said.

Ivar's dinner party included Jonah, two of the Merovingian women Ivar had rescued from getting killed as adulteresses, Pierre, Lucius and the older man who'd been with him at Three Mile Island, and Ivar's apparent manservant, James the cabman. Pierre brought another man, who wore now-time clothes but spoke Latin too fluently to be a native Philadelphian. The Merovingian women couldn't talk much of anything that anyone recognized, but they had learned some English.

Ivar wore an early-twentieth-century tailored suit, blue against his blond hair. He was clean-shaven, his hair cut short, and he seemed tired. Benedetta wondered what Iceland in now-time had shown him. "We all made history," he said. "And we share history." Hearing Ivar say that, she caught Pierre's eye and smiled.

The food was as hard to place in time as the bread, garlic, and oil on South Street: baked leaven bread, roast beef, fava beans, a salad of shredded cabbage with tiny seeds and raisins, and a stew of eggplants, tomatoes, and garbanzo beans. The meal didn't feature whey-pickled meat of any kind, or flat bread.

"I heard from Mr. Wythe recently," Benedetta said. Ivar looked away, muscles in his jaw moving. Jonah was grinning. Ivar looked at Jonah, then back at Benedetta.

"How was he doing?" Ivar asked. "Life as a captive would be harsh in any time."

"Not happy," Benedetta said.

"Jonah is grinning," Ivar said.

"Perhaps he knows more than I do," Benedetta said.

Ivar made a movement with his hands, then picked up a carving knife and fork and cut the roast carefully into very thin slices. He looked at James, who smiled and nodded. James had taught Ivar to carve like a proper eighteenth-century gentleman.

Benedetta caught James's eye, but he held his face bland—vastly experienced, she supposed, in not showing his thoughts to clients or their suspicious spouses when he was a Bath chairman.

Jonah appeared to enjoy their discomfort so much that Benedetta felt sorry for Ivar. She decided to talk to him. Maybe seeing Iceland now changed him?

"So what was Iceland like?"

"Strange," Ivar said. "Some things are so much like Norway was. But they've had fifteen hundred years of lava, plagues, volcanoes, and greenhouses. The sagas they still read, but they went beyond the sagas and became a different people. The language and the food are the only things that didn't change. And the horses. They have lovely horses, but no horse fights."

"They no longer burn a slave girl in her master's pyre," Jonah said.

Ivar didn't even get angry, just worked on eating his roast beef for a moment and looked at the Merovingian girls who were drinking and gossiping in their own language. Then he said, "It was about not dying alone."

Pierre said, "Why don't you work on not living alone?"

James said, "He rarely is alone these days."

Pierre said, "I don't mean casual affairs. I mean something more than that. And you and James are close but not in that way."

James shrugged an I've-seen-everything-and-I-don't-judge shrug.

Ivar said, "I feel close to all of you."

"It's more like having gone through a war together," Pierre said before Benedetta could say almost the same thing.

"Yes," Ivar said. "Perhaps I should have stayed in Iceland after all. Going through wars is intense, but better relived in memory than gone through again."

"Philadelphia is one Iceland beside another Iceland, on top of another Iceland, on top of another Iceland, on to twelve to fifteen Icelands laid out side by side," Benedetta said. "There's a lot for you here."

Ivar said, "You ran away to cities. My family was leaving Norway because a king and probably the beginnings of cities as power centers were dominating the social life. In Iceland, almost everyone who lived in Reykjavik died three hundred years ago. They were back to sixteen thousand people and farming."

"Somehow I don't think you really want to be a farmer," Lucius said.

Ivar smiled for the first time since the dinner started. "I love the technical challenges. I was helping Iceland set up time machines and wireless networks with the rest of the Scandinavians. I learned how to tap heat from lava flows, and how to use geothermal energy to break water into hydrogen and oxygen."

"Do you ever wonder which Ivar is real?" Pierre said. "The person you have become in these days, or who you'd been before?"

Benedetta realized that she didn't have as huge a discontinuity in her life, because she'd moved into Leonardo's world in her imagination well before she moved to the future. She was the product of the age that was moving quickly to the eighteenth-century's clockworks and steam engines. And she hadn't particularly believed anything: Catholics, Valdensians, Moors, Jews, whatever. Ivar's world had been fighting a rear-guard action against kings and central government and state churches.

Ivar said, "I've been this Ivar longer than I was Ivar the boy who was moving with his family to Iceland. My family died out in Iceland."

Jonah said, "Can they really tell that?"

"Yes, they're doing DNA work. I enjoy the skull-work problems. I just miss … I finally arrived in Iceland and realized what I'd lost, how many years, how much Iceland had itself changed in fifteen hundred years. Three thousand meters of change."

"The oceans have changed, too. Higher," Pierre said.

"That's why I couldn't stay there. I didn't want to be reminded every day of how much time …" Ivar stared at the roast beef. Benedetta realized he was trying not to cry.

"I lost my family twice," Jonah said, "but there are probably other Kirkpatricks around. And I have all sorts of crap around me to remind me of what I lost."

Benedetta said, "You lost your children and your wife. That is real."

They all were quiet for a while, even the two people from West Philly, who were born in now-time. The Merovingian girls picked up the mood of the rest of the party and stopped chattering. One of them touched Ivar's leg, but more to comfort him than to seduce, Benedetta thought.

James said, "Well, with that, shall I get more wine and bring out dessert?"

Ivar nodded.

Benedetta realized how much she'd been trying not to think of the past lately, even though she dealt with people freshly in from the old times almost every month. She asked the now-time engineer, who hadn't said anything earlier, "How are now-time people taking all of us showing up?"

"Hard to speak in generalities," he said. "The biggest fear is that you'll change our political life. We finally got something that pleased the best of the Quakers."

Pierre said, "Either you've mastered ways to deflect the passions of people to dominate others, or not. If you can keep those passions from changing your ways of living, you've learned a new political skill since the days of medieval communes. If not, your ways weren't that stable to begin with."

Jonah said, "Nothing human is stable."

"On that note," James said, "dessert." Dessert was a huge cake in tiers with white icing.

Jonah appeared to recognize the cake as something humorous.

"What is it, Jonah?" Benedetta said.

"If it had two little dolls on top, I'd call it a wedding cake."

"Ceremony cake for Pierre and his fiancé," Ivar said. "Put some of it under your pillow and you'll have dreams about your future. We're all invited to the wedding."

Pierre said, "I would never have imagined such a wedding possible in my time. If the politics changes so that I face the rack again, that will be it for me."

His fiancé took Pierre's wounded hand and put some oil on it before rubbing it between the two of his. "You need to have surgery on that," the man said.

"I need to get my nerve up to stand pain to get rid of brokenness, just not yet," Pierre said.

"Well, this is a surprise to me," Benedetta said.

Pierre said, "I told James first. I wanted it to be a surprise to both Ivar and you, but James told Ivar."

"I wanted to make sure Ivar was sensible," James said. "I have always been sensible."

"I hope he makes you happier than Salai made Leonardo," Benedetta said.

Jonah said, "Benedetta, you were a slut, so you should be sympathetic. And you're now a net cop, with your stupid encryption. Net cop." Jonah made that sound worse than being a fuckhead. "So, Ivar, why did you trap Mr. Wythe? He'd helped us earlier."

Ivar waved a hand as though to shut Jonah up. Benedetta was beginning to feel protective of Ivar.

Pierre, his fiancé, Lucius, and the older engineer all rose and told Ivar what a lovely dinner it had been, but they all had things to do in the morning to get ready for the wedding. James left with the Merovingian girls.

Benedetta didn't want to leave Jonah alone with Ivar.

Ivar said, "He fucked with me. He got the Welsh to attack me dishonorably. So I got him back."

"Really." Jonah looked like he didn't believe it. "Maybe you were jealous of him? He had established trade relationships, didn't show off his wealth in any vulgar way, didn't let the petty local constabulary bully him, and had very good taste, better than my kin, actually."

Ivar said, "Bullshit."

Jonah said, "I'm so glad Pierre and his boyfriend left."

Benedetta said, "Stop, both of you."

Jonah said, "Ivar, would you care if someone stuck his dick up your butt? Are you jealous of Pierre's friend?"

Ivar was turning very pale and was quivering slightly. Benedetta hoped that James would be back soon to get Jonah out of here. She said, "Jonah, stop it."

"Why? Do you approve of his killing a woman so he doesn't get buried or burned or whatever they do to corpses alone? Ugly, stupid little Viking, isn't he? Flattered by spies from New York who pretended to be all interested in his old-time religion."

Ivar said, "Jonah, stop."

"What are you going to do to me if I don't stop?"

Benedetta said, "Jonah, I'll call you a cab."

"Why? Ivar's pet cabbie will be back sooner or later."

Ivar said, "James isn't coming back here tonight."

"So, you're throwing me out? How are you going to do that? You're going to beat up on someone who's more than twice your age?"

Benedetta said, "Jonah, what the fuck?"

"I had to hear all these obscene murderous fantasies . . ."

"No," Ivar said. "When did I tell you any of this?"

"About having a girl murdered when you died?"

"It was our custom. Then."

"Fucking ugly custom," Jonah said. "Did your sister expose her bastards, too?" He stood up swaying and moved too close to Ivar, who backed up slightly.

"Ivar, don't hit him. That's what he wants."

"I know."

Jonah went right up into Ivar's face and said, "You have some interesting troll tendencies, Ivar. If you were better with words and less emotional, you might pull that Loki side out more and do something interesting with it now instead of fantasizing about your friends fucking your slave girl in memory of you before they kill her and burn her with you."

Benedetta said, "Jonah, leave now or I'll call the watch."

"I was invited here. I don't want you to be alone with him. I've shamed him and he might kill you before he kills himself. Ivar has to ask me to leave."

Ivar turned red after being pale for so long a time. "You're the one with the fucked imagination. You can't shame me."

"No, you've shamed yourself by betraying someone who'd helped you. You should have given him that time machine after all he'd done for you. He knew you didn't trust him."

Benedetta said, "Jonah, leave now." She held the carving knife in one hand, twisting its point slightly against the platter. Jonah looked at the point, looked at her. *Try me,* she thought.

Jonah said, "Are you good with that?"

"Probably not as good now as I used to be. You ever played with knives, Jonah?"

Jonah said, "Do you need a woman to defend you, Ivar?"

"Ivar, don't be baited by a troll."

Ivar said nothing. He sat down and gripped his chair on either side of his legs, staring at the table. Jonah smiled.

Someone knocked on the door, then. Jonah said, "Who is it?"

"Me, James. Thought you might need a ride, Jonah."

"I was having a nice conversation with your master."

James opened the door. "He's not my master. I'm an independent cabbie. But I think you'd better come with me."

Ivar nodded.

"Well, damn," Jonah said. "Benedetta ought to come too."

James said, "Benedetta?"

"Ivar?"

"I'd like to talk to you," Ivar said to Benedetta.

"Well, Jonah, I think you need to leave these two people alone."

"Fuckheads," Jonah said, but he wasn't physically brave enough to take the three of them, Benedetta thought. She'd been around people who could drive words like needles, not so much as to justify daggers in return, and Jonah was good, but the main reason he scored hits on Ivar was that Ivar hadn't realized that the troll could turn on him. James would be impenetrable.

After James closed the door behind him, Benedetta said, "Do you still want someone to be killed when you die?"

Ivar took his hands away from the chair and almost put them against his face. "No, of course not."

"What Pierre said, about being torn between who you were raised to be and what you've become since, is that true?"

"Oh, yeah. With teeth."

"I hate to say this, but I feel almost like your mom now."

"Don't do that to me."

"It's not shameful to cry. Why are you so afraid of tears?"

"I'm afraid if I start crying, I won't be able to stop."

"Eventually, you wear out and fall asleep. When you wake up, you feel better. At least that's the way most of the people I knew wept."

Ivar put his face to his hands and began crying, rocking back and forth, talking in Norse. Benedetta didn't know if she should cuddle him or what, so she began cleaning up the remains of dinner. He began wailing louder. *Argh, the neighbors,* she thought, so she took him into his bedroom and laid him facedown on the bed. He muffled his face with the pillow and cried on, somewhat aware that he shouldn't disturb the neighbors in an apartment building at this hour. She left the bedroom door open while she finished cleaning up. He came out, barefooted and in a tunic top and linen breeches, tears still brimming in his eyes, and stood leaning against the doorway, his arms folded across his chest, shuddering slightly. "I really don't embarrass you?"

"No. You lost everything at, what, fifteen, sixteen. You're still young. I'm still older than you are, and by these people's standards, I'm even sort of young."

"Perhaps I just imagined that you and Jonah were friends."

"I am your friend. Jonah uses words to hurt for fun. He could have baited Mr. Wythe into thinking he had to steal the time machine from you, or made bad blood between you. He tried to tell me you lied to me, that you worked with New York agents."

"Flitings. Word battle. I was more hurt because I thought he was a friend."

"Think of Jonah as a professional duelist, egging on men into attacking him."

"But I could have killed him."

"'Oh, the embarrassment,'" Benedetta quoted from some ancient media.

"Would he have won if I'd killed him?"

"Yes. And that's a concept you understood, too, isn't it?"

Ivar nodded. "I'm glad you were here. And I'm glad you didn't kill him, either."

"Yeah, if I'd killed him, he would have been killed by a girl. That would have really hurt."

Ivar giggled. "Shit, how do I make myself whole again, in one time?"

"Staying busy helps, but you've been doing that."

"I shouldn't have turned Iceland down. They offered me landed status."

"Maybe, maybe not. You can always reconsider."

"Would you go up-time to the future of this future if you could?"

"I am curious about whether we've made human life better or not, and for whom. Wouldn't it be marvelous to skip up-time a couple of centuries, live there for a decade, go further yet, stay another decade, and die ten thousand years from when you were born?"

"Iceland would be bigger yet." Ivar went to the sink and washed his face, then felt his chin with his fingertips. "Beards have some advantages to being clean-shaven. I'll need to shave again."

"Beard or no beard. Just don't be stubbly."

"I'll shave again, then. Who makes the stainless steel blades?" He went into the bathroom and brought out his shaving gear. Benedetta realized Ivar wanted to keep talking to her.

"We do, with Pennsylvania coal, recycled steel, and imported chromium. Yay, Philadelphia."

Ivar shaved his chin carefully, and then said, "Jonah doesn't believe the way the city has been run will work once more people show up and start organizing more complex economic structures." He continued shaving.

"I don't know. Do people want King Log or King Stork? The people who survived the first round of plagues were people who didn't believe the official stories told to keep people from panicking." Benedetta was budgeting four hours twice a week for learning about the city she was now helping govern. She sat watching Ivar finish shaving and then asked, "What do you want?"

Ivar rinsed his face and turned to look back at her, leaning against the sink. He looked like he was thinking about the age difference between them. He said, "We started to get close at Three Mile Island. Jonah was jealous."

"Jonah reminds me way too much of Salai, Leonardo's boyfriend. And he's worse, because he doesn't have the excuses Salai had. He helped me escape, but he was using me as a test subject. Would I get to the end of the program? Would I die of now-time diseases? Would the silly soap mask even work at all?" She went back to the table and sat down.

Ivar sat down at the table, next to her. "Thanks for cleaning up. I didn't really expect you to do that now that you're a councilwoman."

Benedetta laughed. "That's okay." He seemed like he wasn't sure quite how to bed someone older and with a political position, a female gytha. She didn't know if she wanted to make it easier for him or not, but Ivar vulnerable was more charming than Ivar acting like a Norse brat.

"If I went further forward in time, I'd be even more behind than I was when I began to learn now-time technology. I've made my mark in history. Machines and computers are what swords and boats were."

"So that's the way you go Viking these days?"

He smiled, finally. "Yes. Do you still see me as one of those sorts of people you prayed not to have come into your country?"

"I'm glad you didn't kill Jonah, not that Jonah isn't nasty."

Ivar said, "I can't undo my past."

"You don't want to scare me, do you?"

"I'm scared of you."

That was too vulnerable, Benedetta thought. He couldn't get hard for her if he was frightened. "I lived in a world where any woman who wanted to be safe and free, not in the brothel or the nunnery, had to make an alliance with a man. I loved Emelio, so that alliance was good for me. The artillery wives were among the freest in Lombardy and Burgundy. But all that's in the past now."

"I'm still scared of you." Ivar laughed a little. "It would be like . . ." He blushed slightly.

Don't you dare tell me it would be like fucking your mother, Benedetta thought. She wasn't that much older than Ivar in biological years. "No dead slave girls murdered for your funeral. Promise?"

"I'll have tons of company in the city crematorium."

"Ashes aren't important. The funeral, who comes to remember you, is."

"Okay."

They didn't speak for a while. Benedetta felt the sexual tension growing between them. Ivar got up, his hand over his breeches, too casually. "If you are going, I can call a cab. James will be asleep now, but there are some other cabs that work all night."

"Do you want me to go home?" Benedetta said. "Or do you want to keep talking?" Seducing someone who was afraid of her appealed to her at the moment.

"I . . ."

Benedetta went to him and held him, feeling his spine under the thin linen shirt. They were both shorter than now-time people, but she was almost as tall as he was, tall for a peasant girl. She decided to kiss him first and see how he took it.

When she moved back, he grinned, almost in fear. He scared her some, too. She thought that she shouldn't do this while he's still in mourning for the friendship he thought he had with Jonah and for his past, but she peeled the tunic off him. He began pulling at her clothes, but she was determined to get him naked first and did, running her fingers lightly down his hip. He had a scar on his belly. She tapped it, feeling the muscles underneath the scar.

"Fell out of an apple tree," he said, as though he were ashamed it wasn't a battle scar.

Benedetta pulled off her blouse and bra and put his hand on her breast. He clutched down on it, breathing hard, almost hurting her. Then he felt her own scars where the French had stabbed her, and backed off to look at them. "Wow," he said.

"Are you freaked out?"

He ran his fingers down the scars and then knelt to kiss one at her belly. She was ready to sink to the floor. He said, voice thick, "Let's go to bed."

Okay, he's in charge now, Benedetta thought. *And he accepted the scars.* She realized she'd been afraid of a man's reaction to those.

Once they were on his bed, Ivar moved between her legs and began sucking on her clit as though it was a tiny penis, his tongue rolled around it. Emelio hadn't done this that well.

His finger felt her up and she felt her muscles down there clamping on his fingers as she came. He pushed into her. For a second, she was annoyed, but he began licking her ears and she stopped caring.

They lay back for a while, dozed off. In the morning, she sucked his balls into her mouth while he was barely awake. He looked down startled, and she grinned back at him. A woman learned a lot in an artillery group.

Ivar might not have been the right person to be with, but Benedetta realized how much she'd missed sex and all that.

Ivar spurted into her mouth. He tasted of cod and something like wormwood and salt. Afterward, Ivar seemed almost shy around her. Benedetta wasn't sure if he hadn't really intended to sleep with her, because of age or her prior sexual experience, or whether he was embarrassed about the emotional vulnerability he'd shown before they had sex.

She didn't know quite whether she should have slept with him, because she'd forgotten how much she could enjoy it and want more of it. *Someone my own age, perhaps from my own age,* she thought as she took a shower.

Ivar dressed in his Edwardian suit before walking her down to catch a cab. She'd grown used to fresh clothes every day, so felt sticky in yesterday's underwear. Ivar gave her a hand into the pedicab, something Benedetta expected he'd learned from James.

The cab passed the Archives as it went down Fourth Street. *Lots of history here,* Benedetta thought. She wondered if sleeping with Ivar was going to wreck the friendship they'd had. They'd gotten fairly close at Three Mile Island, but she felt Jonah watching them almost jealously.

Jonah was a fuckhead. Benedetta didn't expect to see much of him again at all after last night.

Two days later, Ivar, James, the men from West Philadelphia, and she went to City Hall as witnesses for Pierre's and Lucellus's marriage. Afterward, they went to the Italian Market and drank and danced, eating bread dipped in oil, seal flippers pickled in whey, and devoured a second cake with two little male figures on top.

Pierre asked, "Where's Jonah?"

Benedetta said, "I don't care."

She and Ivar found a larger house and moved in together, and decorated it in silver, amber, and brightly colored ceramics.

A Real Tiny Dragon

Ivar didn't know if he could keep Benedetta as his woman even though they'd started living together or if they were war buddies who were fucking each other for comfort.

Neither Ivar nor Benedetta ever saw Jonah alive again. Representatives of the watch informed them that Jonah had been killed up in Fishtown, in a small row house that some Merovingian women used as a brothel. Did they know other friends who might want to come to the memorial service before the cremation? Did either of them want to go to the hearing on the shooter?

Ivar thought, *Well, Jonah had finally trolled himself to death.* But he had to see Jonah dead to believe that Jonah had truly died and hadn't faked a death so he could slide away unnoticed into the new city, with its old industries gearing up and people getting too anxious for luxuries to care about being quite as suspicious of their neighbors and workmates as they had been.

So, he dressed in a black suit styled after Edwardian mourning clothes. Benedetta wore ankle-skimming black and a hat with a veil that went down to her chin. They got in James's pedicab to go out to West Philly, where Jonah's linguistics studies community was saying good-bye to him.

"Seems odd," Ivar said.

"You want to make sure he's really dead, don't you?"

"Ah, yeah. Any idea what happened?"

"He insulted someone. She shot him."

"Yeah? I came close to killing him myself," Ivar said. "What you said at the time stopped me. He wanted me to kill him. I would have ruined my life if I had."

Benedetta said, "Life in my day was just too easy to throw away. But I think he was looking for someone to kill him."

Ivar nodded.

Jonah looked vaguely annoyed at being dead in a coffin in the Baltimore Avenue Place of Seeing the Dead. The room was cold. Philadelphia didn't pollute the dead—no natron, formaldehyde, desiccants, or bodies frozen in liquid nitrogen. The head wound was covered with a small piece of cotton. Some of the people in the viewing room asked Ivar and Benedetta if bodies had been preserved and viewed at room temperature in their days.

"No," Ivar said. "That was after our time."

"We used to burn them quicker than this," a woman said, "but we haven't had a good outbreak of plagues recently."

Ivar felt odd about leaving Jonah alone in the cold to go upstairs to a warmer room to speak in his memory. Who would have anything to say about him? What could he say about Jonah? He didn't want to speak ill of the dead.

Benedetta said, just to Ivar, "He tried to get out without paying, and the woman had just decided she'd had enough of him. But we're not going to tell his work people that."

Ivar thought it was strange that Jonah didn't die when New York sent helicopters to get them, but died at a woman's hands in a bawdy house.

Everyone was polite, nodding to each other. One of the women asked everyone to say something about Jonah, and everyone spoke. He was smart; he didn't ask much of others; he did his work.

"Not a wet eye in the house," Benedetta said as they left.

Ivar wanted to follow the corpse to the crematorium, but that wasn't done here. He said, "Jonah knew how to make people really uncomfortable when he wanted to."

Benedetta said, "He should have paid the girl."

Ivar asked, "One of the women I rescued?"

Benedetta said, "Whore by trade there and here. Nobody's wife, so no vows broken and not someone you dug up from a crossroads."

Ivar said, in memory of Jonah, "Just the kind you could kill and put on his pyre."

Benedetta looked at him very hard, then shrugged. "Don't you try being a troll."

Ivar thought she was going to leave him, not for another man, not right away, but for the work she was doing with Pierre and because they'd been through too much together. Life would be duller without her, but he could go back to Iceland, knowing in advance what familiarities came mixed with radical change. The men from Norway changed in Iceland. He would have changed wherever and whenever he lived.

They were in bed after Jonah's cremation. Benedetta asked, "Do you want to make this work? Or have we been through too much together?"

Ivar said, "I don't know. Do you want it to work?"

"What are the alternatives? Could you explain yourself to someone new?"

Ivar, his arms folded behind his head, thought for a few minutes. Just as Benedetta moved as though she was going to say more, he said, "What if we had a child? How could we explain all the past to a child?"

"The kid would just think we were people from the past, like a lot of other kids he knew. We'd be more interesting than some parents and more boring than others."

"We don't need to have a child."

"We don't need to split up either unless you think you want some-one …"

"No, I'm just sad about Jonah, I think. About losing my bearings in time."

Benedetta, beside him, shrugged as best she could while lying down. "Yeah."

Ivar spent half his time with the geeks from all times and some time learning Latin, which became one of more useful ways to talk to people across time and nations again. And he played fighting games with the gladiators, who, like many other entertainers, had gotten lost on the roads between then and now. Now-time was just another venue. Modify the act a bit. Fake being killed more comically.

He came to appreciate the value of being comfortable at home and wondered if that, in the end, was love. They didn't need a child.

Five years after Jonah died, Ivar watched more people from the past settle in the abandoned neighborhoods.

Other places were growing, whether they brought people in from the past or not. Chinese and Africans sold drugs against the latest plagues, nanotech they invented or which some future gave them.

Benedetta discovered gene play and ordered a small dragon in memory of Leonardo who'd tried to build one from bird's wings and a lizard. Hers was real, gaudy, and could fly. It swooped down from the tops of cabinets to catch mice and snatch bits of food off people's plates.

Ivar wondered which future they'd have gotten if he hadn't brought in the Knights Templar. Pierre and the others had just been tortured, so whether they stayed Christian or not, they hated rule by fear and force.

But everyone tended to pick up Philadelphia's politics as soon as they crossed the time flux. The present was contagious: food, drink, sex, warm places to sleep, and peace.

So now-time got its old-new genetic material, and remade the future in the image of everyone.

One spring morning, Benedetta, James, and Ivar rented an internal-combustion car and picked up Pierre de Bologna. They drove to Three Mile Island to show Pierre where the first time-hackers discovered how the time machines worked.

Abandoned sleeping bags littered their old rooms along with jars of local canned produce they hadn't finished.

"If I haven't thanked you both earlier, thank you," Pierre said. "It's been a great pleasure to be here." He'd finally risked the pain and had his hand repaired.

Ivar looked at the interior of the tower where they'd skateboarded and wondered if he'd dare try that again. But the skateboards had rusted since they'd been here last. The skateboard ramp had rotted.

Ivar looked at Benedetta and saw signs of both age and an almost sexual bloom on her, and wondered if she feared those few years between them, but he, too, was getting older.

Pierre said, "Some days, the past seems like a nightmare. Other days, the present seems like a dream."

When Benedetta picked up the edge of one of the sleeping bags, mice jumped out of it, having built a nest there. She smiled and eased the bag down carefully. "They're not bothering anyone. They're not city mice."

Ivar wondered when she would tell him that she was pregnant, or if she just had.

REBECCA ORE is the author of *Outlaw School, Gaia's Toys, Slow Funeral, The Illegal Rebirth of Billy the Kid,* and the Becoming Alien trilogy. She teaches at Drexel University and lives in Philadelphia.